Harold Frederic, William Randolph Hearst, John C. Eckel

In The Valley

Harold Frederic, William Randolph Hearst, John C. Eckel

In The Valley

ISBN/EAN: 9783743367593

Manufactured in Europe, USA, Canada, Australia, Japa

Cover: Foto ©Andreas Hilbeck / pixelio.de

Manufactured and distributed by brebook publishing software (www.brebook.com)

Harold Frederic, William Randolph Hearst, John C. Eckel

In The Valley

IN THE VALLEY

BY

HAROLD FREDERIC

ILLUSTRATED BY HOWARD PYLE

NEW YORK
CHARLES SCRIBNER'S SONS
1890

Press of J. J. Little & Co.,
Astor Place, New York.

DEDICATION.

When, after years of preparation, the pleasant task of writing this tale was begun, I had my chief delight in the hope that the completed book would gratify a venerable friend, to whose inspiration my first idea of the work was due, and that I might be allowed to place his honored name upon this page. The ambition was at once lofty and intelligible. While he was the foremost citizen of New York State, we of the Mohawk Valley thought of him as peculiarly our own. Although born elsewhere, his whole adult life was spent among us, and he led all others in his love for the Valley, his pride in its noble history, and his broad aspirations for the welfare and progress in wise and good ways of its people. His approval of this book would have been the highest honor it could possibly have won. Long before it was finished, he had been laid in his last sleep upon the bosom of the hills that watch over our beautiful river. With reverent affection the volume is brought now to lay as a wreath upon his grave—dedicated to the memory of Horatio Seymour.

H. F.

LONDON, *September 11, 1890.*

CONTENTS.

viii   *Contents.*

CHAPTER IX.

CHAPTER X.

CHAPTER XI.

CHAPTER XII.

CHAPTER XIII.

CHAPTER XIV.

CHAPTER XV.

CHAPTER XVI.

CHAPTER XVII.

CHAPTER XVIII.

CHAPTER XIX.

CHAPTER XX.

CHAPTER XXI.

CHAPTER XXII.

CHAPTER XXIII.

CHAPTER XXIV.

CHAPTER XXV.

CHAPTER XXVI.

CHAPTER XXVII.

CHAPTER XXVIII.

LIST OF ILLUSTRATIONS.

From original drawings by Howard Pyle.

IN THE VALLEY.

IN THE VALLEY.

CHAPTER I.

"THE FRENCH ARE IN THE VALLEY!"

IT may easily be that, during the many years which have come and gone since the eventful time of my childhood, Memory has played tricks upon me to the prejudice of Truth. I am indeed admonished of this by study of my son, for whose children in turn this tale is indited, and who is now able to remember many incidents of his youth—chiefly beatings and like parental cruelties—which I know very well never happened at all. He is good enough to forgive me these mythical stripes and buffetings, but he nurses their memory with ostentatious and increasingly succinct recollection, whereas for my own part, and for his mother's, our enduring fear was lest we had spoiled him through weak fondness. By good fortune the reverse has been true. He is grown into a man of whom any parents might be proud—tall, well-featured, strong, tolerably learned, honorable, and of influence among his fellows. His affection for us, too, is very great. Yet in the fashion of this new generation, which speaks without waiting to be addressed, and does not scruple to instruct on all subjects its elders, he will have it that he feared me when a lad—and with cause! If fancy can so distort impressions within such short span, it does not become me to be too set about events which come back slowly through the mist and darkness of nearly threescore years.

Yet they return to me so full of color, and cut in such precision and keenness of outline, that at no point can I bring myself to say, " Perhaps I am in error concerning this," or to ask, " Has this perchance been confused with other matters?" Moreover, there are few now remaining who of their own memory could controvert or correct me. And if they essay to do so, why should not my word be at least as weighty as theirs? And so to the story:

I was in my eighth year, and there was snow on the ground.

The day is recorded in history as November 13, A.D. 1757, but I am afraid that I did not know much about years then, and certainly the month seems now to have been one of midwinter. The Mohawk, a larger stream then by far than in these days, was not yet frozen over, but its frothy flood ran very dark and chill between the white banks, and the muskrats and the beavers were all snug in their winter holes. Although no big fragments of ice floated on the current, there had already been a prodigious scattering of the bateaux and canoes which through all the open season made a thriving thoroughfare of the river. This meant that the trading was over, and that the trappers and hunters, white and red, were either getting ready to go or had gone northward into the wilderness, where might be had during the winter the skins of dangerous animals—bears, wolves, catamounts, and lynx—and where moose and deer could be chased and yarded over the crust, not to refer to smaller furred beasts to be taken in traps.

I was not at all saddened by the departure of these rude, foul men, of whom those of Caucasian race were not always the least savage, for they did not fail to lay hands upon traps or nets left by the heedless within their reach, and even were not beyond making off with our boats, cursing and beating children who came unprotected in their path, and putting the women in terror of their very lives. The cold weather was welcome not only for clearing us of these pests, but for driving off the black flies, mosquitoes, and gnats which at that time, with the great forests so close behind us, often rendered existence a burden, particularly just after rains.

Other changes were less grateful to the mind. It was true I would no longer be held near the house by the task of keeping alight the smoking kettles of dried fungus, designed to ward off the insects, but at the same time had disappeared many of the enticements which in summer oft made this duty irksome. The partridges were almost the sole birds remaining in the bleak woods, and, much as their curious ways of hiding in the snow, and the resounding thunder of their strange drumming, mystified and attracted me, I was not alert enough to catch

them. All my devices of horse-hair and deer-hide
snares were foolishness in their sharp eyes. The
water-fowl, too—the geese, ducks, cranes, pokes,
fish-hawks, and others—had flown, sometimes darkening the sky over our clearing by the density of
their flocks, and filling the air with clamor. The
owls, indeed, remained, but I hated them.

The very night before the day of which I speak, I
was awakened by one of these stupid, perverse birds,
which must have been in the cedars on the knoll
close behind the house, and which disturbed my very
soul by his ceaseless and melancholy hooting. For
some reason it affected me more than commonly,
and I lay for a long time nearly on the point of tears
with vexation—and, it is likely, some of that terror
with which uncanny noises inspire children in the
darkness. I was warm enough under my fox-robe,
snuggled into the husks, but I was very wretched.
I could hear, between the intervals of the owl's sinister cries, the distant yelping of the timber wolves,
first from the Schoharie side of the river, and then
from our own woods. Once there rose, awfully near
the log wall against which I nestled, a panther's
shrill scream, followed by a long silence, as if the
lesser wild things outside shared for the time my
fright. I remember that I held my breath.

It was during this hush, and while I lay striving,
poor little fellow, to dispel my alarm by fixing my
thoughts resolutely on a rabbit-trap I had set under
some running hemlock out on the side hill, that there
rose the noise of a horse being ridden swiftly down
the frosty highway outside. The hoof-beats came

pounding up close to our gate. A moment later
there was a great hammering on the oak door, as
with a cudgel or pistol handle, and I heard a voice
call out in German (its echoes ring still in my old
ears):

" The French are in the Valley ! "

I drew my head down under the fox-skin as if it
had been smitten sharply, and quaked in solitude. I
desired to hear no more.

Although so very young a boy, I knew quite well
who the French were, and what their visitations por-
tended. Even at that age one has recollections. I
could recall my father, peaceful man of God though
he was, taking down his gun some years before at
the rumor of a French approach, and my mother
clinging to his coat as he stood in the doorway, suc-
cessfully pleading with him not to go forth. I had
more than once seen Mrs. Markell of Minden, with
her black knit cap worn to conceal the absence of
her scalp, which had been taken only the previous
summer by the Indians, who sold it to the French
for ten livres, along with the scalps of her murdered
husband and babe. So it seemed that adults sometimes parted with this portion of their heads without
losing also their lives. I wondered if small boys
were ever equally fortunate. I felt softly of my hair
and wept.

How the crowding thoughts of that dismal hour
return to me! I recall considering in my mind the
idea of bequeathing my tame squirrel to Hendrick
Getman, and the works of an old clock, with their
delightful mystery of wooden cogs and turned wheels,

which was my chief treasure, to my negro friend
Tulp—and then reflecting that they too would share
my fate, and would thus be precluded from enjoy-
ing my legacies. The whimsical aspect of the task
of getting hold upon Tulp's close, woolly scalp was
momentarily apparent to me, but I did not laugh.
Instead, the very suggestion of humor converted my
tears into vehement sobbings.

When at last I ventured to lift my head and
listen again, it was to hear another voice, an English-speaking voice which I knew very well, saying
gravely from within the door:

" It is well to warn, but not to terrify. There are
many leagues between us and danger, and many
good fighting men. When you have told your tidings to Sir William, add that I have heard it all and
have gone back to bed."

Then the door was closed and barred, and the
hoof-beats died away down the Valley.

These few words had sufficed to shame me heartily of my cowardice. I ought to have remembered
that we were almost within hail of Fort Johnson and
its great owner the General ; that there was a long
line of forts between us and the usual point of invasion, with many soldiers ; and—most important of
all—that I was in the house of Mr. Stewart.

If these seem over-mature reflections for one of
my age, it should be explained, that, while a veritable
child in matters of heart and impulse, I was in education and association much advanced beyond my
years. The master of the house, Mr. Thomas Stewart, whose kind favor had provided me with a home

after my father's sad demise, had diverted his leisure
with my instruction, and given me the great advantage of daily conversation both in English and
Dutch with him.   I was known to Sir William and
to Mr. Butler and other gentlemen, and was often
privileged to listen when they conversed with Mr.
Stewart. Thus I had grown wise in certain respects,
while remaining extremely childish in others. Thus
it was that I trembled first at the common hooting
of an owl, and then cried as if to die at hearing the
French were coming, and lastly recovered all my
spirits at the reassuring sound of Mr. Stewart's voice,
and the knowledge that he was content to return to
his sleep.

I went soundly to sleep myself, presently, and
cannot remember to have dreamed at all.

CHAPTER II.

SETTING FORTH HOW THE GIRL CHILD WAS
BROUGHT TO US.

WHEN I came out of my nest next morning—my
bed was on the floor of a small recess back of the
great fireplace, made, I suspect, because the original
builders lacked either the skill or the inclination,
whichever it might be, to more neatly skirt the chimney with the logs—it was quite late. Some meat
and corn-bread were laid for me on the table in Mr.
Stewart's room, which was the chief chamber of the
house. Despite the big fire roaring on the hearth,
it was so cold that the grease had hardened white
about the meat in the pan, and it had to be warmed
again before I could sop my bread.

During the solitary meal it occurred to me to question my aunt, the housekeeper, as to the alarm of
the night, which lay heavily once more upon my
mind. But I could hear her humming to herself in
the back room, which did not indicate acquaintance
with any danger. Moreover, it might as well be
stated here that my aunt, good soul though she was,
did not command especial admiration for the clear-
ness of her wits, having been cruelly stricken with
the small-pox many years before, and owing her employment, be it confessed, much more to Mr. Stew-

art's excellence of heart than to her own abilities.
She was probably the last person in the Valley whose
judgment upon the question of a French invasion,
or indeed any other large matter, I would have
valued.

Having donned my coon-skin cap, and drawn on
my thick pelisse over my apron, I put another beech-
knot on the fire and went outside. The stinging air
bit my nostrils and drove my hands into my pockets.
Mr. Stewart was at the work which had occupied
him for some weeks previously—hewing out logs on
the side hill. His axe strokes rang through the
frosty atmosphere now with a sharp reverberation
which made it seem much colder, and yet more
cheerful. Winter had come, indeed, but I began to
feel that I liked it. I almost skipped as I went along
the hard, narrow path to join him.

He was up among the cedars, under a close-woven
net of boughs, which, themselves heavily capped
with snow, had kept the ground free. He nodded
pleasantly to me when I wished him good-morning,
then returned to his labor. Although I placed
myself in front of him, in the hope that he would
speak, and thus possibly put me in the way to learn
something about this French business, he said nothing, but continued whacking at the deeply notched
trunk. The temptation to begin the talk myself
came near mastering me, so oppressed with curiosity
was I; and finally, to resist it the better, I walked
away and stood on the brow of the knoll, whence
one could look up and down the Valley.

γ It was the only world I knew—this expanse of

flats, broken by wedges of forest stretching down
from the hills on the horizon to the very water's
edge. Straight, glistening lines of thin ice ran out
here and there from the banks of the stream this
morning, formed on the breast of the flood through
the cold night.

To the left, in the direction of the sun, lay, at the
distance of a mile or so, Mount Johnson, or Fort
Johnson, as one chose to call it. It could not be
seen for the intervening hills, but so important was
the fact of its presence to me that I never looked
eastward without seeming to behold its gray stone
walls with their windows and loopholes, its stockade
of logs, its two little houses on either side, its barracks for the guard upon the ridge back of the gristmill, and its accustomed groups of grinning black
slaves, all eyeballs and white teeth, of saturnine
Indians in blankets, and of bold-faced fur-traders.
Beyond this place I had never been, but I knew
vaguely that Schenectady was in that direction,
where the French once wrought such misery, and
beyond that Albany, the great town of our parts,
and then the big ocean which separated us from
England and Holland. Civilization lay that way,
and all the luxurious things which, being shown or
talked of by travellers, made our own rough life
seem ruder still by contrast.

Turning to the right I looked on the skirts of
savagery. Some few adventurous villages of poor
Palatine-German farmers and traders there were up
along the stream, I knew, hidden in the embrace of
the wilderness, and with them were forts and soldiers.

But these latter did not prevent houses being sacked and their inmates tomahawked every now and then.

It astonished me, that, for the sake of mere furs and ginseng and potash, men should be moved to settle in these perilous wilds, and subject their wives and families to such dangers, when they might live in peace at Albany, or, for that matter, in the old countries whence they came. For my part, I thought I would much rather be oppressed by the Grand Duke's tax-collectors, or even be caned now and again by the Grand Duke himself, than undergo these privations and panics in a savage land. I was too little then to understand the grandeur of the motives which impelled men to expatriate themselves and suffer all things rather than submit to religious persecution or civil tyranny. Sometimes even now, in my old age, I feel that I do not wholly comprehend it. But that it was a grand thing, I trust there can be no doubt.

While I still stood on the brow of the hill, my young head filled with these musings, and my heart weighed down almost to crushing by the sense of vast loneliness and peril which the spectacle of naked marsh-lands and dark, threatening forests inspired, the sound of the chopping ceased, and there followed, a few seconds later, a great swish and crash down the hill.

As I looked to note where the tree had fallen, I saw Mr. Stewart lay down his axe, and take into his hands the gun which stood near by. He motioned to me to preserve silence, and himself stood in an attitude of deep attention. Then my slow ears caught the noise he had already heard—a mixed babel of groans, curses, and cries of fear, on the road to the westward of us, and growing louder momentarily.

After a minute or two of listening he said to me, " It is nothing. The cries are German, but the oaths are all English—as they generally are."

All the same he put his gun over his arm as he walked down to the stockade, and out through the gate upon the road, to discover the cause of the commotion.

Five red-coated soldiers on horseback, with another, cloaked to the eyes and bearing himself proudly, riding at their heels; a negro following on, also mounted, with a huge bundle in his arms before him, and a shivering, yellow-haired lad of about my own age on a pillion behind him ; clustering about these, a motley score of poor people, young and old, some bearing household goods, and all frightened out of their five senses—this is what we saw on the highway.

What we heard it would be beyond my power to recount. From the chaos of terrified exclamations in German, and angry cursing in English, I gathered generally that the scared mob of Palatines were all for flying the Valley, or at the least crowding into Fort Johnson, and that the troopers were somewhat vigorously endeavoring to reassure and dissuade them.

Mr. Stewart stepped forward—I following close in his rear—and began phrasing in German to these

Five red-coated soldiers on horse back, with another cloaked to the eyes. . . . clustering . . . a motley score of poor people, young and old.

poor souls the words of the soldiers, leaving out the
blasphemies with which they were laden. How
much he had known before I cannot guess, but the
confidence with which he told them that the French
and Indian marauders had come no farther than the
Palatine Village above Fort Kouarie, that they were
but a small force, and that Honikol Herkimer had
already started out to drive them back, seemed to
his simple auditors born of knowledge. They at all
events listened to him, which they had not done to
the soldiers, and plied him with anxious queries,
which he in turn referred to the mounted men and
then translated their sulky answers. This was done
to such good purpose that before long the wiser
of the Palatines were agreed to return to their
homes up the Valley, and the others had become
calm.

As the clamor ceased, the soldier whom I took to
be an officer removed his cloak a little from his face
and called out gruffly :

" Tell this fellow to fetch me some brandy, or
whatever cordial is to be had in this God-forgotten
country, and stir his bones about it, too ! "

To speak to Mr. Thomas Stewart in this fashion !
I looked at my protector in pained wrath and apprehension, knowing his fiery temper.

With a swift movement he pushed his way between the sleepy soldiers straight to the officer. I
trembled in every joint, expecting to see him cut
down where he stood, here in front of his own house!

He plucked the officer's cloak down from his face
with a laugh, and then put his hands on his hips, his

gun under his arm, looked the other square in the face, and laughed again.

All this was done so quickly that the soldiers, being drowsy with their all-night ride, scarcely understood what was going forward. The officer himself strove to unwrap the muffled cloak that he might grasp his sword, puffing out his cheeks with amazement and indignation meanwhile, and staring down fiercely at Mr. Stewart. The fair-haired boy on the horse with the negro was almost as greatly excited, and cried out, " Kill him, some one! Strike him down ! " in a stout voice. At this some of the soldiers wheeled about, prepared to take part in the trouble when they should comprehend it, while their horses plunged and reared into the others.

The only cool one was Mr. Stewart, who still stood at his ease, smiling at the red-faced, blustering officer, to whom he now said :

" When you are free of your cloak, Tony Cross, dismount and let us embrace."

The gentleman thus addressed peered at the speaker, gave an exclamation or two of impatience, then looked again still more closely. All at once his face brightened, and he slapped his round, tight thigh with a noise like the rending of an ice-gorge.

" Tom Lynch ! " he shouted. " Saints' breeches ! 'tis he ! " and off his horse came the officer, and into Mr. Stewart's arms, before I could catch my breath. It seemed that the twain were old comrades, and had been like brothers in foreign wars, now long past. They walked affectionately, hand in hand, to the house. The negro followed, bringing the two

horses into the stockade, and then coming inside
with the bundle and the boy, the soldiers being despatched onward to the fort. ⋎ ι ⸍

While my aunt, Dame Kronk, busied herself in
bringing bottles and glasses, and swinging the kettle
over the fire, the two gentlemen could not keep eyes
off each other, and had more to say than there were
words for.   It was eleven years since they had met,
and, although Mr. Stewart had learned (from Sir
William) of the other's presence in the Valley, Major
Cross had long since supposed his friend to be dead.
Conceive, then, the warmth of their greeting, the
fondness of their glances, the fervor of the reminiscences into which they straightway launched, sitting
wide-kneed by the roaring hearth, steaming glass in
hand.

The Major sat massively upright on the bench,
letting his thick cloak fall backward from his broad
shoulders to the floor, for, though the heat of the
flames might well-nigh singe one's eyebrows, it would
be cold behind.   I looked upon his great girth of
chest, upon his strong hands, which yet showed delicately fair when they were ungloved, and upon his
round, full-colored, amiable face with much satisfaction.   I seemed to swell with pride when he un-
buckled his sword, belt and all, and handed it to me,
I being nearest, to put aside for him.   It was a ponderous, severe-looking weapon, and I bore it to the
bed with awe, asking myself how many people it was
likely to have killed in its day.   I had before this
handled other swords—including Sir William's—but
never such a one as this.   Nor had I ever before seen

a soldier who seemed to my boyish eyes so like what a warrior should be.

It was not our habit to expend much liking upon English officers or troopers, who were indeed quite content to go on without our friendship, and treated us Dutch and Palatines in turn with contumacy and roughness, as being no better than their inferiors. But no one could help liking Major Anthony Cross —at least when they saw him under his old friend's roof-tree, expanding with genial pleasure.

For the yellow-haired boy, who was the Major's son, I cared much less. I believe truly that I disliked him from the very first moment out on the frosty road, and that when I saw him shivering there with the cold, I was not a whit sorry. This may be imagination, but it is certain that he did not get into my favor after we came inside.

Under this Master Philip's commands the negro squatted on his haunches and unrolled the blankets from the bundle I had seen him carrying. Out of this bundle, to my considerable amazement, was revealed a little child, perhaps between three and four years of age.

This tiny girl blinked in the light thus suddenly surrounding her, and looked about the room piteously, with her little lips trembling and her eyes filled with tears. She was very small for her years, and had long, tumbled hair. Her dress was a home-spun frock in a single piece, and her feet were wrapped for warmth in wool stockings of a grown woman's measure. She looked about the room, I say, until she saw me. No doubt my Dutch face was of the sort she was accustomed to, for she stretched out her hands to me. Thereupon I went and took her in my arms, the negro smiling upon us both.

I had thought to bear her to the fire-place, where Master Philip was already toasting himself, standing between Mr. Stewart's knees, and boldly spreading his hands over the heat. But when he espied me bringing forward the child he darted to us and sharply bade me leave the girl alone.

"Is she not to be warmed, then?" I asked, puzzled alike at his rude behavior and at his words.

"I will do it myself," he answered shortly, and made to take the child.

He alarmed her with his imperious gesture, and she turned from him, clinging to my neck. I was vexed now, and, much as I feared discourtesy to one of Mr. Stewart's guests, felt like holding my own. Keeping the little girl tight in my arms, I pushed past him toward the fire. To my great wrath he began pulling at her shawl as I went, shouting that he would have her, while to make matters worse the babe herself set up a loud wail. Thus you may imagine I was in a fine state of confusion and temper when I stood finally at the side of the hearth and felt Mr. Stewart's eyes upon me. But I had the girl.

"What is the tumult?" he demanded, in a vexed tone. "What are you doing, Douw, and what child is this?"

"It is my child, sir!" young Philip spoke up, panting from his exertions, and red with color.

2

The two men broke out in loud laughter at this, so long sustained that Philip himself joined it, and grinned reluctantly. I was too angry to even feel relieved that the altercation was to have no serious consequences for me—much less to laugh myself. I opened the shawl, that the little one might feel the heat, and said nothing.

"Well, the lad is right, in a way," finally chuckled the Major. "It's as much his child as it is anybody's this side of heaven."

The phrase checked his mirth, and he went on more seriously :

"She is the child of a young couple who had come to the Palatine Village only a few weeks before. The man was a cooper or wheelwright, one or the other, and his name was Peet or Peek, or some such Dutch name. When Bellêtre fell upon the town at night, the man was killed in the first attack. The woman with her child ran with the others to the ford. There in the darkness and panic she was crushed under and drowned ; but strange enough— who can tell how these matters are ordered?—the infant was in some way got across the river safe, and fetched to the Fort. But there, so great is the throng, both of those who escaped and those who now, alarmed for their lives, flock in from the farms round about, that no one had time to care for a mere infant. Her parents were new-comers, and had no friends. Besides, every one up there is distracted with mourning or frantic with preparation for the morrow. The child stood about among the cattle, trying to get warm in the straw, when we came out last night to start. She looked so beseechingly at us, and so like my own little Cordelia, by God! I couldn't bear it! I cursed a trifle about their brutality, and one of 'em offered at that to take her in; but my boy here said, 'Let's bring her with us, father,' and up she came on to Bob's saddle, and off we started. At Herkimer's I found blankets for her, and one of the girls gave us some hose, big enough for Bob, which we bundled her in."

"There! said I not truly she was mine?" broke in the boy, shaking his yellow hair proudly, and looking Mr. Stewart confidently in the eye.

"Rightly enough," replied Mr. Stewart, kindly. "And so you are my old friend Anthony Cross's son, eh? A good, hearty lad, seeing the world young. Can you realize easily, Master Philip, looking at us two old people, that we were once as small as you, and played together then on the Galway hills, never knowing there could be such a place as America? And that later we slept together in the same tent, and thanked our stars for not being bundled together into the same trench, years upon years?"

"Yes, and I know who you are, what's more!" said the pert boy, unabashed.

"Why, that's wisdom itself," said Mr. Stewart, pleasantly.

"You are Tom Lynch, and your grandfather was a king——"

"No more," interposed Mr. Stewart, frowning and lifting his finger. "That folly is dead and in its grave.   Not even so fair a youth as you must give it resurrection."

"Here, Bob," said the Major, with sudden alacrity.   "Go outside with these children, and help them to some games."

CHAPTER III.

MASTER PHILIP MAKES HIS BOW—AND BEHAVES BADLY.

MY protector and chief friend was at this time, as near as may be, fifty years of age ; yet he bore these years so sturdily that, if one should see him side by side with his gossip and neighbor, Sir William Johnson, there would be great doubt which was the elder —and the Baronet was not above forty-two. Mr. Stewart was not tall, and seemed of somewhat slight frame, yet he had not only grace of movement, but prodigious strength of wrist and shoulders. For walking he was not much, but he rode like a knight. He was of strictest neatness and method concerning his clothes; not so much, let me explain, as to their original texture, for they were always plain, ordinary garments, but regarding their cleanliness and order. He had a swift and ready temper, and could not brook to be disputed by his equals, much less by his inferiors, yet had a most perfect and winning politeness when agreed with.

All these, I had come to know, were traits of a soldier, yet he had many other qualities which puzzled me, not being observable in other troopers. He swore very rarely, he was abstemious with wines and spirits, and he loved books better than food

itself. Of not even Sir William, great warrior and
excellent scholar though he was, could all these
things be said. Mr. Stewart had often related to
me, during the long winter days and evenings spent
of necessity by the fire, stories drawn from his campaigns in the Netherlands and France and Scotland,
speaking freely and most instructively. But he had
never helped me to unravel the mystery why he, so
unlike other soldiers in habits and tastes, should
have chosen the profession of arms.

A ray of light was thrown upon the question this
very day by the forward prattle of the boy Philip.
In after years the full illumination came, and I understood it all. It is as well, perhaps, to outline the
story here, although at the time I was in ignorance
of it.

In Ireland, nearly eighty years before, that is to
say in 1679, there had been born a boy to whom was
given the name of James Lynch. His mother was
the smooth-faced, light-hearted daughter of a broken
Irish gentleman, who loved her boy after a gusty
fashion, and bore a fierce life of scorn and sneers on
his behalf. His father was—who? There were no
proofs in court, of course, but it seems never to have
been doubted by any one that the father was no
other than the same worthless prince to wear whose
titles the two chief towns of my State were despoiled
of their honest Dutch names—I mean the Duke of
York and Albany.

Little James Lynch, unlike so many of his luckier
brothers and cousins, got neither a peerage nor a
gentle breeding. Instead he was reared meagrely,

if not harshly, under the maternal roof and name,
until he grew old enough to realize that he was on
an island where bad birth is not forgiven, even if the
taint be royal.   Then he ran away, reached the coast
of France, and made his way to the French court,
where his father was now, and properly enough, an
exile.   He was a fine youth, with a prompt tongue
and clever head, and some attention was finally shown
him.   They gave him a sword and a company, and
he went with the French through all the wars of
Marlborough, gaining distinction, and, what is more,
a fat purse.

With his money he returned to Ireland, wedded a
maid of whom he had dreamed during all his exile,
and settled down there to beggar himself in a life of
bibulous ease, gaming, fox-hunting, and wastefulness
generally.   After some years the wife died, and
James Lynch drifted naturally into the conspiracy
which led to the first rising for the Pretender, involv-
ing himself as deeply as possible, and at its collapse
flying once more to France, never to return.

He bore with him this time a son of eight years
—my Mr. Stewart.   This boy, called Thomas, was
reared on the skirts of the vicious French court, now
in a Jesuit school, now a poor relation in a palace,
always reflecting in the vicissitudes of his condition
the phases of his sire's vagrant existence.   Sometimes this father would be moneyed and prodigal,
anon destitute and mean, but always selfish to the
core, and merrily regardless alike of canons and of
consequences.   He died, did this adventurous gentleman, in the very year which took off the first

George in Hanover, and left his son a very little
money, a mountain of debts, and an injunction of
loyalty to the Stewarts.

Young Thomas, then nearly twenty, thought much
for a time of becoming a priest, and was always a
favorite with the British Jesuits about Versailles,
but this in the end came to nothing. He abandoned
the religious vocation, though not the scholar's
tastes, and became a soldier, for the sake of a beautiful face which he saw once when on a secret visit
to England. He fell greatly in love, and ventured
to believe that the emotion was reciprocated. As
Isaac served Laban for his daughter, so did Tom
Lynch serve the Pretender's cause for the hope of
some day returning, honored and powerful, to ask
the hand of that sweet daughter of the Jacobite
gentleman.

One day there came to him at Paris, to offer his
sword to the Stewarts, a young Irish gentleman who
had been Tom's playmate in childhood—Anthony
Cross. This gallant, fresh-faced, handsome youth
was all ablaze with ardor; he burned to achieve impossible deeds, to attain glory at a stroke. He confessed to Tom over their dinner, or the wine afterward perhaps, that his needs were great because
Love drove. He was partly betrothed to the
daughter of an English Jacobite—yet she would
marry none but one who had gained his spurs under
his rightful king. They drank to the health of this
exacting, loyal maiden, and Cross gave her name.
Then Tom Lynch rose from the table, sick at heart,
and went away in silence.

Cross never knew of the hopes and joys he had unwittingly crushed. The two young men became friends, intimates, brothers, serving in half the lands of Europe side by side. The maiden, an orphan now, and of substance and degree, came over at last to France, and Lynch stood by, calm-faced, and saw her married to his friend. She only pleasantly remembered him ; he never forgot her till his death.

Finally, in 1745, when both men were nearing middle age, the time for striking the great blow was thought to have arrived. The memory of Lynch's lineage was much stronger with the romantic young Pretender of his generation than had been the rightfully closer tie between their more selfish fathers, and princely favor gave him a prominent position among those who arranged that brilliant melodrama of Glenfinnan and Edinburgh and Preston Pans; which was to be so swiftly succeeded by the tragedy of Culloden. The two friends were together through it all—in its triumph, its disaster, its rout—but they became separated afterward in the Highlands, when they were hiding for their lives. Cross, it seems, was able to lie secure until his wife's relatives, through some Whig influence, I know not what, obtained for him amnesty first, then leave to live in England, and finally a commission under the very sovereign he had fought. His comrade, less fortunate, at least contrived to make way to Ireland and then to France. There, angered and chagrined at unjust and peevish rebukes offered him, he renounced the bad cause, took the name of Stewart, and set sail to the New World.

This was my patron's story, as I gathered it in later years, and which perhaps I have erred in bringing forward here among my childish recollections. But it seems to belong in truth much more to this day on which, for the first and last time, I beheld Major Cross, than to the succeeding period when his son became an actor in the drama of my life.

The sun was now well up in the sky, and the snow was melting. While I still moodily eyed my young enemy, and wondered how I should go about to acquit myself of the task laid upon me—to play with him—he solved the question by kicking into the moist snow with his boots and calling out:

"Aha! we can build a fort with this, and have a fine attack. Bob, make me a fort!"

Seeing that he bore no malice, my temper softened toward him a little, and I set to helping the negro in his work. There was a great pile of logs in the clearing, close to the house, and on the sunny side near this the little girl was placed, in a warm, dry spot; and here we two, with sticks and balls of snow, soon reared a mock block-house. The English boy did no work, but stood by and directed us with enthusiasm. When the structure was to his mind, he said:

"Now we will make up some snowballs, and have an attack. I will be the Englishman and defend the fort; you must be the Frenchman and come to drive me out. You can have Bob with you for a savage, if you like; only he must throw no balls, but stop back in the woods and whoop. But first we must have some hard balls made, so that I may hit you good when you come up.—Bob, help this boy make some balls for me!"

Thus outlined, the game did not attract me. I did not so much mind doing his work for him, since he was company, so to speak, but it did go against my grain to have to manufacture the missiles for my own hurt.

"Why should I be the Frenchman?" I said, grumblingly. "I am no more a Frenchman than you are yourself."

"You're a Dutchman, then, and it's quite the same," he replied. "All foreigners are the same."

"It is you who are the foreigner," I retorted with heat. "How can I be a foreigner in my own country, here where I was born?"

He did not take umbrage at this, but replied with argument: "Why, of course you're a foreigner. You wear an apron, and you are not able to even speak English properly."

This reflection upon my speech pained even more than it nettled me. Mr. Stewart had been at great pains to teach me English, and I had begun to hope that he felt rewarded by my proficiency. Years afterward he was wont to laughingly tell me that I never would live long enough to use English correctly, and that as a boy I spoke it abominably, which I dare say was true enough. But just then my childish pride was grievously piqued by Philip's criticism.

"Very well, I'll be on the outside, then," I said. "I won't be a Frenchman, but I'll come all the same,

and do you look out for yourself when I *do* come,"
or words to that purport.

We had a good, long contest over the snow wall.
I seem to remember it all better than I remember
any other struggle of my life, although there were
some to come in which existence itself was at stake,
but boys' mimic fights are not subjects upon which
a writer may profitably dwell. It is enough to say
that he defended himself very stoutly, hurling the
balls which Bob had made for him with great swiftness and accuracy, so that my head was sore for a
week. But my blood was up, and at last over the
wall I forced my way, pushing a good deal of it down
as I went, and, grappling him by the waist, wrestled
with and finally threw him. We were both down,
with our faces in the snow, and I held him tight. I
expected that he would be angry, and hot to turn
the play into a real fight; but he said instead, mumbling with his mouth full of snow:

" Now you must pretend to scalp me, you know."

My aunt called us at this, and we all trooped into
the house again. The little girl had crowed and
clapped her hands during our struggle, all unconscious of the dreadful event of which it was a juve-
nile travesty. We two boys admired her as she
was borne in on the negro's shoulder, and Philip
said :

" I am going to take her to England, for a playmate. Papa has said I may. My brother Digby
has no sport in him, and he is much bigger than me,
besides. So I shall have her all for my own. Only
I wish she weren't Dutch."

When we entered the house the two gentlemen were seated at the table, eating their dinner, and my aunt had spread for us, in the chimney-corner, a like repast. She took the little girl off to her own room, the kitchen, and we fell like famished wolves upon the smoking venison and onions.

The talk of our elders was mainly about a personage of whom I could not know anything then, but whom I now see to have been the Young Pretender. They spoke of him as "he," and as leading a painfully worthless and disreputable life. This Mr. Stewart, who was twelve years the Chevalier's senior, and, as I learned later, had been greatly attached to his person, deplored with affectionate regret. But Major Cross, who related incidents of debauchery and selfishness which, being in Europe, had come to his knowledge about the prince, did not seem particularly cast down.

"It's but what might have been looked for," he said, lightly, in answer to some sad words of my patron's. "Five generations of honest men have trusted to their sorrow in the breed, and given their heads or their estates or their peace for not so much as a single promise kept, or a single smile without speculation in it. Let them rot out, I say, and be damned to them!"

"But he was such a goodly lad, Tony. Think of him as we knew him—and now!"

"No, I'll *not* think, Tom," broke in the officer, "for, when I do, then I too get soft-hearted. And I'll waste no more feeling or faith on any of 'em— on any of 'em, save the only true man of the lot,

who's had the wit to put the ocean 'twixt him and
them.   And you're content here, Tom?"

"Oh, ay!   Why not?" said Mr. Stewart.   "It is
a rude life in some ways, no doubt, but it's free and
it's honest.   I have my own roof, such as it is, and
no one to gainsay me under it.   I hunt, I fish, I
work, I study, I dream—precisely what pleases me
best."

"Ay, but the loneliness of it!"

"Why, no! I see much of Johnson, and there are
others round about to talk with, when I'm driven to
it.   And then there's my young Dutchman—Douw,
yonder—who bears me company, and fits me so well
that he's like a second self."

The Major looked over toward my corner with a
benevolent glance, but without comment. Presently
he said, while he took more meat upon his plate:

"You've no thought of marrying, I suppose?"

"None!" said my patron, gravely and with em-
phasis.

The Major nodded his handsome head meditatively.   "Well, there's a deal to be said on that
side," he remarked.   "Still, children about the hearth
help one to grow old pleasantly.   And you always
had a weakness for brats."

Mr. Stewart said again: "I have my young
Dutchman."

Once more the soldier looked at me, and, I'll be
bound, saw me blushing furiously.   He smiled and
said:

"He seems an honest chap.   He has something
of your mouth, methinks."

My patron pushed his dish back with a gesture of vexation.

" No!" he said, sharply. " There's none of that. His father was a dominie over the river; his mother, a good, hard-working lady, left a widow, struggles to put bread in a dozen mouths by teaching a little home-school for infants. I have the boy here because I like him—because I want him. We shall live together—he and I. As he gets older this hut will doubtless grow into a house fit for gentlemen. Indeed, already I have the logs cut out in part for an addition, on the other side of the chimney."

The Major rose at this, smiling again, and frankly put out his hand.

"I meant no harm, you know, Tom, by my barracks jest. Faith! I envy the lad the privilege of living here with you. The happiest days of my life, dear friend, were those we spent together while I was waiting for my bride."

Mr. Stewart returned his smile rather sadly, and took his hand.

The time for parting had come. The two men stood hand in hand, with moistened eyes and slow-coming words, meeting for perhaps the last time in this life; for the Major was to stop but an hour at Fort Johnson, and thence hasten on to New York and to England, bearing with him weighty despatches.

While they still stood, and the negro was tying Master Philip's hat over his ears, my aunt entered the room, bearing in her arms the poor little waif from the massacre. The child had been washed and warmed, and wore over her dress and feet a sort of mantle, which the good woman had hastily and somewhat rudely fashioned meantime.

"Oh, we came near forgetting her!" cried Philip. "Wrap her snug and warm, Bob, for the journey."

The Major looked blank at sight of the child, who nestled in my aunt's arms. "What am I to do with her?" he said to my patron.

"Why, papa, you know she is going to England with us," said the boy.

"Tut, lad!" spoke the Major, peremptorily; then, to Mr. Stewart: "Could Sir William place her, think you, or does that half-breed swarm of his fill the house? It seemed right enough to bring her out from the Palatine country, but now that she's out, damme! I almost wish she was back again. What a fool not to leave her at Herkimer's!"

I do not know if I had any clear idea of what was springing up in Mr. Stewart's mind, but it seems to me that I must have looked at him pleadingly and with great hope in my eyes, during the moment of silence which followed. Mr. Stewart in turn regarded the child attentively.

"Would it please you to keep her here, Dame Kronk?" he asked at last.

As my aunt made glad assent, I could scarcely refrain from dancing. I walked over to the little girl and took her hand in mine, filled with deep joy.

"You render me very grateful, Tom," said Major Cross, heartily. "It's a load off my mind.—Come, Philip, make your farewells. We must be off."

"And isn't the child to be mine—to go with us?" the boy asked, vehemently.

"Why be childish, Philip?" demanded the Major. "Of course it's out of the question."

The English lad, muffled up now for the ride, with his large flat hat pressed down comically at the sides by the great knitted comforter which Bob had tied under his chin, scowled in a savage fashion, bit his lips, and started for the door, too angry to say good-by. When he passed me, red-faced and wrathful, I could not keep from smiling, but truly rather at his swaddled appearance than at his discomfiture. He had sneered at my apron, besides.

With a cry of rage he whirled around and struck me full in the face, knocking me head over heels into the ashes on the hearth. Then he burst into a fit of violent weeping, or rather convulsions more befitting a wild-cat than a human being, stamping furiously with his feet, and screaming that he *would* have the child.

I picked myself out of the ashes, where my hair had been singed a trifle by the embers, in time to see the Major soundly cuff his offspring, and then lead him by the arm, still screaming, out of the door. There Bob enveloped him in his arms, struggling and kicking, and put him on the horse.

Major Cross, returning for a final farewell word, gave me a shilling as a salve for my hurts, physical and mental, and said:

"I am sorry to have so ill-tempered a son. He cannot brook denial, when once he fixes his heart on a thing. However, he'll get that beaten out of

3

him before he's done with the world.   And so, Tom,
dear, dear old comrade, a last good-by.   God bless
you, Tom!   Farewell."

"God bless you—and yours, *mon frère!*"

We stood, Mr. Stewart and I, at the outer gate,
and watched them down the river road, until the
jutting headland intervened.   As we walked slowly
back toward the house, my guardian said, as if talking partly to himself:

"There is nothing clearer in natural law than that
sons inherit from their mothers.   I know of only two
cases in all history where an able man had a father
superior in brain and energy to the mother—Martin
Luther and the present King of Prussia.   Perhaps
it was all for the best."

To this I of course offered no answer, but trudged
along through the melting snow by his side.

Presently, as we reached the house, he stopped
and looked the log structure critically over.

"You heard what I said, Douw, upon your belonging henceforth to this house—to me?"

"Yes, Mr. Stewart."

"And now, lo and behold, I have a daughter as
well!   To-morrow we must plan out still another
room for our abode."

Thus ended the day on which my story properly
and prophetically begins—the day when I first met
Master Philip Cross.

CHAPTER IV.

IN WHICH I BECOME THE SON OF THE HOUSE.

THE French, for some reason or other, did not follow up their advantage and descend upon the lower Valley; but had they done so there could scarcely have been a greater panic among the Palatines. All during the year there had been seen at times, darkly flitting through the woods near the sparse settlements, little bands of hostile Indians. It was said that their purpose was to seize and abduct Sir William; failing in this, they did what other mischief they could, so that the whole Valley was kept in constant alarm. No household knew, on going to bed, that they would not be roused before morning by savage war-cries. No man ventured out of sight of his home without entertaining the idea that he might never get back alive. Hence, when the long-expected blow was really struck, and the town on the German Flatts devastated, everybody was in an agony of fear. To make matters worse, Sir William was at his home ill in bed, and there was some trouble between him and the English commanders, which stood in the way of troops being sent to our aid.

Those few days following the dreadful news of the

attack above us seem still like a nightmare. The settlers up the river began sending their household goods down to Albany; women and children, too, passed us in great parties, to take refuge in Fort Hunter or at Schenectady. The river suddenly became covered with boats once more, but this time representing the affrighted flight of whole communities instead of a peaceful commerce.

During this season of terror I was, as may be conceived, indeed unhappy. I had no stomach even for play with the new addition to our household, yet scarcely dared to show my nose outside the stockade. Mr. Stewart spent his days abroad, either with Sir William, or up at Caughnawaga concerting means of defence with our friends the Fondas. He did, however, find time to cross the river and reassure my mother, who trembled with apprehension for her great brood of young, but was brave as a lion for herself. Weeks afterward, when I visited her once more, I saw baskets of lime in the attic which this devoted woman had stored there, to throw with water on the Indians when they came. This device she had learned from the family traditions of her ancestors' doings, when the Spaniards were in Holland.

Gradually the alarm wore away. The French and Indians, after killing fifty Palatines and taking thrice that number prisoners, turned tail and marched back to the Lake again, with some of Honikol Herkimer's lead in their miserable bodies. The Valley was rarely to be cursed with their presence again. It was as if a long fever had come to its climax in

a tremendous convulsion, and then gone off altogether. We regained confidence, and faced the long
winter of '57 with content.✓ ⌐

Before the next snowfall succeeded to that first
November flurry, and the season closed in in earnest,
Mr. Stewart was able, by the aid of a number of
neighbors, to build and roof over two additions to
his house. The structure was still all of logs, but
with its new wings became almost as large, if not as
imposing, as any frame-house round about. One of
these wings was set aside for Dame Kronk and the
little girl. The other, much to my surprise, was
given to me. At the same time my benefactor formally presented me with my little black playmate,
Tulp. He had heretofore been my friend ; henceforth he was my slave, yet, let me add, none the less
my friend.

All this was equivalent to my formal adoption as
Mr. Stewart's son. It was the custom in those days,
when a slave child came of a certain age, to present
it to the child of the family who should be of the
same age and sex. The presentation was made at
New Year's, ordinarily, and the white child acknowledged it by giving the little black a piece of money
and a pair of shoes. My mother rather illogically
shed some tears at this token that I was to belong
henceforth to Mr. Stewart ; but she gave me a bright
Spanish dollar out of her small hoard, for Tulp, and
she had old William Dietz, the itinerant cobbler of
Schoharie, construct for him a very notable pair
of shoes, which did him no good since his father
promptly sold them over at Fort Hunter for rum.

The old rascal would have made away with the coin as well, no doubt, but that Mr. Stewart threatened him with a hiding, and so Tulp wore it on a leather string about his neck.

I did not change my name, but continued to be Douw Mauverensen. This was at the wish of both Mr. Stewart and my mother, for the name I bore was an honorable one. My father had been for years a clergyman in the Valley, preaching now in Dutch, now in German, according to the nationality of the people, and leading a life of much hardship, travelling up and down among them. It is not my business to insist that he was a great man, but it is certain that through all my younger years I received kindnesses from many people because I was my father's son. For my own part I but faintly remember him, he having been killed by a fractious horse when I was a very small boy.

As he had had no fixed charge during life, but had ministered to half a dozen communities, so it was nobody's business in particular to care for his family after his death. The owner of the horse did send my mother a bushel of apples, and the congregation at Stone Arabia took up a little money for her. But they were all poor people in those days, wresting a scanty livelihood from the wilderness, and besides, I have never noticed that to be free with their money is in the nature of either the Dutch or the Palatines. The new dominie, too, who came up from Albany to take my father's place, was of the opinion that there was quite little enough coming in for the living pastor, without shearing it, as he said, to keep alive dead folk's memories. Thus sadly a prospect of great destitution opened before my mother.

But she was, if I say it myself, a superior woman. Her father, Captain Baltus Van Hoorn, had been a burgher of substance in old Dorp, until the knavery of a sea-captain who turned pirate with a ship owned by my grandfather drove the old gentleman into poverty and idleness. For years his younger daughter, my mother, kept watch over him, contrived by hook or by crook to collect his old credits outstanding, and maintained at least enough of his business to ward the wolf from the door. It was only after his death, and after her older sister Margaret had gone to Coeymans with her husband, Kronk, that my mother married the elderly Dominie Mauverensen. When he was so untowardly killed, fifteen years later, she was left with eight children, of whom I, a toddling urchin, was among the youngest. She had no money save the pittance from Stone Arabia, no means of livelihood, nor even a roof of her own over her head, since the new dominie made harsh remarks about her keeping him out of his own every time he visited our village. To add to the wretchedness of her plight, at this very time her sister Margaret came back in destitution and weakness to her, having been both widowed and sorely shaken in wits by the small-pox.

It was then that Mr. Stewart, who had known my father, came to our relief. He first lent my mother a small sum of money—she would take no more, and was afterward very proud to repay him penny for penny. He further interested Sir William Johnson, Mr. Douw Fonda, Mr. John Butler, and others in the project of aiding her to establish a small school at Fort Hunter, where little children might be taught pure Dutch.

This language, which I have lived to see almost entirely fade from use, was even then thought to be most probably the tongue of the future in the colony, and there was the more need to teach it correctly, since, by the barbarous commingling of Rhenish peasant dialects, Irish and Scotch perversions of English, Indian phrases, the lingo of the slaves, and the curious expressions of the Yankees from the East, the most villanous jargon ever heard was commonly spoken in our Valley. My mother knew the noble language of her fathers in all its strength and sweetness, and her teaching was so highly prized that soon the school became a source of steady support to us all. Old " Uncle " Conrad— or Coonrod as we used to call him—the high-shouldered old pedagogue who was at once teacher, tithing-man, herb-doctor, and fiddler for our section, grumbled a little at the start ; but either he had not the heart to take the bread from our mouths, or his own lips were soon silenced by the persuasion of our patrons.

It was out of respect for one of these, good old Douw Fonda, who came from Schenectady to live at Caughnawaga when I was two years old, that I had been named. But even more we all owed to the quiet, lonely man who had built the log house opposite Aries Creek, and who used so often to come over on Sunday afternoons in the warm weather and pay us a friendly visit.

My earliest recollections are of this Mr. Stewart, out of whom my boyish fancy created a beneficent sort of St. Nicholas, who could be good all the year round instead of only at New Year's. As I grew older his visits seemed more and more to be connected with me, for he paid little attention to my sisters, and rarely missed taking me on his knee, or, later on, leading me out for a walk. Finally I was asked to go over and stay with him for a week, and this practically was the last of my life with my mother. Soon afterward my aunt was engaged as his housekeeper, and I tacitly became a part of the household as well. Last of all, on my eighth birthday, in this same November of '57, I was formally installed as son of the house.

It was a memorable day, as I have said, in that Tulp was given me for my own. But I think that at the time I was even more affected by the fact that I was presented with a coat, and allowed to forever lay aside my odious aprons. These garments, made by my mother's own hands, had long been the bane of my existence. To all my entreaties to be dressed as the other boys of my age were, like Matthew Wormuth or Walter Butler instead of like a Dutch infant, she was accustomed to retort that young Peter Hansenius, the son of the dominie at Schenectady, had worn aprons until he was twelve. I had never seen Peter Hansenius, nor has it ever since been my fortune so to do, but I hated him bitterly as the cause of my humiliation.

Yet when I had got my coat, and wore it, along with breeches of the same pearl-gray color, dark woollen stockings, copper buckles on my shoes, and plain lace at my wrists and neck and on my new hat, I somehow did not feel any more like the other boys than before.

It was my bringing up, I fancy, which made me a solitary lad. Continual contact with Mr. Stewart had made me older than my years. I knew the history of Holland almost as well, I imagine, as any grown man in the neighborhood, and I had read many valuable books on the history of other countries and the lives of famous men, which were in Mr. Stewart's possession. Sir William also loaned me numerous books, including the *Gentleman's Magazine*, which I studied with delight. I had also from him *Roderick Random*, which I did not at all enjoy, nor do I even now understand how it, or for that matter any of its rowdy fellows, found favor with sensible people.

My reading was all very serious—strangely so, no doubt, for a little boy—but in truth reading of any sort would have served to make me an odd sheep among my comrades. I wonder still at the unlettered condition of the boys about me. John Johnson, though seven years my senior, was so ignorant as scarcely to be able to tell the difference between the Dutch and the Germans, and whence they respectively came. He told me once, some years after this, when I was bringing an armful of volumes from his father's mansion, that a boy was a fool to pore over books when he could ride and fish and hunt instead. Young Butler was of a better sort mentally, but he too never cared to read much. Both he and the Groats, the Nellises, the Cosselmans, young Wormuth—in fact, all the boys of good families I knew in the Valley—derided education, and preferred instead to go into the woods with a negro, and hunt squirrels while he chopped, or to play with their traps.

Perhaps they were not to be blamed much, for the attractions of the rough out-of-door life which they saw men leading all about them might very easily outweigh the quiet pleasures of a book. But it was a misfortune none the less in after-years to some of them, when they allowed uninformed prejudices to lead them into a terrible course of crime against their country and their neighbors, and paid their estates or their lives as the penalty for their ignorance and folly.

Fortunately, things are better ordered for the youth of the land in these days.

CHAPTER V.

IT was on the morrow after my birthday that we
became finally convinced of the French retreat.
Mr. Stewart had returned from his journeys, contented, and sat now, after his hot supper, smoking
by the fire. I lay at his feet on a bear-skin, I
remember, reading by the light of the flames, when
my aunt brought the baby-girl in.

During the week that she had been with us, I had
been too much terrified by the menace of invasion
to take much interest in her, and Mr. Stewart had
scarcely seen her. He smiled now, and held out his
hands to her. She went to him very freely, and
looked him over with a wise, wondering expression
when he took her on his knee. It could be seen that
she was very pretty. Her little white rows of teeth
were as regular and pearly as the upper kernels on an
ear of fresh sweet corn. She had a ribbon in her
long, glossy hair, and her face shone pleasantly with
soap. My aunt had made her some shoes out of
deer-hide, which Mr. Stewart chuckled over.

"What a people the Dutch are!" he said, with a
smile. "The child is polished like the barrel of a
gun. What's your name, little one?"

The girl made no answer, from timidity I suppose.

"Has she no name? I should think she would have one," said I. It was the first time I had ever spoken to Mr. Stewart without having been addressed. But my new position in the house seemed to entitle me to this much liberty, for once.

"No," he replied, "your aunt is not able to discover that she has a name—except that she calls herself Pulkey, or something like that."

"That is not a good name to the ear," I said, in comment.

"No; doubtless it is a nickname. I have thought," he added, musingly, "of calling her Desideria."

I sat bolt upright at this. It did not become me to protest, but I could not keep the dismay from my face, evidently, for Mr. Stewart laughed aloud.

"What is it, Douw? Is it not to your liking?"

"Y-e-s, sir—but she is such a very little girl!"

"And the name is so great, eh? She'll grow to it, lad, she'll grow to it. And what kind of a Dutchman are you, sir, who are unwilling to do honor to the greatest of all Dutchmen? The Dr. Erasmus upon whose letters you are to try your Latin this winter—his name was Desiderius. Can you tell what it means? It signifies 'desired,' as of a mother's heart, and he took a form of the Greek verb *erao*, meaning about the same thing, instead. It's a goodly famous name, you see. We mean to make our little girl the truest lady, and love her the best, of all the women in the Valley. And so we'll give her a name—a fair-sounding, gracious, classical name— which no other woman bears, and one that shall always suggest home love—eh, boy?"

"But if it be so good a name, sir," I said, gingerly, being conscious of presumption, "why did Dr. Erasmus not keep it himself instead of turning it into Greek?"

My patron laughed heartily at this. "A Dutchman for obstinacy!" he said, and leaned over to rub the top of my head, which he did when I specially pleased him.

Late that night, as I lay awake in my new room, listening to the whistling of the wind in the snow-laden branches outside, an idea came to me which I determined to put into action. So next evening, when the little girl was brought in after our supper, I begged that she might be put down on the fur before the fire, to play with me, and I watched my opportunity. Mr. Stewart was reading by the candles on the table. Save for the singing of the kettle on the crane—for the mixing of his night-drink later on—and the click of my aunt's knitting-needles, there was perfect silence. I mustered my bravery, and called my wee playmate "Daisy."

I dared not look at the master, and could not tell if he had heard or not. Presently I spoke the name again, and this time ventured to steal an apprehensive glance at him, and fancied I saw the workings of a smile repressed in the deep lines about his mouth. "A Dutchman for obstinacy" truly, since two days afterward Mr. Stewart himself called the girl "Daisy"—and there was an end of it. Until confirmation time, when she played a queenly part at the head of the little class of farmers' and villagers' daughters whom Dominie Romeyn baptized into full communion, the ponderous Latin name was never heard of again. Then it indeed emerged for but a single day, to dignify a state occasion, and disappeared forever. Except alone on the confirmation register of the Stone Church at Caughnawaga, she was Daisy thenceforth for all time and to all men.

ᐱ The winter of 1757–58 is still spoken of by us old people as a season of great severity and consequent privation. The snow was drifted over the roads up to the first branches of the trees, yet rarely formed a good crust upon which one could move with snowshoes. Hence the outlying settlements, like Cherry Valley and Tribes Hill, had hard work to get food.

I do not remember that our household stood in any such need, but occasionally some Indian who had been across the hills carrying venison would come in and rest, begging for a drink of raw rum, and giving forth a strong smell like that of a tame bear as he toasted himself by the fire. Mr. Stewart was often amused by these fellows, and delighted to talk with them as far as their knowledge of language and inclination to use it went, but I never could abide them.

It has become the fashion now to be sentimental about the red man, and young people who never knew what he really was like find it easy to extol his virtues, and to create for him a chivalrous character. No doubt there were some honest creatures among them; even in Sodom and Gomorrah a few just people were found. It is true that in later life I once had occasion to depend greatly upon the fidelity of two Oneidas, and they did not fail me. But as a whole the race was a bad one—full of laziness and lies and cowardly ferocity. From earliest childhood I saw a good deal of them, and I know what I say.

Probably there was no place on the whole continent where these Indians could be better studied than in the Mohawk Valley, near to Sir William's place. They came to him in great numbers, not only from the Six Nations, but often from far-distant tribes living beyond the Lakes and north of the St. Lawrence. They were on their best behavior with him, and no doubt had an affection for him in their way, but it was because he flattered their egregious vanity by acting and dressing in Indian fashion, and made it worth their while by constantly giving them presents and rum. Their liking seemed always to me to be that of the selfish, treacherous cat, rather than of the honest dog. Their teeth and claws were always ready for your flesh, if you did not give them enough, and if they dared to strike. And they were cowards, too, for all their boasting. Not even Sir William could get them to face any enemy in the open. Their notion of war was midnight skulking and shooting from behind safe cover. Even in battle they were murderers, not warriors.

In peace they were next to useless. There was a little colony of them in our orchard one summer which I watched with much interest. The men never did one stroke of honest work all the season long, except to trot on errands when they felt like it, and occasionally salt and smoke fish which they caught in the river.

But the wretched squaws—my word but *they* worked enough for both! These women, wrinkled, dirty, sore-eyed from the smoke in their miserable huts, toiled on patiently, ceaselessly, making a great variety of wooden utensils and things of deer-hide, like snow-shoes, moccasins, and shirts, which they bartered with the whites for milk and vegetables and rum. Even the little girls among them had to gather berries and mandrake, and, in the fall, the sumach blows which the Indians used for savoring their food. And if these poor creatures obtained in their bartering too much bread and milk and too little rum and tobacco, they were beaten by their men as no white man would beat the meanest animal.

Doubtless much of my dislike for the Indian came from his ridiculous and hateful assumption of superiority over the negro. To my mind, and to all sensible minds I fancy, one simple, honest, devoted black was worth a score of these conceited, childish brutes. I was so fond of my boy Tulp, that, even as a little fellow, I deeply resented the slights and cuffs which he used to receive at the hands of the savages who lounged about in the sunshine in our vicinity. His father, mother, and brothers, who herded together in a shanty at the edge of the clearing back of us, had their faults, no doubt; but they would work when they were bid, and they were grateful to those who fed and clothed and cared for them. These were reasons for their being despised by the

Indians—and they seemed also reasons why I should like them, as I always did.

There were other reasons why I should be very fond of Tulp. He was a queer, droll little darky as a boy, full of curious fancies and comical sayings, and I never can remember a time when he would not, I veritably believe, have laid down his life for me. We were always together, indoors or out. He was exceedingly proud of his name, which was in a way a badge of ancient descent—having been borne by a long line of slaves, his ancestors, since that far-back time when the Dutch went crazy over collecting tulip-bulbs.

His father had started in life with this name, too, but, passing into the possession of an unromantic Yankee at Albany, had been re-christened Eli—a name which he loathed yet perforce retained when Mr. Stewart bought him. He was a drunken, larcenous old rascal, but as sweet-tempered as the day is long, and many's the time I've heard him vow, with maudlin tears in his eyes, that all his evil habits came upon him as the result of changing his name. If he had continued to be Tulp, he argued, he would have had some incentive to an honorable life; but what self-respecting nigger could have so low-down a name as Eli, and· be good for anything? All this warranted my boy in being proud of his name, and, so to speak, living up to it.

I have gossiped along without telling much of the long winter of 1757. In truth, there is little to tell. I happen to remember that it was a season of cruel hardship to many of our neighbors. But it was a happy time for me. What mattered it that the snow was piled outside high above my head; that food in the forest was so scarce that the wolves crept yelping close to our stockade; that we had to eat cranberries to keep off the scurvy, until I grew for all time to hate their very color; or that for five long months I never saw my mother and sisters, or went to church? It was very pleasant inside.

I seem still to see the square, home-like central room of the old house, with Mr. Stewart's bed in one corner, covered with a great robe of pieced panther skins. The smoky rafters above were hung with strings of onions, red-peppers, and long ears of Indian corn, the gold of which shone through pale parted husks and glowed in the firelight. The rude home-made table, chairs, and stools stood in those days upon a rough floor of hewn planks, on projecting corners of which an unlucky toe was often stubbed. There were various skins spread on this floor, and others on the log walls, hung up to dry. Over the great stone mantel were suspended Mr. Stewart's guns, along with his sword and pistols. Back in the corners of the fireplace were hung traps, nets, and the like, while on the opposite side of the room was the master's bookcase, well filled with volumes in English, Latin, and other tongues. Three doors, low and unpanelled, opened from this room to the other chambers of the house—leading respectively to the kitchen, to my room, and to the room now set apart for my aunt and little Daisy.

No doubt it was a poor abode, and scantily enough furnished, judged by present standards, but we were

very comfortable in it, none the less. I worked
pretty hard that winter on my Latin, conning Cæsar
for labor and Dr. Erasmus for play, and kept up my
other studies as well, reading for the first time, I
remember, the adventures of Robinson Crusoe. For
the rest, I busied myself learning to make snow-
shoes, to twist cords out of flax, to mould bullets,
and to write legibly, or else played with Daisy and
Tulp.

To confess how simply we amused ourselves, we
three little ones, would be to speak in an unknown
tongue, I fear, to modern children. Our stock of
playthings was very limited. We had, as the basis
of everything, the wooden works of the old clock,
which served now for a gristmill like that of the
Groats, now for a fort, again for a church. Then
there were the spindles of a discarded spinning-
wheel, and a small army of spools which my aunt
used for winding linen thread. These we dressed in
odd rags for dolls—soldiers, Indians, and fine ladies,
and knights of old. To our contented fancy,
there was endless interest in the lives and doings of
these poor puppets. I made them illustrate the
things I read, and the slave boy and tiny orphan girl
assisted and followed on with equal enthusiasm,
whether the play was of Alexander of Macedon, or
Captain Kidd, or only a war-council of Delaware
Indians, based upon Mr. Colden's book.

Sometimes, when it was warm enough to leave the
hearth, and Mr. Stewart desired not to be disturbed,
we would transport ourselves and our games to my
aunt's room. This would be a dingy enough place,

I suppose, even to my eyes now, but it had a great charm then.   Here from the rafters hung the dried, odoriferous herbs—sage, summer-savory, and mother-wort; bottles of cucumber ointment and of a liniment made from angle-worms—famous for cuts and bruises; strings of dried apples and pumpkins; black beans in their withered pods; sweet clover for the linen—and I know not what else besides.   On the wall were two Dutch engravings of the killing of Jan and Cornelis de Wit by the citizens of The Hague, which, despite their hideous fidelity to details, had a great fascination for me.

My childhood comes back vividly indeed to me as I recall the good old woman, in her white cap and short gown (which she had to lift to get at the pocket tied over her petticoat by a string to her waist), walking up and down with the yarn taut from the huge, buzzing wheel, crooning Dutch hymns to herself the while, and thinking about our dinner.

CHAPTER VI.

WITHIN SOUND OF THE SHOUTING WATERS.

IF I relied upon my memory, I could not tell when the French war ended. It had practically terminated, so far as our Valley was concerned, with the episode already related. Sir William Johnson was away much of the time with the army, and several of the boys older than myself—John Johnson, John Frey, and Adam Fonda among them—went with him. We heard vague news of battles at distant places, at Niagara, at Quebec, and elsewhere. Once, indeed, a band of Roman Catholic Indians appeared at Fort Herkimer and did bloody work before they were driven off, but this time there was no panic in the lower settlements.

Large troops of soldiers continually passed up and down on the river in the open seasons, some of them in very handsome clothes.

I remember one body of Highlanders in particular whose dress and mien impressed me greatly. Mr. Stewart, too, was much excited by the memories this noble uniform evoked, and had the officers into the house to eat and drink with him. I watched and listened to these tall, fierce, bare-kneed warriors in awe, from a distance. He brought out bottles from his rare stock of Madeira, and they drank it

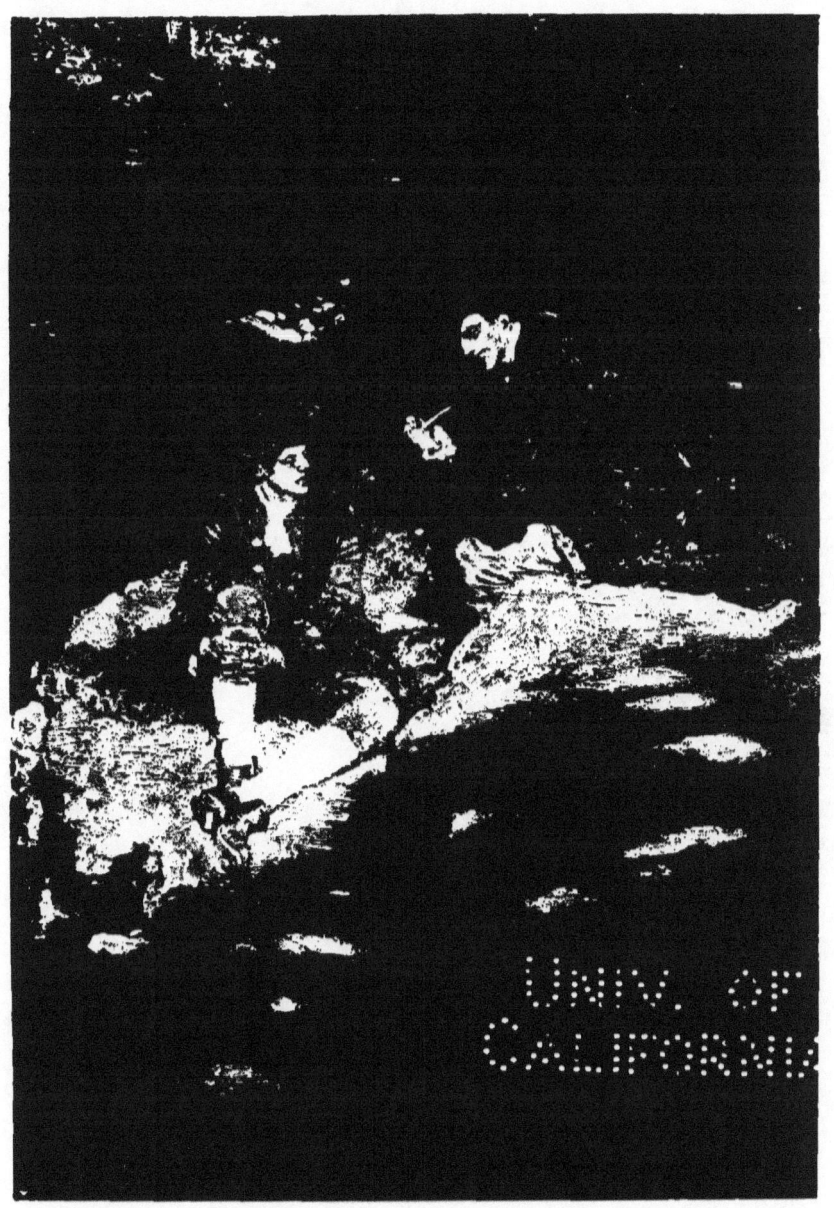

Within sound of the snouting waters. *p. 61*

amid exclamations which, if I mistake not, were highly treasonable. This was almost the last occasion on which I heard references made to his descent, and he did his best to discourage them then. Most of these fine red-haired men, I learned afterward, laid their bones on the bloody plateau overlooking Quebec.

Far fresher in my recollection than these rumors of war is the fact that my Tulp caught the small-pox, in the spring of '60, the malady having been spread by a Yankee who came up the Valley selling sap-spouts that were turned with a lathe instead of being whittled. The poor little chap was carried off to a sheep-shed on the meadow clearing, a long walk from our house, and he had to remain there by himself for six weeks. At my urgent request, I was allowed to take his food to him daily, leaving it on a stone outside and then discreetly retiring. He would come out and get it, and then we would shout to each other across the creek. I took up some of our dolls to him, but he did not get much comfort out of them, being unable to remember any of the stories which I illustrated with them, or to invent any for himself. At his suggestion I brought him instead a piece of tanned calf-skin, with a sailor's needle and some twine, and the little fellow made out of this a lot of wallets for his friends, which had to be buried a long time before they could be safely used. I have one of these yet—mildewed with age, and most rudely stitched, but still a very precious possession.

Tulp came out finally, scarred and twisted so that he was ever afterward repellent to the eye, and as crooked as Richard the Third. I fear that Daisy never altogether liked him after this. To me he was dearer than ever, not because my heart was tenderer than hers, of course, but because women are more delicately made, and must perforce shudder at ugliness.

How happily the years went by! The pictures in my memory, save those of the snug winter rooms already referred to, are all of a beautiful Valley, embowered in green, radiant with sunshine—each day live-long with delight.

There was first of all in the spring, when the chorus of returning song-birds began, the gathering of maple-sap, still sacred to boyhood. The sheep were to be washed and sheared, too, and the awkward, weak-kneed calves to be fed. While the spring floods ran high, ducks and geese covered the water, and musk-rats came out, driven from their holes. Then appeared great flocks of pigeons, well fattened from their winter's sojourn in the South, and everybody, young and old, gave himself up to their slaughter; while this lasted, the crack! crack! of guns was heard all the forenoon long, particularly if the day was cloudy and the birds were flying low—and ah! the buttered pigeon pies my aunt made, too.

As the floods went down, and the snow-water disappeared, the fishing began, first with the big, silly suckers, then with wiser and more valued fish. The woods became dry, and then in long, joyous rambles we set traps and snares, hunted for nests among the low branches and in the marsh-grass, smoked woodchucks out of their holes, gathered wild flowers, winter-green, and dye-plants, or built great fires of the dead leaves and pithless, scattered branches, as boys to the end of time will delight to do.

When autumn came, there were mushrooms, and beech-nuts, butter-nuts, hickory-nuts, wild grapes, pucker-berries, not to speak of loads of elder-berries for making wine. And the pigeons, flying southward, darkened the sky once more; and then the horses were unshod for treading out the wheat, and we children fanned away the chaff with big palm-leaves; and the combs of honey were gathered and shelved; and the October husking began by our having the first kettleful of white corn, swollen and hulled by being boiled in lye of wood ashes, spooned steaming into our porringers of milk by my aunt.

Ah, they were happy times indeed!

Every other Sunday, granted tolerable weather, I crossed the river early in the morning to attend church with my mother and sisters. It is no reflection upon my filial respect, I hope, to confess that these are wearisome memories. We went in solemn procession, the family being invariably ready and waiting when I arrived. We sat in a long row in a pew quite in front of the slate-colored pulpit—my mother sitting sternly upright at the outer end, my tallest sister next, and so on, in regular progression, down to wretched baby Gertrude and me. The very color of the pew, a dull Spanish brown, was enough to send one to sleep, and its high, uncompromising back made all my bones ache.

Yet I was forced to keep awake, and more, to look deeply interested. I was a clergyman's son, and the ward of an important man; I was the best-dressed youngster in the congregation, and brought a slave of my own to church with me. So Dominie Romeyn always fixed his lack-lustre eye on me, and seemed to develop all his long, prosy arguments one by one to me personally. Even when he turned the hour-glass in front of him, he seemed to indicate that it was quite as much my affair as his. I dared not twist clear around, to see Tulp sitting among the negroes and Indians, on one of the backless benches under the end gallery; it was scarcely possible even to steal glances up to the side galleries, where the boys of lower degree were at their mischief, and where fits of giggling and horse-play rose and spread from time to time until the tithing-man, old Conrad to wit, burst in and laid his hickory gad over their irreverent heads.

When at last I could escape without discredit, and get across the river again, it was with the consoling thought that the next Sunday would be Mr. Stewart's Sunday.

This meant a good long walk with my patron. Sometimes we would go down to Mount Johnson, if Sir William was at home, or to Mr. Butler's, or some other English-speaking house, where I would hear much profitable conversation, and then be encouraged to talk about it during our leisurely homeward stroll. But more often, if the day were fine, we would leave roads and civilization behind us, and climb the gradual elevation to the north of the house, through the woodland to an old Indian trail which led to our favorite haunt—a wonderful ravine.

The place has still a local fame, and picnic parties go there to play at forestry, but it gives scarcely a suggestion now of its ancient wildness. As my boyish eyes saw it, it was nothing short of awe-inspiring. The creek, then a powerful stream, had cut a deep gorge in its exultant leap over the limestone barrier. On the cliffs above, giant hemlocks seemed to brush the very sky with their black, tufted boughs. Away below, on the shadowed bottomland, which could be reached only by feet trained to difficult descents, strange plants grew rank in the moisture of the waterfall, and misshapen rocks wrapped their nakedness in heavy folds of unknown mosses and nameless fern-growths. Above all was the ceaseless shout of the tumbling waters, which had in my ears ever a barbaric message from the Spirit of the Wilderness.

The older Mohawks told Mr. Stewart that in their childhood this weird spot was held to be sacred to the Great Wolf, the totem of their tribe. Here, for more generations than any could count, their wise men had gathered about the mystic birch flame, in grave council of war. Here the tribe had assembled to seek strength of arm, hardness of heart, cunning of brain, for its warriors, in solemn incantations and offerings to the Unknown. Here hostile prisoners had been tortured and burned. Some mishap or omen or shift of superstitious feeling had led to the abandonment of this council place. Even the trail, winding its tortuous way from the Valley over the hills toward the Adirondack fastnesses, had been deserted for another long before—so long, in fact, that the young brave who chanced to follow the

lounging tracks of the black bear down the creek to
the gorge, or who turned aside from the stealthy
pursuit of the eagle's flight to learn what this muffled roar might signify, looked upon the remains of
the council fire's circle of stone seats above the cata-
ract, and down into the chasm of mist and foam
underneath, with no knowledge that they were a part
of his ancestral history.

Mr. Stewart told me that when he first settled in
the Valley, a disappointed and angry man, this gulf
had much the satisfaction for him that men in great
grief or wrath find in breasting a sharp storm. There
was something congenial to his ugly unrest in this
place, with its violent clamor, its swift dashing of
waters, its dismal shadows, and damp chilliness of
depths.

But we were fallen now upon calmer, brighter
days. He was no longer the discouraged, sullen
misanthropist, but had come to be instead a pacific,
contented, even happy, gentleman. And lo! the
meaning of the wild gorge changed to reflect his
mood. There was no stain of savagery upon the
delight we had in coming to this spot. As he said,
once listened rightly to, the music of the falling
waters gave suggestions which, if they were sober-
ing, were still not sad.

This place was all our own, and hither we most
frequently bent our steps on Sundays, after the
snow-water had left the creek, and the danger of
lurking colds had been coaxed from the earth by
the May sun. Here he would sit for hours on one
of the stones in the great Druid-like circle which

some dead generation of savages had toiled to construct. Sometimes I would scour the steep sides of
the ravine and the moist bottom for curious plants
to fetch to him, and he would tell me of their structure and design. More often I would sit at his feet,
and he, between whiffs at his pipe, would discourse
to me of the differences between his Old World and
this new one, into which I providentially had been
born. He talked of his past, of my future, and
together with this was put forth an indescribable
wealth of reminiscence, reflection, and helpful
anecdote.

On this spot, with the gaunt outlines of mam-
moth primeval trunks and twisted boughs above us,
with the sacred memorials of extinct rites about
us, and with the waters crashing down through the
solitude beneath us on their way to turn Sir William's mill-wheel, one could get broad, comprehensive ideas of what things really meant. One could
see wherein the age of Pitt differed from and
advanced upon the age of Colbert, on this new
continent, and could as in prophecy dream of the
age of Jefferson yet to come. Did I as a lad feel
these things? Truly it seems to me that I did.

Half a century before, the medicine-man's fire had
blazed in this circle, its smoky incense crackling
upward in offering to the gods of the pagan tribe.
Here, too, upon this charred, barren spot, had been
heaped the blazing fagots about the limbs of the
captive brave, and the victim bound to the stake
had nerved himself to show the encircling brutes
that not even the horrors of this death could shake

his will, or wring a groan from his heaving breast.
Here, too, above the unending din of the waterfall
and the whisper of these hemlocks overhead, had
often risen some such shrill-voiced, defiant death-
song, from the smoke and anguish of the stake, as
that chant of the Algonquin son of Alknomuk
which my grandchildren still sing at their school.
This dead and horrible past of heathendom I saw as
in a mirror, looking upon these council-stones.

The children's children of these savages were
still in the Valley. Their council fires were still
lighted, no further distant than the Salt Springs.
In their hearts burned all the old lust for torture
and massacre, and the awful joys of rending enemies
limb by limb. But the spell of Europe was upon
them, and, in good part or otherwise, they bowed
under it. So much had been gained, and two peaceful white people could come and talk in perfect safety
on the ancient site of their sacrifices and cruelties.

Yet this spell of Europe, accomplishing so much,
left much to be desired. It was still possible to
burn a slave to death by legal process, here in
our Valley; and it was still within the power of
careless, greedy noblemen in London, who did not
know the Mohawk from the Mississippi, to sign
away great patents of our land, robbing honest
settlers of their all. There was to come the spell of
America, which should remedy these things. I cannot get it out of my head that I learned to foresee
this, to feel and to look for its coming, there in the
gorge as a boy.

But there are other reasons why I should remember the place—to be told later on.

The part little Daisy played in all these childhood enjoyments of mine is hardly to be described in words, much less portrayed in incidents. I can recall next to nothing to relate. Her presence as my sister, my comrade, and my pupil seems only an indefinable part of the sunshine which gilds these old memories. We were happy together—that is all.

I taught her to read and write and cipher, and to tell mushrooms from toadstools, to eschew poisonous berries, and to know the weather signs. For her part, she taught me so much more that it seems effrontery to call her my pupil. It was from her gentle, softening companionship that I learned in turn to be merciful to helpless creatures, and to be honest and cleanly in my thoughts and talk. She would help me to seek for birds' nests with genuine enthusiasm, but it was her pity which prevented their being plundered afterward. Her pretty love for all living things, her delight in innocent, simple amusements, her innate repugnance to coarse and cruel actions—all served to make me different from the rough boys about me.

Thus we grew up together, glad in each other's constant company, and holding our common benefactor, Mr. Stewart, in the greatest love and veneration.

CHAPTER VII.

As we two children became slowly transformed into youths, the Valley with no less steadiness developed in activity, population, and wealth. Good roads were built; new settlements sprang up; the sense of being in the hollow of the hand of savagery wore off. Primitive conditions lapsed, disappeared one by one. We came to smile at the uncouth dress and unshaven faces of the "bush-bauer" Palatines—once so familiar, now well nigh outlandish. Families from Connecticut and the Providence Plantations began to come in numbers, and their English tongue grew more and more to be the common language. People spoke now of the Winchester bushel, instead of the Schoharie spint and skipple. The bounty on wolves' heads went up to a pound sterling. The number of gentlemen who shaved every day, wore ruffles, and even wigs or powder on great occasions, and maintained hunting with hounds and horse-racing, increased yearly —so much so that some innocent people thought England itself could not offer more attractions.

There was much envy when John Johnson, now twenty-three years old, was sent on a visit to England, to learn how still better to play the gentleman—and even more when he came back a knight, with splendid London clothes, and stories of what the King and the princes had said to him.

The Johnsons were a great family now, receiving visits from notable people all over the colony at their new hall, which Sir William had built on the hills back of his new Scotch settlement. Nothing could have better shown how powerful Sir William had become, and how much his favor was to be courted, than the fact that ladies of quality and strict propriety, who fancied themselves very fine folk indeed, the De Lanceys and Phillipses and the like, would come visiting the widower baronet in his hall, and close their eyes to the presence there of Miss Molly and her half-breed children. Sir William's neighbors, indeed, overlooked this from their love for the man, and their reliance in his sense and strength. But the others, the aristocrats, held their tongues from fear of his wrath, and of his influence in London.

They never liked him entirely; he in turn had so little regard for them and their pretensions that, when they came, he would suffer none of them to markedly avoid or affront the Brant squaw, whom indeed they had often to meet as an associate and equal. Yet this bold, independent, really great man, so shrewdly strong in his own attitude toward these gilded water-flies, was weak enough to rear his own son to be one of them, to value the baubles they valued, to view men and things through their painted spectacles—and thus to come to grief.

Two years after Johnson Hall was built, Mr.

5

Stewart all at once decided that he too would have
a new house; and before snow flew the handsome,
spacious " Cedars," as it was called, proudly fronted
the Valley highway. Of course it was not, in size,
a rival of the Hall at Johnstown, but it none the
less was among the half-dozen best houses in the
Mohawk Valley, and continued so to be until John
Johnson burned it to the ground fifteen years later.
It stood in front of our old log structure, now
turned over to the slaves. It was of two stories,
with lofty and spacious rooms, and from the road it
presented a noble appearance, now that the old
stockade had given place to a wall of low, regular
masonry.

With this new residence came a prodigious change
in our way of life. Daisy was barely twelve years
old, but we already thought of her as the lady of the
house, for whom nothing was too good. The walls
were plastered, and stiff paper from Antwerp with
great sprawling arabesques, and figures of nymphs
and fauns chasing one another up and down with
ceaseless, fruitless persistency, was hung upon them,
at least in the larger rooms. The floors were laid
smoothly, each board lapping into the next by a
then novel joiner's trick.

On the floor in Daisy's room there was a carpet,
too, a rare and remarkable thing in those days, and
also from the Netherlands. In this same chamber,
as well, were set up a bed of mahogany, cunningly
carved and decorated, and a tall foreign cabinet of
some rich dark wood, for linen, frocks, and the like.
Here, likewise, were two gilt cages from Paris, in

which a heart-breaking succession of native birds drooped and died, until four Dublin finches were at last imported for Daisy's special delight ; and a case with glass doors and a lock, made in Boston, wherein to store her books; and, best of all, a piano—or was it a harpsichord?—standing on its own legs, which Mr. Stewart heard of as for sale in New York and bought at a pretty high figure. This last was indeed a rickety, jangling old box, but Daisy learned in a way to play upon it, and we men-folk, sitting in her room in the candle-light, and listening to her voice cooing to its shrill tinkle of accompaniment, thought the music as sweet as that of the cherubim.

Mr. Stewart and I lived in far less splendor. There was no foreign furniture to speak of in our portions of the house ; we slept on beds the cords of which creaked through honest American maple posts ; we walked on floors which offered gritty sand to the tread instead of carpet-stuffs. But there were two great stands laden with good books in our living-room ; we had servants now within sound of a bell ; we habitually wore garments befitting men of refinement and substance ; we rode our own horses, and we could have given Daisy a chaise had the condition of our roads made it desirable.

I say " we " because I had come to be a responsible factor in the control of the property. Mr. Stewart had never been poor ; he was now close upon being wealthy. Upon me little by little had devolved the superintendence of affairs. I directed the burning over and clearing of land, which every year added scores of tillable acres to our credit ; saw to the

planting, care, and harvesting of crops ; bought, bred,
and sold the stock; watched prices, dickered with
travelling traders, provisioned the house—in a word,
grew to be the manager of all, and this when I was
barely twenty.

Mr. Stewart bore his years with great strength,
physically, but he readily gave over to me, as fast as
I could assume them, the details of out-door work.
The taste for sitting in-doors or in the garden, and
reading, or talking with Daisy—the charm of simply
living in a home made beautiful by a good and clever
young girl—gained yearly upon him.

Side by side with this sedentary habit, curiously
enough, came up a second growth of old-world, me-
diæval notions—a sort of aristocratic aftermath.　It
was natural, no doubt.　His inborn feudal ideas had
not been killed by ingratitude, exile, or his rough-
and-ready existence on the edge of the wilderness,
but only chilled to dormancy ; they warmed now into
life under the genial radiance of a civilized home.
But it is not my purpose to dwell upon this change,
or rather upon its results, at this stage of the
story.

Social position was now a matter for consideration.　With improved means of intercourse and traffic, each year found some family thrifty enough to
thrust its head above the rude level of settlers'
equality, and take on the airs of superiority.　Twenty
years before, it had been Colonel Johnson first, and
nobody else second.　Now the Baronet-General was
still preëminently first ; but every little community
in the Valley chain had its two or three families

We men-folk thought the music as sweet as that of the cherubim.

holding themselves only a trifle lower than the Johnsons.

Five or six nationalities were represented. Of the Germans, there were the Herkimers up above the Falls, the Lawyers at Schoharie, the Freys (who were commonly thus classed, though they came originally from Switzerland), and many others. Of important Dutch families, there were the Fondas at Caughnawaga, the Mabies and Groats at Rotterdam, below us, and the Quackenbosses to the west of us, across the river. The Johnsons and Butlers were Irish. Over at Cherry Valley the Campbells and Clydes were Scotch—the former being, indeed, close blood relatives of the great Argyll house. Colonel Isaac Paris, a prominent merchant near Stone Arabia, came from Strasbourg, and accounted himself a Frenchman, though he spoke German better than French, and attended the Dutch Calvinistic church. There were also English families of quality. I mention them all to show how curious was the admixture of races in our Valley. One cannot understand the terrible trouble which came upon us later without some knowledge of these race divisions.

Mr. Stewart held a place in social estimation rather apart from any of these cliques. He was both Scotch and Irish by ancestry; he was French by education; he had lived and served in the Netherlands and sundry German states. Thus he could be all things to all men—yet he would not. He indeed became more solitary as he grew older, for the reasons I have already mentioned. He once had been friendly with all his intelligent neighbors, no matter what their

nationality. Gradually he came to be intimate with
only the Johnsons and Butlers, on the theory that
they were alone well born. Hours upon hours he
talked with them of the Warrens and the Ormund-
Butlers in Ireland, from whom they claimed descent,
and of the assurance of Dutch and German cobblers
and tinkers, in setting up for gentlemen.

Sir William, in truth, had too much sense to often
join or sympathize with these notions. But young
Sir John and the Butlers, father and son, adopted
them with enthusiasm, and I am sorry to say there
were both Dutch and German residents, here and
there, mean-spirited enough to accept these reflections upon their ancestry, and strive to atone for
their assumed lack of birth by aping the manners,
and fawning for the friendship, of their critics.

But let me defer these painful matters as long as
possible. There are still the joys of youth to recall.

I had grown now into a tall, strong young man,
and I was in the way of meeting no one who did not
treat me as an equal. It seems to me now that I was
not particularly popular among my fellows, but I was
conscious of no loneliness then. I had many things
to occupy my mind, besides my regular tasks. Both
natural history and botany interested me greatly,
and I was privileged also to assist Sir William's in-
vestigations in the noble paths of astronomy. He
had both large information and many fine thoughts
on the subject, and used laughingly to say that if he
were not too lazy he would write a book thereon.
This was his way of saying that he had more labor
to get through than any other man in the Colony.

It was his idea that some time I should write the work instead ; upon the Sacondaga hills, he said, we saw and read the heavens without Old-World dust in our eyes, and our book that was to be should teach the European moles the very alphabet of planets. Alas! I also was too indolent—truly, not figura- tively ; the book was never written.

In those days there was royal sport for rod and gun, but books also had a solid worth. We did not visit other houses much—Daisy and I—but held ourselves to a degree apart. The British people were, as a whole, nearer our station than the others, and had more ideas in common with us; but they were not of our blood, and we were not drawn toward many of them. As they looked down upon the Dutch, so the Dutch, in turn, were supercilious to- ward the Germans. I was Dutch, Daisy was Ger- man ; but by a sort of tacit consent we identified ourselves with neither race, and this aided our iso- lation.

There was also the question of religion. Mr. Stewart had been bred a Papist, and at the time of which I write, after the French war, Jesuit priests of that nation several times visited him to renew old European friendships. But he never went to mass, and never allowed them or anybody else to speak with him on the subject, no matter how deftly they approached it. This was prudent, from a worldly point of view, because the Valley, and for that mat- ter the whole upper Colony, was bitterly opposed to Romish pretensions, and the first Scotch Highlanders who brought the mass into the Valley above Johnstown were openly denounced as idolaters. But it was certainly not caution which induced Mr. Stewart's backsliding. He was not the man to defer in that way to the prejudices of others. The truth was that he had no religious beliefs or faith whatever. But his scepticism was that of the French noble of the time, that of Voltaire and Mirabeau, rather than of the English plebeian and democrat, Thomas Paine.

Naturally Daisy and I were not reared as theologians. We nominally belonged to the Calvinistic church, but not being obliged to attend its services, rarely did so. This tended to further separate us from our neighbors, who were mainly prodigious church-goers.

But, more than all else, we lived by ourselves because, by constant contact with refined associations, we had grown to shrink from the coarseness which ruled outside. All about us marriages were made between mere children, each boy setting up for himself and taking a wife as soon as he had made a voyage to the Lakes and obtained a start in fur-trading. There was precious little sentiment or delicacy in these early courtships and matches, or in the state of society which they reflected—uncultured, sordid, rough, unsympathetic, with all its elementary instincts bluntly exposed and expressed. This was of course a subject not to be discussed by us. Up to the spring of 1772, when I was twenty-three years of age and Daisy was eighteen, no word of all the countless words which young men and women have from the dawn of language spoken on this great engrossing topic had ever been exchanged between us.

In earlier years, when we were on the threshold of our teens, Mr. Stewart had more than once thought aloud in our hearing upon the time when we should inherit his home and fortune as a married couple. Nothing of that talk, though, had been heard for a long while.

I had not entirely forgotten it ; but I carried the idea along in the attic of my mind, as a thing not to be thrown away, yet of no present use or value or interest.

Occasionally, indeed, I did recall it for the moment, and cast a diffident conjecture as to whether Daisy also remembered. Who shall say? I have been young and now am old, yet have I not learned the trick of reading a woman's mind. Very far indeed was I from it in those callow days.

And now, after what I fear has been a tiresome enough prologue, my story awaits.

CHAPTER VIII.

IT is averred that all the evils and miseries of our existence were entailed upon us by the meddlesome and altogether gratuitous perverseness of one weak-headed woman. Although faith in the personal influence of Eve upon the ages is visibly waning in these incredulous, iconoclastic times, there still remains enough respect for the possibilities for mischief inherent within a single silly woman to render Lady Berenicia Cross and her works intelligible, even to the fifth and sixth generations.

I knew that she was a fool the moment I first laid eyes on her—as she stood courtesying and simpering to us on the lawn in front of Johnson Hall, her patched and raddled cheeks mocking the honest morning sunlight. I take no credit that my eyes had a clearer vision than those of my companions, but grieve instead that it was not ordered otherwise.

We had ridden up to the hall, this bright, warm May forenoon, on our first visit of the spring to the Johnsons. There is a radiant picture of this morning ride still fresh in my memory. Daisy, I remember, sat on a pillion behind Mr. Stewart, holding him by the shoulder, and jogging pleasantly along with the motion of the old horse. Our patron looked old in

this full, broad light; the winter had obviously aged
him. His white, queued hair no longer needed powder; his light blue eyes seemed larger than ever under the bristling brows, still dark in color; the pro-
file of his lean face, which had always been so nobly
commanding in outline, had grown sharper of late;
and bended nose and pointed chin were closer together, from the shrinking of the lips. But he sat
erect as of old, proud of himself and of the beautiful girl behind him.

And she *was* beautiful, was our Daisy! Her
rounded, innocent face beamed with pleasure from
its camlet hood, as sweet and suggestive of fragrance,
as a damask rose against the blue sky. It was almost a childish face in its simplicity and frankness,
yet already beginning to take on a woman's thought-
fulness and a woman's charm of tint and texture.
We often thought that her parents must have had
other than Palatine peasant blood, so delicate and
refined were her features, not realizing that books
and thoughts help far more toward making faces than
does ancestry. Just the edge of her wavy light-
brown hair could be seen under the frill of the hood,
with lines of gold upon it painted by the sun.

She laughed and talked gayly as our horses climbed
the hills. I thought, as I rode by their side, how
happy we all were, and how beautiful was she—this
flower plucked from the rapine and massacre of the
Old War! And I fancy the notion that we were no
longer children began dancing in my head a little,
too.

It would have been strange otherwise, for the day

and the scene must have stirred the coldest pulse.
We moved through a pale velvety panorama of green
—woodland and roadside and river reflections and
shadows, all of living yet young and softening green ;
the birds all about us filled the warm air with song ;
the tapping of the woodpeckers and the shrill chatter of squirrels came from every thicket ; there was
nothing which did not reflect our joyous, buoyant
delight that spring had come again. And I rode by
Daisy's side, and thought more of her, I'm bound,
than I did of the flood-dismantled dike on the river-
bend at home which I had left unrestored for the
day.

Over the heads of the negroes, who, spying us,
came headlong to take our horses, we saw Sir William standing in the garden with an unknown lady.
The baronet himself, walking a little heavily with
his cane, approached us with hearty salutations,
helped Daisy to unmount, and presented us to this
stranger—Lady Berenicia Cross.

I am not so sure that people can fall in love at first
sight. But never doubt their ability to dislike from
the beginning! I know that I felt indignantly intolerant of this woman even before, hat in hand, I
had finished my bow to her.

Yet it might well have been that I was over-harsh
in my judgment. She had been a pretty woman in
her time, and still might be thought well-favored.
At least *she* must have thought so, for she wore more
paint and ribbons, and fal-lals generally, than ever I
saw on another woman, before or since. Her face was
high, narrow, and very regular ; oddly enough, it was

in outline, with its thin, pursed-up mouth, straight
nose, and full eyelids and brows, very like a face one
would expect to see in a nun's hood. Yet so little
in the character of the cloister did this countenance
keep, that it was plastered thick with chalk and rouge,
and sprinkled with ridiculous black patches, and bore,
as it rose from the low courtesy before me, an unnatural smile half-way between a leer and a grin.

I may say that I was a wholesome-enough looking
young fellow, very tall and broad-shouldered, with a
long, dark face, which was ugly in childhood, but
had grown now into something like comeliness. I
am not parading special innocence either, but no
woman had ever looked into my eyes with so bold,
I might say impudent, an expression as this fine lady
put on to greet me. And she was old enough to be
my mother, almost, into the bargain.

But even more than her free glances, which, after
all, meant no harm, but only reflected London manners, her dress grated upon me. We were not unac-
customed to good raiment in the Valley. Johnson
Hall, which reared its broad bulk through the trees
on the knoll above us, had many a time sported richer
and costlier toilets in its chambers than this before
us. But on my lady the gay stuffs seemed painfully
out of place—like her feather fan, and smelling-salts,
and dainty netted purse. The mountains and girdling forests were real; the strong-faced, burly, handsome baronet, whose words spoken here in the back-
woods were law to British king and Parliament, was
real; we ourselves, suitably and decently clad, and
knowing our position, were also genuine parts of the

scene. The English lady was pinchbeck by contrast
with all about her.

"Will you give the ladies an arm, Douw?" said
Sir William. "We were walking to see the lilacs I
planted a year ago. We old fellows, with so much
to say to each other, will lead the way."

Nothing occurred to me to say to the new acquaintance, who further annoyed me by clinging
to my arm with a zeal unpleasantly different from
Daisy's soft touch on the other side. I walked silent, and more or less sulky, between them down the
gravelled path. Lady Berenicia chattered steadily.

"And so this is the dear little Mistress Daisy of
whom Sir William talks so much. How happy one
must be to be such a favorite everywhere! And you
content to live here, too, leading this simple, pastoral life! How sweet! And you never weary of
it—never sigh when it is time to return to it from
New York?"

"I never have been to New York, nor Albany
either," Daisy made answer.

Lady Berenicia held up her fan in pretended as-
tonishment.

"Never to New York! nor even to Albany! *Une
vraie belle sauvage!* How you amaze me, poor
child!"

"Oh, I crave no pity, madam," our dear girl answered, cheerily. "My father and brother are so
good to me—just like a true father and brother—
that if I but hinted a wish to visit the moon, they
would at once set about to arrange the voyage. I
do not always stay at home. Twice I have been on

a visit to Mr. Campbell, at Cherry Valley, over the hills yonder. And then once we made a grand excursion up the river, way to Fort Herkimer, and beyond to the place where my poor parents lost their lives."

As we stood regarding the lilac bushes, planted in a circle on the slope, and I was congratulating myself that my elbows were free again, two gentlemen approached us from the direction of the Hall.

Daisy was telling the story of her parents' death, which relation Lady Berenicia had urgently pressed, but now interrupted by saying: "There, that is my husband, with young Mr. Butler."

Mr. Jonathan Cross seemed a very honest and sensible gentleman when we came to converse with him; somewhat austere, in the presence of his rattle-headed spouse at least, but polite and well-informed. He spoke pleasantly with me, saying that he was on his way to the farther Lake country on business, and that his wife was to remain, until his return, at Johnson Hall.

His companion was Walter Butler, and of him I ought to speak more closely, since long generations after this tale is forgotten his name will remain written, blood-red, in the Valley's chronicles. I walked away from the lilacs with him, I recall, discussing some unremembered subject. I always liked Walter: even now, despite everything, there continues a soft spot in my memory for him.

He was about my own age, and, oh! such a handsome youth, with features cut as in a cameo, and pale-brown smooth skin, and large deep eyes, that look upon me still sometimes in dreams with ineffable melancholy. He was somewhat beneath my stature, but formed with perfect delicacy.

In those old days of breeches and long hose, a man's leg went for a good deal. I have often thought that there must be a much closer connection between trousers and democracy than has ever been publicly traced. A man like myself, with heavy knee-joints and a thick ankle, was almost always a Whig in the Revolutionary time—as if by natural prejudice against the would-be aristocrats, who liked to sport a straight-sinking knee-cap and dapper calf. When the Whigs, after the peace, became masters of their own country, and divided into parties again on their own account, it was still largely a matter of lower limbs. The faction which stood nearest Old-World ideas and monarchical tastes are said to have had great delight in the symmetry of Mr. Adams's underpinning, so daintily displayed in satin and silk. And when the plainer majority finally triumphed with the induction of Mr. Jefferson, some fifteen years since, was it not truly a victory of republican trousers—a popular decree that henceforth all men should be equal as to legs?

To return. Walter Butler was most perfectly built—a living picture of grace.\ He dressed, too, with remarkable taste, contriving always to appear the gentleman, yet not out of place in the wilderness. He wore his own black hair, carelessly tied or flowing, and with no thought of powder.

We had always liked each other, doubtless in that we were both of a solemn and meditative nature.

We had not much else in common, it is true, for he was filled to the nostrils with pride about the Ormond-Butlers, whom he held to be his ancestors, and took it rather hard that I should not also be able to revere them for upholding a false-tongued king against the rights of his people. For my own part, I did not pin much faith upon his descent, being able to remember his grandfather, the old licutenant, who seemed a peasant to the marrow of his bones.

Nor could I see any special value in the fact of descent, even were it unquestioned. Walter, it seemed to me, would do much better to work at the law, to which he was bred, and make a name for himself by his own exertions. Alas, he did make a name!

But though our paths would presently diverge, we still were good friends, and as we walked he told me what he had heard that day of Lady Berenicia Cross. It was not much. She had been the daughter of a penniless, disreputable Irish earl, and had wedded early in life to escape the wretchedness of her paternal home. She had played quite a splendid part for a time in the vanities of London court-life, after her husband gained his wealth, but had latterly found her hold upon fashion's favor loosened. Why she had accompanied her serious spouse on this rough and wearisome journey was not clear. It might be that she came because he did not care for her company. It might be that he thought it wisest not to leave her in London to her own devices. In any case, here she indubitably was, and Walter was dis-

6

posed to think her rather a fine woman for her years, which he took to be about twoscore.

We strolled back again to the lilacs, where the two women were seated on a bench, with Mr. Cross and Colonel Claus—the brighter and better of Sir William's two sons-in-law—standing over them. Lady Berenicia beckoned to my companion with her fan.

"Pray come and amuse us, Mr. Butler," she said, in her high, mincing tones. "Were it not for the fear of ministering to your vanity, I might confess we two have been languishing for an hour for your company. Mistress Daisy and I venerate these cavaliers of ours vastly—we hold their grave wisdom in high regard—but our frivolous palates need lighter things than East India Companies and political quarrels in Boston. I command you to discourse nonsense, Mr. Butler—pure, giddy nonsense."

Walter bowed, and with a tinge of irony acknowledged the compliment, but all pleasantly enough. I glanced at our Daisy, expecting to discover my own distaste for this silly speech mirrored on her face. It vexed me a little to see that she seemed instead to be pleased with the London lady.

"What shall it be, my lady?" smiled Walter; "what shall be the shuttlecock—the May races, the ball, the Klock scandal, the——"

If it was rude, it is too late to be helped now. I interrupted the foolish talk by asking Colonel Claus what the news from Boston was, for the post-boy had brought papers to the Hall that morning.

" The anniversary speech is reported. Some apothecary, named Warren, held forth this year, and his seems the boldest tongue yet. If his talk stinks not of treason in every line, why then I have no smelling sense. They are talking of it in the library now ; but I am no statesman, and it suits me better out here in the sun."

" But," I replied, " I have heard of this Dr. Warren, and he is not reputed to be a rash or thoughtless speaker."

Young Butler burst into the conversation with eager bitterness :

" Thoughtless ! Rash ! No—the dogs know better ! There'll be no word that can be laid hold upon —all circumspect outside, with hell itself underneath. Do we not know the canters ? Oh, but I'd smash through letter and seal of the law alike to get at them, were I in power ! There'll be no peace till some strong hand does do it."

Walter's deep eyes flashed and glowed as he spoke, and his face was shadowed with grave intensity of feeling.

There was a moment's silence—broken by the thin voice of the London lady : " *Bravo !* admirable ! Always be in a rage, Mr. Butler, it suits you so much.—Isn't he handsome, Daisy, with his feathers all on end ? "

While our girl, unused to such bold talk, looked blushingly at the young grass, Mr. Cross spoke :

" Doubtless you gentry of New York have your own good reasons for disliking Boston men, as I find you do. But why rasp your nerves and spoil your digestion by so fuming over their politics? I am an Englishman: if I can keep calm on the subject, you who are only collaterally aggrieved, as it were, should surely be able to do so. My word for it, young men, life brings vexations enough to one's very door, without setting out in quest of them."

" Pray, Mr. Cross," languidly sneered my lady, " what is there in the heavens or on the earth, or in the waters under the earth, which could stir your blood by one added beat an hour, save indigo and spices? "

There was so distinct a menace of domestic discord in this iced query that Butler hastened to take up the talk:

" Ah, yes, *you* can keep cool! There are thousands of miles of water between you English and the nest where this treason is hatched. It's close to us. Do you think you can fence in a sentiment as you can cattle? No: it will spread. Soon what is shouted in Boston will be spoken in Albany, whispered in Philadelphia, winked and nodded in Williamsburg, thought in Charleston. And how will it be here, with us? Let me tell you, Mr. Cross, we are really in an alien country here. The high Germans above us, like that Herkimer you saw here Tuesday, do you think they care a pistareen for the King? And these damned sour-faced Dutch traders below, have they forgotten that this province was their grandfathers'? The moment it becomes clear to their niggard souls that there's no money to be lost by treason, will they not delight to help on any trouble the Yankees contrive to make for England?

I tell you, sir, if you knew these Dutch as I know them—their silent treachery, their jealousy of us, their greed——"

This seemed to have gone far enough. "Come, you forget that I am a Dutchman," I said, putting my hand on Butler's shoulder.

Quivering with the excitement into which he had worked himself, he shook off my touch, and took a backward step, eying me angrily. I returned his gaze, and I dare say it was about as wrathful as his own.

Lady Berenicia made a diversion. "It grows cool," she said. "Come inside with me, Mistress Daisy, and I will show you all my chests and boxes. Mr. Cross made a great to-do about bringing them, but——"

As the ladies rose, Walter came to me with outstretched hand. "I was at fault, Douw," said he, frankly. "Don't think more about it."

I took his hand, though I was not altogether sure about forgetting his words.

Lady Berenicia looked at us over her shoulder, as she moved away, with disappointment mantling through the chalk on her cheeks.

"My word! I protest they're not going to fight, after all," she said.

CHAPTER IX.

I SEE MY SWEET SISTER DRESSED IN STRANGE ATTIRE.

IN the library room of the Hall, across from the dining-chamber, and at the foot of the great staircase, on the bannister of which you may still see the marks of Joseph Brant's hatchet, we men had a long talk in the afternoon. I recall but indifferently the lesser topics of conversation. There was, of course, some political debate, in which Sir William and I were alone on the side of the Colonist feeling, and Mr. Stewart, the two Butlers, and Sir John Johnson were all for choking discontent with the rope. Nothing very much to the point was said, on our part at least; for the growing discord pained Sir William too deeply to allow him pleasure in its discussion, and I shrank from appearing to oppose Mr. Stewart, hateful as his notions seemed.

Young Sir John stood by the window, I remember, sulkily drumming on the diapered panes, and purposely making his interjections as disagreeable to me as he could; at least, I thought so. So, apparently, did his father think, for several times I caught the wise old baronet glancing at his son in reproof, with a look in his grave gray eyes as of dawning doubt about the future of his heir.

Young Johnson was now a man of thirty, blond, aquiline-faced, with cold blue eyes and thin, tight lips, which pouted more readily than they smiled. His hair was the pale color of bleached hay, a legacy from his low born German mother, and his complexion was growing evenly florid from too much Madeira wine. We were not friends, and we both knew it.

There was other talk—about the recent creation of our part into a county by itself to be named after the Governor; about the behavior of the French traders at Oswego and Detroit, and a report from Europe in the latest gazettes that the "Young" Pretender, now a broken old rake, was at last to be married. This last was a subject upon which Mr. Stewart spoke most entertainingly, but with more willingness to let it be known that he had a kinsman's interest in the matter than he would formerly have shown. He was getting old, in fact, and an almost childish pride in his equivocal ancestry was growing upon him. Still his talk and reminiscences were extremely interesting.

They fade in my recollection, however, before the fact that it was at this little gathering, this afternoon, that my career was settled for me. There had been some talk about me while I remained alone outside to confer with Sir William's head farmer, and Mr. Cross had agreed with Mr. Stewart and Sir William that I was to accompany him on his trip to the far Western region the following week. My patron had explained that I needed some added knowledge of the world and its affairs, yet was of too serious a

turn to gather this in the guise of amusement, as Mr.
John Butler advised I should, by being sent on a
holiday to New York. Mr. Cross had been good
enough to say that he liked what he had seen of me,
and should be glad of my company.

Of all this I knew nothing when I entered the
library. The air was heavy with tobacco-smoke, and
the table bore more bottles and glasses than books.

" Find a chair, Douw," said Sir William. " I have
sent for my man, Enoch Wade, who is to go westward with Mr. Cross next week. If he's drunk enough
there'll be some sport."

There entered the room a middle-aged man, tall,
erect, well-knit in frame, with a thin, Yankeeish face,
deeply browned, and shrewd hazel eyes. He bowed
to nobody, but stood straight, looking like an Indian
in his clothes of deer-hide.

" This is Enoch Wade, gentlemen," said the baronet, indicating the new-comer with a wave of his
glass, and stretching out his legs to enjoy the scene
the more.   " He is my land-sailor.   Between his last
sale at Albany, and his first foot westward from here,
he professes all the vices and draws never a sober
breath.   Yet when he is in the woods he is abstemious, amiable, wise, resourceful, virtuous as a statue
—a paragon of trappers. You can see him for yourselves. Yet, I warn you, appearances are deceitful ;
he is always drunker than he looks. He was, I know,
most sinfully tipsy last night."

" It was in excellent good company, General,"
said the hunter, drawling his words and no whit
abashed.

"This is Enoch Wade, gentlemen," said the baronet.

" He has no manners to speak of," continued the baronet, evidently with much satisfaction to himself; " he can outlie a Frontenac half-breed, he is more greedy of gain than a Kinderhook Dutchman, he can drink all the Mohawks of both castles under the bench, and my niggers are veritable Josephs in comparison with him—wait a moment, Enoch!— this is while he is in contact with civilization. Yet once on the trail, so to speak, he is probity personi- fied.) I know this, since he has twice accompanied me to Detroit."

"Oh, in the woods, you know, some one of the party must remain sober," said Enoch, readily, still stiffly erect, but with a faint grin twitching on the saturnine corners of his mouth.

This time Sir William laughed aloud, and pointed to a decanter and glass, from which the trapper helped himself with dignity.

" Look you, rogue," said the host, " there is a young gentleman to be added to your party next week, and doubtless he will of needs have a nigger with him. See to it that the boat and provision arrangements are altered to meet this, and to-morrow be sober enough to advise him as to his outfit. For to-night, soak as deep as you like."

Enoch poured out for himself a second tumbler of rum, but not showing the first signs of unsteadiness in gait or gesture.

" This young gentleman "—he said, gravely smacking his lips—"about him ; is he a temperate person, one of the sort who can turn a steadfast back upon the bottle?"

A burst of Homeric laughter was Sir William's reply—laughter in which all were fain to join.

"It's all right, General," said Enoch, as he turned to go ; "don't mind my asking. One never can tell, you know, what kind of company he is like to pick up with here at the Hall."

My surprise and delight when I learned that I was the young gentleman in question, and that I was really to go to the Lakes and beyond, may be imagined. I seemed to walk on air, so great was my elation. You will not marvel now that I fail to recall very distinctly the general talk which followed.

Conversation finally lagged, as the promptings of hunger, not less than the Ethiopian shouting and scolding from the kitchen below, warned us of approaching dinner.

The drinking moderated somewhat, and the pipes were one by one laid aside, in tacit preparation for the meal. The Butlers rose to go, and were persuaded to remain. Mr. Stewart, who had an Old-World prejudice against tippling during the day, was induced by the baronet to taste a thimble of hollands, for appetite's sake. So we waited, with only a decent pretence of interest in the fitful talk.

There came a sharp double knock on the door, which a second later was pushed partly open. Some of us rose, pulling our ruffles into place, and ready to start at once, for there were famous appetites in the wild Valley of those days. But the voice from behind the door was not a servant's, nor did it convey the intelligence we all awaited. It was, instead,

the sharp, surface voice of Lady Berenicia, and it
said :

" We are weary of waiting for you in civilized
quarters of the Hall. May we come in here, or are
you too much ashamed of your vices to court inspection ? "

Walter Butler hastened to open the door, bowing
low as he did so, and delivering himself of some
gallant nonsense or other.

The London lady entered the room with a mincing, kittenish affectation of carriage, casting bold
smirks about her, like an Italian dancer.

If her morning attire had seemed over-splendid,
what shall I say of her appearance now? I looked
in amazement upon her imposing tower of whitened
hair, upon the great fluffs of lace, the brocaded
stomacher and train, the shining satin petticoat
front, the dazzling, creamy surfaces of throat and
shoulders and forearms, all rather freely set forth.

If the effect was bewildering, it was not unpleasant.
The smoke-laden air of the dim old room seemed
suddenly clarified, made radiant. A movement of
chairs and of their occupants ran through the chamber, like a murmur of applause, as we rose to greet
the resplendent apparition. But there came a veritable outburst of admiration when my lady's companion appeared in view.

It was our Daisy, robed like a princess, who
dawned upon our vision. She was blushing as much
from embarrassment as from novel pride, yet managed to keep her pretty head up, smiling at us all,
and to bear herself with grace.

Lady Berenicia, from the wealth of finery in those bulky chests which honest Mr. Cross in vain had protested against bringing over the ocean and up to this savage outpost, had tricked out the girl in wondrous fashion. Her gown was not satin, like the other, but of a soft, lustreless stuff, whose delicate lavender folds fell into the sweetest of violet shadows. I was glad to see that her neck and arms were properly covered. The laces on the sleeves were tawny with age ; the ribbon by which the little white shawl was decorously gathered at the bosom carried the faint suggestion of yellow to a distinct tone, repeated and deepened above by the color of the maiden's hair. This hair, too, was a marvel of the dresser's art—reared straight and tight from the forehead over a high-arched roll, and losing strictness of form behind in ingenious wavy curls, which seemed the very triumph of artlessness; it was less wholly powdered than Lady Berenicia's, so that the warm gold shone through the white dust in soft gradations of half tints ; at the side, well up, was a single salmon tea-rose, that served to make everything else more beautiful.

Picture to yourself this delicious figure—this face which had seemed lovely before, and now, with deft cosmetics, and a solitary tiny patch, and the glow of exquisite enjoyment in the sweet hazel eyes, was nothing less than a Greuze's dream—picture our Daisy to yourself, I say, and you may guess in part how flattering was her reception, how high and fast rose the gallant congratulations that the Valley boasted such a beauteous daughter. Sir William himself gave her his arm, jovially protesting that this was not the Mohawk country, but France—not Johnson Hall, but Versailles.

I came on at the tail of the dinner procession, not quite easy in my mind about all this.

CHAPTER X.

THE MASQUERADE BRINGS ME NOTHING BUT PAIN.

THERE were, in all, ten of us at the table. Sir William beamed upon us from the end nearest the windows, with Daisy on his left hand and the London dame on the other—in the place of distinction to which she was, I suppose, entitled. Below Lady Berenicia sat Mr. Stewart, Sir John, and Walter Butler. I was on the left side below Mr. Cross. These details come back to me as if they were of yesterday, when I think of that dinner.

I could not see Daisy from where I sat, but all through the meal I watched the effect she was producing upon those opposite us. To do her justice, Lady Berenicia seemed to have no alloy of jealousy in the delight with which she regarded the result of her handiwork. Mr. Stewart could not keep his fond eyes off the girl; they fairly glowed with satisfied pride and affection. Both Sir John and Walter gave more attention to our beautiful maiden than they did to their plates, and both faces told an open tale of admiration, each after its kind.

There was plenty of gay talk at the head of the table—merry chatter of which I recall nothing, save vaguely that it was about the triumph of art over unadorned nature at which we were assisting.

Mr. Cross and I bore our small part in the celebration in silence for a time. Then we fell to talking quietly of the journey upon which we were so soon to embark; but our minds were not on the subject, and after a little its discussion lapsed. All at once he said, as if speaking the thoughts which tied my tongue :

"To my mind the young woman is not improved by these furbelows and fal-lals my wife has put upon her. What wit or reason is there in a homely, sensible little maiden like this—a pretty flower growing, as God designed it to, in modest sweetness on its own soil—being garnished out in the stale foppery of the last London season?"

"But it is only a masquerade, sir," I pleaded—as much to my own judgment as to his—"and it does make her very beautiful, does it not?"

"She *was* beautiful before," he replied, in the same low tones. "Can a few trumpery laces and ribbons, a foolish patch, a little powder, affect what is real about a woman, think you? And do any but empty heads value unreal things?"

"True enough, sir; but this is nothing more than harmless pleasantry. Women are that way. See how pleased she is—how full of smiles and happiness she seems. It's a dull sort of life here in the woods. Poor Daisy, she sees so little of gayety, it would be cruel to begrudge her this innocent pleasure."

"Innocent—yes, no doubt ; but, do you know, she will never be the same girl again. She will never feel quite the same pretty little Mistress Daisy, in

her woollen gown and her puttical kerchief. She will
never get the taste of this triumph out of her
mouth. You do not know women, young man,
as I do. I have studied the sex in a very celebrated and costly school. Mark my words, ideas
have been put into her head that will never come
out."

I tried to believe that this was not so. "Ah," I
said, "to know other women is not to know our
Daisy. Why, she is good sense itself—so prudent
and modest and thoughtful that she makes the other
girls roundabout seem all hoydens or simpletons.
She has read the most serious books—never anything else. Her heart is as good as her mind is rich.
Never fear, Mr. Cross! not all the silks in China or
velvets in Genoa could turn her dear head."

He smiled, somewhat compassionately I thought,
and made no answer.

Was I so firm in my faith, after all? The doubt
rose in my thoughts, and would not down, as the
gallant talk flowed and bubbled around me. *Would*
this Daisy be quite the same next day, or next week,
singing to us at the old harpsichord in the twilight,
with the glare of the blaze on the hearth making red
gold of that hair, plaited once more in simple braids?
I tried with all my might to call up this sweet familiar figure before my mental vision: it would not
freely come.

She was laughing now, with a clear ripple of joy-
ousness, at some passing quip between our host and
sharp-tongued Lady Berenicia, both of whom em-
ployed pretty liberally their Irish knack of saying

witty, biting things. The sound came strangely to my ears, as if it were some other than Daisy laughing.

I was still in this brown study when Sir William called the health of the ladies, with some jocose words of compliment to them, congratulation to ourselves. I rose (mechanically after the other gentlemen, glass in hand, to hear Mr. Stewart make pleasant and courtly acknowledgment, and to see the two women pass out in a great rustling of draperies and hoops, with Walter Butler holding open the door and bowing profoundly. The faint scent of powder left on the air annoyed me, as something stifling those thoughts of the good little adopted sister, whom I had brought to the Hall and lost there, which I would fain dwell upon.

We sat over our Madeira and pipes longer than usual. Candles were brought in by Sir William's young body-servant Pontiac, for there was a full moon, and we might thus prolong our stay after nightfall. The talk was chiefly about our coming trip—a very serious undertaking. Sir William and Mr. Butler had adventures of their own early trading days to recall, and they gave us great stores of advice drawn from experience, and ranging from choice of shirts and spirits to needful diplomacy with the Algonquins and Sakis.

Then the company drank the health of Mr. Cross, and were good enough to couple mine with it. A comical little yellow boy danced for us before the hearth—an admiring wall of black faces and rolling white eyeballs filling up the open door meanwhile.

7

Walter Butler sang a pretty song—everybody, negroes and all, swelling the chorus. Rum was brought
in, and mixed in hot glasses, with spice, molasses,
and scalding water from the kettle on the crane.
So evening deepened to night ; but I never for a
moment, not even when they drank my health,
shook off the sense of unrest born of Daisy's masquerade.

It was Molly Brant herself, nobly erect and handsome in her dark, sinister way, who came to us with
word that the moon was up over the pine-ridged
hills, and that Mistress Daisy was attired for the
homeward ride, and waiting.

Of all the pictures in Memory's portfolio, none is
more distinct than this of the departure that evening from the Hall. A dozen negroes were about the
steps, two or three mounted ready to escort us home,
others bearing horn lanterns which the moonlight
darkened into inutility, still others pulling the restive
horses about on the gravel. Mr. Stewart swung himself into the saddle, and Daisy stepped out to mount
behind him. She wore her own garments once
more, but there was just a trace of powder on the
hair under the hood, and the patch was still on her
chin. I moved forward to lift her to the pillion as
I had done hundreds of times before, but she did
not see me. Instead, I was almost pushed away by
the rush of Sir John and young Butler to her side,
both eager to assist. It was the knight, flushed and
a little unsteady with wine, who won the privilege,
and held Daisy's foot. I climbed into my saddle
moodily, getting offence out of even this.

So we rode away, pursued down the path to the lilacs by shouts of "Good-night! Safe home!" Looking back to lift my hat for the last adieu, I saw the honest old baronet, bareheaded in the clear moonlight, waving his hand from the lowest step, with Lady Berenicia and the others standing above him, outlined upon the illumined doorway, and the negroes grouped on either side, obscurely gesticulating in the shadows of the broad, dark front of the Hall, which glowed against the white sky.

As I recall the scene, it seems to me that then and there I said farewell, not alone to pleasant friends, but to the Daisy of my childhood and youth.

The Hall slaves rode well ahead in the narrow road; we could just hear faintly the harmony of the tune they were humming in concert, as one hears the murmur of an Æolian harp. As a guard, they were of course ridiculous: the veriest suspicion of peril would have sent them all galloping helter-skelter, with frantic shrieks of fright. But the road was perfectly safe, and these merry fellows were to defend us from loneliness, not danger.

I did indeed rest my free hand on the pistol in my holster as I jogged along close behind the old gray horse and his double burden; but the act was more an unconscious reflection of my saturnine mood, I fear, than a recognition of need. There was every reason why I should dwell with delight upon the prospect opening before me—upon the idea of the great journey so close at hand; but I scarcely thought of it at all, and I was not happy. The moon threw a jaundiced light over my mind, and in its discolored glare I saw things wrongly, and with gratuitous pain to myself.

In fact, my brooding was the creature of the last few hours, born of a childish pique. But as I rode gloomily silent behind my companions, it seemed as if I had long suffered a growing separation from them. "Three is a clumsy number," I said to myself, "in family affection not less than in love; there was never any triad of friends since the world began, no matter how fond their ties, in which two did not build a little interior court of thoughts and sympathies from which the third was shut out. These two people whom I hold dearer than everything else on earth—this good gentleman to whom I owe all, this sweet girl who has grown up from babyhood in my heart—would scout the idea that there was any line of division running through our household. They do not see it—cannot see it. Yet they have a whole world of ideas and sentiments in common, a whole world of communion, which I may never enter."

This was what, in sulky, inchoate fashion, I said to myself, under the spur of the jealous spirits which sometimes get rein over the thoughts of the best of us. And it was all because the London woman had tricked out our Daisy, for but a little hour or two, in the presentment of a court lady!

Conversation went briskly forward, meanwhile, from the stout back of the gray horse.

"Did you note, papa, how white and soft her

hands were ?" said Daisy. "Mine were so red beside
them ! It is working in the garden, I believe,
although Mary Johnson always wore gloves when she
was out among the flowers and vegetables, and her
hands were red, too. And Lady Berenicia was so
surprised to learn that I had never read any of the
romances which they write now in England! She
says ladies in London, and in the provinces too, do
not deem themselves fit to converse unless they
keep abreast of all these. She has some of them in
her chests, and there are others in the Hall, she has
found, and I am to read them, and welcome."

"You are old enough now, my girl," replied Mr.
Stewart. "They seem to me to be trivial enough
things, but no doubt they have their use. I would
not have you seem as inferior to other ladies in
knowledge of the matters they talk of, as they are
inferior to you in honest information."

"How interested she was when I told her of the
serious books I read, and of my daily occupations—
moulding the candles, brewing the beer, carding
wool, making butter, and then caring for the garden !
She had never seen celery in trenches, she said, and
would not know beans from gourds if she saw them
growing. It seems that in England ladies have
nothing to do with their gardens—when, indeed,
they have any at all—save to pluck a rose now and
then, or give tea to their gentlemen under the
shrubbery when it is fine. And I told her of our
quilting and spinning bees, and the coasting on clear
winter evenings, and of watching the blacks on
Pinkster night, and the picnics in the woods, and

she vowed London had no pleasures like them.
She was jesting though, I think. Oh, shall we ever
go to London, papa?"

"By all means, let us go," chuckled Mr. Stewart.
"You would see something there she never saw—
my grizzled old head upon Temple Bar. Shall we
be off to-morrow? My neck tingles with anticipa-
tion."

"Old tease!" laughed Daisy, patting his shoulder.
"You know there have been no heads put there
since long before I was born. Never flatter yourself that they would begin again now with yours.
They've forgotten there was ever such a body as you."

"Faith ! the world doesn't go round so fast as you
young people think. Only to-day I read in the London mail that two months ago one of the polls that
had been there since '46 fell down ; but if it was
Fletcher's or Townley's no one can tell—like enough
not even they themselves by this time. So there's
a vacant spike now for mine. No, child—I doubt
these old bones will ever get across the sea again.
But who knows?—it may be your fortune to go
some time."

"Lady Berenicia says I must come to the Hall
often, papa, while she is there," said the girl, returning to the subject which bewitched her ; "and you
must fetch me, of course. She admires you greatly ;
she says gentlemen in London have quite lost the
fine manner that you keep up here, with your bow
and your compliments. You must practise them on
me now. We are to keep each other company as
much as possible, she and I, while her husband and

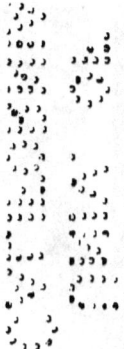

Douw go off together. You should have seen her mimic them—the two solemn, long-faced men boring each other in the depths of the wilderness."

The talk had at last got around to me. Daisy laughed gayly at recollection of the London woman's jesting. Surely never a more innocent, less malicious laugh came from a maiden's merry lips, but it fell sourly on my ears.

" It is easy for people to be clever who do not scruple to be disagreeable," I said, without much relevancy.

" What is this, Douw?" Mr. Stewart turned half-way in his saddle and glanced inquiry back at me. "What is wrong with you? You were as glum all the evening long as a Tuscarora. Isn't the trip with Mr. Cross to your liking?"

"Oh, ay! I shall be glad to go."

It was on my perverse tongue's end to add the peevish thought that nobody would specially miss me, but I held it back.

" He has had a perfect Dutch fit on to-day," said Daisy, with good-natured sisterly frankness; " for all the world such as old Hon Yost Polhemus has when his yeast goes bitter. Whenever I looked down the table to him, at dinner, he was scowling across at poor Walter Butler or Sir John, as if he would presently eat them both. He was the only one who failed to tell me I looked well in the—the citified costume."

" Rather say I was the only one whose opinion you did not care for."

She was too sweet-tempered to take umbrage at my morose rejoinder, and went on with her mock-serious catalogue of my crimes:

"And what do you think, papa? Who should it be but our patient, equable Master Douw that was near quarrelling with Walter Butler, out by the lilacs, this very morning—and in the presence of ladies, too."

"No one ever saw me quarrel, 'ladies' or anybody else," I replied.

"Faith! then I did myself," Mr. Stewart laughingly called out. "And it was before a lady too—or the small beginnings of one. I saw him with my own eyes, Daisy, get knocked into the ashes by a young man, and jump up and run at him with both fists out—and all on your account, too, my lady; and then——"

"Oh, I am reminded!"

It was Daisy who cried out, and with visible excitement. Then she clapped her hand to her mouth with a pretty gesture; then she said:

"Or no! I will not tell you yet. It is so famous a secret, it must come out little by little. Tell me, papa, did you know that this Mr. Cross up at the Hall—Lady Berenicia's husband—is a cousin to the old Major who brought me to you, out of the rout at Kouarie?"

"Is *that* your secret, miss? I knew it hours ago."

"How wise! And perhaps you knew that the Major became a Colonel, and then a General, and died last winter, poor man."

"Alas, yes, poor Tony! I heard that too from his cousin. Heigh-ho! We all walk that way."

Daisy bent forward to kiss the old man. "Not you, for many a long year, papa. And now tell me, did not this Major—*my* Major, though I do not remember him—take up a patent of land here, or hereabouts, through Sir William, while he was on this side of the water?"

"Why, we should be on his land now," said Mr. Stewart, reining up the horse.

We sat thus in the moonlight while he pointed out to us, as nearly as he knew them, the confines of the Cross patent. To the left of us, over a tract covered thick with low, gnarled undergrowth, the estate stretched beyond the brow of the hill, distant a mile or more. On our right, masked by a dense tangle of fir-boughs, lay a ravine, also a part of the property. We could hear, as we passed there, the gurgle of the water running at the gulf's bottom, on its way to the great leap over the rock wall, farther down, of which I have already written.

"Yes, this was what Tony Cross took up. I doubt he ever saw it. Why do you ask, girl?"

"*Now* for my secret," said Daisy. "The Major's elder son, Digby, inherits the English house and lands. The other son, Philip—the boy you fought with, Douw—is given this American land, and money to clear and settle it. He sailed with the others—he is in New York—he is coming here to live!"

"We'll make him welcome," cried Mr. Stewart, heartily.

" I hope his temper is bettered since last he was here," was the civillest comment I could screw my tongue to.

Clouds dimmed the radiance of the moon, threatening darkness, and we quickened our pace. There was no further talk on the homeward ride.

CHAPTER XI.

WHEN the eventful day of departure came, what with the last packing, the searches to see that nothing should be forgotten, the awkwardness and slowness of hands unnerved by the excitement of a great occasion, it was high noon before I was ready to start. I stood idly in the hall, while my aunt put final touches to my traps, my mind swinging like a pendulum) between fear that Mr. Cross, whom I was to join at Caughnawaga, would be vexed at my delay, and genuine pain at leaving my dear home and its inmates, now that the hour had arrived.

I had made my farewells over at my mother's house the previous day, dutifully kissing her and all the sisters who happened to be at home, but without much emotion on either side. Blood is thicker than water, the adage runs. Perhaps that is why it flowed so calmly in all our Dutch veins while we said good-by. But here in my adopted home—my true home—my heart quivered and sank at thought of departure.

"I could not have chosen a better or safer man for you to travel with than Jonathan Cross," Mr. Stewart was saying to me. "He does not look on all things as I do, perhaps, for our breeding was as different as the desk is different from the drum. But he is honest and courteous, well informed after his way, and as like what you will be later on as two peas in a pod. You were born for a trader, a merchant, a man of affairs; and you will be at a good school with him."

He went on in his grave, affectionate manner, telling me in a hundred indirect ways that I belonged to the useful rather than to the ornamental order of mankind, with never a thought in his good heart of wounding my feelings, or of letting me know that in his inmost soul he would have preferred me to be a soldier or an idler with race-horses and a velvet coat. Nor did he wound me, for I had too great a love for him, and yet felt too thorough a knowledge of myself to allow the two to clash. I listened silently, with tears almost ready at my eyes, but with thoughts vagrantly straying from his words to the garden outside.

Tulp was to go with me, and his parents and kin were filling the air with advice and lamentations in about equal measure, and all in the major key. Their shouts and wailing—they could not have made more ado if he had just been sold to Jamaica—came through the open door. It was not of this din I thought, though, nor of the cart which the negroes, while they wept, were piling high with my goods, and which I could see in the highway beyond.

I was thinking of Daisy, my sweet sister, who had gone into the garden to gather a nosegay for me.

Through the door I could see her among the bushes, her lithe form bending in the quest of

blossoms. Were it midsummer, I thought, and
the garden filled with the whole season's wealth
of flowers, it could hold nothing more beautiful
than she. Perhaps there was some shadow of my
moody fit, the evening after the dinner at the Hall,
remaining to sadden my thoughts of parting from
her. I cannot tell. I only know that they were
indeed sad thoughts. I caught myself wondering
if she would miss me much—this dear girl who had
known no life in which I had not had daily share.
Yes, the tears *were* coming, I felt. I wrung my
good old patron's hand, and turned my head away.

There came a clattering of hoofs on the road and
the sound of male voices. Tulp ran in agape with
the tidings that Sir John and a strange gentleman
had ridden up, and desired to see Mr. Stewart. We
at once walked out to the garden, a little relieved
perhaps by the interruption.

Both visitors had had time to alight and leave
their horses outside the wall. The younger Johnson stood in the centre path of the garden, present-
ing his companion to Daisy, who, surprised at her
task, and with her back to us, was courtesying.
Even to the nape of her neck she was blushing.

There was enough for her to blush at. The
stranger was bowing very low, putting one hand
up to his breast. With the other he had taken
her fingers and raised them formally to his lips.
This was not a custom in our parts. Sir William
did it now and then on state occasions, but young
men, particularly strangers, did not.

As we advanced, this gallant morning-caller drew

himself up and turned toward us. You may be sure
I looked him over attentively.

I have seen few handsomer young men. In a
way, so far as light hair, blue eyes, ruddy and regular face went, he was not unlike Sir John. But he
was much taller, and his neck and shoulders were
squared proudly—a trick Johnson never learned.
The fine effect of his figure was enhanced by a
fawn-colored top-coat, with a graceful little cape
falling over the shoulders. His clothes beneath,
from the garnet coat with mother-of-pearl buttons
down to his shining Hessians, all fitted him as if
he had been run into them as into a mould. He
held his hat, a glossy sugar-loaf beaver, in one hand,
along with whip and gloves. The other hand, white
and shapely in its ruffles, he stretched out now toward Mr. Stewart with a free, pleasant gesture.

"With my father's oldest friend," he said, " I
must not wait for ceremony. I am Philip Cross,
from England, and I hope you will be my friend,
sir, now that my father is gone."

That this speech found instant favor need not be
doubted. Mr. Stewart shook him again and again
by the hand, and warmly bade him welcome to the
Valley and the Cedars a dozen times in as many
breaths. Young Cross managed to explain between
these cordial ejaculations, that he had journeyed up
from New York with the youthful Stephen Watts
—to whose sister Sir John was already betrothed;
that they had reached Guy Park the previous evening; that Watts was too wearied this morning to
think of stirring out, but that hardly illness itself

could have prevented him, Cross, from promptly paying his respects to his father's ancient comrade.

The young man spoke easily and fluently, looking Mr. Stewart frankly in the eye, with smiling sincerity in glance and tone. He went on:

"How changed everything is roundabout!—all save you, who look scarcely older or less strong. When I was here as a boy it was winter, cold and bleak. There was a stockade surrounded by wilderness then, I remember, and a log-house hardly bigger than the fireplace inside it. Where we stand now the ground was covered with brush and chips, half hidden by snow. Now—*presto!* there is a mansion in the midst of fields, and a garden neatly made, and"—turning with a bow to Daisy—"a fair mistress for them all, who would adorn any palace or park in Europe, and whom I remember as a frightened little baby, with stockings either one of which would have held her entire."

"I saw the cart laden outside," put in Sir John, "and fancied perhaps we should miss you."

"Why, no," said Mr. Stewart; "I had forgotten for the moment that this was a house of mourning. Douw is starting to the Lake country this very day. Mr. Cross, you must remember my boy, my Douw?"

The young Englishman turned toward me, as I was indicated by Mr. Stewart's gesture. He looked me over briefly, with a half-smile about his eyes, nodded to me, and said:

"You were the Dutch boy with the apron, weren't you?"

I assented by a sign of the head, as slight as I could politely make it.

"Oh, yes, I recall you quite distinctly. I used to make my brother Digby laugh by telling about your aprons. He made quite a good picture of you in one of them, drawn from my descriptions. We had a fort of snow, too, did we not? and I beat you, or you me, I forget which. I got snow down the back of my neck, I know, and shivered all the way to the fort."

He turned lightly at this to Mr. Stewart, and began conversation again. I went over to where Daisy stood, by the edge of the flower-bed.

"I must go now, dear sister," I said. The words were choking me.

We walked slowly to the house, she and I. When I had said good-by to my aunt, and gathered together my hat, coats, and the like, I stood speechless, looking at Daisy. The moment was here, and I had no word for it which did not seem a mockery.

She raised herself on tiptoe to be kissed. "Good-by, big brother," she said, softly. "Come back to us well and strong, and altogether homesick, won't you? It will not be like home, without you, to either of us."

And so the farewells were all made, and I stood in the road prepared to mount. Tulp was already on the cart, along with another negro who was to bring back my horse and the vehicle after we had embarked in the boats. There was nothing more to say—time pressed—yet I lingered dumb and irresolute. At the moment I seemed to be exchanging

"Good-bye, big brother," she said, softly.

everything for nothing—committing domestic suicide.) I looked at them both, the girl and the old
man, with the gloomy thought that I might never
lay eyes on them again. I dare say I wore my
grief upon my face, for Mr. Stewart tried cheerily
to hearten me with, "Courage, lad! We shall all
be waiting for you, rejoiced to welcome you back
safe and sound."

Daisy came to me now again, as I put my hand
on the pommel, and pinned upon my lapel some of
the pale blue blossoms she had gathered.

"There's 'rosemary for remembrance,'" she murmured. "Poor Ophelia could scarce have been sadder than we feel, Douw, at your going."

"And may I be decorated too—for remembrance'
sake?" asked handsome young Philip Cross, gayly.

"Surely, sir," the maiden answered, with a smile
of sweet sorrowfulness. "You have a rightful part
in the old memories—in a sense, perhaps, the greatest part of all."

"Ay, you two were friends before ever you came
to us, dear," said Mr. Stewart.

So as I rode away, with smarting eyes and a heart
weighing like lead, my last picture of the good old
home was of Daisy fastening flowers on the young
Englishman's breast, just as she had put these of
mine in their place.

8

CHAPTER XII.

OLD-TIME POLITICS PONDERED UNDER THE FOREST STARLIGHT.

AMONG the numerous books which at one time or another I had resolved to write, and which the evening twilight of my life finds still unwritten, was one on Fur-trading. This volume, indeed, came somewhat nearer to a state of actual existence than any of its unborn brethren, since I have yet a great store of notes and memoranda gathered for its construction in earlier years. My other works, such as the great treatise on Astronomical Delusions—which Herschel and La Place afterward rendered unnecessary—and the "History of the Dutch in America," never even progressed to this point of preparation. I mention this to show that I resist a genuine temptation now in deciding not to put into this narrative a great deal about my experiences in, and information concerning, the almost trackless West of my youth. My diary of this first and momentous journey with Mr. Jonathan Cross, yellow with age and stained by damp and mildew, lies here before me; along with it are many odd and curious incidents and reflections jotted down, mirroring that strange, rude, perilous past which seems so far away to the genera-

tion now directing a safe and almost eventless commerce to the Pacific and the Gulf. But I will draw
from my stock only the barest outlines, sufficient to
keep in continuity the movement of my story.

When we reached Caughnawaga Mr. Cross and his
party were waiting for us at the trading store of my
godfather, good old Douw Fonda. I was relieved to
learn that I had not delayed them; for it was still
undecided, I found, whether we should all take to
the river here, or send the boats forward with the
men, and ourselves proceed to the Great Carrying
Place at Fort Stanwix by the road. Although it
was so early in the season, the Mohawk ran very low
between its banks. Major Jelles Fonda, the eldest
son of my godfather, and by this time the true head
of the business, had only returned from the Lakes,
and it was by his advice that we settled upon riding
and carting as far as we could, and leaving the light-
ened boats to follow. So we set out in the saddle,
my friend and I, stopping one night with crazy old
John Abeel—he who is still remembered as the father
of the Seneca half-breed chieftain Corn-Planter—and
the next night with Honnikol Herkimer.

This man, I recall, greatly impressed Mr. Cross.
We were now in an exclusively German section of
the Valley, where no Dutch and very little English
was to be heard. Herkimer himself conversed with
us in a dialect that must often have puzzled my English friend, though he gravely forbore showing it.
I had known Colonel Herkimer all my life; doubtless it was this familiarity with his person and speech
which had prevented my recognizing his real merit,

for I was not a little surprised when Mr. Cross said
to me that night : "Our host is one of the strongest
and most sagacious men I have ever encountered in
the Colonies ; he is worth a thousand of your Butlers or Sir Johns."

It became clear in later years that my friend was
right. I remember that I regarded the hospitable
Colonel, at breakfast next morning, with a closer and
more respectful attention than ever before, but it
was not easy to discern any new elements of greatness in his talk.

Herkimer was then a middle-aged, undersized man,
very swart and sharp-eyed, and with a quick, almost
vehement way of speaking. It took no time at all
to discover that he watched the course of politics in
the Colonies pretty closely, and was heart and soul
on the anti-English side. One thing which he said,
in his effort to make my friend understand the difference between his position and the more abstract and
educated discontent of New England and Virginia,
sticks in my memory.

"We Germans," he said, "are not like the rest.
Our fathers and mothers remember their sufferings
in the old country, kept ragged and hungry and
wretched, in such way as my negroes do not dream
of, all that some scoundrel baron might have gilding
on his carriage, and that the Elector might enjoy
himself in his palace. They were beaten, hanged,
robbed of their daughters, worked to death, frozen
by the cold in their nakedness, dragged off into the
armies to be sold to any prince who could pay for
their blood and broken bones. The French who

overran the Palatinate were bad enough; the native
rulers were even more to be hated. The exiles of
our race have not forgotten this; they have told it
all to us, their children and grandchildren born here
in this Valley. We have made a new home for ourselves over here, and we owe no one but God anything for it. If they try to make here another aris-
tocracy over us, then we will die first before we will
submit."

The case for the Mohawk Valley's part in the
great revolt has never been more truly stated, I think,
than it was thus, by the rough, uneducated, little
frontier trader, in his broken English, on that May
morning years before the storm broke.

We rode away westward in the full sunshine that
morning, in high spirits. The sky was pure blue
overhead; the birds carolled from every clump of
foliage about us; the scenery, to which Mr. Cross
paid much delighted attention, first grew nobly wild
and impressive when we skirted the Little Falls—as
grand and gloomy in its effect of towering jagged
cliffs and foaming cataracts as one of Jacob Ruys-
dael's pictures—and then softened into a dream of
beauty as it spread out before us the smiling, embowered expanses of the German Flatts. Time and
time again my companion and I reined up our horses
to contemplate the charms of this lovely scene.

We had forded the river near Fort Herkimer,
where old Hon Yost Herkimer, the father of the
Colonel, lived, and were now once more on the north
side. From an open knoll I pointed out to my friend,
by the apple and pear blossoms whitening the de-

serted orchards, the site of the Palatines' village
where Daisy's father had been killed, fifteen years
ago, in the midnight rout and massacre.

" It was over those hills that the French stole in
darkness. Back yonder, at the very ford we crossed,
her poor mother was trampled under foot and
drowned in the frightened throng. It was at the
fort there, where we had the buttermilk and *Kuchen*,
that your cousin, Major Cross, found the little
girl. I wonder if he ever knew how deeply grateful
to him we were—and are."

This brought once more to my mind—where indeed it had often enough before intruded itself—the
recollection of young Philip's arrival at the Cedars.
For some reason I had disliked to speak of it before,
but now I told Mr. Cross of it as we walked our
horses along over the rough, muddy road, under the
arching roof of thicket.

" I'll be bound Mr. Stewart welcomed him with
open arms," said my companion.

" Ay, indeed! No son could have asked a fonder
greeting."

" Yes, the lad is very like his mother; that of it-
self would suffice to warm the old gentleman's heart.
You knew he was a suitor for her hand long before
Tony Cross ever saw her?"

I didn't know this, but I nodded silently.

" Curious creature she was," mused he, as if to
himself. " Selfish, suspicious, swift to offence, jealous of everything and everybody about her—yet
with moods when she seemed to all she met the most
amiable and delightful of women. She had her fine

side, too. She would have given her life gladly for
the success of the Jacobites, of that I'm sure. And
proud!—no duchess could have carried her head
higher."

"You say her son is very like her?"

"As like as two leaves on a twig. Perhaps he has
something of his father's Irish openness of manner as
well. His father belonged to the younger, what we
call the Irish, branch of our family, you know, though
it is as English in the matter of blood as I am. We
were only second cousins, in point of fact, and his
grandfather was set up in Ireland by the bounty of
mine. Yet Master Philip condescends to me, patron-
izes me, as if the case had been reversed."

Mr. Cross did not speak as if he at all resented
this, but in a calm, analytical manner, and with a
wholly impersonal interest. I have never known
another man who was so totally without individual
bias, and regarded all persons and things with so
little reference to his own feelings. If he had either
prejudices or crotchets on any point, I never discovered them. He was, I feel assured, a scrupulously
honest and virtuous gentleman, yet he never seemed
to hate people who were not so. He was careful not
to let them get an advantage over him, but for the
rest he studied them and observed their weaknesses
and craft, with the same quiet interest he displayed
toward worthier objects. A thoroughly equable
nature was his—with little capacity for righteous indignation on the one side, and no small tendencies
toward envy or peevishness on the other. There
was not a wrinkle on his calm countenance, nor any

power of angry flashing in his steadfast, wide-apart, gray eyes. But his tongue could cut deep on occasion.

We were now well beyond the last civilized habitation in the Valley of the Mohawk, and we encamped that night above the bank of a little rivulet that crossed the highway some four miles to the east of Fort Stanwix. Tulp and the Dutchman, Barent Coppernol, whom Mr. Cross had brought along, partially unpacked the cart, and set to with their axes. Soon there had been constructed a shelter for us, half canvas, half logs and brush, under a big beech-tree which stood half-way up the western incline from the brook, and canopied with its low boughs a smooth surface of clear ground. We had supper here, and then four huge night-fires were built as an outer wall of defence, and Barent went to sleep, while young Tulp, crouching and crooning by the blaze, began his portion of the dreary watch to keep up the fires.

We lay awake for a long time on our bed of hemlock twigs and brake, well wrapped up, our heads close to the beech-trunk, our knees raised to keep the fierce heat of the flames from our faces. From time to time we heard the barking of the wolves, now distant, now uncomfortably near. When the moon came up, much later, the woods seemed alive with strange vocal noises and ominous rustlings in the leaves and brakes. It was my London companion's first night in the open wilderness; but while he was very acute to note new sounds and inquire their origin, he seemed to be in no degree nervous.

We talked of many things, more particularly, I remember, of what Herkimer had said at breakfast. And it is a very remarkable thing that, as we talked thus of the German merchant-farmer and his politics, we were lying on the very spot where, five years later, I was to behold him sitting, wounded but imperturbable, smoking his pipe and giving orders of battle, under the most hellish rain of bullets from which man ever shrank affrighted. And the tranquil moon above us was to look down again upon this little vale, and turn livid to see its marsh and swale choked with fresh corpses, and its brook rippling red with blood. And the very wolves we heard snapping and baying in the thicket were to raise a ghastly halloo, here among these same echoes, as they feasted on the flesh of my friends and comrades.

(We did not guess this fearsome future,) but instead lay peacefully, contentedly under the leaves, with the balmy softness of the firs in the air we breathed, and the flaming firelight in our eyes. Perhaps lank, uncouth Barent Coppernol may have dreamed of it, as he snored by the outer heap of blazing logs. If so, did he, as in prophecy, see his own form, with cleft skull, stretched on the hill-side?

" I spoke about Philip's having some of his father's adopted Irish traits," said Mr. Cross, after a longer interval of silence than usual. " One of them is the desire to have subordinates, dependents, about him. There is no Irishman so poor or lowly that he will not, if possible, encourage some still poorer, lowlier Irishman to hang to his skirts. It is a reflection of their old Gaelic tribal system, I suppose, which, between its chiefs above and its clansmen below, left no place for a free yeomanry. I note this same thing in the Valley, with the Johnsons and the Butlers. So far as Sir William is concerned, the quality I speak of has been of service to the Colony, for he has used his fondness and faculty for attracting retainers and domineering over subordinates to public advantage. But then he is an exceptional and noteworthy man—one among ten thousand. But his son Sir John, and his son-in-law Guy Johnson, and the Butlers, father and son, and now to them added our masterful young Master Philip—these own no such steadying balance-wheel of common-sense. They have no restraining notion of public interest. Their sole idea is to play the aristocrat, to surround themselves with menials, to make their neighbors concede to them submission and reverence. It was of them that Herkimer spoke, plainly enough, though he gave no names. Mark my words, they will come to grief with that man, if the question be ever put to the test."

I had not seen enough of Englishmen to understand very clearly the differences between them and the Irish, and I said so. The conversation drifted upon race questions and distinctions, as they were presented by the curiously mixed population of New York province.

My companion was of the impression that the distinctly British settlements, like those of Massachusetts and Virginia, were far more powerful and promising than my own polyglot province. No doubt from his point of view this notion was natural, but it nettled me. To this day I cannot read or listen to the inflated accounts this New England and this Southern State combine to give of their own greatness, of their wonderful patriotism and intelligence, and of the tremendous part they played in the Revolution, without smashing my pipe in wrath. Yet I am old enough now to see that all this is largely the fault of the New Yorkers themselves. We have given our time and attention to the making of money, and have left it to others to make the histories. If they write themselves down large, and us small, it is only what might have been expected. But at the time of which I am telling I was very young, and full of confidence in not only the existing superiority but the future supremacy of my race. I could not foresee how we were to be snowed under by the Yankees in our own State, and, what is worse, accept our subjugation without a protest—so that to-day the New York schoolboy supposes Fisher Ames, or any other of a dozen Boston talkers, to have been a greater man than Philip Schuyler.

I remember that I greatly vaunted the good qualities of the Dutch that night. I pointed out how they alone had learned the idea of religious toleration toward others in the cruel school of European persecution ; how their faith in liberty and in popular institutions, nobly exemplified at home in the marvellous struggle with Spain, had planted roots of civil and religious freedom in the New World which he could find neither to the east nor to the south of us ; and how even the early Plymouth Puritans had imbibed all they knew of clemency and liberty during their stay in Holland.

I fear that Mr. Cross inwardly smiled more or less at my enthusiasm and extravagance, but his comments were all serious and kindly. He conceded the justice of much that I said, particularly as to the admirable resolution, tenacity, and breadth of character the Dutch had displayed always in Europe. But then he went on to declare that the Dutch could not hope to hold their own in strange lands against the extraordinary conquering and colonizing power of the more numerous English, who, by sheer force of will and energy, were destined in the end to dominate everything they touched. Note how Clive and the English had gradually undermined or overthrown French, Portuguese, and Dutch alike in the Indies, he said ; the same thing has happened here, either by bloodshed or barter. No nation could resist the English in war; no people could maintain themselves in trade or the peaceful arts against the English.

"But you yourself predicted, not an hour ago, that the young gentry down the Valley would come to grief in their effort to lord it over the Dutch and Palatines."

"Oh, that indeed," my friend replied. "They are silly sprouts, grown up weak and spindling under the shadow of Sir William ; when he is cut down the sun will shrivel them, no doubt. But the hardier, healthier plants which finally take their place will be of English stock—not Dutch or German."

I hope devoutly that this lengthened digression into politics has not proved wearisome. I have touched upon but one of a hundred like conversations which we two had together on our slow journey, and this because I wanted to set forth the manner of things we discussed, and the views we severally had. Events proved that we both were partially right. The United States of the Netherlands was the real parent of the United States of America, and the constitution which the Dutch made for the infant State of New York served as the model in breadth and in freedom for our present noble Federal Constitution. In that much my faith was justified. But it is also true that my State is no longer Dutch, but English, and that the language of my mother has died out from among us.

Before noon next day we reached Fort Stanwix, the forest-girdled block-house commanding the Great Carrying Place. Here we waited one day for the boats to come up, and half of another to get them through the sluices into Wood Creek. Then, as the horses and carts returned, we embarked and set our faces toward the Lakes.

CHAPTER XIII.

WE had left what it pleases us to call civilization behind. Until our return we were scarcely again to see the blackened fields of stumps surrounding clearings, or potash kettles, or girdled trees, or chimneys.

Not that our course lay wholly through unbroken solitude ; but the men we for the most part encoun-' tered were of the strange sort who had pushed westward farther and farther to be alone—to get away from their fellows. The axe to them did not signify the pearlash of commerce, but firewood and honey and coon-skins for their own personal wants. They traded a little, in a careless, desultory fashion, with the proceeds of their traps and rifles. But their desires were few—a pan and kettle, a case of needles and cord, some rum or brandy from cider or wild grapes, tobacco, lead, and powder—chiefly the last three. They fed themselves, adding to their own fish and game only a little pounded maize which they got mostly from the Indians, and cooked in mush or on a baking stone. In the infrequent cases where there were women with them, we sometimes saw candles, either dips or of the wax of myrtle-berries, but more often the pine-knot was used. Occasionally they had log-houses, with even here and there a second story above the puncheon-floor, reached by a ladder; but in the main their habitations were half-faced camps, secured in front at night by fires. They were rough, coarse, hardened, drunken men as a rule, generally disagreeable and taciturn; insolent, lazy, and miserable from my point of view, but I judge both industrious and contented from their own.

We should have had little favor or countenance from these fellows, I doubt not, but for Enoch Wade. He seemed to know all the saturnine, shaggy, lounging outcasts whom we met in unexpected places; if he did not, they knew him at a glance for one of their own kidney, which came to the same thing. It was on his account that we were tolerated, nay, even advised and helped and entertained.

Enoch had been a prodigious traveller—or else was a still more prodigious liar—I never quite decided which. He told them, when we chanced to sit around their fires of an evening, most remarkable stories of field and forest—of caribou and seals killed in the North; of vast herds of bison on far Western prairies; of ice-bound winters spent in the Hudson Bay Company's preserves beyond the Lakes; of houses built of oyster-shells and cement 'on the Carolina coast. They listened gravely, smoking their cob-and-reed pipes, and eying him attentively. They liked him, and they did not seem to dislike Coppernol and our other white servants. But they showed no friendliness toward my poor Tulp, and exhibited only scant, frigid courtesy to Mr. Cross and me.

The fact that my companion was a power in the East India Company, and a director in the new Northwestern Fur Company, did not interest them, at least favorably. It was indeed not until after we had got beyond the Sandusky that Enoch often volunteered this information, for the trappers of the East had little love for companies, or organized commerce and property of any sort.

I like better to recall the purely physical side of our journey. Now our little flotilla would move for hours on broad, placid, still waters, flanked on each side by expanses of sedge and flags—in which great broods of water-fowl lived—and beyond by majestic avenues formed of pines, towering mast-like sheer sixty feet before they burst into intertwining branches. Again, we would pass through darkened, narrow channels, where adverse waters sped swiftly, and where we battled not only with deep currents, but had often to chop our way through barriers of green tree-trunks, hickory, ash, and birch, which the soft soil on the banks had been unable to longer hold erect. Now we flew merrily along under sail or energetic oars ; now we toiled laboriously against strong tides, by poles or by difficult towing.

But it was all healthful, heartening work, and we enjoyed it to the full. Toward sundown we would begin to look for a brook upon which to pitch our camp. When one was found which did not run black, showing its origin in a tamarack swamp, a

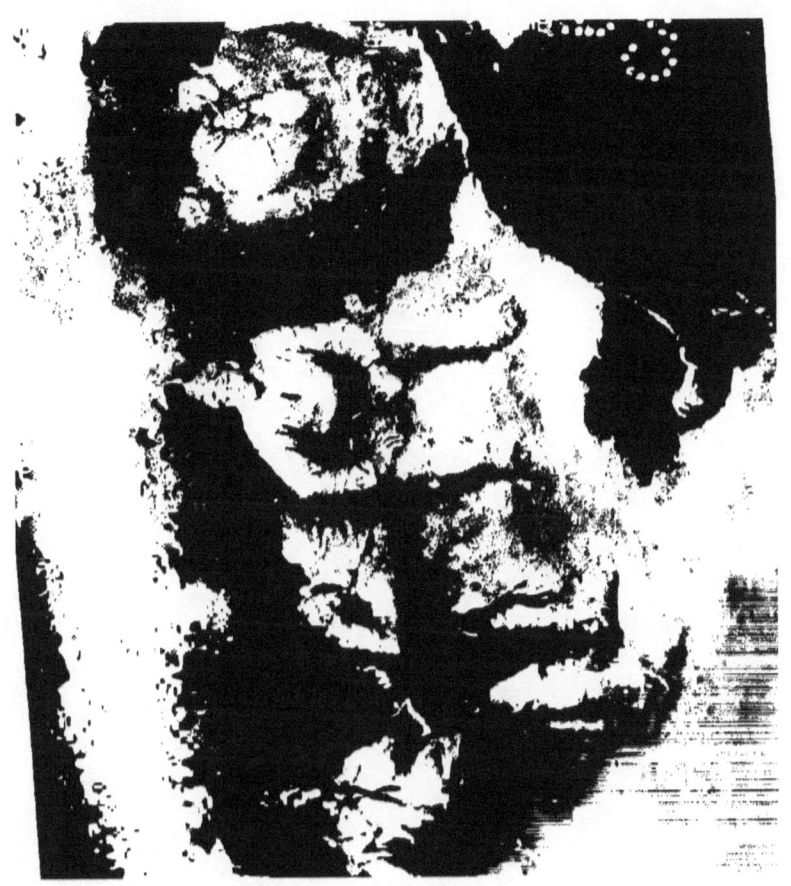

landing was made with all the five boats. These secured, axes were out with, and a shelter soon constructed, while others heaped the fire, prepared the food and utensils, and cooked the welcome meal. How good everything tasted! how big and bright the stars looked! how sweet was the odor of the balsam in the air, later, as we lay on our blankets, looking skyward, and talked! Or, if the night was wild and wet, how cheerily the great fires roared in the draught, and how snugly we lay in our shelter, blinking at the fierce blaze!

When in early July we drew near the country of the Outagamis, having left the Detroit settlement behind us, not to speak of Oswego and Niagara, which seemed as far off now as the moon, an element of personal danger was added to our experiences. Both white hunters and Indians were warmly affected toward the French interest, and often enough we found reason to fear that we would be made to feel this, though luckily it never came to anything serious. It was a novel experience to me to be disliked on account of the English, whom I had myself never regarded with friendship. I was able, fortunately, being thus between the two rival races, as it were, to measure them each against the other.

I had no prejudice in favor of either, God knows. My earliest recollections were of the savage cruelty with which the French had devastated, butchered, and burned among the hapless settlements at the head of the Mohawk Valley. My maturer feelings were all colored with the strong repulsion we Dutch felt for the English rule, which so scornfully mis-

9

governed and plundered our province, granting away
our lands to court favorites and pimps, shipping to
us the worst and most degraded of Old-World crimi-
nals, quartering upon us soldiers whose rude vices
made them even more obnoxious than the convicts,
and destroying our commerce by selfish and senseless laws.

From the Straits west I saw the Frenchman for
the first time, and read the reasons for his failure to
stand against the English. Even while we suspected
grounds for fearing his hostility, we found him a
more courteous and affable man than the Englishman or Yankee. To be pleasant with us seemed a
genuine concern, though it may really have been
otherwise. The Indians about him, too, were a
far more satisfactory lot than I had known in the
Valley. Although many of our Mohawks could
read, and some few write, and although the pains
and devotion of my friend Samuel Kirkland had
done much for the Oneidas, still these French-
spoken, Jesuit-taught Indians seemed a much better
and soberer class than my neighbors of the Iroquois.
They drank little or no rum, save as English traders
furtively plied them with it, for the French laws
were against its sale. They lived most amicably
with the French, too, neither hating nor fearing
them ; and this was in agreeable contrast to the
wearisome bickering eternally going on in New
York between the Indians striving to keep their
land, and the English and Dutch forever planning
to trick them out of it. So much for the good side.

The medal had a reverse. The Frenchman contrived to get on with the Indian by deferring to him, cultivating his better and more generous side, and treating him as an equal. This had the effect of improving and softening the savage, but it inevitably tended to weaken and lower the Frenchman— at least, judged by the standard of fitness to maintain himself in a war of races. No doubt the French and Indians lived together much more quietly and civilly than did the English and Indians. But when these two systems came to be tested by results, it was shown that the Frenchman's policy and kindliness had only enervated and emasculated him, while the Englishman's rough domineering and rule of force had hardened his muscles and fired his resolution. To be sure, measured by the received laws of humanity, the Frenchman was right and the other wrong. But is it so certain, after all, that the right invariably wins?

It was well along in September when, standing on the eminence to the east of Fort Stanwix, I first looked again on my beloved Mohawk.

The trip had been a highly successful one. Enoch was bringing back four bateaux well packed under thin oilskin covers with rare peltries, including some choice black-beaver skins and sea-otter furs from the remote West, which would fetch extravagant prices. On the best estimate of his outward cargo of tea, spirits, powder, traps, calico, duffle, and silver earbobs, breast-buckles, and crosses, he had multiplied its value twenty-fold.

Of course, this was of secondary importance. The

true object of the journey had been to enable Mr. Jonathan Cross to see for himself the prospects of the new Northwestern Company—to look over the territory embraced in its grants, estimate its probable trade, mark points for the establishment of its forts and posts, and secure the information necessary to guard the company from the frauds or failings of agents. He professed himself vastly gratified at the results, physical as well as financial, of his experience, and that was the great thing.

Or no!—perhaps for the purposes of this story there was something more important still. It is even now very pleasant to me to recall that he liked me well enough, after this long, enforced intimacy, to proffer me the responsible and exacting post of the company's agent at Albany.

To say that the offer made me proud and glad would be to feebly understate my emotions. I could not be expected to decide all at once. Independent of the necessity of submitting the proposition to Mr. Stewart, there was a very deep distaste within me for fur-trading at Albany—of the meanness and fraudulency of which I had heard from boyhood. A good many hard stories are told of the Albanians, which, aside from all possible bias of race, I take the liberty of doubting. I do not, for instance, believe all the Yankee tales that the Albany Dutchmen bought from the Indians the silver plate which the latter seized in New England on the occasions of the French and Indian incursions —if for no other reason than the absence of proof that they ever had any plate in New England. But that the Indians used to be most shamefully drugged and cheated out of their eye-teeth in Albany, I fear there can be no reasonable doubt. An evil repute attached to the trade there, and I shrank from embarking in it, even under such splendid auspices. All the same, the offer gratified me greatly.

To be in the woods with a man, day in and day out, is to know him through and through. If I had borne this closest of all conceivable forms of scrutiny, in the factor's estimation, there must be something good in me.

So there was pride as well as joy in this first glance I cast upon the soft-flowing, shadowed water, upon the spreading, stately willows, upon the far-off furrow in the hazy lines of foliage— which spoke to me of home. Here at last was my dear Valley, always to me the loveliest on earth, but now transfigured in my eyes, and radiant beyond all dreams of beauty—because in it was my home, and in that home was the sweet maid I loved.

Yes—I was returned a man, with the pride and the self-reliance and the heart of a man. As I thought upon myself, it was to recognize that the swaddlings of youth had fallen from me. I had never been conscious of their pressure; I had not rebelled against them, nor torn them asunder. Yet somehow they were gone, and my breast swelled with a longer, deeper breath for their absence. I had almost wept with excess of boyish feeling when I left the Valley—my fond old mother and pro-

tector.   I gazed upon it now with an altogether
variant emotion—as of one coming to take possession.   Ah, the calm elation of that one moment,
there alone on the knoll, with the sinking September
sun behind me, and in front but the trifle of sixty
miles of river route—when I realized that I was a
man!

Perhaps it was at this moment that I first knew
I loved Daisy ; perhaps it had been the truly domi-
nant thought in my mind for months, gathering
vigor and form from every tender, longing memory
of the Cedars.   I cannot decide, nor is it needful
that I should.   At least now my head was full of
the triumphant thoughts that I returned successful and in high favor with my companion, that I
had a flattering career opened for me, that the
people at home would be pleased with me—and
that I should marry Daisy.

These remaining twenty leagues grew really very
tedious before they were done with.   We went down
with the boats this time.   I fear that Mr. Cross
found me but poor company these last three days,
for I sat mute in the bow most of the time, twisted
around to look forward down the winding course,
as if this would bring the Cedars nearer.   I had not
the heart to talk.   " Now she is winding the yarn
for my aunt," I would think ; " now she is scattering
oats for the pigeons, or filling Mr. Stewart's pipe,
or running the candles into the moulds.   Dear girl,
does she wonder when I am coming ?   If she could
know that I was here—here on the river speeding to
her—what would she think ? "

And I pictured to myself the pretty glance of surprise, mantling into a flush of joyous welcome, which would greet me on her face, as she ran gladly to my arms. Good old Mr. Stewart, my more than father, would stare at me, then smile with pleasure, and take both my hands in his, with warm, honest words straight from his great heart. What an evening it would be when, seated snugly around the huge blaze—Mr. Stewart in his arm-chair to the right, Daisy nestling on the stool at his knee and looking up into my face, and Dame Kronk knitting in the chimney-shadow to the left—I should tell of my adventures! How goodly a recital I could make of them, though they had been even tamer than they were, with such an audience! And how happy, how gratified they would be when I came to the climax, artfully postponed, of Mr. Cross's offer to me of the Albany agency!

And then how natural, how easy, while these dear people were still smiling with pride and satisfaction at my good fortune, to say calmly—yes, calmly in tone, though my heart should be beating its way through my breast:

"Even more, sir, I prize the hope that Daisy will share it with me—as my wife!"

What with the delay at Caughnawaga, where Mr. Cross debarked, and Major Fonda would have us eat and drink while he told us the news, and Tulp's crazy rowing later, through excitement at nearing home, it was twilight before the boat was run up into our little cove, and I set my foot on land. The Cedars stood before us as yet lightless

against the northern sky.   The gate was open.
The sweet voice of a negro singing arose from the
cabins on the dusky hill-side.   Tears came to my
eyes as I turned to Tulp, who was gathering up the
things in the boat, and said:

   "Do you see, boy?   We're home—home at last!"

CHAPTER XIV.

HOW I SEEM TO FEEL A WANTING NOTE IN THE
CHORUS OF WELCOME.

I COULD hear the noisy clamor among the negroes over the advent of Tulp, whom I had sent off,
desiring to be alone, while I still stood irresolute on
the porch. My hand was on the familiar, well-worn
latch, yet I almost hesitated to enter, so excited was
I with eager anticipations of welcome.

The spacious hall — our sitting-room — was deserted. A fire was blazing on the hearth, and plates
were laid on the oak table as in preparation for a
meal, but there was no one to speak to me. I lighted
a candle, and opened the door to the kitchen; here
too there was a fire, but my aunt was not visible.
Mr. Stewart's room to the right of the hall, and mine
to the left, were alike unoccupied. I threw aside
my hat and watch-coat here, and then with the light
went up-stairs, whistling as was my wont to warn
Daisy of my coming. There was no sound or sign
of movement. The door of her outer room stood
open, and I entered and looked about.

The furniture and appointments had been changed
in position somewhat, so that the chamber seemed
strange to me. There were numerous novel objects

scattered through the rooms as well. A Spanish guitar which I had never seen before stood beside the old piano. There were several elegantly bound books, new to me, on the table; on the mantel-shelf were three miniatures, delicately painted, depicting a florid officer in scarlet, a handsome, proud-looking lady with towering powdered coiffure, and a fair-haired, proud-looking youth. This last I knew in an instant to be the likeness of Master Philip Cross, though it seemingly portrayed him at an age half-way between the two times I had seen him as boy and man. His resemblance to the lady, and then my own recurring recollection of the officer's features, helped me to place them as his parents.

I called out " Daisy ! " My voice had a faltering, mournful sound, and there was no answer.

I came down the stairs again, burdened with a sudden sense of mental discomfort. Already the visions I had had of an enthusiastic welcome were but vague outlines of dreams. There had sprung up in my mind instead a sudden, novel doubt of my position in this house—a cruel idea that perhaps the affection which had so swelled and buoyed my heart was not reciprocated. I put this notion away as foolish and baseless, but all the same the silent hall-room down-stairs seemed now larger and colder, and the flames curled and writhed toward the flue with a chill, metallic aspect, instead of the bright, honest glow of greeting.

While I stood before the fire-place, still holding the candle in my hand, my aunt entered the room from the kitchen door. At sight of me the good soul gave a guttural exclamation, dropped flat an apronful of chips she was bringing in, and stared at me open-mouthed. When she was at last persuaded that I was in proper person and not the spirit, she submitted to be kissed by me—it was not a fervent proceeding, I am bound to add—but it was evident the shock had sent her wits wool-gathering. Her hands were a bright brown from the butternut dye, and the pungent, acrid odor she brought in with her garments made unnecessary her halting explanation that she had been out in the smoke-house.

" Philip sent down two haunches yesterday by Marinus Folts," she said, apologetically, " and this muggy weather I was afraid they wouldn't keep."

" This is the Dutch conception of a welcome after five months! " I could not help thinking to myself, uncharitably forgetting for the. moment my aunt's infirmities. Aloud I said :

" How are they all—Mr. Stewart and Daisy? And where are they? And how have the farms been doing?"

" Well," answered Dame Kronk, upon reflection, " I maintain that the wool is the worst we ever clipped. Was the shearing after you went? Yes, of course it was. Well, how I'm going to get out enough fine for the stockings alone, is more than I can see. It's downright poor."

" But Mr. Stewart and Daisy—are they well? Where are they ? "

" But the niggers have gathered five times as much ginseng as they ever did before. The pigs are fattening fit to eat alive. Eli's been drunk some, but

his girls are really a good deal of help.   There are
going to be more elder-berries this fall than you can
shake a stick at ; they're just breaking the branches.
And the——"

"Oh, aunt," I broke in, "do tell me!   Are Daisy
and Mr. Stewart well?"

"Why, of course they are," she answered; "that
is, they were when they left here a week come
Thursday.   And Marinus Folts didn't say anything
to the contrary yesterday.   Why shouldn't they be
well?   They don't do anything but gad about, these
days.   Daisy hasn't done a stitch of work all summer but knit a couple of comforters—and the time
she's been about it!   When I was her age I could
have knit the whole side of a house in less time.
One of them is for you."

Dear girl, I had wronged her, then.   She had been
thinking of me—working for me.   My heart felt
lighter.

"But where *are* they?" I repeated.

"Oh, where are they?   Up at Sir William's new
summer-house that he's just built.   I don't know
just where it is, but it's fourteen miles from the
Hall, up somewhere on the Sacondaga Vlaie, where
two creeks join.   He's made a corduroy road out to
it, and he's painted it white and green, and he's been
having a sort of fandango out there—a house-warming, I take it.   Marinus Folts says he never saw so
much drinking in his born days.   He'd had his full
share himself, I should judge.   They're coming back
to-night."

I sat down at this, and stared into the fire.   It was

not just the home-coming which I had looked forward to, but it would be all right when they returned. Ah, but would it? Yes, I forced myself
to believe so, and began to find comfort of mind
again.

My aunt picked up the chips and dumped them
into the wood-box. Then she came over and stood
for a long time looking at me. Once she said: "I'm
going to get supper for them when they get back.
Can you wait till then, or shall I cook you something
now?" Upon my thanking her and saying I would
wait, she relapsed into silence, but still keeping her
eyes on me. I was growing nervous under this
phlegmatic inspection, and idly investing it with
some occult and sinister significance, when she broke
out with:

"Oh, I know what it was I wanted to ask you.
Is it really true that the trappers and men in the
woods out there eat the hind-quarters of frogs and
toads?"

This was the sum of my relative's interest in my
voyage. When I had answered her, she gathered
up my luggage and bundles and took them off to
the kitchen, there to be overhauled, washed, and
mended.

I got into my slippers and a loose coat, lighted a
pipe, and settled myself in front of the fire to wait.
Tulp came over, grinning with delight at being
among his own once more, to see if I wanted anything. I sent him off, rather irritably I fear, but I
couldn't bear the contrast which his jocose bearing
enforced on my moody mind, between my reception

and his. This slave of mine had kin and friends who rushed to fall upon his neck, and made the night echoes ring again with their shouts of welcome. I could hear that old Eli had got down his fiddle, and between the faint squeaking strains I could distinguish choruses of happy guffaws and bursts of childlike merriment. Tulp's return caused joy, while mine——

Then I grew vexed at my peevish injustice in complaining because my dear ones, not being gifted with second-sight, had failed to exactly anticipate my coming ; and in blaming my poor aunt for behaving just as the dear old slow-witted creature had always behaved since she was stricken with small-pox, twenty years before. Yet this course of candid self-reproach upon which I entered brought me small relief. I was unhappy, and whether it was my own fault or that of somebody else did not at all help the matter. And I had thought to be so exaltedly happy, on this of all the nights of my life!

At length I heard the sound of hoofs clattering down the road, and of voices lifted in laughing converse. Eli's fiddle ceased its droning, and on going to the window I saw lanterns scudding along to the gate from the slaves' cabins, like fireflies in a gale. I opened the window softly, enough to hear. Not much was to be seen, for the night had set in dark; but there were evidently a number of horsemen outside the gate, and, judging from the noise, all were talking together. The bulk of the party, I understood at once, were going on down the river road, to make a night of it at Sir John's bachelor quarters in old Fort Johnson, or at one of the houses of his two brothers-in-law. I was relieved to hear these roisterers severally decline the invitations to enter the Cedars for a time, and presently out of the gloom became distinguishable the forms of the two for whom I had been waiting. Both were muffled to the eyes, for the air had turned cold, but it seemed as if I should have recognized them in any disguise.

I heard Tulp and Eli jointly shouting out the news of my arrival—for which premature disclosure I could have knocked their woolly heads together— but it seemed that the tidings had reached them before. In fact, they had met Mr. Cross and Enoch on the road down from Johnstown, as I learned afterward.

All my doubts vanished in the warm effusion of their welcome to me, as sincere and honest as it was affectionate. I had pictured it to myself almost aright. Mr. Stewart did come to me with outstretched arms, and wring my hands, and pat my shoulder, and well-nigh weep for joy at seeing me returned, safe and hale. Daisy did not indeed throw herself upon my breast, but she ran to me and took my hands, and lifted her face to be kissed with a smile of pleasure in which there was no reservation.

And it was a merry supper-table around which we sat, too, half an hour later, and gossiped gayly, while the wind rose outside, and the sparks flew the swifter and higher for it. There was so much to tell on both sides.

Somehow, doubtless because of my slowness of tongue, my side did not seem very big compared

with theirs. One day had been very much like another with me, and, besides, the scenes through which
I had passed did not possess the novelty for these
frontier folk that they would have for people nowadays.

But their budget of news was fairly prodigious,
alike in range and quantity. The cream of this, so
to speak, had been taken off by hospitable Jelles
Fonda at Caughnawaga, yet still a portentous substance remained. Some of my friends were dead,
others were married. George Klock was in fresh
trouble through his evil tricks with the Indians. A
young half-breed had come down from the Seneca
nation and claimed John Abeel as his father. Daniel
Claus had set up a pack of hounds, equal in breed
to Sir William's. It was really true that Sir John
was to marry Miss Polly Watts of New York, and
soon too. Walter Butler had been crossed in love,
and was very melancholy and moody, so much so
that he had refused to join the house-warming party
at the new summer-house on Sacondaga Vlaie, which
Sir William had christened Mount Joy Pleasure Hall
—an ambitious enough name, surely, for a forest
fishing-cottage.

Naturally a great deal was told me concerning this
festival from which they had just returned. It seems
that Lady Berenicia Cross and Daisy were the only
ladies there. They were given one of the two sleep-
ing-rooms, while Sir William and Mr. Stewart shared
the other. The younger men had ridden over to
Fish House each night, returning next day. Without its being said in so many words, I could see that

the drinking and carousing there had disturbed and displeased Daisy. There had even, I fancied, been a dispute on this subject between her and our guardian, for he was at pains several times to insist upon telling me incidents which it was plain she desired left unmentioned, and to rather pointedly yet good-humoredly laugh at her as a little puritan, who did not realize that young gentlemen had their own particular ways, as proper and natural to them as were other habits and ways to young foxes or fishes. Her manner said clearly enough that she did not like these ways, but he pleasantly joked her down.

I noted some slight changes in Mr. Stewart, which gave me a sense of uneasiness. He seemed paler than before, and there were darker pits under his prominent, bright eyes. He had been visibly exhausted on entering the house, but revived his strength and spirits under the influence of the food and wine. But the spirits struck, somehow, a false note on my ear. They seemed not to come from a natural and wholesome fund, as of old, but to have a ring of artificiality in them. I could not help thinking, as I looked at him, of the aged French noblemen we read about, who, at an age and an hour which ought to have found them nightcapped and asleep, nourishing their waning vitality, were dancing attendance in ladies' boudoirs, painted, rouged, padded, and wigged, aping the youth they had parted with so long ago. Of course, the comparison was ridiculous, but still it suggested itself, and, once framed in my mind, clung there.

It dawned upon me after a time that it was con-

10

tact with that Lady Berenicia which had wrought this change in him, or, rather, had brought forth in his old age a development of his early associations, that, but for her, would to the end have lain hidden, unsuspected, under the manly cover of his simple middle life.

If there were alterations of a similar sort in Daisy, I could not see them this night. I had regard only for the beauty of the fire-glow on her fair cheek, for the sweet, maidenly light in her hazel eyes, for the soft smile which melted over her face when she looked upon me. If she was quieter and more reserved in her manner than of old, doubtless the same was true of me, for I did not notice it.

I had learned at Fonda's that young Philip Cross was cutting a great swath, socially, in the Valley, and that he was building a grand mansion, fully as large as Johnson Hall, nearly at the summit of the eminence which crowned his patent. Major Fonda was, indeed, contracting to furnish the bricks for what he called the "shimlies," and the house was, by all accounts, to be a wonderful affair. I heard much more about it, in detail, this evening, chiefly from Mr. Stewart. Nay, I might say entirely, for Daisy never once mentioned Philip's name if it could be avoided. Mr. Stewart was evidently much captivated by the young man's spirit and social qualities and demeanor generally.

" He is his father's own boy, ay, and his mother's too," said the old man, with sparkling eyes. " Not much for books, perhaps, though no dullard. But he can break a wild colt, or turn a bottle inside out, or bore a pencilled hole with a pistol-bullet at thirty paces, or tell a story, or sing a song, or ride, dance, box, cross swords, with any gentleman in the Colony. You should have seen him stand Walrath the black-smith on his head at the races a fortnight ago ! I never saw it better done in the Tweed country."

" A highly accomplished gentleman, truly," I said, with as little obvious satire as possible.

" Ah, but he has mind as well as muscle," put in Mr. Stewart. " He is a very Bolingbroke with the ladies. It carries me back to my days at the play, I swear, to hear him and Lady Berenicia clashing rapiers in badinage. You shall hear them, my boy, and judge. And there's a sweet side to his tongue, too, or many a pretty, blushing cheek belies the little ear behind it."

The old gentleman chuckled amiably to himself as he spoke, and poured more Madeira into my glass and his. Daisy somewhat hurriedly rose, bade us " good-night," and left us to ourselves.

Oh, if I had only spoken the word that night !

CHAPTER XV.

I LOOK back now upon the week which followed this home-coming as a season of much dejection and unhappiness. Perhaps at the time it was not all unmixed tribulation. There was a great deal to do, naturally, and occupation to a healthful and vigorous young man is of itself a sovereign barrier against undue gloom. Yet I think of it now as all sadness.

Mr. Stewart had really grown aged and feeble. For the first time, too, there was a petulant vein in his attitude toward me. Heretofore he had treated my failure to grow up into his precise ideal of a gentleman with affectionate philosophy, being at pains to conceal from me whatever disappointment he felt, and, indeed, I think, honestly trying to persuade himself that it was all for the best.

But these five months had created a certain change in the social conditions of the Valley. For years the gulf had been insensibly widening, here under our noses, between the workers and the idlers; during my absence there had come, as it were, a landslide, and the chasm was now manifest to us all. Something of this was true all over the Colonies: no doubt what I noticed was but a phase of the general movement, part social, part religious, part political, now carrying us along with a perceptible glide toward the crisis of revolution. But here in the Valley, more than elsewhere, this broadening fissure of division ran through farms, through houses, ay, even through the group gathered in front of the family fire-place—separating servants from employers, sons from fathers, husbands from wives. And, alas! when I realized now for the first time the existence of this abyss, it was to discover that my dearest friend, the man to whom I most owed duty and esteem and love, stood on one side of it and I on the other.

This was made clear to me by his comments—and even more by his manner—when I told him next day of the great offer which Mr. Cross had made. Not unnaturally I expected that he would be gratified by this proof of the confidence I had inspired, even if he did not favor my acceptance of the proffered post. Instead, the whole matter seemed to vex him. When I ventured to press him for a decision, he spoke unjustly and impatiently to me, for the first time.

"Oh, ay! that will serve as well as anything else, I suppose," he said. "If you are resolute and stubborn to insist upon leaving me, and tossing aside the career it has been my pleasure to plan for you, by all means go to Albany with the other Dutchmen, and barter and cheapen to your heart's content. You know it's no choice of mine, but please yourself!"

This was so gratuitously unfair and unlike him, and so utterly at variance with the reception I had expected for my tidings, that I stood astounded, looking at him. He went on:

"What the need is for your going off and mixing yourself up with these people, I fail for the life of me to see. I suppose it is in the blood. Any other young man but a Dutchman, reared and educated as you have been, given the society and friendship of gentlefolk from boyhood, and placed, by Heaven! as you are here, with a home and an estate to inherit, and people about you to respect and love —I say nothing of obeying them—would have appreciated his fortune, and asked no more. But no! You must, forsooth, pine and languish to be off tricking drunken Indians out of their peltry, and charging some other Dutchman a shilling for fourpence worth of goods!"

What could I say? What could I do but go away sorrowfully, and with a heavy heart take up farm affairs where I had left them? It was very hard to realize that these rough words, still rasping my ears, had issued from Mr. Stewart's lips. I said to myself that he must have had causes for irritation of which I knew nothing, and that he must unconsciously have visited upon me the peevishness which the actions of others had engendered. All the same, it was not easy to bear.

Daily contact with Daisy showed changes, too, in her which disturbed me. Little shades of formalism had crept here and there into her manner, even toward me. She was more distant, I fancied, and mistress-like, toward my poor old aunt. She rose later, and spent more of her leisure time up-stairs in her rooms alone. Her dress was notably more careful and elegant, now, and she habitually wore her hair twisted upon the crown of her head, instead of in a simple braid as of old.

If she was not the Daisy I had so learned to love in my months of absence, it seemed that my heart went out in even greater measure to this new Daisy. She was more beautiful than ever, and she was very gentle and soft with me. A sense of tender pity vaguely colored my devotion, for the dear girl seemed to my watchful solicitude to be secretly unhappy. Once or twice I strove to so shape our conversation that she would be impelled to confide in me—to throw herself upon my old brotherly fondness, if she suspected no deeper passion. But she either saw through my clumsy devices, or else in her innocence evaded them ; for she hugged the sorrow closer to her heart, and was only pensively pleasant with me.

I may explain now, in advance of my story, what I came to learn long afterward ; namely, that the poor little maiden was truly in sore distress at this time—torn by the conflict between her inclination and her judgment, between her heart and her head. She was, in fact, hesitating between the glamour which the young Englishman and Lady Berenicia, with their polished ways, their glistening surfaces, and their attractive, idlers' views of existence, had thrown over her, and her own innate, womanly repugnance to the shallowness and indulgence, not to say license, beneath it all. It was this battle the progress of which I unwittingly watched. Had I but known what emotions were fighting for mastery behind those sweetly grave hazel eyes—had I but realized how slight a pressure might have tipped the scales my way—how much would have been different!

But I, slow Frisian that I was, comprehended nothing of it all, and so was by turns futilely compassionate—and sulky.

For again, at intervals, she would be as gay and bright as a June rose, tripping up and down through the house with a song on her lips, and the old laugh rippling like sunbeams about her. Then she would deftly perch herself on the arm of Mr. Stewart's chair, and dazzle us both with the joyous merriment of her talk, and the sparkle in her eyes—or sing for us of an evening, up-stairs, playing the while upon the lute (which young Cross had given her) instead of the discarded piano. Then she would wear a bunch of flowers—I never suspecting whence they came—upon her breast, and an extra ribbon in her hair. And then I would be wretched, and gloomily say to myself that I preferred her unhappy, and next morning, when the cloud had gathered afresh upon her face, would long again to see her cheerful once more.

And so the week went by miserably, and I did not tell my love.

One morning, after breakfast, Mr. Stewart asked Daisy to what conclusion she had come about our accepting Philip Cross's invitation to join a luncheon-party on his estate that day. I had heard this gathering mentioned several times before, as a forthcoming event of great promise, and I did not quite under-

stand either the reluctance with which Daisy seemed
to regard the thought of going, or the old gentleman's mingled insistence and deference to her wishes
in the matter.

To be sure, I had almost given up in weary heart-
sickness the attempt to understand his new moods.
Since his harsh words to me, I had had nothing but
amiable civility from him—now and then coming
very near to his old-time fond cordiality—but it was
none the less grievously apparent to me that our
relations would never again be on the same footing.
I could no longer anticipate his wishes, I found, or
foresee what he would think or say upon matters as
they came up. We two were wholly out of chord,
be the fault whose it might. And so, I say, I was
rather puzzled than surprised to see how much stress
was laid between them upon the question whether
or not Daisy would go that day to Cairncross, as the
place was to be called.

Finally, without definitely having said "yes," she
appeared dressed for the walk, and put on a mock
air of surprise at not finding us also ready. She
blushed, I remember, as she did so. There was no
disposition on my part to make one of the party,
but when I pleaded that I had not been invited, and
that there was occupation for me at home, Mr.
Stewart seemed so much annoyed that I hastened
to join them.

It was a perfect autumn day, with the sweet scent
of burning leaves in the air, and the foliage above
the forest path putting on its first pale changes toward scarlet and gold. Here and there, when the

tortuous way approached half-clearings, we caught glimpses of the round sun, opaquely red through the smoky haze.

Our road was the old familiar trail northward over which Mr. Stewart and I, in the happy days, had so often walked to reach our favorite haunt the gulf. The path was wider and more worn now—almost a thoroughfare, in fact. It came to the creek at the very head of the chasm, skirting the mysterious circle of sacred stones, then crossing the swift water on a new bridge of logs, then climbing the farther side of the ravine by a steep zigzag course which hung dangerously close to the precipitous wall of dark rocks. I remarked at the time, as we made our way up, that there ought to be a chain, or outer guard of some sort, for safety. Mr. Stewart said he would speak to Philip about it, and added the information that this side of the gulf was Philip's property.

"It is rough enough land," he went on to say, "and would never be worth clearing. He has some plan of keeping it in all its wildness, and building a little summer-house down below by the bridge, within full sound of the waterfall. No doubt we shall arrange to share the enterprise together. You know I have bought on the other side straight to the creek."

Once the road at the top was gained, Cairncross was but a pleasant walking measure, over paths well smoothed and made. Of the mansion in process of erection, which, like Johnson Hall, was to be of wood, not much except the skeleton framework met the eye, but this promised a massive and imposing edifice. A host of masons, carpenters, and laborers, sufficient to have quite depopulated Johnstown during the daylight hours, were hammering, hewing, or clinking the chimney-bricks with their trowels, within and about the structure.

At a sufficient distance from this tumult of construction, and on a level, high plot of lawn, was a pretty marquee tent. Here the guests were assembled, and thither we bent our steps.

Young Cross came forth eagerly to greet us—or, rather, my companions—with outstretched hands and a glowing face. He was bareheaded, and very beautifully, though not garishly clad. In the reddish, dimmed sunlight, with his yellow hair and his fresh, beaming face, he certainly was handsome.

He bowed ceremoniously to Mr. Stewart, and then took him warmly by the hand. Then with a frank gesture, as if to gayly confess that the real delight was at hand, he bent low before Daisy and touched her fingers with his lips.

" You make me your slave, your very happy slave, dear lady, by coming," he murmured, loud enough for me to hear. She blushed, and smiled with pleasure at him.

To me our young host was civil enough. He called me " Morrison," it is true, without any " Mr.," but he shook hands with me, and said affably that he was glad to see me back safe and sound. Thereafter he paid no attention whatsoever to me, but hung by Daisy's side in the cheerful circle outside the tent.

Sir William was there, and Lady Berenicia, of course, and a dozen others. By all I was welcomed home with cordiality—by all save the Lady, who was distant, not to say supercilious in her manner, and Sir John Johnson, who took the trouble only to nod at me.

Inquiring after Mr. Jonathan Cross, I learned that my late companion was confined to the Hall, if not to his room, by a sprained ankle. There being nothing to attract me at the gathering, save, indeed, the girl who was monopolized by my host, and the spectacle of this affording me more discomfort than satisfaction, the condition of my friend at the Hall occurred to me as a pretext for absenting myself. I mentioned it to Mr. Stewart, who had been this hour or so in great spirits, and who now was chuckling with the Lady and one or two others over some tale she was telling.

"Quite right," he said, without turning his head; and so, beckoning to Tulp to follow me, I started.

It was a brisk hour's walk to the Hall, and I strode along at a pace which forced my companion now and again into a trot. I took rather a savage comfort in this, as one likes to bite hard on an aching tooth; for I had a profound friendship for this poor black boy, and to put a hardship upon him was to suffer myself even more than he did. Tulp had come up misshapen and undersized from his long siege with the small-pox, and with very rickety and unstable legs. I could scarcely have sold him for a hundred dollars, and would not have parted with him for ten thousand, if for no other reason than his deep and dog-like devotion to me. Hence, when I made this poor fellow run and pant, I must have been possessed of an unusually resolute desire to be disagreeable to myself. And in truth I was.

Mr. Jonathan Cross made me very welcome. His accident had befallen on the very day following his return, and he had seen nobody save the inmates of the Hall since that time. We had many things to talk about—among others, of my going to Albany to take the agency. I told him that this had not been quite decided as yet, but avoided giving reasons. I could not well tell this born-and-bred merchant that my guardian thought I ought to feel above trade. His calm eyes permitted themselves a solitary twinkle as I stumbled over the subject, but he said nothing.

He did express some interest, however, when I told him whence I had come, and what company I had quitted to visit him.

" So Mistress Daisy is there with the rest, is she ? " he said, with more vigor in his voice than I had ever heard there before. " So, so ! The apple has fallen with less shaking than I thought for."

I do not think that I made any remark in reply. If I did, it must have been inconsequential in the extreme, for my impression is of a long, heartaching silence, during which I stared at my companion, and saw nothing.

At last I know that he said to me—I recall the very tone to this day :

" You ought to be told, I think. Yes, you ought

to know. Philip Cross asked her to be his wife a fortnight ago. She gave no decided answer. From what Philip and Lady Berenicia have said to each other here, since, I know it was understood that if she went to him to-day it meant 'yes.' "

This time I know I kept silence for a long time.

I found myself finally holding the hand he had extended to me, and saying, in a voice which sounded like a stranger's:

" I will go to Albany whenever you like."

I left the Hall somehow, kicking the drunken Enoch Wade fiercely out of my path, I remember, and walking straight ahead as if blindfolded.

CHAPTER XVI.

TULP GETS A BROKEN ·HEAD TO MATCH MY HEART.

WITHOUT heed as to the direction, I started at a furious pace up the road which I found myself upon —Tulp at my heels. If he had not, from utter weariness, cried out after a time, I should have followed the track straight, unceasing, over the four leagues and more to the Sacondaga. As it was, I had presently to stop and retrace my steps to where he sat on a wayside stump, dead beat.

" Don't you wait for me, Mass' Douw, if you're bound to get there quick," he said, gasping for breath. " Don't mind me. I'll follow along the best I can."

The phrase "get there"—it was almost the only English which poor Tulp had put into the polyglot sentence he really uttered—arrested my attention. " Get where?" I had been headed for the mountains—for the black water which dashed foaming down their defiles, and eddied in sinister depths at their bases. I could see the faint blue peaks on the horizon from where I stood, by the side of the tired slave. The sight sobered me. To this day I cannot truly say whether I had known where I was going, and if there had not been in my burning brain the latent impulse to throw myself into the

Sacondaga. But I could still find the spot—altered beyond recollection as the face of the country is—where Tulp's fatigue compelled me to stop, and where I stood gazing out of new eyes, as it were, upon the pale Adirondack outlines.

As I looked, the aspect of the day had changed. The soft, somnolent haze had vanished from the air. Dark clouds were lifting themselves in the east and north beyond the mountains, and a chill breeze was blowing from them upon my brow. I took off my hat, and held up my face to get all its cooling touch. Tulp, between heavy breaths, still begged that his infirmity might not be allowed to delay me.

"Why, boy," I laughed bitterly at him, "I have no place to go to. Nobody is waiting for me—nobody wants me."

The black looked hopeless bewilderment at me, and offered no comment. Long afterward I learned that he at the moment reached the reluctant conclusion that I had taken too much drink in the Hall.

"Or no!" I went on, a thought coming to the surface in the hurly-burly of my mind. "We are going to Albany. That's where we're going."

Tulp's sooty face took on a more dubious look, if that were possible. He humbly suggested that I had chosen a roundabout route; perhaps I was going by the way of the Healing Springs. But it must be a long, lonesome road, and the rain was coming on.

Sure enough the sky was darkening: a storm was in the air, and already the distant mountain-tops were hidden from view by the rain-mist.

Without more words I put on my hat, and we turned back toward the settlements. The disposition to walk swiftly, which before had been a controlling thing, was gone. My pace was slow enough now, descending the hill, for even Tulp, who followed close upon my heels. But my head was not much clearer. It was not from inability to think: to the contrary, the vividness and swift succession of my thoughts, as they raced through my brain, almost frightened me.

I had fancied myself miserable that very morning, because Mr. Stewart had spoken carelessly to me, and she had been only ordinarily pleasant. Ah, fool! My estate that morning had been that of a king, of a god, in contrast to this present wretchedness. Then I still had a home—still nourished in my heart a hope—and these *were* happiness! I laughed aloud at my folly in having deemed them less.

She had put her hand in his—given herself to him! She had with her eyes open promised to marry this Englishman—fop! dullard! roisterer! insolent cub!—so the rough words tumbled to my tongue. In a hundred ways I pictured her—called up her beauty, her delicacy, her innocence, her grace, the refined softness of her bearing, the sweet purity of her smile, the high dignity of her thoughts—and then ground my teeth as I placed against them the solitary image my mind consented to limn of him— a brawling dandy with fashionable smirk and false blue eyes, flushed with wine, and proud of no better achievement than throwing a smith in a drunken

11

wrestling-bout.⁾ It was a sin—a desecration! Where
were their eyes, that they did not read this fellow's
worthlessness, and bid him stand back when he
sought to lay his coarse hands upon her?

Yet who were these that should have saved her?
Ah! were they not all of his class, or of his pretence
to class?

Some of them had been my life-long friends. To
Mr. Stewart—and I could not feel bitterly toward
him even now—I owed home, education, rearing,
everything; Sir William had been the earliest and
kindest of my other friends, eager and glad always
to assist, instruct, encourage me; John Butler had
given me my first gun, and had petted me in his
rough way from boyhood. Yet now, at a touch
of that hateful, impalpable thing "class," these all
vanished away from my support, and were to me
as if they had never been. I saw them over on the
other side, across the abyss from me, grouped smiling about this new-comer, praising his brute ability
to drink and race and wrestle, complimenting him
upon his position among the gentry—save the mark!
—of Tryon County, and proud that they had by
never so little aided him to secure for a wife this poor
trembling, timid, fascinated girl. Doubtless they
felt that a great honor had been done her; it might
be that even she dreamed this, too, as she heard
their congratulations.

And these men, honest, fair-minded gentlemen as
they were in other affairs, would toss me aside like
a broken pipe if I ventured to challenge their sympathy as against this empty-headed, satined, and pow-

dered stranger. They had known and watched me all my life. My smallest action, my most trivial habit, was familiar to them. They had seen me grow before their eyes—dutiful, obedient, diligent, honest, sober, truthful. In their hearts they knew that I deserved all these epithets. They themselves time out of mind had applied them to me. I stood now, at my early age, and on my own account, on the threshold of a career of honorable trade, surely as worthy now as it was when Sir William began at it far more humbly. Yet with all these creditable things known to them, I could not stand for a moment in their estimation against this characterless new-comer!

Why? He was a "gentleman," and I was not.

Not that he was better born—a thousand times no! But I had drawn from the self-sacrificing, modest, devoted man of God, my father, and the resolute, tireless, hard working, sternly honest housewife, my mother, the fatal notion that it was not beneath the dignity of a Mauverensen or a Van Hoorn to be of use in the world. My ancestors had fought for their little country, nobly and through whole generations, to free it from the accursed rule of that nest of aristocrats, Spain; but they had not been ashamed also to work, in either the Old World or the New. This other, this Englishman—I found myself calling him that as the most comprehensive expletive I could use—the son of a professional butcher and of an intriguing woman, was my superior here, in truth, where I had lived

all my life and he had but shown his nose, because
he preferred idleness to employment!

It was a mistake, then, was it, to be temperate
and industrious? It was more honorable to ride at
races, to play high stakes, and drain three bottles at
dinner, than to study and to do one's duty? To
be a gentleman was a matter of silk breeches and
perukes and late hours? Out upon the blundering
playwright who made Bassanio win with the leaden
casket! Portia was a woman, and would have
wrapped her picture—nay, herself—in tinsel gilt,
the gaudier the better!

But why strive to trace further my wrathful meditations? There is nothing pleasant or profitable in
the contemplation of anger, even when reason runs
abreast of it. And I especially have no pride in
this three hours' wild fury. There were moments
in it, I fear, when my rage was well-nigh murderous
in its fierceness.

The storm came—a cold, thin, driving rain, with
faint mutterings of thunder far behind. I did not
care to quicken my pace or fasten my coat. The
inclemency fitted and echoed my mood.

On the road we came suddenly upon the Hall
party, returning in haste from the interrupted picnic. The baronet's carriage, with the hood drawn,
rumbled past without a sign of recognition from
driver or inmates. A half-dozen horsemen cantered
behind, their chins buried in their collars, and their
hats pulled down over their eyes. One of the last
of these—it was Bryan Lefferty—reined up long
enough to inform me that Mr. Stewart and Daisy

had long before started by the forest path for
their home, and that young Cross had made short
work of his other guests in order to accompany
them.

" We're not after complaining, though," said the
jovial Irishman; "it's human nature to desert ordinary mortals like us when youth and beauty beckon
the other way."

I made some indifferent answer, and he rode away
after his companions.   We resumed our tramp over
the muddy track, with the rain and wind gloomily
pelting upon our backs.

When we turned off into the woods, to descend
the steep side-hill to the water-fall, it was no easy
matter to keep our footing.   The narrow trail was
slippery with wet leaves and moss.   Looking over
the dizzy edge, you could see the tops of tall trees
far below.   The depths were an indistinct mass of
dripping foliage, dark green and russet.   We made
our way gingerly and with extreme care, with the
distant clamor of the falls in our ears, and the peril
of tumbling headlong keeping all our senses painfully alert.

At a turn in the path, I came sharply upon Philip
Cross.

He was returning from the Cedars: he carried a
broken bough to use as a walking-stick in the difficult ascent, and was panting with the exertion ; yet
the lightness of his heart impelled him to hum broken
snatches of a song as he climbed.   The wet verdure
under foot had so deadened sound that neither suspected the presence of the other till we suddenly

stood, on this slightly widened, overhanging plat-
form, face to face!

He seemed to observe an unusual something on
my face, but it did not interest him enough to affect
his customary cool, off-hand civility toward me.

"Oh, Morrison, is that you?" he said, noncha-
lantly. "You're drenched, I see, like the rest of us.
Odd that so fine a day should end like this"—and
made as if to pass me on the inner side.

I blocked his way and said, with an involuntary
shake in my voice which I could only hope he failed
to note:

"You have miscalled me twice to-day. I will
teach you my true name, if you like—here! now!"

He looked at me curiously for an instant—then
with a frown. "You are drunk," he cried, angrily.
"Out of my way!"

"No, you are again wrong," I said, keeping my
voice down, and looking him square in the eye.
"I'm not of the drunken set in the Valley. No man
was ever soberer. But I am going to spell my name
out for you, in such manner that you will be in no
danger of forgetting it to your dying day."

The young Englishman threw a swift glance about
him, to measure his surroundings. Then he laid
down his cudgel, and proceeded to unbutton his
great-coat, which by some strange freak of irony
happened to be one of mine that they had lent
him at the Cedars for his homeward journey.

If the words may be coupled, I watched him with
an enraged admiration. There was no sign of fear
manifest in his face or bearing. With all his knowl-

edge of wrestling, he could not but have felt that, against my superior size and weight, and long familiarity with woodland footing, there were not many chances of his escaping with his life: if I went over, he certainly would go too—and he might go alone. Yet he unfastened his coats with a fine air of unconcern, and turned back his ruffles carefully. I could not maintain the same calm in throwing off my hat and coat, and was vexed with myself for it.

We faced each other thus in our waistcoats in the drizzling rain for a final moment, exchanging a crossfire sweep of glances which took in not only antagonist, but every varying foot of the treacherous ground we stood upon, and God knows what else beside—when I was conscious of a swift movement past me from behind.

I had so completely forgotten Tulp's presence that for the second that followed I scarcely realized what was happening. Probably the faithful slave had no other thought, as he glided in front of me, than to thus place himself between me and what he believed to be certain death.

To the Englishman the sudden movement may easily have seemed an attack.

There was an instant's waving to and fro of a light and a dark body close before my startled eyes. Then, with a scream which froze the very marrow in my bones, the negro boy, arms whirling wide in air, shot over the side of the cliff!

Friends of mine in later years, when they heard this story from my lips over a pipe and bowl, used to express surprise that I did not that very moment throw myself upon Cross, and fiercely bring the quarrel to an end, one way or the other. I remember that when General Arnold came up the Valley, five years after, and I recounted to him this incident, which recent events had recalled, he did not conceal his opinion that I had chosen the timid part. " By God ! " he cried, striking the camp-table till the candlesticks rattled, " I would have killed him or he would have killed me, before the nigger struck bottom ! " Very likely he would have done as he said. I have never seen a man with a swifter temper and resolution than poor, brave, choleric, handsome Arnold had ; and into a hideously hopeless morass of infamy they landed him, too ! No doubt it will seem to my readers, as well, that in nature I ought upon the instant to have grappled the Englishman.

The fact was, however, that this unforeseen event took every atom of fight out of both of us as completely as if we had been struck by lightning.

With a cry of horror I knelt and hung over the shelving edge as far as possible, striving to discover some trace of my boy through the misty masses of foliage below. I could see nothing—could hear nothing but the far-off dashing of the waters, which had now in my ears an unspeakably sinister sound. It was only when I rose to my feet again that I caught sight of Tulp, slowly making his way up the other side of the ravine, limping and holding one hand to his head. He had evidently been hurt, but it was a great deal to know that he was alive. I turned to my antagonist—it seemed that a long time had passed since I last looked at him.

The same idea that the struggle was postponed had come to him, evidently, for he had put on his coats again, and had folded his arms. He too had been alarmed for the fate of the boy, but he affected now not to see him.

I drew back to the rock now, and Cross passed me in silence, with his chin defiantly in the air. He turned when he had gained the path above, and stood for a moment frowning down at me.

" I am going to marry Miss Stewart," he called out. "The sooner you find a new master, and take yourself off, the better. I don't want to see you again."

" When you do see me again," I made answer, "be sure that I will break every bone in your body."

With this not very heroic interchange of compliments we parted. I continued the descent, and crossed the creek to where the unfortunate Tulp was waiting for me.

CHAPTER XVII.

THE slave sat upon one of the bowlders in the old Indian circle, holding his jaw with his hand, and rocking himself like a child with the colic.

He could give me no account whatever of the marvellous escape he had had from instant death, and I was forced to conclude that his fall had been more than once broken by the interposition of branches or clumps of vines. He seemed to have fortunately landed on his head. His jaw was broken, and some of his teeth loosened, but none of his limbs were fractured, though all were bruised. I bound up his chin with my handkerchief, and put my neckcloth over one of his eyes, which was scratched and swollen shut, as by some poisonous thing.) Thus bandaged, he hobbled along behind me over the short remaining distance. The rain and cold increased as nightfall came on, and, no longer sustained by my anger, I found the walk a very wet and miserable affair.

When I reached the Cedars, and had sent Tulp to his parents with a promise to look in upon him later, I was still without any definite plan of what to say or do upon entering. The immensity of the crisis which had overtaken me had not shut my mind to the fact that the others, so far from being similarly overwhelmed, did not even suspect any reason on my part for revolt or sorrow. I had given neither of them any cause, by word or sign, to regard me as a rival to Cross—at least, of late years. So far as they were concerned, I had no ground to stand upon in making a protest. Yet when did this consideration restrain an angry lover? I had a savage feeling they they ought to have known, if they didn't. And reflection upon the late scene on the gulf side— upon the altercation, upon the abortive way in which I had allowed mastery of the situation to slip through my fingers, and upon poor Tulp's sufferings—only served to swell my mortification and rage.

When I entered—after a momentary temptation to make a stranger of myself by knocking at the door—Daisy was sitting by the fire beside Mr. Stewart; both were looking meditatively into the fire, which gave the only light in the room, and she was holding his hand. My heart melted for a second as this pretty, home-like picture met my eyes, and a sob came into my throat at the thought that I was no longer a part of this dear home-circle. Then sulkiness rose to the top again. I muttered something about the weather, lighted a candle at the fire, and moved past them to the door of my room.

" Why, Douw," asked Daisy, half rising as she spoke, " what has happened? There's blood on your ruffles! Where is your neckcloth?"

I made answer, standing with my hand upon the latch, and glowering at her:

" The blood comes from my Tulp's broken head;

I used my neckcloth to tie it up. He was thrown over the side of Kayaderosseros gulf, an hour ago, by the gentleman whom it is announced you are going to marry!"

Without waiting to note the effect of these words, I went into my room, closing the door behind me sharply. I spent a wretched hour or so, sorting over my clothes and possessions, trinkets and the like, and packing them for a journey. Nothing was very clear in my mind, between bitter repining at the misery which had come upon me and the growing repulsion I felt for making these two unhappy, but it was at least obvious that I must as soon as possible leave the Cedars.

When at last I reëntered the outer room, the table was spread for supper. Only Mr. Stewart was in the room, and he stood in his favorite attitude, with his back to the fire and his hands behind him. He preserved a complete silence, not even looking at me, until my aunt had brought in the simple evening meal. To her he said briefly that Mistress Daisy had gone to her room, weary and with a headache, and would take no supper. I felt the smart of reproof to me in every word he uttered, and even more in his curt tone. I stood at the window with my back to him, looking through the dripping little panes at the scattered lights across the river, and not ceasing for an instant to think forebodingly of the scene which was impendent.

Dame Kronk had been out of the room some moments when he said, testily:

"Well, sir! will you do me the honor to come to

the table, or is it your wish that I should fetch your supper to you?" The least trace of softness in his voice would, I think, have broken down my temper. If he had been only grieved at my behavior, and had shown to me sorrow instead of truculent rebuke, I would have been ready, I believe, to fall at his feet. But his scornful sternness hardened me.

"Thank you, sir," I replied, "I have no wish for supper."

More seconds of silence ensued. The streaming windows and blurred fragments of light, against the blackness outside, seemed to mirror the chaotic state of my mind. I ought to turn to him—a thousand times over, I knew I ought—and yet for my life I could not. At last he spoke again:

"Perhaps, then, you will have the politeness to face me. My association has chiefly been with gentlemen, and I should mayhap be embarrassed by want of experience if I essayed to address you to your back."

I had wheeled around before half his first sentence was out, thoroughly ashamed of myself. In my contrition I had put forth my hand as I moved toward him. He did not deign to notice—or rather to respond to—the apologetic overture, and I dropped the hand and halted. He looked me over now, searchingly and with a glance of mingled curiosity and anger. He seemed to be searching for words sufficiently formal and harsh, meanwhile, and he was some time in finding them.

"In the days when I wore a sword for use, young man, and moved among my equals," he began, deliberately, " it was not held to be a safe or small matter to offer me affront. Other times, other manners. The treatment which then I would not have brooked from Cardinal York himself, I find myself forced to submit to, under my own roof, at the hands of a person who, to state it most lightly, should for decency's sake put on the appearance of respect for my gray hairs."

He paused here, and I would have spoken, but he held up his slender, ruffled hand with a peremptory " Pray, allow me ! " and presently went on :

" In speaking to you as I ought to speak, I am at the disadvantage of being wholly unable to comprehend the strange and malevolent change which has come over you. Through nearly twenty years of close and even daily observation, rendered at once keen and kindly by an affection to which I will not now refer, you had produced upon me the impression of a dutiful, respectful, honorable, and polite young man. If, as was the case, you developed some of the to me less attractive and less generous virtues of your race, I still did not fail to see that they were, in their way, virtues, and that they inured both to my material profit and to your credit among your neighbors. I had said to myself, after much consideration, that if you had not come up wholly the sort of gentleman I had looked for, still you were a gentleman, and had qualities which, taken altogether, would make you a creditable successor to me on the portions of my estate which it was my purpose to entail upon you and yours."

" Believe me, Mr. Stewart," I interposed here,

with a broken voice, as he paused again, " I am deeply—very deeply grateful to you."

He went on as if I had not spoken :

"Judge, then, my amazement and grief to find you returning from your voyage to the West intent upon leaving me, upon casting aside the position and duties for which I had trained you, and upon going down to Albany to dicker for pence and ha'pence with the other Dutchmen there. I did not forbid your going. I contented myself by making known to you my disappointment at your selection of a career so much inferior to your education and position in life. Whereupon you have no better conception of what is due to me and to yourself than to begin a season of sulky pouting and sullenness, culminating in the incredible rudeness of open insults to me, and, what is worse, to my daughter in my presence. She has gone to her chamber sick in head and heart alike from your boorish behavior. I would fain have retired also, in equal sorrow and disgust, had it not seemed my duty to demand an explanation from you before the night passed."

The blow—the whole crushing series of blows— had fallen. How I suffered under them, how each separate lash tore savagely through heart and soul and flesh, it would be vain to attempt to tell.

Yet with the anguish there came no weakening. I had been wrong and foolish, and clearly enough I saw it, but this was not the way to correct or chastise me. A solitary sad word would have unmanned me ; this long, stately, satirical speech, this ironically elaborate travesty of my actions and motives, had an opposite effect. I suffered, but I stubbornly stood my ground.

"If I have disappointed you, sir, I am more grieved than you can possibly be," I replied. "If what I said was in fact an affront to you, and to—her—then I would tear out my tongue to recall the words. But how can the simple truth affront?"

"What was this you called out so rudely about the gulf—about Tulp's being thrown over by—by the gentleman my daughter is to marry? since you choose to describe him thus."

"I spoke the literal truth, sir. It was fairly by a miracle that the poor devil escaped with his life."

"How did it happen? What was the provocation? Even in Caligula's days slaves were not thrown over cliffs without some reason."

"Tulp suffered for the folly of being faithful to me—for not understanding that it was the fashion to desert me," I replied, with rising temerity. "He threw himself between me and this Cross of yours, as we faced each other on the ledge—where we spoke this morning of the need for a chain—and the Englishman flung him off."

"Threw himself between you! Were you quarrelling, you two, then?"

"I dare say it would be described as a quarrel. I think I should have killed him, or he killed me, if the calamity of poor Tulp's tumble had not put other things in our heads."

"My faith!" was Mr. Stewart's only comment. He stared at me for a time, then seated himself before the fire, and looked at the blaze and smoke

The bow—the whole crushing series of blows—had fallen

in apparent meditation. Finally he said, in a somewhat milder voice than before: "Draw a chair up
here and sit down. Doubtless there is more in this
than I thought. Explain it to me."

I felt less at my ease, seated now for a more or
less moderate conference, than I had been on my
feet, bearing my part in a quarrel.

"What am I to explain?" I asked.

"Why were you quarrelling with Philip?"

"Because I felt like it—because I hate him!"

"Tut, tut! That is a child's answer. What is
the trouble between you two? I demand to
know!"

"If you will have it"—and all my resentment and
sense of loss burst forth in the explanation—"because he has destroyed my home for me; because he
has ousted me from the place I used to have, and
strove so hard to be worthy of, in your affections;
because, after a few months here, with his fine
clothes and his dashing, wasteful ways, he is more
regarded by you and your friends than I am, who
have tried faithfully all my life to deserve your regard; because he has taken—" But I broke down
here. My throat choked the sound in sobs, and I
turned my face away that he might not see the tears
which I felt scalding my eyes.

My companion kept silent, but he poked the
damp, smudging sticks about in the fire-place vigorously, took his spectacles out of their case, rubbed
them, and put them back in his pocket, and in other
ways long since familiar to me betrayed his uneasy
interest. These slight signs of growing sympathy

12

—or, at least, comprehension—encouraged me to proceed, and my voice came back to me.

" If you could know," I went mournfully on, "the joy I felt when I first looked on the Valley—*our* Valley—again at Fort Stanwix ; if you could only realize how I counted the hours and minutes which separated me from this home, from you and her, and how I cried out at their slowness ; if you could guess how my heart beat when I walked up the path out there that evening, and opened that door, and looked to see you two welcome me—ah, then you could feel the bitterness I have felt since ! I came home burning with eagerness, homesickness, to be in my old place again near you and her—and the place was filled by another ! If I have seemed rude and sullen, *that* is the reason. If I had set less store upon your love, and upon her—her—liking for me, then doubtless I should have borne the displacement with better grace. But it put me on the rack. Believe me, if I have behaved to your displeasure, and hers, it has been from very excess of tenderness trampled underfoot."

At least the misunderstanding had been cleared up, and for a time, at all events, the heart of my life-long friend had warmed again to me as of old. He put his hand paternally upon my knee, and patted it softly.

" My poor boy," he said, with a sympathetic half-smile, and in his old-time gravely gentle voice : " even in your tribulation you must be Dutch ! Why not have said this to me—or what then occurred to you of it—at the outset, the first day after you came? Why, then it could all have been put right in a twinkling. But no! in your secretive Dutch fashion you must needs go aloof, and worry your heart sore by all sorts of suspicions and jealousies and fears that you have been supplanted—until, see for yourself what a melancholy pass you have brought us all to! Suppose by chance, while these sullen devils were driving you to despair, you had done injury to Philip—perhaps even killed him! Think what your feelings, and ours, would be now. And all might have been cleared up, set right, by a word at the beginning."

I looked hard into the fire, and clinched my teeth.

"Would a word have given me Daisy?" I asked from between them.

He withdrew his hand from my knee, and pushed one of the logs petulantly with his foot. "What do you mean?" he demanded.

"I mean that for five years I have desired—for the past six months have, waking or sleeping, thought of nothing else but this desire of my heart —to have Daisy for my wife."

As he did not speak, I went on with an impassioned volubility altogether strange to my custom, recalling to him the tender intimacy in which she and I had grown up from babyhood; the early tacit understanding that we were to inherit the Cedars and all its belongings, and his own not infrequent allusions in those days to the vision of our sharing it, and all else in life, together. Then I pictured to him the brotherly fondness of my later years, blossoming suddenly, luxuriantly, into the fervor of a lover's devotion while I was far away in the wilds, with no gracious, civilizing presence (save always Mr. Cross) near me except the dear image of her which I carried in my heart of hearts. I told him, too, of the delicious excitement with which, day by day, I drew nearer to the home that held her, trembling now with nervousness at my slow progress, now with timidity lest, grasping this vast happiness too swiftly, I should crush it from very ecstasy of possession. I made clear to him, moreover, that I had come without ever dreaming of the possibility of a rival—as innocently, serenely confident of right, as would be a little child approaching to kiss its mother.

"Fancy this child struck violently in the face by this mother, from whom it had never before received so much as a frown," I concluded; "then you will understand something of the blow which has sent me reeling."

His answering words, when finally he spoke, were sympathetic and friendly enough, but not very much to the point. This was, doubtless, due to no fault of his; consolation at such times is not within the power of the very wisest to bestow.

He pointed out to me that these were a class of disappointments exceedingly common to the lot of young men; it was the way of the world. In the process of pairing off a generation, probably ninety-nine out of every hundred couples would secretly have preferred some other distribution; yet they made the best of it, and the world wagged on just the same as before. With all these and many other jarring commonplaces he essayed to soothe me—to the inevitable increase of my bitter discontent. He added, I remember, a personal parallel :

" I have never spoken of it to you, or to any other, but I too had my grievous disappointment. I was in love with the mother of this young Philip Cross. I worshipped her reverently from afar ; I had no other thought or aim in life but to win her favor, to gain a position worthy of her ; I would have crossed the Channel, and marched into St. James's, and hacked off the Hanoverian's heavy head with my father's broadsword, I verily believe, to have had one smile from her lips. Yet I had to pocket this all, and stand smilingly by and see her wedded to my tent-mate, Tony Cross. I thought the world had come to an end—but it hadn't. Women are kittle cattle, my boy. They must have their head, or their blood turns sour. Come ! where is the gen-uineness of your affection for our girl, if you would deny her the gallant of her choice ? "

" If I believed," I blurted out, " that it *was* her own free choice ! "

" Whose else, then, pray ? "

" If I felt that she truly, deliberately preferred him—that she had not been decoyed and misled by that Lady Ber——"

" Fie upon such talk ! " said the old gentleman, with a shade of returning testiness in his tone. " Do you comprehend our Daisy so slightly, after all these years ? Is she a girl not to know her own mind ? Tut ! she loves the youngster ; she has chosen him.

If you had stopped at home, if you had spoken earlier instead of mooning, Dutch fashion, in your own mind, it might have been different. Who can say? But it may not be altered now. We who are left must still plan to promote her happiness. A hundred bridegrooms could not make her less our Daisy than she was. There must be no more quarrels between you boys, remember! I forbid it, your own judgment will forbid it. He will make a good husband to the girl, and I mistake much if he does not make a great man of himself in the Colony. Perhaps—who knows?—he may bring her a title, or even a coronet, some of these days. The Crown will have need of all its loyal gentlemen here, soon enough, too, as the current runs now, and rewards and honors will flow freely. Philip will lose no chance to turn the stream Cairncross way."

My aunt came in to take away the untouched dishes—Mr. Stewart could never abide negroes in their capacity as domestics—and soon thereafter we went to bed; I, for one, to lie sleepless and disconsolate till twilight came.

The next morning we two again had the table to ourselves, for Daisy sent down word that her head was still aching, and we must not wait the meal for her. It was a silent and constrained affair, this breakfast, and we hurried through it as one speeds a distasteful task.

It was afterward, as we walked forth together into the garden, where the wet earth already steamed under the warm downpour of sunlight, that I told Mr.

Stewart of my resolution to go as soon as possible to Albany, and take up the proffered agency.

He seemed to have prepared himself for this, and offered no strong opposition. We had both, indeed, reached the conclusion that it was the best way out of the embarrassment which hung over us. He still clung, or made a show of clinging, to his regret that I had not been satisfied with my position at the Cedars. But in his heart, I am sure, he was relieved by my perseverance in the project.

Two or three days were consumed in preparations at home and in conferences with Jonathan Cross, either at Johnson Hall or at our place, whither he was twice able to drive. He furnished me with several letters, and with voluminous suggestions and advice. Sir William, too, gave me letters, and much valuable information as to Albany ways and prejudices. I had, among others from him, I remember, a letter of presentation to Governor Tryon, who with his lady had visited the baronet during my absence, but which I never presented, and another to the uncle of the boy-Patroon, which was of more utility.

In the hurry and occupation of making ready for so rapid and momentous a departure, I had not many opportunities of seeing Daisy. During the few times that we were alone together, no allusion was made to the scene of that night, or to my words, or to her betrothal. How much she knew of the incident on the gulf-side, or of my later explanation and confession to Mr. Stewart, I could not guess. She was somewhat reserved in her manner, I fancied, and she seemed to quietly avoid being alone in the room with me. At the final parting, too, she proffered me only her cheek to touch with my lips. Yet I could not honestly say that, deep in her heart, shè was not sorry for me and tender toward me, and grieved to have me go.

It was on the morning of the last day of September, 1772, that I began life alone, for myself, by starting on the journey to Albany. If I carried with me a sad heart, there yet were already visible the dawnings of compensation. At least, I had not quarrelled with the dear twain of the Cedars.

As for Philip Cross, I strove not to think of him at all.

CHAPTER XVIII.

THE life in Albany was to me as if I had become
a citizen of some new world. I had seen the old
burgh once or twice before, fleetingly and with but
a stranger's eyes; now it was my home. As I think
upon it at this distance, it seems as if I grew accustomed to the novel environment almost at the outset. At least, I did not pine overmuch for the
Valley I had left behind.

For one thing, there was plenty of hard work to
keep my mind from moping. I had entirely to create
both my position and my business. This latter was,
in some regards, as broad as the continent ; in others
it was pitifully circumscribed and narrow. It is hard
for us now, with our eager national passion for opening up the wilderness and peopling waste places, to
realize that the great trading companies of Colonial
days had exactly the contrary desire. It was the
chief anxiety of the fur companies to prevent im-
migration—to preserve the forests in as savage a
state as possible. One can see now that it was a
fatal error in England's policy to encourage these
vast conservators of barbarism, instead of wholesome settlement by families—a policy which was
avowedly adopted because it was easier to sell

ñunopolies to a few companies than to collect taxes from scattered communities. I do not know that I thought much upon this then, however. I was too busy in fitting myself to Albany.

Others who saw the city in these primitive Dutch days have found much in it and its inhabitants to revile and scoff at. To my mind it was a most delightful place. Its Yankee critics assail a host of features which were to me sources of great satisfaction—doubtless because they and I were equally Dutch. I loved its narrow-gabled houses, with their yellow pressed brick, and iron girders, and high, hospitable stoops, and projecting water-spouts—which all spoke to me of the dear, brave, good old Holland I had never seen. It is true that these eaves-troughs, which in the Netherlands discharged the rainfall into the canal in front of the houses, here poured their contents upon the middle of the sidewalks, and New England carpers have made much of this. But to me there was always a pretty pathos in this resolution to reproduce, here in the wilderness, the conditions of the dear old home, even if one got drenched for it.

And Albany was then almost as much in the wilderness as Caughnawaga. There were a full score of good oil-lamps set up in the streets; some Scotchmen had established a newspaper the year before, which print was to be had weekly; the city had had its dramatic baptism, too, and people still told of the theatrical band who had come and performed for a month at the hospital, and of the fierce sermon against them which Dominie Freylinghuysen had preached three years before. · Albany now is a great town, having over ten thousand souls within its boundaries; then its population was less than one-third of that number. But the three or four hundred houses of the city were spread over such an area of ground, and were so surrounded by trim gardens and embowered in trees, that the effect was that of a vastly larger place. Upon its borders, one stepped off the grassy street into the wild country-road or wilder forest-trail. The wilderness stretched its dark shadows to our very thresholds. It is thought worthy of note now by travellers that one can hear, from the steps of our new State House, the drumming of partridges in the woods beyond. Then we could hear, in addition, the barking of wolves skulking down from the Helderbergs, and on occasion the scream of a panther.

Yet here there was a feeling of perfect security and peace. The days when men bore their guns to church were now but a memory among the elders. The only Indians we saw were those who came in, under strict espionage, to barter their furs for merchandise and drink—principally drink—and occasional delegations of chiefs who came here to meet the governor or his representatives—these latter journeying up from New York for the purpose. For the rest, a goodly and profitable traffic went sedately and comfortably forward. We sent ships to Europe and the West Indies, and even to the slave-yielding coast of Guinea. In both the whaling and deep-sea fisheries we had our part. As for furs and leather and lumber, no other town in the colonies compared with Albany. We did this business in our own way, to be sure, with-out bustle or boasting, and so were accounted slow by our noisier neighbors to the east and south.

There were numerous holidays in this honest, happy old time, although the firing of guns on New Year's was rather churlishly forbidden by the Assembly the year after my arrival. It gives me no pleasure now, in my old age, to see Pinkster forgotten, and Vrouwen-dagh and Easter pass un-noticed, under the growing sway of the New Eng-land invaders, who know how neither to rest nor to play.

But my chief enjoyment lay, I think, in the people I came to know. Up in the Valley, if exception were made of four or five families already sketched in this tale, there were no associates for me who knew aught of books or polite matters in general. Of late, indeed, I had felt myself almost wholly alone, since my few educated companions or ac-quaintances were on the Tory side of the widening division, and I, much as I was repelled by their politics, could find small intellectual equivalent for them among the Dutch and German Whigs whose cause and political sympathies were mine.

But here in Albany I could hate the English and denounce their rule and rulers in excellent and prof-itable company. I was fortunate enough at the out-set to produce a favorable impression upon Abraham Ten Broeck, the uncle and guardian of the boy-Patroon, and in some respects the foremost citizen of the town. Through him I speedily became ac-

quainted with others not less worthy of friendship
—Colonel Philip Schuyler, whom I had seen before
and spoken with in the Valley once or twice, but
now came upon terms of intimacy with; John Tay-
ler and Jeremiah Van Rensselaer, younger men, and
trusted friends of his; Peter Gansevoort, who was
of my own age, and whom I grew to love like a
brother—and so on, through a long list.

These and their associates were educated and
refined gentlemen, not inferior in any way to the
Johnsons and Butlers I had left behind me, or to
the De Lanceys, Phillipses, Wattses, and other Tory
gentry whom I had seen. If they did not drink as
deep, they read a good deal more, and were masters
of as courteous and distinguished a manner. Heretofore I had suffered not a little from the notion—
enforced upon me by all my surroundings—that gen-
tility and good-breeding went hand in hand with loyalty to everything England did, and that disaffection
was but another name for vulgarity and ignorance.
Despite this notion, I had still chosen disaffection,
but I cannot say that I was altogether pleased with
the ostracism from congenial companionship which
this seemed to involve. Hence the charm of my
discovery in Albany that the best and wisest of its
citizens, the natural leaders of its social, commercial,
and political life, were of my way of thinking.

More than this, I soon came to realize that this question for and against England was a deeper and graver
matter than I had dreamed it to be. Up in our
slow, pastoral, uninformed Valley the division was of
recent growth, and, as I have tried to show, was even

now more an affair of race and social affiliations than
of politics. The trial of Zenger, the Stamp Act
crisis, the Boston Massacre—all the great events
which were so bitterly discussed in the outer Colonial world—had created scarcely a ripple in our isolated chain of frontier settlements. We rustics had
been conscious of disturbances and changes in the
atmosphere, so to speak, but had lacked the skill and
information—perhaps the interest as well—to inter-
pret these signs of impending storm aright. Here
in Albany I suddenly found myself among able and
prudent men who had as distinct ideas of the evils
of English control, and as deep-seated a resolution
to put an end to it, as our common ancestors had
held in Holland toward the detested Spaniards.
Need I say that I drank in all this with enthusiastic
relish, and became the most ardent of Whigs?

Of my business it is not needful to speak at length.
Once established, there was nothing specially laborious or notable about it. The whole current of the
company's traffic to and fro passed under my eye.
There were many separate accounts to keep, and a
small army of agents to govern, to supply, to pay,
and to restrain from fraud—for which they had a considerable talent, and even more inclination. There
were cargoes of provisions and merchandise to receive from our company's vessels at Albany, and prepare for transportation across country to the West;
and there were return-cargoes of peltries and other
products to be shipped hence to England. Of all
this I had charge and oversight, but with no obligation upon me to do more of the labor than was fit,

or to spare expense in securing a proper perform-
ance of the residue by others.

Mr. Jonathan Cross and his lady came down to
Albany shortly after I had entered upon my duties
there, and made a stay of some days. He was as
kind and thoughtful as ever, approving much that I
had done, suggesting alterations and amendments
here and there, but for the most part talking of me
and my prospects. He had little to say about the
people at the Cedars, or about the young master of
Cairncross, which was now approaching completion,
and I had small heart to ask him for more than
he volunteered. Both Mr. Stewart and Daisy had
charged him with affectionate messages for me, and
that was some consolation ; but I was still sore enough
over the collapse of my hopes, and still held enough
wrath in my heart against Philip, to make me wish
to recall neither more often than could be helped.
The truth is, I think that I was already becoming
reconciled to my disappointment and to my change
of life, and was secretly ashamed of myself for it,
and so liked best to keep my thoughts and talk upon
other things.

Lady Berenicia I saw but once, and that was once
too often. It pleased her ladyship to pretend to recall me with difficulty, and, after she had established
my poor identity in her mind, to treat me with great
coolness. I am charitable enough to hope that this
gratified her more than it vexed me, which was not
at all.

The ill-assorted twain finally left Albany, taking
passage on one of the company's ships. Mr. Cross's

last words to me were : " Do as much business, push
trade as sharply, as you can.   There is no telling how
long English charters, or the King's writ for that
matter, will continue to run over here."

So they set sail, and I never saw either of them
again.

It was a source of much satisfaction and gain to
me that my position held me far above the bartering and dickering of the small traders.   It is true
that I went through the form of purchasing a license
to trade in the city, for which I paid four pounds
sterling—a restriction which has always seemed to
me as unintelligent as it was harmful to the interests of the town—but it was purely a form.   We
neither·bought nor sold in Albany.   This made it
the easier for me to meet good people on equal
terms—not that I am silly enough to hold trade in
disrespect, but because the merchants who came in
direct contact with the Indians and trappers suffered
in estimation from the cloud of evil repute which
hung over their business.

I lived quietly, and without ostentation, putting
aside some money each quarter, and adventuring my
savings to considerable profit in the company's business—a matter which Mr. Cross had arranged for me.
I went to many of the best houses of the Whig sort.
In some ways, perhaps, my progress in knowledge
and familiarity with worldly things were purchased
at the expense of an innocence which might better
have been retained.   But that is the manner of all
flesh, and I was no worse, I like to hope, than the
best-behaved of my fellows.   I certainly laughed

more now in a year than I had done in all my life before; in truth, I may be said to have learned to laugh here in Albany, for there were merry wights among my companions. One in particular should be spoken of—a second-cousin of mine, named Teunis Van Hoorn, a young physician who had studied at Leyden, and who made jests which were often worthy to be written down.

So two years went by. I had grown somewhat in flesh, being now decently rounded out and solid. Many of my timid and morose ways had been dropped meantime. I could talk now to ladies and to my elders without feeling tongue-tied at my youthful presumption. I was a man of affairs, twenty-five years of age, with some money of my own, an excellent position, and as good a circle of friends as fortune ever gave to mortal man.

Once each month Mr. Stewart and I exchanged letters. Through this correspondence I was informed, in the winter following my departure, of the marriage of Daisy and Philip Cross.

13

CHAPTER XIX.

WE come to a soft, clear night in the Indian sum-
mer-time of 1774—a night not to be forgotten while
memory remains to me.

There was a grand gathering and ball at the Manor
House of the Patroons, and to it I was invited. Cad-
wallader Colden, the octogenarian lieutenant-governor, and chief representative of the Crown now that
Tryon was away in England, had come up to Albany
in state, upon some business which I now forget, and
he was to be entertained at the Van Rensselaer mansion, and with him the rank, beauty, and worth of
all the country roundabout. I had heard that a considerable number of invitations had been despatched
to the Tory families in my old neighborhood, and
that, despite the great distance, sundry of them had
been accepted. Sir William Johnson had now been
dead some months, and it was fitting that his successor, Sir John, newly master of all the vast estates,
should embrace this opportunity to make his first
appearance as baronet in public. In fact, he had
arrived in town with Lady Johnson, and it was said
that they came in company with others. I could
not help wondering, as I attired myself, with more
than ordinary care, in my best maroon coat and

smallclothes and flowered saffron waistcoat, who it was that accompanied the Johnsons. Was I at last to meet Daisy?

Succeeding generations have discovered many tricks of embellishment and decoration of which we old ones never dreamed. But I doubt if even the most favored of progressive moderns has laid eyes upon any sight more beautiful than that which I recall now, as the events of this evening return to me.

You may still see for yourselves how noble, one might say palatial, was the home which young Stephen Van Rensselaer built for himself, there on the lowlands at the end of Broadway, across the Kissing Bridge. But no power of fancy can restore for *you*—sober-clad, pre-occupied, democratic people that you are—the flashing glories of that spectacle : the broad, fine front of the Manor House, with all its windows blazing in welcome ; the tall trees in front aglow with swinging lanterns and colored lights, hung cunningly in their shadowy branches after some Italian device ; the stately carriages sweeping up the gravelled avenue, and discharging their passengers at the block ; the gay procession up the wide stone steps—rich velvets and costly satins, powdered wigs and alabaster throats, bright eyes, and gems on sword-hilts or at fair breasts—all radiant in the hospitable flood of light streaming from the open door ; the throng of gaping slaves with torches, and smartly dressed servants holding the horses or helping with my lady's train and cloak ; the resplendent body of color, and light, and sparkling beauty, which the eye caught in the spacious hall within, beyond the fig-ures of the widowed hostess and her son, the eight-year-old Patroon, who stood forth to greet their guests. No! the scene belongs to its own dead cen-tury and fading generation. You shall strive in vain to reproduce it, even in fancy.

The full harvest-moon, which hung in the lambent heavens above all, pictures itself to my memory as far fairer and more luminous than is the best of nowaday moons. Alas! my old eyes read no romance in the silvery beams now, but suspect rheumatism instead.

This round, lustrous orb, pendant over the Hud-son, was not plainer to every sight that evening than was to every consciousness the fact that this gath-reing was a sort of ceremonial salute before a duel. The storm was soon to break; we all felt it in the air. There was a subdued, almost stiff, politeness in the tone and manner when Dutchman met English-man, when Whig met Tory, which spoke more elo-quently than words. Beneath the formal courtesy, and careful avoidance of debatable topics, one could see sidelong glances cast, and hear muttered sneers. We bowed low to one another, but with anxious faces, knowing that we stood upon the thin crust over the crater, likely at any moment to crash through it.

It was my fortune to be well known to Madame Van Rensselaer, our hostess. She was a Livingston, and a patriot, and she knew me for one as well. "The Tories are here in great muster," she whispered to me, when I bowed before her; "I doubt not it is the

last time you will ever see them under my roof. The
Colonel has news from Philadelphia to-day. There
is trouble brewing."

I could see Colonel Schuyler standing beside one
of the doors to the left, but to reach him was not
easy. First I must pause to exchange a few words
with Dominie Westerlo, the learned and good pastor
of the Dutch church, of whose intended marriage
with the widow, our hostess, there were even then
rumors. And afterward there was the mayor, Abraham Cuyler, whom we all liked personally, despite
his weak leaning toward the English, and it would
not do to pass him by unheeded.

While I still stood with him, talking of I know
not what, the arrival of the lieutenant-governor was
announced. A buzz of whispering ran round the
hall. In the succeeding silence that dignitary walked
toward us, a space clearing about him as he did so.
The mayor advanced to meet him, and I perforce
followed.

I knew much about this remarkable Mr. Colden.
Almost my first English book had been his account
of the Indian tribes, and in later years I had been
equally instructed by his writings on astronomy and
scientific subjects. Even in my boyhood I had heard
of him as a very old man, and here he was now,
eighty-six years of age, the highest representative in
the Colony of English authority. I could feel none
of the hostility I ought from his office to have felt,
when I presently made my obeisance, and he offered
me his hand.

It was a pleasant face and a kindly eye which

met my look. Despite his great age, he seemed scarcely older in countenance and bearing than had Mr. Stewart when last I saw him. He was simply clad, and I saw from his long, waving, untied hair why he was called "Old Silver Locks." His few words to me were amiable commonplaces, and I passed to make room for others, and found my way now to where Schuyler stood.

" The old fox ! " he said, smilingly nodding toward Colden. " One may not but like him, for all his tricks. If England had had the wit to keep that rude boor of a Tryon at home, and make Colden governor, and listen to him, matters would have gone better. Who is that behind him? Oh, yes, De Lancey."

Oliver de Lancey was chiefly notable on account of his late brother James, who had been chief justice and lieutenant-governor, and the most brilliant, unscrupulous, masterful politician of his time. Oliver was himself a man of much energy and ambition. I observed him curiously, for his mother had been a Van Cortlandt, and I had some of that blood in my veins as well. So far as it had contributed to shape his face, I was not proud of it, for he had a selfish and arrogant mien.

It was more satisfactory to watch my companion, as he told me the names of the Tories who followed in Colden's wake, and commented on their characters. I do not recall them, but I remember every line of Philip Schuyler's face, and every inflection of his voice. He was then not quite forty years of age, and almost of my stature—that is to say, a tall man.

He held himself very erect, giving strangers the impression of a haughty air, which his dark face and eyes, and black lines of hair peeping from under the powder, helped to confirm. But no one could speak in amity with him without finding him to be the most affable and sweet-natured of men. If he had had more of the personal vanity and self-love which his bearing seemed to indicate, it would have served him well, perhaps, when New England jealousy assailed and overbore him. But he was too proud to fight for himself, and too patriotic not to fight for his country, whether the just reward came or was withheld.

Colonel Schuyler had been chosen as one of the five delegates of the Colony to attend the first Continental Congress, now sitting at Philadelphia, but ill-health had compelled him to decline the journey. He had since been to New York, however, where he had learned much of the situation, and now was in receipt of tidings from the Congress itself. By a compromise in the New York Assembly, both parties had been represented in our delegation, the Whigs sending Philip Livingston and Isaac Low, the Tories James Duane and John Jay, and the fifth man, one Alsopp, being a neutral-tinted individual to whom neither side could object. The information which Schuyler had received was to the effect that all five, under the tremendous and enthusiastic pressure they had encountered in Philadelphia, had now resolved to act together in all things for the Colonies and against the Crown.

"That means," said he, "that we shall all adopt

Massachusetts's cause as our own. After Virginia led the way with Patrick Henry's speech, there was no other course possible for even Jay and Duane. I should like to hear that man Henry. He must be wonderful."

The space about Mr. Colden had shifted across the room, so that we were now upon its edge, and Schuyler went to him with outstretched hand. The two men exchanged a glance, and each knew what the other was thinking of.

"Your excellency has heard from Philadelphia," said the Colonel, more as a statement of fact than as an inquiry.

"Sad, sad!" exclaimed the aged politician, in a low tone. "It is a grief instead of a joy to have lived so long, if my life must end amid contention and strife."

"He is really sincere in deploring the trouble," said Schuyler, when he had rejoined me. "He knows in his heart that the Ministry are pig-headedly wrong, and that we are in the right. He would do justice if he could, but he is as powerless as I am so far as influencing London goes, and here he is in the hands of the De Lanceys. To give the devil his due, I believe Sir William Johnson was on our side, too, at heart."

We had talked of this before, and out of deference to my sentiments of liking and gratitude to Sir William, he always tried to say amiable things about the late baronet to me. But they did not come easily, for there was an old-time feud between the two families. The dislike dated back to the beginning of young Johnson's career, when, by taking sides shrewdly in a political struggle between Clinton and De Lancey, he had ousted John Schuyler, Philip's grandfather, from the Indian commissionership and secured it for himself. In later years, since the Colonel had come to manhood, he had been forced into rivalry, almost amounting to antagonism at times, with the baronet, in Colonial and Indian affairs; and even now, after the baronet's death, it was hard for him to acknowledge the existence of all the virtues which my boyish liking had found in Sir William. But still he did try, if only to please me.

As we spoke, Sir John Johnson passed us, in company with several younger men, pushing toward the room to the right, where the punch-bowl was placed.

"At least, *he* is no friend of yours?" said Schuyler, indicating the red-faced young baronet.

"No man less so," I replied, promptly. Two years ago I doubt I should have been so certain of my entire enmity toward Sir John. But in the interim all my accumulating political fervor had unconsciously stretched back to include the Johnstown Tories; I found myself now honestly hating them all alike for their former coolness to me and their present odious attitude toward my people. And it was not difficult, recalling all my boyish dislike for John Johnson and his steadily contemptuous treatment of me, to make him the chief object of my aversion.

We talked of him now, and of his wife, a beautiful,

sweet-faced girl of twenty, who had been Polly Watts
of New York. My companion pointed her out to
me, as one of a circle beyond the fire-place. He had
only soft words and pity for her—as if foreseeing the
anguish and travail soon to be brought upon her by
her husband's misdeeds—but he spoke very slight-
ingly and angrily of Sir John. To Schuyler's mind
there was no good in him.

" I have known him more or less since he was a
boy and followed his father in the Lake George
campaign. The officers then could not abide him,
though some were submissive to him because of his
father's position. So now, fifteen years afterward,
although he has many toadies and flatterers, I doubt
his having any real friends. Through all these score
of years, I have yet to learn of any gracious or manly
thing he has done."

" At least he did gallop from the Fort to the Hall
at news of his father's death, and kill his horse by
the pace," I said.

" Heirs can afford to ride swiftly," replied the
Colonel, in a dry tone. " No: he has neither the
honesty to respect the rights of others, nor the wit
to enforce those which he arrogates to himself.
Look at his management in the Mohawk Valley.
Scarce two months after the old baronet's death—
before he was barely warm in his father's bed—all
the Dutch and Palatines and Cherry Valley Scotch
were up in arms against him and his friends. I call
that the work of a fool. Why, Tryon County ought,
by all the rules, to be the Tories' strongest citadel.
There, of all other places, they should be able to

hold their own. Old Sir William would have contrived matters better, believe me. But this sulky, slave-driving cub must needs force the quarrel from the start. Already they have their committee in the Palatine district, with men like Frey and Yates and Paris on it, and their resolutions are as strong as any we have heard."

Others came up at this, and I moved away, thinking to pay my respects to friends in the rooms on the left. The fine hall was almost overcrowded. One's knee struck a sword, or one's foot touched a satin train, at every step. There were many whom I knew, chiefly Albanians, and my progress was thus rendered slow. At the door I met my kinsman, Dr. Teunis Van Hoorn.

"Ha! well met, Cousin Sobriety!" he cried. "Let us cross the hall, and get near the punch-bowl."

"It is my idea that you have had enough," I answered.

"'Too much is enough,' as the Indian said. He was nearer the truth than you are," replied Teunis, taking my arm.

"No, not now! First let me see who is here."

"Who is here? Everybody—from Hendrik Hudson and Killian the First down. Old Centenarian Colden is telling them about William the Silent, whom he remembers very well."

"I have never heard any one speak of Teunis the Silent."

"Nor ever will! It is not my *métier*, as the French students used to say. Well, then, I will turn back with you ; but the punch will all be gone, mark my words. I saw Johnson and Watts and their party headed for the bowl five-and-twenty minutes ago. We shall get not so much as a lemon-seed. But I sacrifice myself."

We entered the room, and my eyes were drawn, as by the force of a million magnets, to the place where Daisy sat.

For the moment she was unattended. She was very beautifully attired, and jewels glistened from her hair and throat. Her eyes were downcast— looking upon the waxed floor as if in meditation. Even to this sudden, momentary glance, her fair face looked thinner and paler than I remembered it —and. ah, how well did I remember it ! With some muttered word of explanation I broke away from my companion, and went straight to her.

She had not noted my presence or approach, and only looked up when I stood before her.   There was not in her face the look of surprise which I had expected. She smiled in a wan way, and gave me her hand.

" I knew you were here," she said, in a soft voice which I scarcely recognized, so changed, I might say saddened, was it by the introduction of some plaintive, minor element. " Philip told me. I thought that sooner or later I should see you."

" And I have thought of little else but the chance of seeing you," I replied, speaking what was in my heart, with no reflection save that this was our Daisy, come into my life again.

She was silent for a moment, her eyes seeking the

floor and a faint glow coming upon her cheeks. Then she raised them to my face, with something of the old sparkle in their glance.

"Well, then," she said, drawing aside her skirts, "sit here, and see me."

CHAPTER XX.

A FOOLISH AND VEXATIOUS QUARREL IS THRUST UPON ME. ·

I SAT beside Daisy, and we talked. It was at the beginning a highly superficial conversation, as I remember it, during which neither looked at the other, and each made haste to fill up any threatened lapse into silence by words of some sort, it mattered not much what.

She told me a great deal about Mr. Stewart's health, which I learned was far less satisfactory than his letters had given reason to suspect. In reply to questions, I told her of my business and my daily life here in Albany. I did not ask her in return about herself. She seemed eager to forestall any possible inquiry on this point, and hastened to inform me as to my old acquaintances in the Valley.

From her words I first realized how grave the situation there had suddenly become. It was not only that opposition to the Johnsons had been openly formulated, but feuds of characteristic bitterness had sprung up within families, and between old-time friends, in consequence. Colonel Henry Frey, who owned the upper Canajoharie mills, took sides with the Tories, and had fiercely quarrelled with his brother John, who was one of the Whig Committee. There was an equally marked division

in the Herkimer family, where one brother, Hon-
yost Herkimer, and his nephew, outraged the others
by espousing the Tory cause. So instances might
be multiplied. Already on one side there were pro-
jects of forcible resistance, and on the other ugly
threats of using the terrible Indian power, which
hung portentous on the western skirt of the Valley,
to coerce the Whigs.

I gained from this recital, more from her manner
than her words, that her sympathies were with the
people and not with the aristocrats. She went on
to say things which seemed to offer an explanation
of this.

The tone of Valley society, at least so far as it was
a reflection of Johnson Hall, had, she said, deterio-
rated wofully since the old baronet's death. A reign
of extravagance and recklessness both as to money
and temper—of gambling, racing, hard drinking, low
sports, and coarse manners—had set in. The friends
of Sir John were now a class by themselves, having
no relations to speak of with the body of Whig farmers, merchants, inn-keepers, and the like. Rather
it seemed to please the Tory clique to defy the good
opinion of their neighbors, and show by very excess
and license contempt for their judgment. Some of
the young men whom I had known were of late
sadly altered. She spoke particularly of Walter
Butler, whose moodiness had now been inflamed, by
dissipation and by the evil spell which seemed to
hang over everything in the Valley, into a sinister
and sombre rage at the Whigs, difficult to distinguish
sometimes from madness.

In all this I found but one reflection—rising again and again as she spoke—and this was that she was telling me, by inference, the story of her own unhappiness.

Daisy would never have done this consciously—of that I am positive. But it was betrayed in every line of her face, and my anxious ear caught it in every word she uttered as to the doings of the Johnson party. Doubtless she did not realize how naturally and closely 1 would associate her husband with that party.

Underneath all our talk there had been, on both sides, I dare say, a sense of awkward constraint. There were so many things which we must not speak of—things which threatened incessantly to force their way to the surface.

I thought of them all, and wondered how much she knew of the events that preceded my departure —how much she guessed of the heart-breaking grief with which I had seen her go to another. It came back to me now, very vividly, as I touched the satin fold of her gown with my shoe, and said to myself, "This is really she."

The two years had not passed so uncomfortably, it is true; work and pre-occupation and the change of surroundings had brought me back my peace of mind and taken the keen edge from my despair— which was to have been life-long, and had faded in a month. Yet now her simple presence—with the vague added feeling that she was unhappy—sufficed to wipe out the whole episode of Albany, and transport me bodily back to the old Valley days. I felt

again all the anguish at losing her, all the bitter
wrath at the triumph of my rival—emphasized and
intensified now by the implied confession that he
had proved unworthy.

To this gloom there presently succeeded, by some
soft, subtle transition, the consciousness that it was
very sweet to sit thus beside her. The air about
us seemed suddenly filled with some delicately be-
numbing influence. The chattering, smiling, moving throng was here, close upon us, enveloping us in
its folds. Yet we were deliciously isolated. Did she
feel it as I did?

I looked up into her face. She had been silent
for I know not how long, following her thoughts as
I had followed mine. It was almost a shock to me
to find that the talk had died away, and I fancied
that I read a kindred embarrassment in her eyes.
I seized upon the first subject which entered my
head.

"Tulp would be glad to see you," I said, foolishly
enough.

She colored slightly, and opened and shut her fan
in a nervous way. "Poor Tulp!" she said, "I don't
think he ever liked me as he did you. Is he well?"

"He has never been quite the same since—since
he came to Albany. He is a faithful body-servant
now—nothing more."

"Yes," she said, softly, with a sigh; then, after
a pause, "Philip spoke of offering to make good
to you your money loss in Tulp, but I told him he
would better not."

"It *was* better not," I answered.

14

Silence menaced us again. I did not find myself indignant at this insolent idea of the Englishman's. Instead, my mind seemed to distinctly close its doors against the admission of his personality. I was near Daisy, and that was enough ; let there be no thoughts of him whatsoever.

"You do Tulp a wrong," I said. " Poor little fellow! Do you remember—" and so we drifted into the happy, sunlit past, with its childish memories for both of games and forest rambles, and innocent pleasures making every day a little blissful lifetime by itself, and all the years behind our parting one sweet prolonged delight.

Words came freely now ; we looked into each other's faces without constraint, and laughed at the pastimes we recalled. It was so pleasant to be together again, and there was so much of charm for us both in the time which we remembered together.

Sir John Johnson and his party had left the punch —or what remained of it—and came suddenly up to us. Behind the baronet I saw young Watts, young De Lancey, one or two others whom I did not know, and, yes!—it was he—Philip Cross.

He had altered in appearance greatly. The two years had added much flesh to his figure, which was now burly, and seemed to have diminished his stature in consequence. His face, which even I had once regarded as handsome, was hardened now in expression, and bore an unhealthy, reddish hue. For that matter, all these young men were flushed with drink, and had entered rather boisterously, attracting attention as they progressed. This attention was not altogether friendly. Some of the ladies had drawn in their skirts impatiently, as they passed, and beyond them I saw a group of Dutch friends of mine, among them Teunis, who were scowling dark looks at the new-comers.

Sir John recognized me as he approached, and deigned to say, "Ha! Mauverensen—you here?" after a cool fashion, and not offering his hand.

I had risen, not knowing what his greeting would be like. It was only decent now to say: "I was much grieved to hear of your honored father's death last summer."

"Well you might be!" said polite Sir John. "He served you many a good purpose. I saw you talking out yonder with Schuyler, that coward who dared not go to Philadelphia and risk his neck for his treason. I dare say he, too, was convulsed with grief over my father's death!"

"Perhaps you would like to tell Philip Schuyler to his face that he is a coward," I retorted, in rising heat at the unprovoked insolence in his tone. "There is no braver man in the Colony."

"But he didn't go to Philadelphia, all the same. He had a very pretty scruple about subscribing his name to the hangman's list."

"He did not go for a reason which is perfectly well known—his illness forbade the journey."

"Yes," sneered the baronet, his pale eyes shifting away from my glance; "too ill for Philadelphia, but not too ill for New York, where, I am told, he has been most of the time since your—what d'ye call it?—Congress assembled."

I grew angry. "He went there to bury General Bradstreet. That, also, is well known. Information seems to reach the Valley but indifferently, Sir John. Everywhere else people understand and appreciate the imperative nature of the summons which called Colonel Schuyler to New York. The friendship of the two men has been a familiar matter of knowledge this fifteen years. I know not your notions of friendship's duties; but for a gentleman like Schuyler, scarcely a mortal illness itself could serve to keep him from paying the last respect to a friend whose death was such an affliction to him."

Johnson had begun some response, truculent in tone, when an interruption came from a most unexpected source. Philip Cross, who had looked at me closely without betraying any sign of recognition, put his hand now on Sir John's shoulder.

"Bradstreet?" he said. "Did I not know him? Surely he is the man who found his friend's wife so charming that he sent that friend to distant posts —to England, to Quebec, to Oswego, and Detroit— and amused himself here at home during the husband's absence. I am told he even built a mansion for her while the spouse was in London *on business.* So he is dead, eh?"

I had felt the bitter purport of his words, almost before they were out. It was a familiar scandal in the mouths of the Johnson coterie—this foul assertion that Mrs. Schuyler, one of the best and most faithful of helpmates, as witty as she was beautiful, as good as she was diligent, in truth, an ideal wife, had pursued through many years a course of deceit and dishonor, and that her husband, the noblest son of our Colony, had been base enough to profit by it. Of all the cruel and malignant things to which the Tories laid their mean tongues, this was the lowest and most false. I could not refrain from putting my hand on my sword-hilt as I answered:

"Such infamous words as these are an insult to every gentleman, the world over, who has ever presented a friend to his family!"

Doubtless there was apparent in my face, as in the exaggerated formality of my bow to Cross, a plain invitation to fight. If there had not been, then my manner would have wofully belied my intent. It was, in fact, so plain that Daisy, who sat close by my side, and, like some others near at hand, had heard every word that had passed, half-started to her feet and clutched my sleeve, as with an appeal against my passionate purpose.

Her husband had not stirred from his erect and arrogant posture until he saw his wife's frightened action. I could see that he noted this, and that it further angered him. He also laid his hand on his sword now, and frigidly inclined his wigged head toward me.

" I had not the honor of addressing you, sir," he said, in a low voice, very much at variance with the expression in his eyes. " I had no wish to exchange words with you, or with any of your sour-faced tribe. But if you desire a conversation—a lengthy and more private conversation—I am at your disposition. Let me say here, however,"—and he glanced with fierce

meaning at Daisy as he spoke—" I am not a Schuyler; I do not encourage ' friends.' "

Even Sir John saw that this was too much.

" Come, come, Cross !" he said, going to his friend.
" Your tongue runs away with you." Then, in a
murmur, he added : " Damn it, man ! Don't drag
your wife into the thing. Skewer the Dutchman
outside, if you like, and if you are steady enough,
but remember what you are about."

I could hear this muttered exhortation as distinctly as I had heard Cross's outrageous insult. Sir
John's words appealed to me even more than they
did to his companion. I was already ashamed to
have been led into a display of temper and a threat
of quarrelling, here in the company of ladies, and
on such an occasion. We were attracting attention,
moreover, and Teunis and some of his Dutch friends
had drawn nearer, evidently understanding that a
dispute was at hand. The baronet's hint about
Daisy completed my mortification. *I* should have
been the one to think of her, to be restrained by her
presence, and to prevent, at any cost, her name being associated with the quarrel by so much as the
remotest inference.

So I stood irresolute, with my hand still on
my sword, and black rage still tearing at my
heart, but with a mist of self-reproach and inde-
cision before my eyes, in which lights, costumes,
powdered wigs, gay figures about me, all swam
dizzily.

Stephen Watts, a man in manner, though a mere
stripling in years, had approached me from the

other group, a yard off, in a quiet way to avoid observation. He whispered :

"There must be no quarrel *here*, Mr. Mauverensen. And there must be no notice taken of his last words—spoken in heat, and properly due, I dare say, to the punch rather than to the man."

"I feel that as deeply as you can," I replied.

"I am glad," said Watts, still in a sidelong whisper. "If you must fight, let there be some tolerable pretext."

"We have one ready standing," I whispered back. "When we last met I warned him that at our next encounter I should break every bone in his skin. Is not that enough?"

"Capital! Who is your friend?"

By some remarkable intuition my kinsman Teunis was prompted to advance at this. I introduced the two young men to each other, and they sauntered off, past where Sir John was still arguing with Cross, and into the outer hall. I stood watching them till they disappeared, then looking aimlessly at the people in front of me, who seemed to belong to some strange phantasmagoria.

It was Daisy's voice which awakened me from this species of trance. She spoke from behind her fan, purposely avoiding looking up at me.

"You are going to fight—you two!" she murmured.

I could not answer her directly, and felt myself flushing with embarrassment. "He spoke in heat," I said, stumblingly. "Doubtless he will apologize—to you, at least."

"You do not know him. He would have his tongue torn out before he would admit his wrong, or any sorrow for it."

To this I could find no reply. It was on my tongue's end to say that men who had a pride in combining obstinacy with insolence must reap what they sow, but I wisely kept silence.

She went on:

" Promise me, Douw, that you will not fight. It chills my heart, even the thought of it. Let it pass. Go away now—anything but a quarrel! I beseech you!"

" 'Tis more easily said than done," I muttered back to her. " Men cannot slip out of du—out of quarrels as they may out of coats."

" For my sake!" came the whisper, with a pleading quaver in it, from behind the feathers.

" It is all on one side, Daisy," I protested. " I must be ridden over, insulted, scorned, flouted to my face—and pocket it all! That is a nigger's portion, not a gentleman's. You do not know what I have borne already."

" Do I not? Ah, too well! For my sake, Douw, for the sake of our memories of the dear old home, I implore you to avoid an encounter. Will you not —for me?"

" It makes a coward out of me! Every Tory in the two counties will cackle over the story that a Dutchman, a Whig, was affronted here under the Patroon's very roof, and dared not resent it."

" How much do you value their words? Must a thing be true for them to say it? The real man-

hood is shown in the strength of restraint, not the
weakness of yielding to the impulse of the moment.
And you can be strong if you choose, Douw!"

While I still pondered these words Teunis Van
Hoorn returned to me, having finished his consulta-
tion with Watts, whom I now saw whispering to Sir
John and the others who clustered about Cross.

The doctor was in good spirits. He sidled up to
me, uttering aloud some merry commonplace, and
then adding, in a low tone :

" I was a match for him. He insisted that they
were the aggrieved party, and chose swords. I stuck
to it that we occupied that position, and had the
right to choose pistols. You are no Frenchman, to
spit flesh with a wire ; but you *can* shoot, can't you ?
If we stand to our point, they must yield."

I cast a swift glance toward the sweet, pleading
face at my side, and made answer :

" I will not fight ! "

My kinsman looked at me with surprise and vexation.

" No," I went on, " it is not our way here. You
have lived so long abroad that duelling seems a natural and proper thing. But we stay-at-homes no more
recognize the right of these English fops to force
their fighting customs upon us than we rush to tie
our hair in queues because it is their fashion."

I will not pretend that I was much in love with
the line of action thus lamely defended. To the
contrary, it seemed to me then a cowardly and unworthy course ; but I had chosen it, and I could
not retreat.

There was upon the moment offered temptation enough to test my resolution sorely.

Many of the ladies had in the meantime left the room, not failing to let it be seen that they resented the wrangling scene which had been thrust upon them. Mistress Daisy had crossed the floor to where Lady Johnson stood, with others, and this frightened group were now almost our sole observers.

Philip Cross shook himself loose from the restraining circle of friends, and strode toward me, his face glowing darkly with passion, and his hands clinched.

" You run away, do you ? " he said. " I have a mind, then, to thrash you where you stand, you canting poltroon ! Do you hear me ?—here, where you stand ! "

" I hear you," I made answer, striving hard to keep my voice down and my resolution up. " Others hear you, too. There are ladies in the room. If you have any right to be among gentlemen, it is high time for you to show it. You are acting like a blackguard."

" Hear the preaching Dutchman ! " he called out, with a harsh, scornful laugh, to those behind him. " He will teach me manners, from his hiding-place behind the petticoats.—Come out, you skunk-skin pedler, and I'll break that sword of yours over your back ! "

Where this all would have ended I cannot tell. My friends gathered around beside me, and at my back. Cross advanced a step or two nearer to me, his companions with him. I felt, rather than saw, the gestures preceding the drawing of swords. I cast a single glance toward the group of women across the room—who, huddled together, were gazing at us with pale faces and fixed eyes—and I dare say the purport of my glance was that I had borne all I could, and that the results were beyond my control —when suddenly there came an unlooked-for interruption.

The dignified, sober figure of Abraham Ten Broeck appeared in our wrathful circle. Some one had doubtless told him, in the outer hall, of the quarrel, and he had come to interfere. A hush fell over us all at his advent.

" What have we here, gentlemen ? " asked the merchant, looking from one to another of our heated faces with a grave air of authority. " Are you well advised to hold discussions here, in what ought to be a pleasant and social company? "

No ready answer was forthcoming. The quarrel was none of my manufacture, and it was not my business to explain it to him. The Tories were secretly disgusted, I fancy, with the personal aspects of the dispute, and had nothing to say. Only Cross, who unfortunately did not know the new-comer, and perhaps would not have altered his manner if he had known him, said uncivilly :

" The matter concerns us alone, sir. It is no affair of outsiders."

I saw the blood mount to Mr. Ten Broeck's dark cheeks, and the fire flash in his eyes. But the Dutch gentleman kept tight bit on his tongue and temper.

" Perhaps I am not altogether an outsider, young sir," he replied, calmly. " It might be thought that I would have a right to civil answers here."

" Who is he? " asked Cross, contemptuously turning his head toward Sir John.

Mr. Ten Broeck took the reply upon himself. " I am the uncle and guardian of your boy-host," he said, quietly. " In a certain sense I am myself your host —though it may be an honor which I shall not enjoy again."

There was a stateliness and solidity about this rebuke which seemed to impress even my headstrong antagonist. He did not retort upon the instant, and all who listened felt the tension upon their emotions relaxed. Some on the outskirts began talking of other things, and at least one of the principals changed his posture with a sense of relief.

Philip Cross presently went over to where the ladies stood, exchanged a few words with them, and then with his male friends left the room, affecting great composure and indifference. It was departing time ; the outer hall was beginning to display cloaks, hoods, and tippets, and from without could be heard the voices of the negroes, bawling out demands for carriages.

I had only a momentary chance of saying farewell to Daisy. Doubtless I ought to have held aloof from her altogether, but I felt that to be impossible. She gave me her hand, looking still very pale and distrait, and murmured only, " It was brave of you, Douw."

I did not entirely agree with her, so I said in

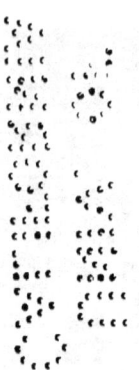

reply: "I hope you will be happy, dear girl; that I truly hope. Give my love and duty to Mr. Stewart, and—and if I may be of service to you, no matter in how exacting or how slight a matter, I pray you command me."

We exchanged good-byes at this, with perfunctory words, and then she left me to join Lady Johnson and to depart with their company.

Later, when I walked homeward with Teunis, sauntering in the moonlight, he imparted something to me which he had heard, in confidence of course, from one of the ladies who had formed the anxious little group that watched our quarrel.

"After Ten Broeck came in, Cross went over to his wife, and brusquely said to her, in the hearing of her friends, that your acquaintance with her was an insult to him, and that he forbade her ever again holding converse with you!"

We walked a considerable time in silence after this, and I will not essay to describe for you my thoughts. We had come into the shadow of the old Dutch church in the square, I know, before Teunis spoke again.

"Be patient yet a little longer, Douw," he said. "The break must come soon now, and then we will drive all these insolent scoundrels before us into the sea!"

I shook hands with him solemnly on this, as we parted.

CHAPTER XXI.

CONTAINING OTHER NEWS BESIDES THAT FROM BUNKER HILL.

To pass from October, 1774, to mid-June of 1775 —from the moonlit streets of sleeping Albany to the broad noonday of open revolt in the Mohawk Valley—is for the reader but the turning of a page with his fingers. To us, in those trying times, these eight months were a painfully long-drawn-out period of anxiety and growing excitement. ·

War was coming surely upon us—and war under strange and sinister conditions. Dull, horse-racing, dog-fighting noblemen were comforting themselves in Parliament, at London, by declaring that the Americans were cowards and would not fight. We boasted little, but we knew ourselves better. There was as yet small talk of independence, of separation. Another year was to elapse before Thomas Paine's *Common Sense* should flash a flood of light as from some new sun upon men's minds, and show us both our real goal and the way to attain it. But about fighting, we had resolved our purpose.

We should have been slaves otherwise.

Turn and turn about, titled imbecile had succeeded distinguished incapable at London in the task of humiliating and bullying us into subjection. Now it was Granville, now Townshend, now Bed-

ford, now North—all tediously alike in their refusal
to understand us, and their slow obstinacy of deter-
mination to rule us in their way, not in ours. To
get justice, or even an intelligent hearing, from these
people, was hopeless. They listened to their own
little clique in the colonies—a coterie of officials,
land-owners, dependents of the Crown, often men of
too worthless a character to be tolerated longer in
England—who lied us impudently and unblushingly
out of court. To please these gentry, the musty
statutes of Tudor despotism were ransacked for a
law by which we were to be haled over the seas for
trial by an English jury for sedition; the port of
Boston was closed to traffic, and troops crowded
into the town to overawe and crush its citizens; a
fleet of war-ships was despatched under Lord Howe
to enforce by broadsides, if needs be, the wicked
and stupid trade and impost laws which we resented;
everywhere the Crown authorities existed to harass
our local government, affront such honest men as
we selected to honor, fetter or destroy our business,
and eat up our substance in wanton taxation.

There had been a chance that the new Parliament,
meeting for the first time in the January of this
1775, would show more sense, and strive to honestly
set matters right. We had appealed from Crown
and Commons to the English people; for a little we
fancied the result might be favorable. But the
hope speedily fell to the ground. The English,
with that strange rushing of blood to the head
which, from age to age, on occasion blinds their
vision, confuses their judgment, and impels them to

rude and brutal courses, decreed in their choler that
we should be flogged at the cart-tail.

To this we said no!

In Albany, on this day in the latter part of June,
when the thread of the story is again resumed, there
were notable, but distressingly vague, tidings. Following upon the blow struck at Concord in April, a
host of armed patriots, roughly organized into something like military form, were investing Boston, and
day by day closing in the cordon around the beleaguered British General Gage. A great battle had
been fought near the town—this only we knew, and
not its result or character. But it meant War, and
the quiet burgh for the nonce buzzed with the hum
of excited comment.

The windows of my upper room were open, and
along with the streaming sunlight came snatches of
echoing words from the street below. Men had
gone across the river, and horses were to be posted
farther on upon the Berkshire turnpike, to catch the
earliest whisper from across the mountains of how
the fight had gone. No one talked of anything else.
Assuredly I too would have been on the street outside, eager to learn and discuss the news from Boston, but that my old friend Major Jelles Fonda had
come down from Caughnawaga, bearing to me almost
as grave intelligence from the Mohawk Valley.

How well I remember him still, the good, square-
set, solid merchant-soldier, with his bold broad face,
resolute mouth, and calm, resourceful, masterful air!
He sat in his woollen shirt-sleeves, for the day was
hot, and slowly unfolded to me his story between

meditative and deliberate whiffs of his pipe. I listened with growing interest, until at last I forgot to keep even one ear upon the sounds from the street, which before had so absorbed me. He had much to tell.

More than a month before, the two contending factions had come to fisticuffs, during a meeting held by the Whigs in and in front of John Veeder's house, at Caughnawaga. They were to raise a liberty pole there, and the crowd must have numbered two hundred or more. While they were deliberating, up rides Guy Johnson, his short, pursy figure waddling in the saddle, his arrogant, high-featured face redder than ever with rage. Back of him rode a whole company of the Hall cabal—Sir John Johnson, Philip Cross, the Butlers, and so on—all resolved upon breaking up the meeting, and supported by a host of servants and dependents, well armed. Many of these were drunk. Colonel Guy pushed his horse into the crowd, and began a violent harangue, imputing the basest motives to those who had summoned them thither. Young Jake Sammons, with the characteristic boldness of his family, stood up to the Indian superintendent and answered him as he deserved, whereat some half-dozen of the Johnson men fell upon Jake, knocked him down, and pummelled him sorely. Some insisted that it was peppery Guy himself who felled the youngster with his loaded riding-whip, but on this point Major Jelles was not clear.

" But what were our people about, to let this happen?" I asked, with some heat.

15

"To tell the truth," he answered, regretfully, "they mostly walked away. Only a few of us held our place. Our men were unarmed, for one thing. Moreover, they are in awe of the power of the Hall. The magistrates, the sheriff, the constables, the assessors—everybody, in fact, who has office in Tryon County—take orders from the Hall. You can't get people to forget that. Besides, if they had resisted, they would have been shot down."

Major Jelles went on to tell me, that, despite this preponderance of armed force on the side of the Johnsons, they were visibly alarmed at the temper of the people and were making preparations to act on the defensive. Sir John had set up cannon on the eminence crowned by the Hall, and his Roman Catholic Highlanders were drilling night and day to perfect themselves as a military body. All sorts of stories came down from Johnstown and up from Guy Park, as to the desperate intentions of the aristocrats and their retainers. Peculiarly conspicuous in the bandying of these threats were Philip Cross and Walter Butler, who had eagerly identified themselves with the most violent party of the Tories. To them, indeed, was directly traceable the terrible rumor, that, if the Valley tribes proved to have been too much spoiled by the missionaries, the wilder Indians were to be called down from the headwaters of the Three Rivers, and from the Lake plains beyond, to coerce the settlements in their well-known fashion, if rebellion was persisted in.

"But they would never dare do that!" I cried, rising to my feet.

" Why not?" asked Jelles, imperturbably sucking at his pipe. "After all, that is their chief strength. Make no mistake! They are at work with the red-skins, poisoning them against us. Guy Johnson is savage at the mealy-mouthed way in which they talked at his last council, at Guy Park, and he has already procured orders from London to remove Dominie Kirkland, the missionary who has kept the Oneidas heretofore friendly to us. That means— You can see as well as the rest of us what it means."

" It means war in the Valley—fighting for your lives."

" Well, let it! My customers owe me three thou-sand pounds and more. I will give every penny of that, and as much besides, and fight with my gun from the windows of my house, sooner than tolerate this Johnson nonsense any longer. And my old father and my brothers say it with me. My brother Adam, he thinks of nothing but war these days ; he can hardly attend to his work, his head is so full of storing powder, and collecting cherry and red maple for gun-stocks, and making bullets. That reminds me—Guy Johnson took all the lead weights out of the windows at Guy Park, and hid them, to keep them from our bullet-moulds, before he ran away."

" Before he ran away? Who ran away?"

"Why, Guy, of course," was the calm reply.

I stared at the man in open-mouthed astonish-ment. "You never mentioned this!" I managed to say at last.

" I hadn't got to it yet," the Dutchman answered,

filling his pipe slowly. "You young people hurry
one so."

By degrees I obtained the whole story from him
—the story which he had purposely come down, I
believe, to tell me. As he progressed, my fancy ran
before him, and pictured the conclave of desperate
plotters in the great Hall on the hill which I knew
so well.

I needed not his assurances to believe that Molly
Brant, who had come down from the upper Mohawk
Castle to attend this consultation, led and spurred on
all the rest into malevolent resolves.

I could conceive her, tall, swart, severely beautiful still, seated at the table where in Sir William's
time she had been mistress, and now was but a
visitor, yet now as then every inch a queen. I
could see her watching with silent intentness—first
the wigged and powdered gentlemen, Sir John, Colonel Guy, the Butlers, Cross, and Claus, and then
her own brother Joseph, tall like herself, and darkly
handsome, but, unlike her, engrafting upon his full
wolf-totem Mohawk blood the restraints of tongue
and of thought learned in the schools of white youth.
No one of the males, Caucasian or aboriginal, spoke
out clearly what was in their minds. Each in turn
befogged his suggestions by deference to what the
world—which to them meant London—would think
of their acts. No one, not even Joseph Brant, uttered
bluntly the one idea which lay covert in their hearts
—to wit: that the recalcitrant Valley should be
swept as with a besom of fire and steel in the hands
of the savage horde at their command. This, when

it came her time, the Indian woman said for them frankly, and with scornful words on their own faint stomachs for bloodshed. I could fancy her darkling glances around the board, and their regards shrinking away from her, as she called them cowards for hesitating to use in his interest the powers with which the king had intrusted them.

It was not hard, either, to imagine young Walter Butler and Philip Cross rising with enthusiasm to approve her words, or how these, speaking hot and fast upon the echo of Mistress Molly's contemptuous rebuke, should have swept away the last restraining fears of the others, and committed all to the use of the Indians.

So that day, just a week since, it had been settled that Colonel Guy and the two Butlers, father and son, should go west, ostensibly to hold a council near Fort Schuyler, but really to organize the tribes against their neighbors; and promptly thereafter, with a body of retainers, they had departed. Guy had taken his wife, because, as a daughter of the great Sir William, she would be of use in the work; but Mrs. John Butler had gone to the Hall—a refuge which she later was to exchange for the lower Indian Castle.

The two houses thus deserted—Guy Park and the Butlers' home on Switzer's Hill—had been in a single night almost despoiled by their owners of their contents; some of which, the least bulky, had been taken with them in their flight, the residue given into safe-keeping in the vicinity, or hidden.

" My brother Adam went to look for the lead in the windows," honest Jelles Fonda concluded, "but it was all gone. So their thoughts were on bullets as well as his. He has his eye now on the church roof at home."

Here was news indeed ! There could be no pretence that the clandestine flight of these men was from fear for their personal safety. To the contrary, Colonel Guy, as Indian superintendent, had fully five hundred fighting men, Indian and otherwise, about his fortified residence. They had clearly gone to enlist further aid, to bring down fresh forces to assist Sir John, Sheriff White, and their Tory minions to hold Tryon County in terror, and, if need be, to flood it with our blood.

We sat silent for a time, as befitted men confronting so grave a situation. At last I said :

"Can I do anything? You all must know up there that I am with you, heart and soul."

Major Jelles looked meditatively at me, through his fog of smoke.

"Yes, we never doubted that. But we are not agreed how you can best serve us. You are our best-schooled young man ; you know how to write well, and to speak English like an Englishman. Some think you can be of most use here, standing between us and the Albany committee ; others say that things would go better if we had you among us. Matters are very bad. John Johnson is stopping travellers on the highways and searching them ; we are trying to watch the river as closely as he does the roads, but he has the courts and the sheriff, and that makes it hard for us. I don't know what to advise you. What do you think?"

While we were still debating the question thus raised by Major Fonda—although I have written it in an English which the worthy soul never attained —my cousin Teunis Van Hoorn burst into the room with tidings from Boston which had just arrived by courier. Almost before he could speak, the sound of cheering in the streets told me the burden of his story. It was the tale of Bunker Hill which he shouted out to us—that story still so splendid in our ears, but then, with all its freshness of vigor and meaning upon us, nothing less than soul-thrilling!

An hour later Major Jelles rose, put on his coat, and said he must be off.

He would sleep that night at Mabie's, so as to have all the Tryon County part of his ride by daylight next day, when the roads would be safer.

It was only when we were shaking hands with him at the door that I found how the secretive Dutchman had kept his greatest, to me most vital, tidings for the last.

"Oh, yes!" he said, as he stood in the doorway; "perhaps I did not mention it. Young Cross has left his home and gone to join Guy Johnson and the Butlers. They say he had angry words with his wife—your Daisy—before he deserted her. She has come back to the Cedars again to live!"

CHAPTER XXII.

THE MASTER AND MISTRESS OF CAIRNCROSS.

THERE is the less need to apologize for now essaying to portray sundry scenes of which I was not an actual witness, in that the reader must by this time be heartily disposed to welcome an escape from my wearisome *ego*, at any expense whatsoever of historical accuracy. Nor is it essential to set forth in this place the means by which I later came to be familiar with the events now to be described —means which will be apparent enough as the tale unfolds.

Dusk is gathering in the great room to the right and rear of the wide hall at Cairncross, and a black servant has just brought in candles, to be placed on the broad marble mantel, and on the oaken table in the centre of the room. The soft light mellows the shadows creeping over the white and gold panelling of the walls, and twinkles faintly in reflection back from the gilt threads in the heavy curtains; but it cannot dispel the gloom which, like an atmosphere, pervades the chamber. Although it is June, and warm of mid-days, a fire burns on the hearth, slowly and spiritlessly, as if the task of imparting cheerfulness to the room were beyond its strength.

Close by the fireplace, holding over it, in fact, his

thin, wrinkled hands, sits an old man. At first glance, one would need to be told that it was Mr. Stewart, so heavily has Time laid his weight upon him in these last four years. There are few enough external suggestions now of the erect, soldierly gentleman, swift of perception, authoritative of tone, the prince of courtiers in bearing, whom we used to know. The white hair is still politely queued, and the close-shaven cheeks glisten with the neat polish of the razor's edge; but, alas! it is scarcely the same face. The luminous glow of the clear blue eyes has faded; the corners of the mouth, eloquently resolute no longer, depend in weakness. As he turns now to speak to his companion, there is a moment's relief: the voice is still calm and full, with perhaps just a thought of change toward the querulous in tone.

"I heard something like the sound of hoofs," he says; "doubtless it is Philip."

"Perhaps, father; but he is wont to be late, nowadays."

Here the change *is* in the voice, if little else be altered. It is Daisy who speaks, standing by his chair, with one hand upon his shoulder, the other hanging listlessly at her side. Like him she looks at the smouldering fire, preferring the silence of her own thoughts to empty efforts at talk. The formal, unsympathetic walls and hangings seem to take up the sad sound of her murmured words and return it to her, as if to emphasize her loneliness.

"The rooms are so large—so cold," she says again, after a long pause, in comment upon a little shiver which shakes the old man's bent shoulders. "If we heaped the fireplace to the top, it could not make them seem homelike."

The last words sink with a sigh into the silence of the great room, and no more are spoken. Both feel, perhaps, that if more were spoken there must be tears as well. Only the poor girl presses her hand upon his arm with a mute caress, and draws closer to his side. There is nothing of novelty to them in this tacitly shared sense of gloom. This Thursday is as Monday was, as any day last year was, as seemingly all days to come will be.

The misery of this marriage has never been discussed between these two. The girl is too fond to impute blame, the old gentleman too proud to accept it; in both minds there is the silent consciousness that into this calamity they walked with eyes open, and must needs bear the results without repining. And more, though there is true sympathy between the two up to a certain point, even Daisy and Mr. Stewart have drifted apart beyond it. Both view Philip within the house with the same eyes; the Philip of the outer world—the little Valley-world of hot passions, strong ambitions, fierce intolerances, growing strife and rancor—they see differently. And this was the saddest thing of all.

Philip Cross entered abruptly, his spurs clanking with a sharp ring at his boot-heels, and nodded with little enough graciousness of manner to the two before the fire.

"I have not ordered supper to be laid," said

Daisy; "your coming was so uncertain. Shall I ring for it now?"

"I have eaten at the Hall," said the young man, unlocking an escritoire at the farther end of the room as he spoke, and taking from it some papers. He presently advanced toward the fire, holding these in his hand. He walked steadily enough, but there was the evil flush upon his temples and neck —a deep suffusion of color, against which his flaxen, powdered hair showed almost white—which both knew too well.

"Who is at the Hall?" asked Mr. Stewart.

"There were good men there to-day—and a woman, too, who topped them all in spirit and worth. We call the Indians an inferior race, but, by God! they at least have not lost the trick of breeding women who do not whine—who would rather show us blood than tears!"

Thus young Mr. Cross spoke, with a sulky inference in his tone, as he held up his papers to the candle, and scanned the writings by its light.

"Ah," Mr. Stewart made answer, dissembling what pique he might have felt, and putting real interest into his words. "Is Molly Brant, then, come down from the Castle? What does she at the Hall? I thought Lady Johnson would have none of her."

"Yes, she is at the Hall, or was when I left. She was sorely needed, too, to put something like resolution into the chicken-hearts there. Things will move now—nay, are moving! As for Lady Johnson, she is too dutiful and wise a woman to have any wishes that are not her husband's. I would to God there were others half so obedient and loyal as Polly Watts!"

Again there was the obvious double meaning in his sullen tone. A swift glance flashed back and forth between Mr. Stewart and the pale-faced young wife, and again Mr. Stewart avoided the subject at which Cross hinted. Instead he turned his chair toward the young man, and said:

"Things are moving, you say. What is new?"

"Why, this is new," answered Cross, lowering the papers for the moment, and looking down upon his questioner: "blood runs now at last instead of milk in the veins of the king's men. We will know where we stand. We will master and punish disloyalty; we will brook not another syllable of rebellion!"

"Yes, it has been let to run overlong," said Mr. Stewart. "Often enough, since Sir William died, have I wished that I were a score of years younger. Perhaps I might have served in unravelling this unhappy tangle of misunderstandings. The new fingers that are picking at the knot are honest enough, but they have small cunning."

"That as you will; but there is to be no more fumbling at the knot. We will cut it now at a blow —cut it clean and sharp with the tomahawk!"

An almost splendid animation glowed in the young man's eyes as he spoke, and for the nonce lit up the dogged hardness of his face. So might the stolid purple visage of some ancestral Cross have become illumined, over his heavy beef and tubs of ale, at the stray thought of spearing a boar at bay,

or roasting ducats out of a Jew. The thick rank
blood of centuries of gluttonous, hunting, maraud-
ing progenitors, men whose sum of delights lay in
working the violent death of some creature—wild
beast or human, it mattered little which—warmed
in the veins of the young man now, at the prospect
of slaughter. The varnish of civilization melted
from his surface; one saw in him only the historic
fierce, blood-letting islander, true son of the men
who for thirty years murdered one another by tens
of thousands all over England, nominally for a York
or a Lancaster, but truly from the utter wantonness
of the butcher's instinct, the while we Dutch were
discovering oil-painting and perfecting the noble
craft of printing with types.

"Yes!" he repeated, with a stormy smile. "We
will cut the knot with the tomahawk!"

The quicker wit of the young woman first scented
his meaning.

"You are going to bring down the savages?" she
asked, with dilated eyes, and in her emotion forgetting that it was not her recent habit to interrogate
her husband.

He vouchsafed her no answer, but made a pretence of again being engrossed with his papers.

After a moment or two of silence the old gentleman rose to his feet, walked over to Philip, and put
his hand on the young man's arm.

"I will take my leave now," he said, in a low
voice; "Eli is here waiting for me, and the evenings
grow cold."

"Nay, do not hasten your going, Mr. Stewart,"

said Philip, with a perfunctory return to the usages of politeness. "You are ever welcome here."

"Yes, I know," replied Mr. Stewart, not in a tone of complete conviction. "But old bones are best couched at home."

There was another pause, the old gentleman still resting his hand affectionately, almost deprecatingly, on the other's sleeve.

"I would speak plainly to you before I go, Philip," he said, at last. "I pray you, listen to the honest advice of an old man, who speaks to you, God knows, from the very fulness of his heart. I mislike this adventure at which you hint. It has an evil source of inspiration. It is a gloomy day for us here, and for the Colony, and for the cause of order, when the counsels of common-sense and civilization are tossed aside, and the words of that red she-devil regarded instead. No good will come out of it—no good, believe me. Be warned in time! I doubt you were born when I first came into this Valley. I have known it for decades, almost, where you have known it for years. I have watched its settlements grow, its fields push steadily, season after season, upon the heels of the forest. I understand its people as you cannot possibly do. Much there is that I do not like. Many things I would change, as you would change them. But those err cruelly, criminally, who would work this change by the use of the savages."

"All other means have been tried, short of crawling on our bellies to these Dutch hinds!" muttered the young man.

"You do not know what the coming of the tribes

in hostility means," continued Mr. Stewart, with increasing solemnity of earnestness. "You were too young to realize what little you saw, as a child here in the Valley, of Bellêtre's raid. Sir John and Guy know scarcely more of it than you. Twenty years, almost, have passed since the Valley last heard the Mohawk yell rise through the night-air above the rifle's crack, and woke in terror to see the sky red with the blaze of roof-trees. All over the world men shudder still at hearing of the things done then. Will you be a willing party to bringing these horrors again upon us? Think what it is that you would do!"

"It is not I alone," Philip replied, in sullen defence. "I but cast my lot on the king's side, as you yourself do. Only you are not called upon to fit your action to your words; I am! Besides," he went on, sulkily, "I have already chosen not to go with Guy and the Butlers. Doubtless they deem me a coward for my resolution. That ought to please you."

"Go with them? Where are they going?"

"Up the river; perhaps only to the Upper Castle; perhaps to Oswego; perhaps to Montreal—at all events, to get the tribes well in hand, and hold them ready to strike. That is," he added, as an afterthought, "if it really becomes necessary to strike at all. It may not come to that, you know."

"And this flight is actually resolved upon?"

"If you call it a flight, yes! The Indian superintendent goes to see the Indians; some friends go with him—that is all. What more natural? They have in truth started by this time, well on their way. I was sorely pressed to accompany them ; for hours Walter Butler urged all the pleas at his command to shake my will."

"Of course you could not go; that would have been madness!" said Mr. Stewart, testily. Both men looked toward the young wife, with instinctive concert of thought.

She sat by the fire, with her fair head bent forward in meditation ; if she had heard the conversation, or knew now that they were thinking of her, she signified it not by glance or gesture.

"No, of course," said Philip, with a faltering disclaimer. "Yet they urged me strenuously. Even now they are to wait two days at Thompson's on Cosby's Manor, for my final word—they choosing still to regard my coming as possible."

"Fools!" broke in the old gentleman. "It is not enough to force war upon their neighbors, but they must strive to destroy what little happiness I have remaining to me!" His tone softened to one of sadness, and again he glanced toward Daisy. "Alas, Philip," he said, mournfully, "that it *should* be so little!"

The young man shifted his attitude impatiently, and began scanning his papers once more. A moment later he remarked, from behind the manuscripts :

"It is not we who begin this trouble. These committees of the rebel scoundrels have been active for months, all about us. Lying accounts to our prejudice are ceaselessly sent down to the commit-

tees at Schenectady and Albany, and from these
towns comes back constant encouragement to dis-
order and bad blood. If they will have it so, are we
to blame? You yourself spoke often to me, formerly, of the dangerous opinions held by the Dutch
here, and the Palatines up the river, and, worst of
all, by those canting Scotch-Irish Presbyterians over
Cherry Valley way. Yet now that we must meet
this thing, you draw back, and would tie my hands
as well. But doubtless you are unaware of the
lengths to which the Albany conspirators are pushing their schemes."

"I am not without information," replied Mr.
Stewart, perhaps in his desire to repudiate the im-
putation of ignorance revealing things which upon
reflection he would have reserved. "I have letters
from my boy Douw regularly, and of late he has told
me much of the doings of the Albany committee."

Young Cross put his papers down from before his
face with a swift gesture. Whether he had laid a
trap for Mr. Stewart or not, is doubtful; we who
knew him best have ever differed on that point.
But it is certain that his manner and tone had
changed utterly in the instant before he spoke.

"Yes!" he said, with a hard, sharp inflection; "it
is known that you hold regular correspondence with
this peculiarly offensive young sneak and spy. Let
me tell you frankly, Mr. Stewart, that this thing is
not liked overmuch. These are times when men,
even old men, must choose their side and stand
to it. People who talk in one camp and write
to the other subject themselves to uncomfortable

16

suspicions. Men are beginning to recall that you were in arms against His Majesty King George the Second, and to hint that perhaps you are not precisely overflowing with loyalty to his grandson, though you give him lip-service readily enough. As you were pleased to say to me a few minutes ago, ' Be warned in time,' Mr. Stewart ! "

The old gentleman had started back as if struck by a whip at the first haughty word's inflection. Gradually, as the impertinent sentences followed, he had drawn up his bent, slender frame until he stood now erect, his hooked nose in the air, and his blue eyes flashing. Only the shrunken lips quivered with the weakness of years, as he looked tall young Mr. Cross full in the face.

" Death of my life ! " he stammered. " *You* are saying these things to *me !* It is Tony Cross's son whom I listen to—and *her* son—the young man to whom I gave my soul's treasure ! "

Then he stopped, and while his eyes still glowed fiery wrath the trembling lips became piteous in their inability to form words. For a full minute the fine old soldier stood, squared and quivering with indignation. What he would have said, had he spoken, we can only guess. But no utterance came. He half-raised his hand to his head with a startled movement; then, seeming to recover himself, walked over to where Daisy sat, ceremoniously stooped to kiss her forehead, and, with a painfully obvious effort to keep his gait from tottering, moved proudly out of the room.

When Philip, who had dumbly watched the effect

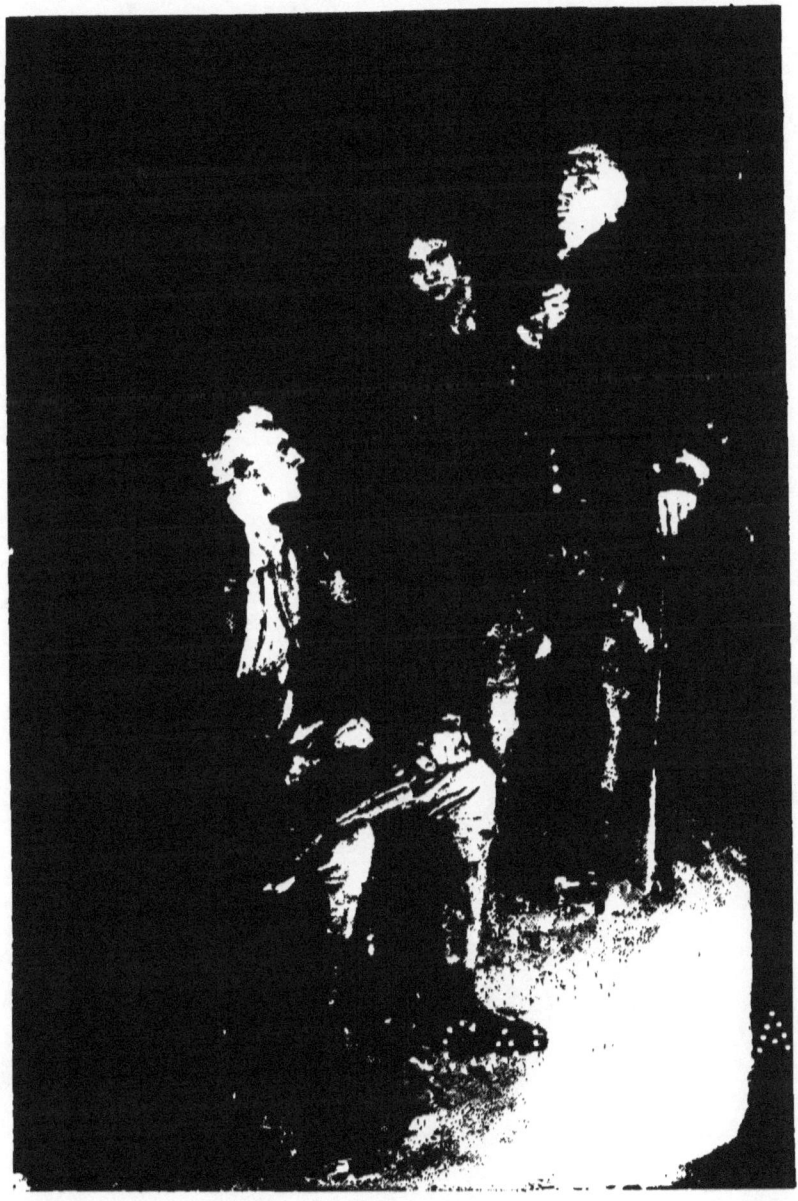

While his eyes still glowed fiery wrath, the trembling lips became piteous in their inability to form words.

of his words, turned about, he found himself confronted with a woman whom he scarcely knew to be his wife, so deadly pale and drawn was her face, so novel and startling were the glance and gesture with which she reared herself before him.

CHAPTER XXIII.

"You are, then, not even a gentleman !"

The ungracious words came almost unbidden from
Daisy's pallid lips, as husband and wife for the first
time faced each other in anger. She could not help
it. Passive, patient, long-suffering she had been the
while the mortifications and slights were for herself.
But it was beyond the strength of her control to sit
quietly by when Mr. Stewart was also affronted.

Through all the years of her life she had been
either so happy in her first home, or so silently loyal
to duty in her second, that no one had discovered
in Daisy the existence of a strong spirit. Sweet-
tempered, acquiescent, gentle, every one had known
her alike in joy or under the burden of disappointment and disillusion. "As docile as Daisy"
might have been a proverb in the neighborhood, so
general was this view of her nature. Least of all
did the selfish, surly-tempered, wilful young Englishman who was her husband, and who had ridden
rough-shod over her tender thoughts and dreams
these two years, suspect that she had in her the
capabilities of flaming, wrathful resistance.

He stared at her now, at first in utter bewilderment, then with the instinct of combat in his scowl.

" Be careful what you say ! " he answered, sharply.
" I am in no mood for folly."

" Nay, mood or no mood, I shall speak. Too long
have I held my peace. You should be ashamed in
every recess of your heart for what you have said
and done this day! " She spoke with a vibrant fer-
vency of feeling which for the moment pierced even
his thick skin.

" He was over-hasty," he muttered, in half-apol-
ogy. " What I said was for his interest. I intended
no offence."

"Will you follow him, and say so ? "

"Certainly not! If he chooses to take umbrage,
let him. It's no affair of mine."

" Then *I* will go—and not return until he comes
with me, invited by you ! "

The woman's figure, scornfully erect, trembled
with the excitement of the position she had on the
moment assumed ; but her beautiful face, refined
and spiritualized of late by the imprint of woman-
hood's saddening wisdom, was coldly resolute. By
contrast with the burly form and red, rough countenance of the man she confronted, she seemed made
of another clay.

"Yes, I will go ! " she went on, hurriedly. " This
last is too much ! It is not fit that I should keep
up the pretence longer."

The husband burst out with a rude and somewhat
hollow laugh. " Pretence, you say ! Nay, madam,
you miscall it. A pretence is a thing that deceives,
and I have never been deceived. Do not flatter
yourself. I have read you like a page of large print,

these twenty months. Like the old gaffer whose feathers I ruffled here a while ago with a few words of truth, your tongue has been here, but your thoughts have been with the Dutchman in Albany!"

The poor girl flushed and recoiled under the coarse insult, and the words did not come readily with which to repel it.

"I know not how to answer insolence of this kind," she said, at last. "I have been badly reared for such purposes."

She felt her calmness deserting her as she spoke; her eyes began to burn with the starting tears. This crisis in her life had sprung into being with such terrible swiftness, and yawned before her now, as reflection came, with such blackness of unknown consequences, that her woman's strength quaked and wavered. The tears found their way to her cheeks now, and through them she saw, not the heavy, half-drunken young husband, but the handsome, slender, soft-voiced younger lover of three years ago. And then the softness came to her voice too.

"How *can* you be so cruel and coarse, Philip, so unworthy of your real self?" She spoke despairingly, not able wholly to believe that the old self was the true self, yet clinging, woman-like, to the hope that she was mistaken.

"Ha! So my lady has thought better of going, has she?"

"Why should you find pleasure in seeking to make this home impossible for me, Philip?" she asked, in grave gentleness of appeal.

" I thought you would change your tune," he
sneered back at her, throwing himself into a chair.
" I have a bit of counsel for you. Do not venture
upon that tone with me again. It serves with Dutch
husbands, no doubt ; but I am not Dutch, and I
don't like it."

She stood for what seemed to be a long time, unoccupied and irresolute, in the centre of the room.
It was almost impossible for her to think clearly or
to see what she ought to do. She had spoken in
haste about leaving the house, and felt now that
that would be an unwise and wrongful step to take.
Yet her husband had deliberately insulted her, and
had coldly interpreted as weak withdrawals her con-
ciliatory words, and it was very hard to let this
state of affairs stand without some attempt at its
improvement. Her pride tugged bitterly against
the notion of addressing him again, yet was it not
right that she should do so ?

The idea occurred to her of ringing for a servant and directing him to draw off his master's
boots. The slave-boy who came in was informed
by a motion of her finger, and, kneeling to the task,
essayed to lift one of the heavy boots from the tiled
hearth. The amiable Mr. Cross allowed the foot to
be raised into the boy's lap. Then he kicked the
lad backward, head over heels, with it, and snapped
out angrily :

" Get away ! When I want you, I'll call ! "

The slave scrambled to his feet and slunk out
of the room. The master sat in silence, moodily
sprawled out before the fire. At last the wife

approached him, and stood at the back of his chair.

"You are no happier than I am, Philip," she said. "Surely there must be some better way to live than this. Can we not find it, and spare ourselves all this misery?"

"What misery?" he growled. "There is none that I know, save the misery of having a wife who hates everything her husband does. The weather-cock on the roof has more sympathy with my purposes and aims than you have. At least once in a while he points my way."

"Wherein have I failed? When have you ever temperately tried to set me aright,ꞌ seeing my errors?"

"There it is—the plausible tongue always. 'When have I done this, or that, or the other?' It is not one thing that has been done, madam, but ten thousand left undone! What did I need—having lands, money, position—to make me the chief gentleman of Tryon County, and this house of mine the foremost mansion west of Albany, once Sir William was dead? Naught but a wife who should share my ambitions, enter into my plans, gladly help to further my ends! I choose for this a wife with a pretty face, a pretty manner, a tidy figure which carries borrowed satins gracefully enough—as I fancy, a wife who will bring sympathy and distinction as well as beauty. Well, I was a fool! This precious wife of mine is a Puritan ghost who gazes gloomily at me when we are alone, and chills my friends to the marrow when they are ill-advised enough to visit me. She looks at the wine I lift to my lips, and it sours in the glass. She looks into my kennels, and it is as if turpentine had been rubbed on the hounds' snouts. This great house of mine, which ought of right to be the gallant centre of Valley life and gayety, stands up here, by God! like a deserted churchyard.) Men avoid it as if a regicide had died here. I might have been Sir Philip before this, and had his Majesty's commission in my pocket, but for this petticoated skeleton which warns off pleasure and promotion. And then she whines, ' What have I done ? ' "

"You are clever enough, Philip, to have been any-thing you wanted to be, if only you had started with more heart and less appetite for pleasure.) It is not your wife, but your wine, that you should blame."

"Ay, there it comes! And even if it were true—as it is not, for I am as temperate as another—it would be you who had driven me to it."

" What folly !"

" Folly, madam ? By Heaven, I will not——"

" Nay, listen to me, Philip, for the once. We may not speak thus frankly again; it would have been better had we freed our minds in this plain fashion long ago. It is not poor me, but something else, that in two years has changed you utterly. To-day you could no more get your mind into the same honest course of thoughts you used to hold than you could your body into your wedding waistcoat. You talk now of ambitions ; for the moment you really think you had ambitions, and because they are only memories, you accuse me. Tell me truly, what were

your ambitions? To do nothing but please yourself
—to ride, hunt, gamble, scatter money, drink till you
could drink no more. Noble aspirations these for
which to win the sympathy of a wife!"

Philip had turned himself around in his chair, and
was looking steadily at her. She found the courage
to stand resolute under the gaze and return it.

"There is one point on which I agree with you,"
he said, slowly: "I am not like ever again to hear
talk of this kind under my roof. But while we are
thus amiably laying our hearts bare to each other,
there is another thing to be said. Everywhere it is
unpleasantly remarked that I am not master in my
own house—that here there are two kinds of politics—that I am loyal and my wife is a rebel."

"Oh, that is unfair! Truly, Philip, I have given no
cause for such speech. Not a word have I spoken,
ever, to warrant this. It would be not only wrong
but presuming to do so, since I am but a woman,
and have no more than a woman's partial knowledge
of these things. If you had ever asked me I would
have told you frankly, that, as against the Johnsons
and Butlers and Whites, my feelings were with the
people of my own flesh and blood; but as to my
having ever spoken——"

"Yes, I know what you would say," he broke in,
with cold, measured words. "I can put it for you
in a breath—I am an English gentleman; you are a
Dutch foundling!"

She looked at him, speechless and mentally staggered. In all her life it had never occurred to her
that this thing could be thought or said. That it

should be flung thus brutally into her face now by her husband—and he the very man who as a boy had saved her life—seemed to her astonished sense so incredible that she could only stare, and say nothing.

While she still stood thus, the young aristocrat rose, jerked the bell-cord fiercely, and strode again to the escritoire, pulling forth papers from its recesses with angry haste.

" Send Rab to me on the instant ! " he called out to the slave who appeared.

The under-sized, evil-faced creature who presently answered this summons was the son of a Scotch dependent of the Johnsons, half tinker, half trapper, and all ruffian, by an Indian wife. Rab, a young-old man, had the cleverness and vices of both strains of blood, and was Philip's most trusted servant, as he was Daisy's especial horror. He came in now, his black eyes sparkling close together like a snake's, and his miscolored hair in uncombed tangle hanging to his brows. He did not so much as glance at his mistress, but went to Philip, with a cool—

" What is it ? "

" There is much to be done to-night, Rab," said the master, assorting papers still as he spoke. " I am leaving Cairncross on a journey. It may be a long one ; it may not."

" It will at least be as long as Thompson's is distant," said the familiar.

" Oh, you know, then," said Philip. " So much the better, when one deals with close tongues. Very

well. I ride to-night. Do you gather the things
I need—clothes, money, trinkets, and what not—to
be taken with me. Have the plate, the china, the
curtains, pictures, peltries, and such like, properly
packed, to be sent over to the Hall with the horses
and dogs in the early morning. I shall ride all
night, and all to-morrow if needs be. When you
have seen the goods safely at the Hall, deliver certain letters which I shall presently write, and return
here. I leave you in charge of the estate; you will
be master—supreme—and will account only to me,
when the king's men come back. I shall take Cæsar
and Sam with me. Have them saddle the roan for
me, and they may take the chestnut pair and lead
Firefly. Look tò the saddle-bags and packs yourself.
Let everything be ready for my start at eleven; the
moon will be up by then."

The creature waited for a moment after Philip
had turned to his papers.

" Will you take my lady's jewels ? " he asked.

" Damnation ! No ! " growled Philip.

"If you do not, they shall be thrown after you !"

It was Daisy who spoke—Daisy, who leaned heavily upon the chair-back to keep erect in the whirling
dream of bewilderment which enveloped her. The
words when they had been uttered seemed from
some other lips than hers. There was no thought
in her mind which they reflected. She was too near
upon swooning to think at all.

Only dimly could she afterward recall having left
the room, and the memory was solely of the wicked
gleam in the serpent eyes of her enemy Rab, and of

the sound of papers being torn by her husband, as she, dazed and fainting, managed to creep away and reach her chamber.

The wakeful June sun had been up for an hour or so, intent upon the self-appointed and gratuitous task of heating still more the sultry, motionless morning air, when consciousness returned to Daisy. All about her the silence was profound. As she rose, the fact that she was already dressed scarcely interested her. She noted that the lace and velvet hangings were gone, and that the apartment had been despoiled of much else besides, and gave this hardly a passing thought.

Mechanically she took from the wardrobe a hooded cloak, put it about her, and left the room. The hallways were strewn with straw and the litter of packing. Doors of half-denuded rooms hung open. In the corridor below two negroes lay asleep, snoring grotesquely, beside some chests at which they had worked. There was no one to speak to her or bar her passage. The door was unbolted. She passed listlessly out, and down the path toward the gulf.

It was more like sleep-walking than waking, conscious progress—this melancholy journey. The dry, parched grass, the leaves depending wilted and sapless, the leaden air, the hot, red globe of dull light hanging before her in the eastern heavens—all seemed a part of the lifeless, hopeless pall which weighed from every point upon her, deadening thought and senses. The difficult descent of the

steep western hill, the passage across the damp
bottom and over the tumbling, shouting waters, the
milder ascent, the cooler, smoother forest walk toward the Cedars beyond—these vaguely reflected
themselves as stages of the crisis through which she
had passed : the heart-aching quarrel, the separation,
the swoon, and now the approaching rest.

Thus at last she stood before her old home, and
opened the familiar gate. The perfume of the
flowers, heavily surcharging the dewless air, seemed
to awaken and impress her. There was less order
in the garden than before, but the plants and shrubs
were of her own setting. A breath of rising zephyr
stirred their blossoms as she regarded them in
passing.

" They nod to me in welcome," her dry lips murmured.

A low, reverberating mutter of distant thunder
came as an echo, and a swifter breeze lifted the
flowers again, and brought a whispered greeting
from the lilac-leaves clustered thick about her.

The door opened at her approach, and she saw
Mr. Stewart standing there on the threshold, awaiting her. It seemed natural enough that he should
be up at this hour, and expecting her. She did not
note the uncommon whiteness of his face, or the
ceaseless twitching of his fallen lips.

" I have come home to you, father," she said,
calmly, wearily.

He gazed at her without seeming to apprehend
her meaning.

" I have no longer any other home," she added.

She saw the pallid face before her turn to wax, shot over with green and brazen tints. The old hands stretched out as if to clutch hers—then fell inert.

Something had dropped shapeless, bulky, at her feet, and she could not see Mr. Stewart. Instead, there was a reeling vision of running slaves, of a form lifted and borne in, and then nothing but a sinking away of self amid the world-shaking roar of thunder and blazing lightning streaks.

CHAPTER XXIV.

OF these sad occurrences it was my fortune not
to be informed for many months. In some senses
this was a beneficent ignorance. Had I known
that, under the dear old roof which so long sheltered me, Mr. Stewart was helplessly stricken with
paralysis, and poor Daisy lay ill unto death with a
brain malady, the knowledge must have gone far
to unfit me for the work which was now given into
my hands. And it was work of great magnitude
and importance.

Close upon the heels of the Bunker Hill intelligence came the news that a Continental army had
been organized ; that Colonel Washington of Virginia had been designated by Congress as its chief,
and had started to assume command at Cambridge ;
and that our own Philip Schuyler was one of the
four officers named at the same time as major-
generals. There was great pleasure in Albany over
the tidings ; the patriot committee began to prepare for earnest action, and our Tory mayor, Abraham Cuyler, sagaciously betook himself off, ascend-
ing the Mohawk in a canoe, and making his way
to Canada.

Among the first wishes expressed by General Schuyler was one that I should assist and accompany him, and this, flattering enough in itself, was made delightful by the facts that my friend Peter Gansevoort was named as another aide, and that my kinsman Dr. Teunis was given a professional place in the general's camp family. We three went with him to the headquarters at Cambridge very shortly after, and thenceforward were too steadily engrossed with our novel duties to give much thought to home affairs.

It was, indeed, a full seven months onward from the June of which I have written that my first information concerning the Cedars, and the dear folk within its walls, came to me in a letter from my mother. This letter found me, of all unlikely places in the world, lying in garrison on the frozen bank of the St. Lawrence—behind us the strange, unnatural silence of the northern waste of snow, before us the black, citadel-crowned, fire-spitting rock of Quebec.

Again there presses upon me the temptation to put into this book the story of what I saw there while we were gathering our strength and resolution for the fatal assault. If I am not altogether proof against its wiles, at least no more shall be told of it than properly belongs here, insomuch as this is the relation of my life's romance.

We had started in September with the expedition against Canada, while it was under the personal command of our general; and when his old sickness came unluckily upon him and forced his return, it was at his request that we still kept on, under his

17

successor, General Richard Montgomery. It was the pleasanter course for us, both because we wanted to see fighting, and because Montgomery, as the son-in-law of Mr. Livingston, was known to us and was our friend. And so with him we saw the long siege of St. John's ended, and Chambly, and then Montreal, Sorel, and Three Rivers, one by one submit, and the *habitants* acclaim us their deliverers as we swept the country clean to the gates of Quebec.

To this place we came in the first week of December, and found bold Arnold and his seven hundred scarecrows awaiting us. These men had been here for a month, yet had scarcely regained their strength from the horrible sufferings they encountered throughout their wilderness march. We were by this time not enamoured of campaigning in any large degree, from our own experience of it. Yet when we saw the men whom Arnold and Morgan had led through the trackless Kennebec forest, and heard them modestly tell the story of that great achievement—of their dreadful sustained battle with cold, exhaustion, famine, with whirling rapids, rivers choked with ice, and dangerous mountain precipices —we felt ashamed at having supposed we knew what soldiering was.

Three weeks we lay waiting. Inside, clever Carleton was straining heaven and earth in his endeavor to strengthen his position ; without, we could only wait. Those of us who were from the Albany and Mohawk country came to learn that some of our old Tory neighbors were within the walls, and the knowledge gave a new zest to our eager watchfulness.

This, it should be said, was more eager than sanguine. It was evident from the outset that, in at least one respect, we had counted without our host. The French-Canadians were at heart on our side, perhaps, but they were not going to openly help us; and we had expected otherwise. Arnold himself, who as an old horse-dealer knew the country, had especially believed in their assistance and sympathy, and we had bills printed in the French language to distribute, calling upon them to rise and join us. That they did not do so was a grievous disappointment from the beginning.

Yet we might have been warned of this. The common people were friendly to us—aided us privily when they could—but they were afraid of their seigneurs and curés. These gentry were our enemies for a good reason—in their eyes we were fighting New England's fight, and intolerant New England had only the year before bitterly protested to Parliament against the favor shown the Papist religion in Quebec. These seigneurs and priests stood together in a common interest. England had been shrewd enough to guarantee them their domains and revenues. Loyalty meant to them the security of their *rentes et dîmes*, and they were not likely to risk these in an adventure with the Papist-hating Yankees. Hence they stood by England, and, what is more, held their people practically aloof from us.

But even then we could have raised Canadian troops, if we had had the wherewithal to feed or

clothe or arm them. But of this Congress had taken
no thought. Our ordnance was ridiculously inade-
quate for a siege; our clothes were ragged and foul,
our guns bad, our powder scanty, and our food
scarce. Yet we were deliberately facing, in this
wretched plight, the most desperate assault of known
warfare.

The weeks went by swiftly enough. Much of the
time I was with the commander at our headquarters
in Holland House, and I grew vastly attached to
the handsome, gracious, devoted young soldier.
Brigadier-General Montgomery had not, perhaps, the
breadth of character that made Schuyler so notable ;
which one of all his contemporaries, save Washington, for that matter, had ? But he was very single-
minded and honorable, and had much charm of
manner. Often, during those weeks, he told me of
his beautiful young wife, waiting for his return at
their new home on the Hudson, and of his hope
soon to be able to abandon the strife and unrest of
war, and settle there in peace. Alas ! it was not to
be so.

And then, again, we would adventure forth at
night, when there was no moon, to note what degree
of vigilance was observed by the beleaguered force.
This was dangerous, for the ingenious defenders
hung out at the ends of poles from the bastions
either lighted lanterns or iron pots filled with blazing balsam, which illuminated the ditch even better
than the moon would have done. Often we were
thus discovered and fired upon, and once the General
had his horse killed under him.

I should say that he was hardly hopeful of the result of the attack already determined upon. But it was the only thing possible to be done, and with all his soul and mind he was resolved to as nearly do it as might be.

The night came, the last night but one of that eventful, momentous year 1775. Men had passed each day for a week between our quarters and Colonel Arnold's at St. Roch, concerting arrangements. There were Frenchmen inside the town from whom we were promised aid. What we did not know was that there were other Frenchmen, in our camp, who advised Carleton of all our plans. The day and evening were spent in silent preparations for the surprise and assault—if so be it the snow-storm came which was agreed upon as the signal. Last words of counsel and instruction were spoken. Suppressed excitement reigned everywhere.

The skies were clear and moonlit in the evening ; now, about midnight, a damp, heavy snowfall began and a fierce wind arose. So much the better for us and our enterprise, we thought.

We left Holland House some hours after midnight, without lights and on foot, and placed ourselves at the head of the three hundred and fifty men whom Colonel Campbell (not the Cherry Valley man, but a vain and cowardly creature from down the Hudson, recently retired from the British army) held in waiting for us. Noiselessly we descended from the heights, passed Wolfe's Cove, and gained the narrow road on the ledge under the mountain.

The General and his aide, McPherson, trudged through the deep snow ahead of all, with Gansevoort and me keeping up to them as well as we could. What with the very difficult walking, the wildness of the gale, and the necessity for silence, I do not remember that anything was said. We panted heavily, I know, and more than once had to stop while the slender and less eager carpenters who formed the van came up.

It was close upon the fence of wooden pickets which stretched across the causeway at Cape Diamond that the last of these halts was made. Through the darkness, rendered doubly dense by the whirling snowflakes with which the wind lashed our faces, we could only vaguely discern the barrier and the outlines of the little block-house beyond it.

" Here is our work ! " whispered the General to the half-dozen nearest him, and pointing ahead with his gauntleted hand. " Once over this and into the guard-house, and we can never be flanked, whatever else betide."

We tore furiously at the posts, even while he spoke —we four with our hands, the carpenters with their tools. It was the work of a moment to lay a dozen of these ; another moment and the first score of us were knee-deep in the snow piled to one side of the guard-house door. There was a murmur from behind which caused us to glance around. The body of Campbell's troops, instead of pressing us closely, had lingered to take down more pickets. Somebody— it may have been I—said, " Cowards ! " Some one else, doubtless the General, said, " Forward ! "

Then the ground shook violently under our feet, a great bursting roar deafened us, and before a scythe-like sweep of fire we at the front tumbled and fell !

I got to my feet again, but had lost both sword and pistol in the snow. I had been hit somewhere —it seemed in the side—but of that I scarcely thought. I heard sharp firing and the sound of oaths and groans all around me, so it behooved me to fight, too. There were dimly visible dark forms issuing from the guard-house, and wrestling or exchanging blows with other forms, now upright, now in the snow. Here and there a flash of fire from some gun or pistol gave an instant's light to this Stygian hurly-burly.

A heavy man, coming from the door of the block-house, fired a pistol straight at me ; the bullet seemed not to have struck me, and I leaped upon him before he could throw the weapon. We struggled fiercely backward toward the pickets, I tearing at him with all my might, and striving with tremendous effort to keep my wits as well as my strength about me, in order to save my life. Curiously enough, I found that the simplest wrestling tricks I tried I had not the power for; even in this swift minute, loss of blood was telling on me. A ferocious last effort I made to swing and hurl him, and, instead, went staggering down into the drift with him on top.

As I strove still to turn, and lifted my head, a voice sounded close in my ear, " It's you, is it ? Damn you ! " and then a great mashing blow on my face ended my fight.

Doubtless some reminiscence in that voice caused my mind to carry on the struggle in the second after sense had fled, for I thought we still were in the snow wrestling, only it was inside a mimic fort in the clearing around Mr. Stewart's old log-house, and I was a little boy in an apron, and my antagonist was a yellow-haired lad with hard fists, with which he beat me cruelly in the face—and so off into utter blackness and void of oblivion.

One morning in the latter half of January, nearly three weeks after, I woke to consciousness again. Wholly innocent of the lapse of time, I seemed to be just awakening from the dream of the snow fort, and of my boyish fight with little Philip Cross. I smiled to myself as I thought of it, but even while I smiled the vague shadows of later happenings came over my mind. Little by little the outlines of that rough December night took shape in my puzzled wits.

I had been wounded, evidently, and had been borne back to Holland House, for I recognized the room in which I lay. My right arm was in stiff splints; with the other hand I felt of my head and discovered that my hair had been cut close, and that my skull and face were fairly thatched with crossing strips of bandage. My chest, too, was girdled by similar medicated bands. My mental faculties moved very sedately, it seemed, and I had been pondering these phenomena for a long time when my cousin Dr. Teunis Van Hoorn came tiptoeing into the room.

This worthy young man was sincerely delighted to find me come by my senses once more. In his joy he allowed me to talk and to listen more than was for my good, probably, for I had some bad days immediately following; but the relapse did not come before I had learned much that was gravely interesting.

It is a story of sufficient sorrow and shame to American ears even now—this tale of how we failed to carry Quebec. Judge how grievously the recital fell upon my ears then, in the little barrack-chamber of Holland House, within hearing of the cannonade by which the farce of a siege was still maintained from day to day! Teunis told me how, by that first volley of grape at the guard-house, the brave and noble Montgomery had been instantly killed; how Arnold, forcing his way from the other direction at the head of his men, and being early shot in the leg, had fought and stormed like a wounded lion in the narrow Sault-au-Matelot; how he and the gallant Morgan had done more than their share in the temerarious adventure, and had held the town and citadel at their mercy if only the miserable Campbell had pushed forward after poor Montgomery fell, and gone on to meet those battling heroes in the Lower Town. But I have not the patience, even at this late day, to write about this melancholy and mortifying failure.

Some of our best men—Montgomery, Hendricks, Humphreys, Captain Cheseman, and other officers, and nearly two hundred men—had been killed outright, and the host of wounded made veritable hos-

pitals of both the headquarters. Nearly half of
our total original force had been taken prisoners.
With the shattered remnants of our little army we
were still keeping up the pretence of a siege, but
there was no heart in our operations, since reverse
had broken the last hope of raising assistance among
the French population. We were too few in numbers to be able now to prevent supplies reaching the
town, and everybody gloomily foresaw that when
the river became free of ice, and open for the British fleet to throw in munitions and re-enforcements,
the game would be up.

All this Dr. Teunis told me, and often during the
narration it seemed as if my indignant blood would
burst off the healing bandages, so angrily did it boil
at the thought of what poltroonery had lost to us.

It was a relief to turn to the question of my own
adventure. It appeared that I had been wounded
by the first and only discharge of the cannon at the
guard-house, for there was discovered, embedded in
the muscles over my ribs, a small iron bolt, which
would have come from no lesser firearm. They
moreover had the honor of finding a bullet in my
right forearm, which was evidently a pistol-ball.
And, lastly, my features had been beaten into an
almost unrecognizable mass of bruised flesh by
either a heavy-ringed fist or a pistol-butt.

" Pete Gansevoort dragged you off on his back,"
my kinsman concluded. " Some of our men wanted
to go back for the poor General, and for Cheseman
and McPherson, but that Campbell creature would
not suffer them. Instead, he and his cowards ran

back as if the whole King's army were at their heels.
You may thank God and Gansevoort that you were
not found frozen stiff with the rest, next morning."

"Ah, you may be sure I do!" I answered. "Can
I see Peter?"

"Why, no—at least not in this God-forgotten
country. He has been made a colonel, and is gone
back to Albany to join General Schuyler. And we
are to go—you and I—as soon as it suits your con-
venience to be able to travel. There are orders to
that purport. So make haste and get well, if you
please."

"I have been dangerously ill, have I not?"

"Scarcely that, I should say. At least, I had
little fear for you after the first week. Neither of
the gunshot wounds was serious. But somebody
must have dealt you some hearty thwacks on the
poll, my boy. It was these, and the wet chill, and
the loss of blood, which threw you into a fever. But
I never feared for you."

Later in the year, long after I was wholly recovered, my cousin confided to me that this was an
amiable lie, designed to instil me with that confidence which is so great a part of the battle gained,
and that for a week or so my chance of life had been
held hardly worth a *sou marquee.* But I did not now
know this, and I tried to fasten my mind upon that
encounter in the drift by the guard-house, which
was my last recollection. Much of it curiously
eluded my mental grasp for a time; then all at once
it came to me.

"Do you know, Teunis," I said, "that I believe

it was Philip Cross who broke my head with his pistol-butt?"

" Nonsense!"

"Yes, it surely was—and he knew me, too!" And I explained the grounds for my confidence.

" Well, young man," said Dr. Teunis, at last, " if you do not find that gentleman out somewhere, sometime, and choke him, and tear him up into fiddle-strings, you've not a drop of Van Hoorn blood in your whole carcass!"

CHAPTER XXV.

FOR a man who had his physician's personal assurance that there was nothing serious in his case, I recovered my strength with vexatious slowness. There was a very painful and wearing week, indeed, before it became clear to me that I was even convalescent, and thereafter my progress was wofully halting and intermittent. Perhaps health would have come more rapidly if with every sound of the guns from the platforms, and every rattle of the drums outside, I had not wrathfully asked myself, " Of what use is all this now, alas ! "

These bad days were nearing their end when Dr. Teunis one afternoon came in with tidings from home. An express had arrived from Albany, bringing the intelligence that General Wooster was shortly to come with re-enforcements, to take over our headless command. There were many letters for the officers as well, and among these were two for me. The physician made some show of keeping these back from me, but the cousin relented, and I was bolstered up in bed to read them.

One was a business epistle from Albany, enclosing a brief memorandum of the disposition of certain moneys and goods belonging to the English trading company whose agent I had been, and setting my mind at ease concerning what remained of its interests.

The other was a much longer missive, written in my mother's neat, painstaking hand, and in my mother's language. My story can be advanced in no better way than by translating freely from the original Dutch document, which I still have, and which shows, if nothing else, that Dame Mauverensen had powers of directness and brevity of statement not inherited by her son.

"*January* 9, A. D. 1776.

" DEARLY BELOVED SON : This I write, being well and contented for the most part, and trusting that you are the same. It is so long since I have seen you—now nearly four years—that your ways are beyond me, and I offer you no advice. People hereabout affect much satisfaction in your promotion to be an officer. I do not conceal my preference that you should have been a God-fearing man. though you were of humbler station. However, that I surrendered your keeping to a papistical infidel is my own blame, and I do not reproach you.

" The nigger Tulp, whom you sent to me upon your departure for the wars, was more trouble than he was worth, to say nothing of his keep. He was both lame and foolish, getting forever in my way, and crying by the hour with fears for your safety. I therefore sent him to his old home, the Cedars, where, as nobody now does any manner of work (your aunt being dead, and an incapable sloven having taken her place), he will not get in the way, and where others can help him to weep.

" When Mistress Cross came down to the Cedars last summer, having been deserted by her worthless husband, and found Mr. Stewart stricken with paralysis, I was moved to offer my assistance while they both lay ill. The burden of their illness was so great that your aunt broke down under it, but she did not die until after Mistress Cross had recovered from her fever, and Mr Stewart had regained his speech and a small portion of his wits. Mistress Cross was in a fair way to be despoiled of all her rightful belongings, for she brought not so much as a clean smock away with her from her husband's house, and there was there in charge an insolent rascal named Rab, who, when I demanded the keys and his mistress's chattels, essayed to turn me away. I lectured him upon his behavior in such terms that he slunk off like a whipped dog, and presently sent to me a servant from whom I received what I came for. She would otherwise have obtained nothing, for, obstinate as she is in some matters, she is a timid soul at best, and stands in mortal fear of Rab's malevolence.

"Mr. Stewart's mind is still in a sad way. He is childish beyond belief, and talks about you as if you were a lad again, and then speaks of foreign matters of which we know nothing, so long past are they, as if they were still proceeding. In bodily health, he seems now somewhat stronger. I knitted him some woollen stockings, but he would not wear them, saying that they scratched his legs. Mistress Cross might have persuaded him out of this nonsense, but did not see fit to do so. She also humors him in the matter of taking him to the Papist church at Johnstown whenever the roads are open, he having become highly devotional in his second childhood. I was vigorously opposed to indulging this idea of his, which is almost as sinful in her as it is superstitious and silly in him ; but she would go her own gait, and so she may for all of me.

"She insisted, too, on having one of Adam Wemple's girls in to do the work when your aunt fell ill. I recommended to her the widow of Dirck Tappan, a worthy and pious woman who could not sleep if there was so much as a speck of dust on the floor under her bed, but she would not listen to me, saying that she liked Moll Wemple and wanted her, and that she did not like Dame Tappan and did not want her. Upon this I came home, seeing clearly that my company was not desired longer.

"I send you the stockings which I knitted for Mr. Stewart, and sundry other woollen trifles. Your sisters are all well, but the troubles in the Valley take young men's thoughts unduly off the subject of marriage. If the committee would only hang John Johnson or themselves, there would be peace, one way or the other, and girls would get husbands again. But all say matters will be worse before they mend.

"Affectionately, your mother,

"KATHARINE MAUVERENSEN."

As I look at this ancient, faded letter, which brought to me in belated and roundabout form the tidings of Mr. Stewart's helpless condition and of Daisy's illness and grief, I can recall that my first impulse was to laugh. There was something so droll, yet so thoroughly characteristic of my honest, bustling, resolute, domineering mother in the thing, that its humor for the moment overbalanced the gravity of the news. There was no more helpful, valuable, or good-hearted woman alive than she, provided always it was permitted her to manage and dictate everything for everybody. There was no limit to the trouble she would undertake, nothing in the world she would not do, for people who would consent to be done for, and would allow her to dominate all their thoughts and deeds. But the moment they revolted, or showed the weakest inclination to do things their own way, she blazed up and was off like a rocket. Her taste for governing was little short of a mania, and I could see, in my mind's eye, just how she had essayed to rule Daisy, and how in her failure she had written to me, unconsciously revealing her pique.

Poor Daisy! My thoughts had swung quickly enough from my mother to her, and, once there, persistently lingered. She had, then, been at the Cedars since June ; she had been very ill, but now was in health again ; she was a fugitive from her rightful home, and stood in fear of her former servants ; she had upon her hands a broken old invalid, and to all his freaks and foibles was a willing slave ; she was the saddened, solitary mistress of a large estate, with all its anxieties multiplied a hundred-fold by the fact that these were war-times, that passions ran peculiarly high and fierce all about her, and that her husband's remaining friends, now her bitter foes perhaps, were in a desperate state of temper and daring.

From this grewsome revery I roused myself to exclaim : " Teunis, every day counts now. The sooner I get home the better."

" Quite so," said he, with ready sarcasm. " We will go on snow-shoes to Sorel to-morrow morning."

" No : you know what I mean. I want to——"

" Oh, yes, entirely so. We might, in fact, start this evening. The wolves are a trifle troublesome just now, but with a strong and active companion, like you, I should fear nothing."

" Will you cease jesting, Teunis ! What I want now is to exhaust all means of gaining strength— to make every hour tell upon the work of my restoration. There is urgent need of me at home. See for yourself ! " And I gave him my mother's letter.

My cousin had had from me, during our long camp intercourse, sufficient details of my early life to enable him to understand all my mother's allusions. He read the letter through carefully, and smiled. Then he went over it again, and turned grave, and began to look out of the window and whistle softly.

" Well," I asked, impatiently, " what is your judgment ? "

" My judgment is that your mother was, without doubt, the daughter of my great-uncle Baltus.

18

When I was fourteen years old my father put me
out of his house because I said that cocoa-nuts grew
on trees, he having been credibly informed by a
sailor that they were dug from the ground like
potatoes. Everybody said of my father, when they
learned of this: 'How much he is like his uncle,
Captain Baltus.' She has the true family piety, too:
The saying in Schenectady used to be: 'The Van
Hoorns are a God-fearing people—and they have
reason to be.'"

I could not but laugh at this, the while I protested that it was his views upon the tidings in the
letter that I wished.

"I agree with you that the sooner you get home
the better," he said, seriously. "The troubles in
the Valley will be ripe ere long. The letters from
Albany, just arrived, are filled, they tell me, with
rumors of the doings of Johnson. General Schuyler
had, at last accounts, gone up toward Johnstown
with a regiment, to discover the baronet's intentions. So get well as fast as you like, and we will
be off."

This was easy enough to say, but nearly two
months went by before I was judged able to travel.
We indeed did not make a start until after General
Wooster arrived with more troops, and assumed command. Our return was accomplished in the company
of the express he sent back with news of his arrival,
and his report of the state of affairs in front of Quebec. From our own knowledge this was very bad,
what with the mutinous character of many of the
men, the total absence of subordination, and the bit-

ter jealousies which existed among the rival officers. Even above the joy of turning our faces once more toward home, there rose in both of us a sense of relief at cutting loose from an expedition which had done no good, and that, too, at such a sad cost of suffering and bloodshed. It was impossible to have any pride whatever in the adventure, and we had small disposition to look people in the face, or talk with them of the siege and attack. To do them justice, the residents of the sparsely settled districts through which we slowly passed were civil enough. But we felt that we were returning like detected impostors, and we had no heart for their courtesies.

Albany was reached at last, and there the news that the British had evacuated Boston put us in better spirits. The spring was backward, but it .was April by the calendar if not by the tree-buds and gardens, and busy preparations for the season's campaign were going forward. General Schuyler took me into his own house, and insisted upon my having a full fortnight's rest, telling me that I needed all my strength for the work he had in mind for me. The repose was in truth grateful, after the long and difficult journey I had performed in my enfeebled condition ; and what with books and pictures, and the journals of events that had transpired during my long absence, and the calls of friends, and the careful kindness of the General and his good wife, I ought to have felt myself indeed happy.

But in some senses it was to me the most vexatious fortnight of the whole spring, for no hour of it all passed in which I was not devoured with anxiety to be among my own people again. The General was so preoccupied and burdened with the stress of public and martial business, always in his case carried on for the most part under the embarrassment of recurring illness, that I shrank from questioning him, and the fear haunted me that it was his intention to send me away again without a visit to my old home. It is true that I might have pleaded an invalid's privileges, but I was really well enough to work with prudence, and I could not offer to shirk duty at such a time.

But in his own good time the General relieved my mind and made me ashamed that I had ever doubted his considerateness. After breakfast one morning —it was the first, I remember, upon which I wore the new uniform with which I had been forced to replace the rags brought from Quebec—he called me to him in his library, and unfolded to me his plans:

"John Johnson lied to me last January, when I went up there, disarmed his Scotchmen, and took his parole. He lied to me here in March, when he came down and denied that he was receiving and despatching spies through the woods to and from Canada. The truth is not in him. During the past month much proof has come to my hands of his hiding arms and powder and lead near the Hall, and of his devil's work among the Mohawks, whom he plots day and night to turn against us. All this time he keeps a smooth tongue for us, but is conspiring with his Tory neighbors, and with those who followed Guy to Canada, to do us a mischief. Now that General Washington is master at Boston, and affairs are moving well elsewhere, there is no reason for further mincing of matters in Tryon County. It is my purpose to send Colonel Dayton to Johnstown with part of his regiment, to settle the thing once for all.   He will have the aid of Herkimer's militia if he needs them, and will arrest Sir John, the leaders of his Scotch followers, and all others, tenants and gentlemen alike, whose freedom is a threat to the neighborhood.   In short, he will stamp out the whole wasps nest.

" You know the Valley well, and your people are there.   It is the place for you just now.   Here is your commission as major.   But you are still attached to my staff.   I lend you merely to the Tryon County committee.   You will go with Dayton as far as you like—either to Caughnawaga or some near place—perhaps your old home would suit you best.   Please yourself.   You need not assist in the arrests at Johnstown ; that might be painful to you. But after Dayton's return with his prisoners you will be my representative in that district.   You have four days in which to make ready.   I see the prospect pleases you.   Good!   To-morrow we will discuss it further."

When I got outside I fairly leaped for joy.

CHAPTER XXVI.

I SEE DAISY AND THE OLD HOME ONCE MORE.

I RODE beside Colonel Elias Dayton one forenoon some ten days later, up the Valley road, my
pulses beating fast at the growing familiarity of the
scene before us. We had crossed the Chuctenunda
Creek, and were within sight of the gray walls of
Guy Park. Beyond rose the hills behind which lay
Fort Johnson. I was on the very threshold of my
boyhood's playfield—within a short hour's walk of
my boyhood's home.

The air was full of sounds. Birds sang with merry
discordance all through the thicket to our right,
flitting among the pale green tangle of spring's
foliage. The May sunshine had lured forth some
pioneer locusts, whose shrill cries came from who
could tell where—the tall swale-grass on the river
edge, erect now again after the April floods, or the
brown broom-corn nearer the road, or from the sky
above? We could hear the squirrels' mocking chatter in the tree-tops, the whir of the kingfishers along
the willow-fringed water—the indefinable chorus of
Nature's myriad small children, all glad that spring
was come. But above these our ears took in the
ceaseless clang of the drums, and the sound of hundreds of armed men's feet, tramping in unison upon
the road before us, behind us, at our side.

For my second return to the Valley was at the head of troops, bringing violence, perhaps bloodshed, in their train. I could not but contrast it in my mind with that other home-coming, four years before, when I sat turned to look eastward in the bow of Enoch's boat, and every soft dip of the oars timed the glad carol in my heart of home and friends—and the sweet maid I loved. I was so happy then!—and now, coming from the other direction, with suggestions of force and cruel purposes in every echo of our soldiers' tread, I was, to tell the plain truth, very miserable withal.

My talk with Colonel Dayton had, in a way, contributed to this gloomy feeling. We had, from choice, ridden side by side for the better part of two days, and, for very need of confiding in some one, I had talked with him concerning my affairs more freely than was my wont. This was the easier, because he was a contemplative, serious, and sensible man, whose words and manner created confidence. Moreover, he was neither Dutchman nor Yankee, but a native Jerseyman, and so considered my story from an equable and fair point of view, without bias.

It was, indeed, passing strange that this man, on his way to seize or crush the Johnson clique, as the case might be, should have been the one to first arouse in my mind the idea that, after all, the Tories had their good side, and were doing what to them seemed right, at tremendous cost and sacrifice to themselves. I had been telling him what a ruffian was Philip Cross, and what grounds I had for hating

him, and despitefully describing the other chief
Tories of the district. He said in reply, I remember:

"You seem to miss the sad phase of all this, my
friend. Your young blood feels only the partisan
promptings of dislike. Some day—soon, perhaps—
you will all at once find this youthful heat gone;
you will begin to walk around men and things, so to
speak, and study them from all sides. This stage
comes to every sober mind; it will come to you.
Then you will realize that this baronet up yonder
is, from his own stand-point, a chivalrous, gallant,
loyal gentleman, who imperils estates, power, peace,
almost life itself, rather than do what he holds to
be weak or wrong. Why, take even this enemy of
yours, this Cross. He was one of the notables of
these parts—rich, popular, influential; he led a life
of utmost luxury and pleasure. All this he has
exchanged for the rough work of a soldier, with its
privations, cold, fatigue, and the risk of death. Ask
yourself why he did it."

"I see what you would enforce," I said. "Your
meaning is that these men, as well as our side, think
the right is theirs."

"Precisely. They have inherited certain ideas.
We disagree with them; we deem it our duty to
silence them, fight them, drive them out of the
country, and, with God's help, we will do it. But let
us do this with our eyes open, and with the understanding that they are not necessarily scoundrels
and heathen because they fail to see things as we
see them."

"But you would not defend, surely, their plotting to use the savages against their neighbors—against helpless women and children. That must be heathenish to any mind."

"Defend it? No! I do not defend any acts of theirs. Rid your mind of the idea that because a man tries to understand a thing he therefore defends it. But I can see how they would defend it to their own consciences—just as these thrifty Whig farmers hereabout explain in their own minds as patriotic and public-spirited their itching to get hold of Johnson's Manor. Try and look at things in this light. Good and bad are relative terms; nothing is positively and unchangeably evil. Each group of men has its own little world of reasons and motives, its own atmosphere, its own standard of right and wrong. If you shut your eyes, and condemn or praise these wholly, without first striving to comprehend them, you may or may not do mischief to them; you assuredly injure yourself."

Thus, and at great length, spoke the philosophical colonel. I could not help suspecting that he had too open a mind to be a very valuable fighter, and, indeed, this proved to be true. He subsequently built some good and serviceable forts along the Mohawk, one of which to this day bears his name, but he attained no distinction as a soldier in the field.

But, none the less, his words impressed me greatly. What he said had never been put to me in clear form before, and at twenty-seven a man's mind is in that receptive frame, trembling upon the verge of the meditative stage, when the presentation of new ideas like these often marks a distinct turn in the progress and direction of his thoughts. It seems strange to confess it, but I still look back to that May day of 1776 as the date of my first notion that there could be anything admirable in my enemies.

At the time, these new views and the tone of our talk helped to disquiet me. The swinging lines of shoulders, the tramp! tramp! in the mud, the sight of the guns and swords about me, were all depressing. They seemed to give a sinister significance to my return. It was my home, the dearest spot on earth—this smiling, peaceful, sunlit Mohawk Valley —and I was entering it with soldiers whose mission was to seize and despoil the son of my boyhood's friend, Sir William. More than one of my old playmates, now grown to man's estate, would note with despair our approach, and curse me for being of it. The lady of Johnson Hall, to whom all this would be horrible nigh unto death, was a close, warm friend of Daisy's. So my thoughts ran gloomily, and I had no joy in any of the now familiar sights around me.

The march up from Schenectady had been a most wearisome one for the men, owing to the miserable condition of the road, never over-smooth and now rendered doubly bad and difficult by the spring freshets and the oozing frost. When we reached the pleasant little hollow in which Fort Johnson nestles, a halt was accordingly ordered, and the tired soldiers prepared to refresh themselves with food by the banks of the creek. It was now afternoon; we were distant but a short mile from the Cedars, and

I could not abide the thought of lingering here, to no purpose, so close to the goal of all my longings. I therefore exchanged some plans and suggestions with Colonel Dayton and his companion Judge Duer, who represented the civil law in the expedition, and so clapped spurs and dashed forward up the road.

"It seems ten years, not four, since I was last here," I was saying to Daisy half an hour later, and unconsciously framing in words the thoughts which her face suggested.

I know not how to describe the changes which this lapse of time had wrought upon her countenance and carriage. In the more obvious, outward sense, it had scarcely aged her. She was now twenty-three years of age, and I doubt a stranger would have deemed her older. Yet, looking upon her and listening to her, I seemed to feel that, instead of being four years her senior, I was in truth the younger of the two. The old buoyant, girlish air was all gone, for one thing. She spoke now with gentle, sweet-toned gravity; and her eyes, frankly meeting mine as of old, had in their glance a soft, reposeful dignity which was new to me.

Almost another Daisy, too, she seemed in face. It was the woman in her features, I dare say, which disconcerted me. I had expected changes, perhaps, but not upon these lines. She had been the prettiest maiden of the Valley, beyond all others. She was not pretty now, I should say, but she *was* beautiful—somewhat pallid, yet not to give an air of unhealth; the delicate chiselling of features yielded now not merely the pleasure of regularity, but the subtler charm of sensitive, thoughtful character. The eyes and hair seemed a deeper hazel, a darker brown, than they had been. The lips had lost something of their childish curve, and met each other in a straight line—fairer than ever, I thought, because more firm.

I am striving now, you see, against great odds, to revive in words the impressions of difference which came to me in those first hours, as I scanned her face. They furnish forth no real portrait of the dear lady: how could I hope they should? But they help to define, even if dimly, the changes toward strength and self-control I found in her.

I was, indeed, all unprepared for what awaited me here at the Cedars. My heart had been torn by all manner of anxieties and concern. I had hastened forward, convinced that my aid and protection were direly needed. I sat now, almost embarrassed, digesting the fact that the fortunes of the Cedars were in sufficient and capable hands.

Mr. Stewart's condition was in truth sad enough. He had greeted me with such cordiality and clear-wittedness of utterance and manner that at first I fancied his misfortunes to have been exaggerated in my mother's letter. His conversation for a moment or two was also coherent and timely. But his mind was prone to wander mysteriously. He presently said: "Assuredly I taught you to shave with both hands. I knew I could not be mistaken." I stole a glance toward Daisy at this, and her answering nod showed me the whole case. It was after old

Eli had come in and wheeled Mr. Stewart in his big chair out into the garden, that I spoke to Daisy of the differences time had wrought.

"Ay," she said, "it must be sadly apparent to you—the change in everything."

How should I approach the subject—the one thing of which I knew we were both thinking? There seemed a wall between us. She had been unaffectedly glad to see me; had, for the instant, I fancied, thought to offer me her cheek to kiss—yet was, with it all, so self-possessed and reserved that I shrank from touching upon her trouble.

"Perhaps not everything is sad," I made answer, falteringly. "Poor Mr. Stewart—that is indeed mournful; but, on the other hand—" I broke off abruptly.

"On the other hand," she took up my words calmly, "you are thinking that I am advantaged by Philip's departure."

My face must have showed that I could not deny it.

"In some respects," she went on, "yes; in others, no. I am glad to be able to speak freely to you, Douw, for you are nearest to me of all that are left. I do not altogether know my own mind; for that matter, does any one? The Philip to whom I gave my heart and whom I married is one person; the Philip who trampled on the heart and fled his home seems quite another and a different man. I hesitate between the two sometimes. I cannot always say to myself: 'The first was all fancy; the second is the reality.' Rather, they blend themselves in my

. mind, and I seem to see the fond lover remaining
still the good husband, if only I had had the knowledge and tenderness to keep him so!"

"In what are you to be reproached, Daisy?" I
said this somewhat testily, for the self-accusation
nettled me.

"It may easily be that I was not wise, Douw.
Indeed, I showed small wisdom from the beginning."

"It was all the doing of that old cat, Lady Berenicia!" I said, with melancholy conviction.

"Nay, blame not her alone. I was the silly girl
to be thus befooled. My heart would have served
me better if it had been all good. The longing for
finery and luxury was my own. I yearned to be set
above the rest. I dreamed to be called ' My lady,'
too, in good time. I forgot that I came from the
poor people, and that I belonged to them. So well
and truly did I forget this that the fact struck me
like a whip when—when it was brought to my
notice."

"He taunted you with it, then!" I burst forth,
my mind working quickly for once.

She made no answer for the time, but rose from
her chair and looked out upon the group in the
garden. From the open door she saw the van of
Dayton's soldiers trudging up the Valley road. I
had previously told her of their mission. and my
business.

"Poor Lady Johnson," she said, resting her head
against her hand on the door-frame, and looking
upon the advancing troops with a weary expression
of face. "Her trouble is coming—mine is past."

Then, after a pause: "Will they be harsh with Sir John, think you? I trust not. They have both been kind to me since—since Philip went. Sir John is not bad at heart, Douw, believe me. You twain never liked each other, I know. He is a bitter man with those who are against him, but his heart is good if you touch it aright."

I had not much to say to this. "I am glad he was good to you," I managed to utter, not over-graciously, I fear.

The troops went by, with no sound of drums now, lest an alarm be raised prematurely. We watched them pass in silence, and soon after I took my leave for the day, saying that I would go up to see the Fondas at Caughnawaga, and cross the river to my mother's home, and would return next morning. We shook hands at parting, almost with constraint.

CHAPTER XXVII.

EARLY the next day, which was May 20th, we heard to our surprise and consternation that on the preceding afternoon, almost as Colonel Dayton and his soldiers were entering Johnstown, Sir John and the bulk of his Highlanders and sympathizers, to the number of one hundred and thirty, had privately taken to the woods at the north of the Hall, and struck out for Canada.

Over six weeks elapsed before we learned definitely that the baronet and his companions had traversed the whole wilderness in safety and reached Montreal, which now was once more in British hands—our ill-starred Quebec expedition having finally quitted Canada earlier in the month. We could understand the stories of Sir John's travail and privations, for the snow was not yet out of the Adirondack trails, and few of his company were skilled in woodmen's craft. But they did accomplish the journey, and that in nineteen days.

I, for one, was not very much grieved at Johnson's escape, for his imprisonment would have been an embarrassment rather than a service to us. But Colonel Dayton was deeply chagrined at finding the bird flown, and I fear that in the first hours of his discomfiture he may have forgotten some of his philosophical toleration for Tories in general. He had, moreover, the delicate question on his hands of what to do with Lady Johnson. Neither Judge Duer nor I could advise him, and so everything was held in suspense for the better part of a week, until General Schuyler's decision could be had.

Meanwhile my time was fairly occupied in the fulfilment of matters intrusted to me by the General. I had to visit Colonel Herkimer at his home below Little Falls, and talk with him about the disagreeable fact that his brother, Hon-Yost Herkimer, had deserted the militia command given him by the Whigs and fled to Canada. The stout old German was free to denounce his brother, however, and I liked the looks and blunt speech of Peter Bellinger, who had been made colonel of the deserted battalion of German Flatts. There were also conversations to be had with Colonel Klock, and Ebenezer Cox, and the Fondas, at their several homes, and a day to spend with my friend John Frey, now sheriff in place of the Tory White. It thus happened that I saw very little of the people at the Cedars, and had no real talk again with Daisy, until a full week had passed.

It was a cool, overcast forenoon when I alighted next at the familiar gate, and gave my horse into Tulp's charge. The boy, though greatly rejoiced to see me back again, had developed a curious taciturnity in these latter years—since his accident, in fact —and no longer shouted out the news to me at sight. Hence I had to ask him, as I neared the door, what strange carriage was that in the yard beyond, and why it was there. As I spoke, a couple of men lounged in view from the rear of the house, and I recognized them as of Dayton's command. Tulp explained that Lady Johnson was being taken away, and that she had tarried here to rest on her journey.

If I had known this at the gate, I doubt I should have stopped at all; but I had been seen from the window, and it was too late now to turn about. So I entered, much wishing that I had left off my uniform, or, still better, that I had stayed away altogether.

There were present in the great room Daisy, Lady Johnson, a young lady who was her sister, two children—and a man in civilian's garb, with some few military touches, such as a belt and sword and a cockade, who sat by the window, his knees impudently spread apart and his hat on his head. I looked at this fellow in indignant inquiry.

Daisy came eagerly to me, with an explanation on her lips:

"It is the officer who is to take Lady Johnson to Albany. He insists upon forcing his presence upon us, and will not suffer us to be alone together in any room in the house."

"Who are you?—and off with your hat!" I said to the man, sharply.

My uniform was of service, after all. He looked me over, and evidently remembered having seen me with his colonel, for he stood up and took off his hat. "I am a lieutenant of the Connecticut line,"

he said, in a Yankee snarl, "and I am doing my duty."

"I am a major in the Continental line, and I should be doing *my* duty if I sent you back in irons to your colonel," I answered. "Get out of here, what time Lady Johnson is to remain, and leave these ladies to themselves!"

He was clearly in two minds about obeying me, and I fancy it was my superior size rather than my rank that induced him to go, which he did in as disagreeable a fashion as possible. I made my bow to Lady Johnson, and said something about being glad that I had come, if I had been of use.

She, poor young woman, was in a sad state of nervous excitement, what with her delicate condition and the distressing circumstances of the past week. She was, moreover, a very beautiful creature, naturally of soft and refined manners, and this made me the readier to overlook the way in which she met my kindly meant phrases.

"I marvel that you are not ashamed, Mr. Mauverensen," she said, heatedly, "to belong to an army made up of such ruffians. Every rag of raiment that man has on he stole from my husband's wardrobe at the Hall. To think of calling such low fellows officers, or consorting with them!"

I answered as gently as I could that, unfortunately, there were many such ill-conditioned men in every service, and pointed out that the man, by his speech, was a New Englander.

"And who fetched them into this province, I should like to know!"

Nothing was further from my thoughts than to hold a political discussion with this poor troubled wife, who saw her husband's peril, her own plight, and the prospective birth of her first child in captivity constantly before her eyes! So I strove to bring the talk upon other grounds, but not with much success. She grew calmer, and with the returning calmness came a fine, cool dignity of manner and tone which curiously reminded me of Lady Berenicia Cross; but she could talk of nothing save her wrongs, or rather those of her husband. She seemed not to have very clear notions of what the trouble was all about, but ascribed it loosely, I gathered, to the jealousy of Philip Livingston, who was vexed that the Scotch did not settle upon his patent instead of on Sir John's land, and to the malice of General Schuyler, whose feud with the Johnsons was notorious.

"And to think, too," she added, "that Mr. Schuyler's mother and my mother's mother were sisters! A very pleasant and valuable cousin he is, to be sure! Driving my husband off into the forest to perhaps die of hunger, and dragging me down to Albany, in my condition, and thrusting a low Connecticut cobbler into my carriage with me! If my sickness overtakes me on the road, and I die, my blood will be on the head of Philip Schuyler."

I read in Daisy's eyes a way out of this painful conversation, and so said: "Lady Johnson, it will perhaps render your journey less harrowing if I have some talk with this officer who is your escort. Let me leave you women-folk together here in peace, the while "—and went out into the garden again.

I found the lieutenant in the garden to the rear of the house, gossiping in familiar style with his half-dozen men, and drew him aside for some private words. He was sensible enough, at bottom, and when I had pointed out to him that his prisoner was a good and kindly soul, who had been, through no fault of her own, nurtured in aristocratic ideas and ways; that those of whatever party who knew her well most heartily esteemed her; and that, moreover, she was nearly related by blood to General Schuyler—he professed himself ready to behave toward her with more politeness.

The trouble with him really lay in his abiding belief that people underestimated his importance, and hence he sought to magnify his position in their eyes by insolent demeanor. Therein I discerned the true Yankee.

That the men of the New England States have many excellent parts, I would be the last to deny; but that they were in the main a quarrelsome, intractable, mutinous, and mischief-making element in our armies during the Revolution, is not to be gainsaid. I know, of my own knowledge, how their fractious and insubordinate conduct grieved and sorely disheartened poor Montgomery while we lay before Quebec. I could tell many tales, too, of the harm they did to the cause in New York State, by their prejudices against us, and their narrow spite against General Schuyler. So mischievous did this attitude become at last—when old General Wooster came to us with his Connecticut troops, and these set themselves up to be independent of all our plans or rules, refusing even to mess with the others or to touch Continental provisions and munitions—that Congress had to interfere and put them sharply back into their proper places. Jerseymen, Pennsylvanians, Virginians, and men from the Carolinas will bear me out in saying these things about the New England soldiery. I speak not in blame or bitterness. The truth is that they were too much akin in blood and conceit to the English not to have in themselves many of the disagreeable qualities which had impelled us all to revolt against British rule.

When the lieutenant had ordered the horses to be brought out for a start, I went back into the house. The women had been weeping, I could see. Lady Johnson had softened in her mood toward me, and spoke now some gentle words of thanks for the little I had done. When I told her, in turn, that her escort would henceforth be more considerate in his conduct toward her, she was for a moment pleased, but then tears filled her eyes at the thoughts of the journey before her.

"When I am out of sight of this house," she said, sadly, "it will seem as if my last friend had been left behind. Why could they not have left me at the Hall? I gave them the keys ; I yielded up everything ! What harm could I have done them —remaining there ? I had no wish to visit my relatives in Albany ! It is a trick—a device ! I doubt I shall ever lay eyes on my dear home again."

And, poor lady, she never did.

We strove to speak words of comfort to her, but they came but feebly, and could not have consoled her much. When the lieutenant opened the door, the women made a tearful adieu, with sobs and kisses upon which I could not bear to look. Lady Johnson shook hands with me, still with a pathetic quivering of the lips. But then in an instant she straightened herself to her full height, bit her lips tight, and walked proudly past the obnoxious escort down the path to the carriage, followed by her weeping sister and the two big-eyed wondering children.

"Will she ever come back?" said Daisy, half in inquiry, half in despairing exclamation, as we saw the last of the carriage and its guard. "How will it all end, Douw?"

"Who can foresee?" I answered. "It is war now, at last, war open and desperate. I can see no peaceful way out of it. These aristocratic landlords, these Johnsons, Butlers, Phillipses, De Lanceys, and the rest, will not give up their estates without a hard fight for them. Of that you may be sure. *They* will come back, if their wives do not, and all that they can do, backed by England, to regain their positions, will be done. They may win, and if they do, it will be our necks that will be put into the yoke —or the halter. At all events, it has gone too far to be patched over now. We can only stand up and fight as stoutly as we may, and leave the rest to fate."

"And it really was necessary to fight—I suppose it could not have been in reason avoided?"

" They would have it so. They clung to the faith that they were by right the masters here, and we the slaves, and so infatuated were they that they brought in English troops and force to back them up. There was no alternative but to fight. Would you have had me on the other side—on the English side, Daisy ? "

" Oh, no, Douw," she answered, in a clear voice. " If war there must be, why, of course, the side of my people is my side."

I was not surprised at this, but I said, " You speak of your people, Daisy—but surely mere birth does not count for more than one's whole training afterward, and you have been bred among another class altogether. Why, I should think nine out of every ten of your friends here in the Mohawk district must be Tories."

" Not so great a proportion as that," she went on, with a faint smile upon her lips, but deep gravity in her eyes. " You do not know the value of these ' friends,' as you call them, as closely as I do. Never have they forgotten on their side, even if I did on mine, that my parents were Palatine peasants. And you speak of my being bred among them ! In what way more than you were? Was I not brought up side by side with you ? Was there any difference in our rearing, in our daily life until—until you left us? Why should I not be a patriot, sir, as well as you ? "

She ended with a little laugh, but the voice quivered beneath it. We both were thinking, I felt, of the dear old days gone by, and of the melancholy

(fate which clouded over and darkened those days, and drove us apart.

We still stood by the open door, whence we had watched the carriage disappear. After some seconds of silence I essayed to bring back the conversation to Lady Johnson, and talked of her narrow, ill-informed, purely one-sided way of regarding the troubles, and of how impossible it was that the class to which she belonged, no matter how amiable and good they might be, could ever adapt themselves to the enlarging social conditions of this new country.

While I talked, there burst forth suddenly the racket of fifes and drums in the road. Some militia companies were marching past on their way to join Colonel Dayton's force. We stood and watched these go by, and in the noise that they made we failed to hear Mr. Stewart's tottering footsteps behind us.

The din of the drums had called him out of his lethargy, and he came forward to watch the yeoman-soldiery.

" They march badly—badly," he said, shielding his eyes from the sun with his hand. " I do not know the uniform. But I have been away so long, and everything is changed since the King of Prussia began his wars. Yet I am happier here as I am— far happier with my fields, and my freedom, and my children."

He had spoken in the tone, half-conversational, half-dreamy, which of late strangely marked most of his speech. He turned now and looked at us ; a pleasant change came over his wan face, and he smiled upon us with a curious reflection of the old fond look.

"You are good children," he said; "you shall be married in due time, and come after me when I am gone. There will be no handsomer, happier twain in the province."

Daisy flushed crimson and looked pained at the old gentleman's childish babbling, and I made haste to get away.

CHAPTER XXVIII.

A TRULY miserable fourteen months' period of thankless labor, and of unending yet aimless anxiety, follows here in my story. It was my business to remain in the Valley, watch its suspected figures, invigorate and encourage its militia, and combat the secret slander and open cowardice which there menaced the cause of liberty. Fortunately I had, from time to time, assurance that my work was of actual advantage to General Schuyler, and occasionally I had leisure hours to spend at the Cedars. If these pleasurable things had been denied me, there would have been in the whole Continental service no more unenviable post than mine.

I have never pretended, least of all to myself, to be much enamoured of fighting; nor have I ever been regardless of personal comfort, and of the satisfaction of having warm clothes, sufficient food, and a good bed in which to sleep. Yet I would gladly have exchanged my state for that of the most wretched private soldier, barefooted and famished, on the frozen Delaware or at Morristown. War is a hateful and repellent enough thing; but it is at least better to be in the thick of it, to smell burning powder and see and feel the enemy, even if he be at your heels, than to be posted far away from the theatre of conflict, spying upon an outwardly peaceful community for signs of treason and disaffection.

I should not like to put down in black and white, here in my old age, all the harsh and malignant things which I thought of my Mohawk Valley neighbors, or some of them, during those fourteen months. I am able to see now that they were not altogether without excuse.

The affairs of the revolted Colonies were, in truth, going very badly. No sooner had Congress summoned the resolution to decree Continental independence than the fates seemed to conspire to show that the declaration was a mistake. Our successes in the field came to a sudden halt; then disasters followed in their place. Public confidence, which had been too lightly raised, first wavered, then collapsed. Against the magnificent army of English and Hessian regulars which Howe mustered in New York, General Washington could not hold his own, and Congress lost the nerve to stand at his back. Our militia threw up the service, disheartened. Our commissariat faded out of existence. The patriot force became the mere skeleton of an army, ragged, ill-fed, discouraged, and almost hopeless. In battle after battle the British won—by overwhelming numbers or superior fortune, it mattered not which; the result was equally lamentable.

There had been, indeed, a notable week at Christmas-time, when the swift strong blows struck at Trenton and Princeton lifted for a moment the cloud which hung over us. But it settled down again, black and threatening, before spring came.

The Colonies quarrelled with one another ; their generals plotted and intrigued, or sullenly held aloof. Cool men, measuring on the one side this lax and inharmonious alliance of jealous States, without money, without public-spirited populations, and, above all, without confidence in their own success, and on the other the imposing power of rich and resolute England, with its splendid armies and fleets in the St. Lawrence and in New York Harbor, and with its limitless supply of hired German auxiliaries —cool men, I say, weighing dispassionately these two opposing forces, came pretty generally to believe that in the end General Washington would find himself laid by the heels in the Tower at London.

I cannot honestly say now whether I ever shared this despondent view or not. But I do know that I chafed bitterly under the orders which kept me in the Valley, and not only prevented my seeing what fighting there was, but put me to no better task than watching in a ten-acre field for rattlesnakes. I can in no apter way describe my employment from May of 1776 to July of the following year. There was unending work, but no visible fruit, either for the cause or for myself. The menace of impending danger hung over us constantly—and nothing came of it, month after month. I grew truly sick of it all. Besides, my wounds did not heal well, and my bad health from time to time induced both melancholy and an irritable mind.

The situation in the Valley was extremely simple. There was a small outspoken Tory party, who made no secret of their sympathies, and kept up communi-

cations with the refugees in Canada.   These talked
openly of the time soon to arrive when the King's
troops would purge the Valley of disloyalty, and loyal-
ists should come by more than their own.   There was
a somewhat larger Whig party, which by word and
deed supported Congress.   Between these two, or
rather, because of their large number, surrounding
them, was the great neutral party, who were chiefly
concerned to so trim their sails that they should ship
no water whichever way the wind blew.

Up to the time of the Declaration of Independence
these peaceful people had leaned rather toward the
Whigs.   But when General Washington evacuated
Long Island, and the Continental prospects seemed
to dwindle, it was wonderful to note how these same
trimmers began again, first furtively, then with less
concealment, to drink the King's health.

Roughly speaking, the majority of the avowed
Tories were in the lower district of Tryon County,
that called the Mohawk district, embracing all east
of Anthony's Nose, including Johnstown, Tribes
Hill, and Caughnawaga.   They had, indeed, out-
numbered the Whigs by five to one before the flights
to Canada began ; and even now enough remained
to give a strong British color to the feeling of the
district.   In the western districts of the county,
where the population was more purely Dutch and
Palatine, the Whig sentiment was very much
stronger.   But here, too, there were Tories, confessed
and defiant ; and everywhere, as time passed, the
dry-rot of doubt spread among those who were of
neither party.   It came at last that nearly every

week brought news of some young man's disappear-
ance from home—which meant another recruit for
the hostile Canadian force; and scarcely a day went
by without the gloomy tidings that this man or the
other, heretofore lukewarm, now spoke in favor of
submission to the King.

It was my function to watch this shifting public
opinion, to sway it where I could, but to watch it
always. No more painful task could have been conceived. I lived in an atmosphere of treachery and
suspicion. Wherever I turned I saw humanity at its
worst. Men doubted their brothers, their sons, even
their wives. The very ground underneath us was
honeycombed with intrigues and conspiracies. Intelligence from Canada, with its burden of promises
to speedily glut the passions of war, circulated
stealthily all about us. How it came, how it was
passed from hearth to hearth, defied our penetration.
We could only feel that it was in the air around us,
and strive to locate it—mainly in vain—and shudder
at its sinister omens.

For all felt a blow to be impending, and only
marvelled at its being so long withheld. It was
two years now since Colonel Guy Johnson, with the
Butlers and Philip Cross, had gone westward to
raise the Indians. It was more than a year since
Sir John and his retainers had joined them. Some
of these had been to England in the interim, and
we vaguely heard of others flitting, now in Quebec,
now at Niagara or Detroit ; yet none doubted that
the dearest purpose of all of them was to return
with troops and savages to reconquer the Valley.

This was the sword which hung daily, nightly, over our heads.

And as the waiting time lengthened out it grew terrible to weak and selfish minds. More and more men sought to learn how they might soften and turn its wrath aside, not how they might meet and repel its stroke.

Congress would not believe in our danger—perhaps could not have helped us if it would. And then our own friends at this lost heart. The flights to Canada multiplied; our volunteer militiamen fell away from the drills and patrols. Stories and rumors grew thicker of British preparations, of Indian approaches, of invasion's red track being cleared up to the very gates of the Valley. And no man saw how the ruin was to be averted.

It was in the second week of July, at almost the darkest hour in that gloomy first part of 1777, that a singular link in the chain of my story was forged.

Affairs were at their worst, abroad and at home. General Washington's call for more troops had fallen on deaf ears, and it seemed impossible that his poor force could withstand the grand army and fleet mustering at New York. The news of St. Clair's wretched evacuation of Ticonderoga had come in, and we scarcely dared look one another in the face when it was told. Apparently matters were nearing a climax, so far at least as we in New York State were involved. For Burgoyne was moving down through the Champlain country upon Albany, with none to stay his progress, and an auxiliary force was somewhere upon the great northern water frontier of our State, intending to sweep through the Mohawk Valley to join him. Once this junction was formed, the Hudson lay open—and after that? We dared not think!

I cannot hope to make young people realize what all this meant to us. To comprehend this, one must have had not only a neck menaced by the halter, but mother, sisters, dear ones, threatened by the tomahawk and knife. Thinking back upon it now, I marvel that men did not go mad under this horrible stress of apprehension. Apparently there was no hope. The old New England spite and prejudice against General Schuyler had stirred up now a fierce chorus of calumny and attack. He was blamed for St. Clair's pusillanimous retreat, for Congressional languor, for the failure of the militia to come forward—for everything, in fact. His hands were tied by suspicion, by treason, by popular lethargy, by lack of money, men, and means. Against these odds he strove like a giant, but I think not even he, with all his great, calm confidence, saw clearly through the black cloud just then.

I had gone to bed late one hot July night, and had hardly fallen asleep, for gloomy musing upon these things, when I was awakened by a loud pounding on the door beneath. I was at my mother's house, fortunately, and the messenger had thus found me out promptly.

Tulp had also been aroused, and saddled my horse while I dressed, in response to the summons. I was wanted at Johnstown by Sheriff Frey, on some mat-

20

ter which would not wait for the morrow. This much I gathered from the messenger, as we rode together in the starlight, but he could tell me little more, save that an emissary from the Tories in Canada had been captured near the Saçondaga, and it was needful that I should see him. I wondered somewhat at this as a reason for routing me out of my sleep, but cantered silently along, too drowsy to be querulous.

Daylight broke before we crossed the river, and the sunrise gun sounded as we rode up into the court-house square at Johnstown. Soldiers were already to be seen moving about outside the block-houses at the corners of the palisade which, since Sir John's flight, had been built around the jail. Our coming seemed to be expected, for one of the soldiers told us to wait while he went inside, and after a few minutes John Frey came out, rubbing his eyes. As I dismounted, he briefly explained matters to me.

It seemed that a Tory spy had made his way in from the woods, had delivered letters both at Cairncross and at the Cedars, and had then started to return, but by the vigilance of one of the Vrooman boys had been headed off and taken.

" He is as close as the bark on a beech-tree," concluded the sheriff. " We could get nothing out of him. Even when I told him he would be hanged this morning after breakfast, he did not change color. He only said that if this was the case he would like first to see you ; it seems he knows you, and has some information for you—probably about

Philip Cross's wife. Perhaps he will tell *you* what was in the letter he brought to her."

It occurred to me on the instant that this was the real reason for my being summoned. These were days of universal suspicion, and the worthy sheriff had his doubts even of Daisy.

"All right! Let me see the man," I said, and we entered the jail.

When the soldier in charge had opened the cell-door, the object of our interest was discovered to be asleep. Frey shook him vigorously by the shoulder. He sat bolt upright on the instant, squinting his eyes to accustom them to the light, but evincing no special concern at our presence.

"Is your hanging-party ready?" he said, and yawned, stretching his arms as freely as the manacles would admit.

I looked curiously at him—a long, slender, wiry figure, with thin, corded neck, and twisted muscles showing on so much of his hairy breast as the open buckskin shirt exposed. The face was pointed and bony, and brown as leather. For the moment I could not place him; then his identity dawned on me. I stepped forward, and said:

"Is that you, Enoch Wade?"

He looked up at me, and nodded recognition, with no show of emotion.

"It might have been my ghost, cap'n," he said, "if you hadn't hurried right along. These friends of yours were bent on spoiling a good man to make bad meat. They wouldn't listen to any kind of reason. Can I have a palaver with you, all by yourself?"

"What does he mean by a 'palaver'?" asked the honest Swiss sheriff.

I explained that it was a common enough Portuguese word, signifying "talk," which Enoch in his wanderings had picked up. Furthermore, I told Frey that I knew the man, and wished to speak with him apart, whereupon the sheriff and the soldier left us.

"It is all in my eye—their hanging me," began Enoch, with a sardonic smile slowly relaxing his thin lips. "I wasn't fooled a minute by that."

"Perhaps you are mistaken there, my man," I said, as sternly as I could.

"Oh, no, not a bit! What's more, they wouldn't have caught me if I hadn't wanted to be caught. You know me. You have travelled with me. Honest Injun, now, do you take me for the kind of a man to be treed by a young Dutch muskrat-trapper if I have a mind not to be?"

I had to admit that my knowledge of his resourceful nature had not prepared me for such an ignoble catastrophe, but I added that all the more his conduct mystified me.

"Quite so!" he remarked, with another grim smile of complacency. "Sit down here on this bed, if you can find room, and I'll tell you all about it."

The tale to which I listened during the next half-hour, full of deep interest as it was for me, would not bear repeating here at length. Its essential points were these:

After Sir William's death Enoch had remained on at the Hall, not feeling particularly bound to the

"Is your hanging party ready?" he said.

new baronet, but having a cat's attachment to the
Hall itself. When Sir John finally resolved to
avoid arrest by flight, Enoch had been in two minds
about accompanying him, but had finally yielded to
the flattering reliance placed by all upon the value
and thoroughness of his knowledge as a woodsman.
It was largely due to his skill that the party got
safely through the great wilderness, and reached
Montreal so soon. Since his arrival in Canada,
however, things had not been at all to his liking.
There was but one thought among all his refugee
companions, which was to return to the Mohawk
Valley and put their old neighbors to fire and sword
—and for this Enoch had no inclination whatever.
He had accordingly resisted all offers to enrol him
in the Tory regiment which Sir John was raising in
Canada, and had looked for an opportunity to get
away quietly and without reproach. This chance
had only come to him a week or so ago, when Philip
Cross offered to pay him well to take two letters
down the Valley—one to his servant Rab, the other
to Mrs. Cross. He had accepted this errand, and
had delivered the letters as in duty bound. There
his responsibility ended. He had no intention to
return, and had allowed himself to be arrested by a
slow and uninventive young man, solely because it
seemed the best way of achieving his purpose.

" What is your purpose, Enoch ? "

" Well, to begin with, it is to make your hair stand
on end. I started from Buck's Island, on the St.
Lawrence, on the 9th of this month. Do you know
who I left there? Seven hundred uniformed soldiers,

English and Tory, with eight cannons, commanded by a British colonel—Sillinger they called him—and Sir John Johnson. They are coming to Oswego, where they will meet the Butlers with more Tories, and Dan Claus with five hundred Indians. Then the whole force is to march on Fort Stanwix, capture it, and come down the Valley!"

You may guess how eagerly I listened to the details which Enoch gave—details of the gravest importance, which I must hasten to send west to Herkimer and east to Schuyler. When this vital talk was ended, I returned to the personal side of the matter with a final query:

"But why get yourself arrested?"

"Because I wanted to see you. My errand wasn't finished till I had given you Philip Cross's message. 'Tell that Dutchman,' he said, 'if you can contrive to do it without peril to yourself, that when I come into the Valley I will cut out his heart, and feed it to a Missisague dog!'"

CHAPTER XXIX.

THE MESSAGE SENT AHEAD FROM THE INVADING ARMY.

THE whole forenoon of this eventful day was occupied in transmitting to the proper authorities the great tidings which had so fortuitously come to us.

For this purpose, after breakfast, John Frey, who was the brigade major as well as sheriff, rode down to Caughnawaga with me, four soldiers bringing Enoch in our train. It was a busy morning at the Fonda house, where we despatched our business, only Jelles Fonda and his brother Captain Adam and the staunch old Samson Sammons being admitted to our counsels.

Here Enoch repeated his story, telling now in addition that one-half of the approaching force was composed of Hanau Chasseurs—skilled marksmen recruited in Germany from the gamekeeper or forester class—and that Joseph Brant was expected to meet them at Oswego with the Iroquois war party, Colonel Claus having command of the Missisagues or Hurons from the Far West. As he mentioned the names of various officers in Sir John's regiment of Tories, we ground our teeth with wrath. They were the names of men we had long known in the Valley —men whose brothers and kinsmen were still among us, some even holding commissions in our militia. Old Sammons could not restrain a snort of rage when the name of Hon-Yost Herkimer was mentioned in this list of men who wore now the traitor's "Royal Green" uniform, and carried commissions from King George to fight against their own blood.

"You saw no Sammons in that damned snake's nest, I'll be bound!" he shouted fiercely at Enoch.

"Nor any Fonda, either," said Major Jelles, .as firmly.

But then both bethought them that these were cruel words to say in the hearing of the stalwart John Frey, who could not help it that his brother, Colonel Hendrick, was on parole as a suspected Tory, and that another brother, Bernard, and a nephew, young Philip Frey, Hendrick's son, were with Johnson in Canada. So the family subject was dropped.

More or less minute reports of all that Enoch revealed, according to the position of those for whom they were intended, were written out by me, and despatched by messenger to General Schuyler at Albany ; to Brigadier-General Herkimer near the Little Falls ; to Colonel Campbell at Cherry Valley ; and to my old comrade Peter Gansevoort, now a full colonel, and since April the commandant at Fort Stanwix. Upon him the first brunt of the coming invasion would fall. He had under him only five hundred men—the Third New York Continentals—and I took it upon myself to urge now upon General Schuyler that more should be speeded to him.

This work finally cleared away, and all done that was proper until the military head of Tryon County, Brigadier Herkimer, should take action, there was time to remember my own affairs.   It had been resolved that no word of what we had learned should be made public.   The haying had begun, and a panic now would work only disaster by interfering with this most important harvest a day sooner than need be.   There was no longer any question of keeping Enoch in prison, but there was a real fear that if he were set at large he might reveal his secret.   Hence John Frey suggested that I keep him under my eye, and this jumped with my inclination.

Accordingly, when the noon-day heat was somewhat abated, we set out down the Valley road toward the Cedars.   There was no horse for him, but he walked with the spring and tirelessness of a greyhound, his hand on the pommel of my saddle.   The four soldiers who had come down from Johnstown followed in our rear, keeping under the shade where they could, and picking berries by the way.

The mysterious letter from Philip to his deserted wife lay heavily upon my thoughts.   I could not ask Enoch if he knew its contents—which it turned out he did not—but I was unable to keep my mind from speculating upon them.

During all these fourteen months Daisy and I had rarely spoken of her recreant ruffian of a husband— or, for that matter, of any other phase of her sad married life.   There had been some little constraint between us for a time, after Mr. Stewart's childish babbling about us as still youth and maiden.   He never happened to repeat it, and the embarrassment gradually wore away. But we had both been warned by it—if indeed I ought to speak of her as possibly needing such a warning—and by tacit consent the whole subject of her situation was avoided. I did not even tell her that I owed the worst and most lasting of my wounds to Philip. It would only have added to her grief, and impeded the freedom of my arm when the chance for revenge should come.

That my heart had been all this while deeply tender toward the poor girl, I need hardly say. I tried to believe that I thought of her only as the dear sister of my childhood, and that I looked upon her when we met with no more than the fondness which may properly glow in a brother's eyes. For the most part I succeeded in believing it, but it is just to add that the neighborhood did not. More than once my mother had angered me by reporting that people talked of my frequent visits to the Cedars, and faint echoes of this gossip had reached my ears from other sources.

"You did not stop to see Mistress Cross open her letter, then?" I asked Enoch.

"No: why should I? Nothing was said about that. He paid me only to deliver it into her hands."

"And what was his mood when he gave it to you?"

"Why, it was what you might call the Madeira mood—his old accustomed temper. He had the hiccoughs, I recall, when he spoke with me. Most generally he does have them. Yet, speak the truth

and shame the devil! he is sober two days to that
Colonel Sillinger's one. If their expedition fails, it
won't be for want of rum. They had twenty barrels
when they started from La Chine, and it went to
my heart to see men make such beasts of themselves."

I could not but smile at this. "The last time I
saw you before to-day," I said, "there could not
well have been less than a quart of rum inside of
you."

"No doubt! But it is quite another thing to
guzzle while your work is still in hand. That I
never would do. And it is that which makes me
doubt these British will win, in the long-run. Rum
is good to rest upon—it is rest itself—when the labor
is done; but it is ruin to drink it when your task is
still ahead of you. To tell the truth, I could not
bear to see these fellows drink, drink, drink, all day
long, with all their hard fighting to come. It made
me uneasy."

"And is it your purpose to join us? We are the
sober ones, you know."

"Well, yes and no. I don't mind giving your
side a lift—it's more my way of thinking than the
other—and you seem to need it powerfully, too.
But "—here he looked critically over my blue and
buff, from cockade to boot-tops—" you don't get
any uniform on me, and I don't join any regiment.
I'd take my chance in the woods first. It suits
you to a 't,' but it would gag me from the first
minute."

We talked thus until we reached the Cedars. I

left Enoch and the escort without, and knocked at the door. I had to rap a second time before Molly Wemple appeared to let me in.

"We were all up-stairs," she said, wiping her hot and dusty brow with her apron, "hard at it! I'll send her down to you. She needs a little breathing-spell."

The girl was gone before I could ask what extra necessity for labor had fallen upon the household this sultry summer afternoon.

Daisy came hurriedly to me, a moment later, and took both my hands in hers. She also bore signs of work and weariness.

"Oh, I am *so* glad you are come!" she said, eagerly. "Twice I have sent Tulp for you across to your mother's. It seemed as if you never would come."

"Why, what is it, my girl? Is it about the letter from—from——"

"You know, then!"

"Only that a letter came to you yesterday from him. The messenger—he is an old friend of ours—told me that much, nothing more."

Daisy turned at this and took a chair, motioning me to another. The pleased excitement at my arrival—apparently so much desired—was succeeded all at once by visible embarrassment.

"Now that you are here, I scarcely know why I wanted you, or—or how to tell you what it is," she said, speaking slowly. "I was full of the idea that nothing could be done without your advice and help —and yet, now you have come, it seems that there

is nothing left for you to say or do." She paused
for a moment, then added : " You know we are going
back to Cairncross."

I stared at her, aghast. The best thing I could
say was, " Nonsense ! "

She smiled wearily. " So I might have known you
would say. But it is the truth, none the less."

" You must be crazy ! "

" No, Douw, only very, very wretched ! "

The poor girl's voice faltered as she spoke, and I
thought I saw the glisten of tears in her eyes. She
had borne so brave and calm a front through all her
trouble, that this suggestion of a sob wrung my
heart with the cruelty of a novel sorrow. I drew
my chair nearer to her.

" Tell me about it all, Daisy—if you can."

Her answer was to impulsively take a letter from
her pocket and hand it to me. She would have
recalled it an instant later.

" No—give it me back, " she cried. " I forgot !
There are things in it you should not see."

But even as I held it out to her, she changed her
mind once again.

" No—read it," she said, sinking back in her chair ;
" it can make no difference—between *us*. You
might as well know all ! "

The " all " could not well have been more hateful.
I smoothed out the folded sheet over my knee, and
read these words, written in a loose, bold character,
with no date or designation of place, and with the
signature scrawled grandly like the sign-manual of a
duke, at least :

" MADAM :—It is my purpose to return to Cairncross forthwith, though you are not to publish it.

" If I fail to find you there residing, as is your duty, upon my arrival, I shall be able to construe the reasons for your absence, and shall act accordingly.

" I am fully informed of your behavior in quitting my house the instant my back was turned, and in consorting publicly with my enemies, and with ruffian foes to law and order generally.

" All these rebels and knaves will shortly be shot or hanged, including without fail your Dutch gallant, who, I am told, now calls himself a major. His daily visits to you have all been faithfully reported to me. After his neck has been properly twisted, I may be in a better humor to listen to such excuses as you can offer in his regard, albeit I make no promise.

" I despatch by this same express my commands to Rab, which will serve as your further instructions.

" PHILIP."

One clearly had a right to time for reflection, after having read such a letter as this. I turned the sheet over and over in my hands, re-reading lines here and there under pretence of study, and preserving silence, until finally she asked me what I thought of it all. Then I had perforce to speak my mind.

" I think, if you wish to know," I said, deliberately, " that this husband of yours is the most odious brute God ever allowed to live ! "

There came now in her reply a curious confirmation of the familiar saying, that no man can ever comprehend a woman. A long life's experience has convinced me that the simplest and most direct of her sex must be, in the inner workings of her mind, an enigma to the wisest man that ever existed ; so impressed am I with this fact that several times in the course of this narrative I have been at pains to disavow all knowledge of why the women folk of my tale did this or that, only recording the fact that they did do it ; and thus to the end of time, I take it, the world's stories must be written.

This is what Daisy actually said:

" But do you not see running through every line of the letter, and but indifferently concealed, the confession that he is sorry for what he has done, and that he still loves me?"

" I certainly see nothing of the kind ! "

She had the letter by heart. " Else why does he wish me to return to his home?" she asked. " And you see he is grieved at my having been friendly with those who are not his friends; that he would not be if he cared nothing for me. Note, too, how at the close, even when he has shown that by the reports that have reached him he is justified in suspecting me, he as much as says that he will forgive me."

" Yes—perhaps—when once he has had his sweet fill of seeing me kicking at the end of a rope! Truly I marvel, Daisy, how you can be so blind, after all the misery and suffering this ruffian has caused you."

" He is my husband, Douw," she said, simply, as if that settled everything.

" Yes, he is your husband—a noble and loving husband, in truth! He first makes your life wretched at home—you know you *were* wretched, Daisy ! Then he deserts you, despoiling your house before your very eyes, humiliating you in the hearing of your servants, and throwing the poverty of your parents in your face as he goes ! He stops away

two years—having you watched meanwhile, it seems
—yet never vouchsafing you so much as a word of
message! Then at last, when these coward Tories
have bought help enough in Germany and in the
Indian camps to embolden them to come down and
look their neighbors in the face, he is pleased to
write you this letter, abounding in coarse insults in
every sentence. He tells you of his coming as he
might notify a tavern wench. He hectors and orders
you as if you were his slave. He pleasantly promises the ignominious death of your chief friends.
And all this you take kindly—sifting his brutal
words in search for even the tiniest grain of manli-
ness. My faith, I am astonished at you! I credited
you with more spirit."

She was not angered at this outburst, which had
in it more harsh phrases than she had heard in all
her life from me before, but, after a little pause, said
to me quite calmly:

"I know you deem him all bad. You never
allowed him any good quality."

"You know him better than I—a thousand times
better, more's the pity. Very well! I rest the case
with you. Tell me, out of all your knowledge of
the man, what 'good quality' he ever showed, how
he showed it, and when!"

"Have you forgotten that he saved my life?"

"No; but he forgot it—or rather made it the subject of taunts, in place of soft thoughts."

"And he loved me—ah! he truly did—for a
little!"

"Yes, he loved you! So he did his horses, his

kennel, his wine cellar; and a hundred-fold more he loved himself and his cursed pride."

" How you hate him !"

" Hate him ? Yes ! Have I not been given cause ? "

" He often said that he was not in fault for throwing Tulp over the gulf-side. He knew no reason, he avowed, why you should have sought a quarrel with him that day, and forced it upon him, there in the gulf; and as for Tulp—why, the foolish boy ran at him. Is it not so? "

"Who speaks of Tulp?" I asked, impatiently. "If he had tossed all Ethiopia over the cliff, and left me *you*—I—I——"

The words were out !

I bit my tongue in shamed regret, and dared not let my glance meet hers. Of all things in the world, this was precisely what I should not have uttered— what I wanted least to say. But it had been said, and I was covered with confusion. The necessity of saying something to bridge over this chasm of insensate indiscretion tugged at my senses, and finally—after what had seemed an age of silence— I stammered on:

" What I mean is, we never liked each other. Why, the first time we ever met, we fought. You cannot remember it, but we did. He knocked me into the ashes. And then there was our dispute at Albany—in the Patroon's mansion, you will recall. And then at Quebec. I have never told you of this," I went on, recklessly, " but we met that morning in the snow, as Montgomery fell. He knew me, dark as it still was, and we grappled. This scar here," I

21

pointed to a reddish seam across my temple and cheek, "this was his doing."

I have said that I could never meet Daisy in these days without feeling that, mere chronology to the opposite notwithstanding, she was much the older and more competent person of the two. This sense of juvenility overwhelmed me now, as she calmly rose and put her hand on my shoulder, and took a restful, as it were maternal, charge of me and my mind.

"My dear Douw," she said, with as fine an assumption of quiet, composed superiority as if she had not up to that moment been talking the veriest nonsense, "I understand just what you mean. Do not think, if I seem sometimes thoughtless or indifferent, that I am not aware of your feelings, or that I fail to appreciate the fondness you have always given me. I know what you would have said——"

"It was exactly what I most of all would *not* have said," I broke in with, in passing.

"Even so. But do you think, silly boy, that the thought was new to me? Of course we shall never speak of it again, but I am not altogether sorry it was referred to. It gives me the chance to say to you"—her voice softened and wavered here, as she looked around the dear old room, reminiscent in every detail of our youth—"to say to you that, wherever my duty may be, my heart is here, here under this roof where I was so happy, and where the two best men I shall ever know loved me so tenderly, so truly, as daughter and sister."

There were tears in her eyes at the end, but she was calm and self-sustained enough.

She was very firmly of opinion that it was her
duty to go to Cairncross at once, and nothing I could
say sufficed to dissuade her.   So it turned out that
the afternoon and evening of this important day were
devoted to convoying across to Cairncross the whole
Cedars establishment, I myself accompanying Daisy
and Mr. Stewart in the carriage around by the Johnstown road.   Rab was civil almost to the point of
servility, but, to make assurance doubly sure, I sent
up a guard of soldiers to the house that very night,
brought Master Rab down to be safely locked up by
the sheriff at Johnstown, and left her Enoch instead.

CHAPTER XXX.

FROM THE SCYTHE AND REAPER TO THE MUSKET.

AND now, with all the desperate energy of men who risked everything that mortal can have in jeopardy, we prepared to meet the invasion.

The tidings of the next few days but amplified what Enoch had told us. Thomas Spencer, the half-breed, forwarded full intelligence of the approaching force ; Oneida runners brought in stories of its magnitude, with which the forest glades began to be vocal ; Colonel Gansevoort, working night and day to put into a proper state of defence the dilapidated fort at the Mohawk's headwaters, sent down urgent demands for supplies, for more men, and for militia support.

At the most, General Schuyler could spare him but two hundred men, for Albany was in sore panic at the fall of Ticonderoga and the menace of Burgoyne's descent in force through the Champlain country. We watched this little troop march up the river road in a cloud of dust, and realized that this was the final thing Congress and the State could do for us. What more was to be done we men of the Valley must do for ourselves.

It was almost welcome, this grim, blood-red reality

of peril which now stared-us in the face, so good and wholesome a change did it work in the spirit of the Valley. Despondency vanished ; the cavillers who had disparaged Washington and Schuyler, sneered at stout Governor Clinton, and doubted all things save that matters would end badly, ceased their grumbling and took heart ; men who had wavered and been luke-warm or suspicious came forward now and threw in their lot with their neighbors. And if here and there on the hillsides were silent houses whence no help was to come, and where, if the enemy once broke through, he would be welcomed the more as a friend if his hands were spattered with our blood—the consciousness, I say, that we had these base traitors in our midst only gave us a deeper resolution not to fail.

General Herkimer presently issued his order to the Tryon militia, apprising them of the imminent danger, and summoning all between sixteen and sixty to arms. There was no doubt now where the blow would fall. Cherry Valley, Unadilla, and the Sacondaga settlements no longer feared raids from the wilderness upon their flanks. The invaders were coming forward in a solid mass, to strike square at the Valley's head. There we must meet them !

It warms my old heart still to recall the earnestness and calm courage of that summer fortnight of preparation. All up and down the Valley bottom-lands the haying was in progress. Young and old, rich and poor, came out to carry forward this work in common. The meadows were taken in their order, some toiling with scythe and sickle, others

standing guard at the forest borders of the field
to protect the workers. It was a goodly yield that
year, I remember, and never in my knowledge was
the harvest gathered and housed better or more
thoroughly than in this period of genuine danger,
when no man knew whose cattle would feed upon
his hay a month hence. The women and girls
worked beside the men, and brought them cooling
drinks of ginger, molasses, and vinegar, and spread
tables of food in the early evening shade for the
weary gleaners. These would march home in
bodies, a little later, those with muskets being at
the front and rear; and then, after a short night's
honest sleep, the rising sun would find them again
at work upon some other farm.

There was something very good and strengthen-
ing in this banding together to get the hay in for all.
During twenty years of peace and security, we had
grown selfish and solitary—each man for himself.
We had forgotten, in the strife for individual gain
and preferment, the true meaning of that fine old
word " neighbor "—the husbandman, or *boer*, who is
nigh, and to whom in nature you first look for help
and sympathy and friendship. It was in this fortnight of common peril that we saw how truly we
shared everything, even life itself, and how good
it was to work for as well as to fight for one another
—each for all, and all for each. Forty years have
gone by since that summer, yet still I seem to discover in the Mohawk Valley the helpful traces of
that fortnight's harvesting in common. The poor
bauers and squatters from the bush came out then

and did their share of the work, and we went back
with them into their forest clearings and beaver-flies
and helped them get in their small crops, in turn.
And to this day there is more brotherly feeling here
between the needy and the well-to-do than I know
of anywhere else.

When the barns were filled, and the sweet-smell-
ing stacks outside properly built and thatched, the
scythe was laid aside for the musket, the sickle for
the sword and pistol. All up the Valley the drums'
rattle drowned the drone of the locusts in the
stubble. The women moulded bullets now and
filled powder-horns instead of making drinks for the
hay-field. There was no thought anywhere save of
preparation for the march. Guns were cleaned,
flints replaced, new hickory ramrods whittled out,
and the grindstones threw off sparks under the pressure of swords and spear-heads. Even the little
children were at work rubbing goose-grease into the
hard leather of their elders' foot-gear, against the
long tramp to Fort Stanwix.

By this time, the first of August, we knew more
about the foe we were to meet. The commander
whom Enoch had heard called Sillinger was learned
to be one Colonel St. Leger, a British officer of distinction, which might have been even greater if he
had not embraced the Old-World military vice of his
day—grievous drunkenness. The gathering of Indians at Oswego under Claus and Brant was larger
than the first reports had made it. The regular
troops, both British and German, intended for our
destruction, were said to alone outnumber the whole

militia force which we could hope to oppose to them.
But most of all we thought of the hundreds of our
old Tory neighbors, who were bringing this army
down upon us to avenge their own fancied wrongs ;
and when we thought of them we moodily rattled
the bullets in our deerskin bags, and bent the steel
more fiercely upon the whirling, hissing stone.

I have read much of war, both ancient and modern.
I declare solemnly that in no chronicle of warfare in
any country, whether it be of great campaigns like
those of Marlborough and the late King of Prussia,
and that strange Buonaparte, half god, half devil,
who has now been caged at last at St. Hélena ;
of brutal invasions by a foreign enemy, as when
the French overran and desolated the Palatinate ;
or of buccaneering and piratical enterprise by the
Spaniards and Portuguese ; or of the fighting of
savages or of the Don Cossacks—in none of these
records, I aver, can you find so much wanton base-
ness and beast-like bloodthirstiness as these native-
born Tories showed toward us. Mankind has not
been capable of more utter cruelty and wickedness
than were in their hearts. Beside them the lowest
painted heathen in their train was a Christian, the
most ignorant Hessian peasant was a nobleman.

Ever since my talk with Colonel Dayton I had
been trying to look upon these Tories as men who,
however mistaken, were acting from a sense of duty.
For a full year it seemed as if I had succeeded ; indeed, more than once, so temperately did I bring myself in my new philosophy to think of them, I was
warned by my elders that it would be better for me

to keep my generous notions to myself. But now, when the stress came, all this philanthropy fell away. These men were leading down to their old home an army of savages and alien soldiers ; they were boasting that we, their relatives or whilom school-fellows, neighbors, friends, should be slaughtered like rats in a pit ; their commander, St. Leger, published at their instigation general orders offering his Indians twenty dollars apiece for the scalps of our men, women, and children ! How could one pretend not to hate such monsters ?

At least I did not pretend any longer, but worked with an ,enthusiasm I had never known before to marshal our yeomanry together.

Under the pelting July sun, in the saddle from morning till night—to Cherry Valley, to Stone Arabia, to the obscure little groups of cabins in the bush, to the remote settlements on the Unadilla and the East Creek—organizing, suggesting, pleading, sometimes, I fear, also cursing a little, my difficult work was at last done. The men of the Mohawk district regiment, who came more directly under my eye, were mustered at Caughnawaga, and some of the companies that were best filled despatched forward under Captain Adam Fonda, who was all impatience to get first to Fort Dayton, the general rendezvous. In all we were likely to gather to- gether in this regiment one hundred and thirty men, and this was better than a fortnight ago had seemed possible.

They were sturdy fellows for the most part, tall, deep-chested, and hard of muscle. They came from the high forest clearings of Kingsland and Tribes Hill, from the lower Valley flatlands near to Schenectady, from the bush settlements scattered back on Aries Creek, from the rich farms and villages of Johnstown, and Caughnawaga, and Spraker's. There were among them all sorts and conditions of men, thrifty and thriftless, cautious and imprudent, the owners of slaves along with poor yokels of scarcely higher estate than the others' niggers. Here were posted thick in the roll-call such names as Fonda, Starin, Yates, Sammons, Gardenier, and Wemple. Many of the officers, and some few of the men, had rough imitations of uniform, such as homemade materials and craft could command, but these varied largely in style and color. The great majority of the privates wore simply their farm homespun, gray and patched, and some had not even their hat-brims turned up with a cockade. But they had a look on their sunburned, gnarled, and honest faces which the Butlers and Johnsons might well have shrunk from.

These men of the Mohawk district spoke more Dutch than anything else, though there were both English and High German tongues among them. They had more old acquaintances among the Tories than had their Palatine friends up the river, for this had been the Johnsons' own district. Hence, though in numbers we were smaller than the regiments that mustered above at Stone Arabia and Zimmerman's, at Canajoharie and Cherry Valley, we were richer in hate.

At daybreak on August 2, the remaining companies of this regiment were to start on their march up the Valley. I rode home to my mother's house late in the afternoon of the 1st, to spend what might be a last night under her roof. On the morrow, Samson Sammons and Jelles Fonda, members of the Committee of Safety, and I, could easily overtake the column on our horses.

I was greatly perplexed and unsettled in mind about Daisy and my duty toward her, and, though I turned this over in my thoughts the whole distance, I could come to no satisfactory conclusion. On the one hand, I yearned to go and say farewell to her; on the other, it was not clear, after that letter of her husband's, that I could do this without unjustly prejudicing her as a wife. For the wife of this viper she still was, and who could tell how soon she might not be in his power again?

I was still wrestling with this vexatious question when I came to my mother's house. I tied the horse to the fence till Tulp should come out for him, and went in, irresolutely. At every step it seemed to me as if I ought instead to be going toward Cairncross.

Guess my surprise at being met, almost upon the threshold, by the very woman of whom of all others I had been thinking! My mother and she had apparently made up their differences, and stood together waiting for me.

"Were you going away, Douw, without coming to see me—to say good-by?" asked Daisy, with a soft reproach in her voice. "Your mother tells me of your starting to-morrow—for the battle."

I took her hand, and, despite my mother's presence, continued to hold it in mine. This was bold, but there was little enough of bravery in my words.

"Yes, we go to-morrow; I wanted to come—all day I have been thinking of little else—yet I feared that my visit might—might——"

Very early in this tale it was my pride to explain that my mother was a superior woman. Faults of temper she may have had, and eke narrow prejudices on sundry points. But she had also great good sense, which she showed now by leaving the room.

"I came to you instead, you see," my dear girl said, trying to smile, yet with a quivering lip; "I could not have slept, I could not have borne to live almost, it seems, if I had let you ride off without a word, without a sign."

We stood thus facing each other for a moment— I mumbling forth some commonplaces of explanation, she looking intently into my eyes. Then with a sudden deep outburst of anguish, moaning piteously, "*Must you truly go?*" she came, nay, almost fell into my arms, burying her face on my shoulder and weeping violently.

It is not meet that I should speak much of the hour that followed. I would, in truth, pass over it wholly in silence—as being too sacred a thing for aught of disclosure or speculation—were it not that some might, in this case, think lightly of the pure and good woman who, unduly wrung by years of grief, disappointment, and trial, now, from very weariness of soul, sobbed upon my breast. And that would be intolerable.

We sat side by side in the little musty parlor. I did not hold her hand, or so much as touch her gown with my knee or foot.

We talked of impersonal things—of the coming invasion, of the chances of relieving Fort Stanwix, of the joy it would be to me if I could bear a good part in rescuing my dear friend Gansevoort, its brave young commandant. I told her about Peter, and of how we two had consorted together in Albany, and later in Quebec. And this led us back—as we had so often returned before during these latter hateful months—to the sweet companionship of our own childhood and youth. She, in turn, talked of Mr. Stewart, who seemed less strong and contented in his new home at Cairncross. He had much enjoyment now, she said, in counting over a rosary of beads which had been his mother's, reiterating a prayer for each one in the Romish fashion, and he was curiously able to remember these long-disused formulas of his boyhood, even while he forgot the things of yesterday. I commented upon this, pointing out to her that this is the strange quality of the Roman faith—that its forms and customs, learned in youth, remain in the affections of Papists to their dying day, even after many years of neglect and unbelief; whereas in the severe, Spanish-drab Protestantism to which I was reared, if one once loses interest in the tenets themselves, there is nothing whatever left upon which the mind may linger pleasantly.

Thus our conversation ran—decorous and harmless enough, in all conscience. And if the thoughts

masked by these words were all of a forbidden subject; if the very air about us was laden with sweet
influences; if, when our eyes met, each read in the
other's glance a whole world of meaning evaded in
our talk—were we to blame?'

I said "no" then, in my own heart, honestly. I
say it now. Why, think you! This love of ours
was as old as our intelligence itself. Looking back,
we could trace its soft touch upon every little
childish incident we had in common memory; the
cadence of its music bore forward, tenderly, sweetly,
the song of all that had been happy in our lives.
We were man and woman now, wise and grave by
reason of sorrow and pain and great trials. These
had come upon us both because neither of us had
frankly said, at a time when to have said it would
have been to alter all, "I love you!" And this we
must not say to each other even now, by all the
bonds of mutual honor and self-respect. But not
any known law, human or divine, could hold our
thoughts in leash. So we sat and talked of common things, calmly and without restraint, and our
minds were leagues away, in fields of their own
choosing, amid sunshine and flowers and the low
chanting of love's cherubim.

We said farewell, instinctively, before my mother
returned. I held her hands in mine, and, as if she
had been a girl again, gently kissed the white forehead she as gently inclined to me.

"Poor old father is to burn candles for your
safety," she said, with a soft smile, "and I will pray
too. Oh, do spare yourself! Come back to us!"

"I feel it in my bones," I answered, stoutly. "Fear nothing, I shall come back."

The tall, bright-eyed, shrewd old dame, my mother, came in at this, and Daisy consented to stop for supper with us, but not to spend the night with one of my sisters as was urged. I read her reason to be that she shrank from a second and public farewell in the morning.

The supper was almost a cheery meal. The women would have readily enough made it doleful, I fancy, but my spirits were too high for that. There were birds singing in my heart. My mother from time to time looked at me searchingly, as if to guess the cause of this elation, but I doubt she was as mystified as I then thought.

At twilight I stood bareheaded and watched Daisy drive away, with Enoch and Tulp as a mounted escort. The latter was also to remain with her during my absence—and Major Mauverensen almost envied his slave.

CHAPTER XXXI.

THE RENDEZVOUS OF FIGHTING MEN AT FORT DAYTON.

I SHALL not easily forget the early breakfast next morning, or the calm yet serious air with which my mother and two unmarried sisters went about the few remaining duties of preparing for my departure. For all they said, they might have been getting me ready for a fishing excursion, but it would be wrong to assume that they did not think as gravely as if they had flooded the kitchen with tears.

Little has been said of these good women in the course of my story, for the reason that Fate gave them very little to do with it, and the narrative is full long as it is, without the burden of extraneous personages. But I would not have it thought that we did not all love one another, and stand up for one another, because we kept cool about it.

During this last year, in truth, my mother and I had seen more of each other than for all the time before since my infancy, and in the main had got on admirably together. Despite the affectation of indifference in her letter, she did not lack for pride in my being a major; it is true that she exhibited little of this emotion to me, fearing its effect upon my vanity, doubtless, but her neighbors and gossips heard a good deal from it, I fancy. It was in her nature to be proud, and she had right to be; for what other widow in the Valley, left in sore poverty with a household of children, had, like her, by individual exertions, thrift, and keen management, brought all that family well up, purchased and paid for her own homestead and farm, and laid by enough for a comfortable old age? Not one! She therefore was justified in respecting herself and exacting respect from others, and it pleased me that she should have satisfaction as well in my advancement. But she did ruffle me sometimes by seeking to manage my business for me—she never for a moment doubting that it was within her ability to make a much better major than I was—and by ever and anon selecting some Valley maiden for me to marry. This last became a veritable infliction, so that I finally assured her I should never marry—my heart being irrevocably fixed upon a hopelessly unattainable ideal.

I desired her to suppose that this referred to some Albany woman, but I was never skilful in indirection, and I do not believe that she was at all deceived.

The time came soon enough when I must say good-by. My carefully packed bags were carried out and fastened to the saddle. Tall, slender, high-browed Margaret sadly sewed a new cockade of her own making upon my hat, and round-faced, red-cheeked Gertrude tied my sash and belt about me in silence. I kissed them both with more feeling than in all their lives before I had known for them, and when my mother followed me to the horse-block, and embraced me again, the tears could not be kept

22

back. After all, I was her only boy, and it was to war in its deadliest form that I was going.

And then the thought came to me—how often in that cruel week it had come to fathers, husbands, brothers, in this sunny Valley of ours, leaving homes they should never see again!—that nothing but our right arms could save these women, my own flesh and blood, from the hatchet and scalping-knife.

I swung myself into the saddle sternly at this thought, and gripped the reins hard and pushed my weight upon the stirrups. By all the gods, I should not take this ride for nothing!

" Be of good heart, mother," I said, between my teeth. " We shall drive the scoundrels back—such as we do not feed to the wolves."

" Ay! And do you your part!" said this fine old daughter of the men who through eighty years of warfare broke the back of Spain. " Remember that you are a Van Hoorn!"

" I shall not forget."

" And is that young Philip Cross—*her* husband—with Johnson's crew?"

" Yes, he is."

" Then if he gets back to Canada alive, you are not the man your grandfather Baltus was!"

These were her last words, and they rang in my ears long after I had joined Fonda and Sammons at Caughnawaga, and we had started westward to overtake the regiment. If I could find this Philip Cross, there was nothing more fixed in my mind than the resolve to kill him.

We rode for the most part without conversation

along the rough, sun-baked road, the ruts of which
had here and there been trampled into fine dust by
the feet of the soldiers marching before.   When we
passed houses near the highway, women and children came to the doors to watch us; other women
and children we could see working in the gardens or
among the rows of tall corn.   But save for now and
then an aged gaffer, sitting in the sunshine with his
pipe, there were no men.   All those who could bear
a musket were gone to meet the invasion.   Two
years of war in other parts had drained the Valley
of many of its young men, who could not bear peace
at home while there were battles at the North or
in the Jerseys, and were serving in every army which
Congress controlled, from Champlain and the Delaware to Charleston.   And now this levy for home
defence had swept the farms clean.

We had late dinner, I remember, at the house of
stout old Peter Wormuth, near the Palatine church.
Both he and his son Matthew—a friend of mine
from boyhood, who was to survive Oriskany only
to be shot down near Cherry Valley next year by
Joseph Brant—had of course gone forward with
the Palatine militia.   The women gave us food and
drink, and I recall that Matthew's young wife, who
had been Gertrude Shoemaker and was General
Herkimer's niece, wept bitterly when we left, and
we shouted back to her promises to keep watch over
her husband.   It is curious to think that when I
next saw this young woman, some years later, she
was the wife of Major John Frey.

It was a stiff ride on to overtake the stalwart yeomen of our regiment, which we did not far from a point opposite the upper Canajoharie Castle. The men had halted here, weary after their long, hot march, and were sprawling on the grass and in the shade of the bushes. The sun was getting low on the distant hills of the Little Falls, and there came up a refreshing stir of air from the river. Some were for encamping here for the night ; others favored going on to the Falls. It annoyed me somewhat to find that this question was apparently to be left to the men themselves, Colonel Visscher not seeming able or disposed to decide for himself.

Across the stream, in the golden August haze, we could see the roofs of the Mohawks' village—or castle as they called it. Some of the men idly proposed to go over and stampede or clear out this nest of red vermin, but the idea was not seriously taken up. Perhaps if it had been, much might have been changed for the better. Nothing is clearer than that Molly Brant, who with her bastard brood and other Mohawk wómen was then living there, sent up an emissary to warn her brother Joseph of our coming, and that it was upon this information he acted to such fell purpose. Doubtless if we had gone over and seized the castle and its inmates then, that messenger would never have been sent. But we are all wise when we look backward.

By the afternoon of the next day, August 3, the mustering at Fort Dayton was complete. No one of the thirty-three companies of Tryon County militia was absent, and though some sent barely a score of men, still no more were to be expected. Such as the little army was, it must suffice. There were of more or less trained militiamen nearly six hundred. Of artisan volunteers, of farmers who had no place in the regular company formations, and of citizens whose anxiety to be present was unfortunately much in excess of their utility, there were enough to bring the entire total up to perhaps two-score over eight hundred. Our real and effective fighting force was about half-way between these two figures — I should say about seven hundred strong.

It was the first time that the whole Tryon militia had been gathered together, and we looked one another over with curiosity. Though called into common action by a common peril, the nearness of which made the Mohawk Valley seem a very small place and its people all close neighbors, the men assembled here represented the partial settlement of a country larger than any one of several European monarchies.

As there were all sorts and grades of dress, ranging from the spruce blue and buff of some of the officers, through the gray homespun and linsey-woolsey of the farmer privates, to the buckskin of the trappers and huntsmen, so there were all manner of weapons, all styles of head-gear and equipment, all fashions of faces. There were Germans of half a dozen different types, there were Dutch, there were Irish and Scotch Presbyterians, there were stray French Huguenots, and even Englishmen, and here and there a Yankee settler from New England.

Many there were who with difficulty understood each other, as when the Scotch Campbells and Clydes of Cherry Valley, for example, essayed to talk with the bush-Germans from above Zimmerman's.

Notable among the chief men of the communities here, so to speak, huddled together for safety, was old Isaac Paris, the foremost man of Stone Arabia. He should now be something over sixty years of age, yet had children at home scarce out of the cradle, and was so hale and strong in bearing that he seemed no less fit for battle and hardship than his strapping son Peter, who was not yet eighteen. These two laid their lives down together within this dread week of which I write. I shall never forget how fine and resolute a man the old colonel looked, with his good clothes of citizen make, as became a member of the State Senate and one of the Committee of Safety, yet with as martial a bearing as any. He was a Frenchman from Strasbourg, but spoke like a German ; no man of us all looked forward to fighting with greater appetite, though he had been always a quiet merchant and God-fearing, peaceful burgher.

Colonel Ebenezer Cox, a somewhat arrogant and solitary man for whom I had small liking, now commanded the Canajoharie regiment in place of Herkimer the Brigadier-General ; there were at the head of the other regiments stout Colonel Peter Bellinger, the capable and determined Colonel Jacob Klock, and our own Colonel Frederick Visscher. Almost all of the Committee of Safety were here—most of them being also officers in the militia ; but others, like Paris, John Dygert, Samson Sammons, Jacob Snell, and Samuel Billington, coming merely as lookers-on. In short, no well-known Whig of the Valley seemed absent as we looked the gathering over, and scarcely a familiar family name was lacking on our lists, which it was now my business to check off.

Whole households of strong men marched together. There were nine Snells, all relatives, in the patriot ranks ; so far as I can remember, there were five Bellingers, five Seebers, five Wagners, and five Wollovers—and it may well be five of more than one other family.

The men of the different settlements formed groups by themselves at the first, and arranged their own separate camping-places for the night. But soon, as was but natural, they discovered acquaintances from other parts, and began to mingle, sitting in knots or strolling about the outer palisades or on the clearing beyond. The older men who had borne a part in the French war told stories of that time, which, indeed, had now a new, deep interest for us, not only in that we were to face an invading force greater and more to be dreaded than was Bellêtre's, but because we were encamped on historic ground.

From the gentle knoll upon which the blockhouse and stockade of Fort Dayton were now reared we could see the site of that first little Palatine settlement that had then been wiped so rudely from the face of the earth ; and our men revived memories of that dreadful night, and talked of them in a low voice as the daylight faded.

The scene affected me most gravely. I looked at the forest-clad range of northern hills over which the French and Indian horde stole in the night, and tried to picture their stealthy approach in my mind.⟩ Below us, flowing tranquilly past the willow-hedged farms of the German Flatts settlers, lay the Mohawk. The white rippling overcast on the water marked the shallow ford through which the panic-stricken refugees crowded in affright in the wintry darkness, and where, in the crush, that poor forgotten woman, the widow of an hour, was trampled under foot, swept away by the current, drowned !

How miraculous it seemed that her baby girl should have been saved, should have been brought to Mr. Stewart's door, and placed in the very sanctuary of my life, by the wilful freak of a little English boy ! And how marvellous that this self-same boy, her husband now, should be among the captains of a new and more sinister invasion of our Valley, and that I should be in arms with my neighbors to stay his progress ! Truly here was food enough for thought.

But there was little time for musing. After supper, when most of the rest were free to please themselves, to gossip, to set night-lines in the river against breakfast, or to carve rough initials on their powder-horns in emulation of the art-work displayed by the ingenious Petrie boys, I was called to the council held by General Herkimer in one of the rooms of the fort. There were present some of those already mentioned, and I think that Colonel Wesson, the Massachusetts officer whose troops garrisoned the place, was from courtesy also invited to take part, though if he was there he said nothing. Thomas Spencer, the Seneca half-breed blacksmith, who had throughout been our best friend, had come down, and with him was Skenandoah, the war-chief of the Oneidas, whom Dominie Kirkland had kept in our interest.

The thing most talked of, I remember, was the help that these Oneidas could render us. General Schuyler had all along shrunk from the use of savages on the Continental side, and hence had required only friendly neutrality of the Oneidas, whose chief villages lay between us and the foe. But these Indians now saw clearly, that, if the invasion succeeded, they would be exterminated not a whit the less ruthlessly by their Iroquois brothers because they had held aloof. In the grim code of the savage, as in the softened law of the Christian, those who were not for him were against him. So the noble old Oneida war-chief had come to us to say that his people, standing as it were between the devil and the deep sea, preferred to at least die like men, fighting for their lives. Skenandoah was reputed even then to be seventy years of age, but he had the square shoulders, full, corded neck, and sharp glance of a man of forty. Only last year he died, at a great age—said to be one hundred and ten years—and was buried on Clinton Hill beside his good friend Kirkland, whom for half a century he had loved so well.

There were no two opinions in the council: let the Oneidas join us with their war-party, by all means.

After this had been agreed upon, other matters came up—the quantity of stores we should take, the precedence of the regiments, the selection of the men to be sent ahead to apprise Gansevoort of our approach. But these do not concern the story.

It was after this little gathering had broken up, and the candles been blown out, that General Herkimer put his hand on my shoulder and said, in his quaint German dialect :

" Come, walk with me outside the fort."

We went together across the parade in the growing dusk. ، Most of those whom we passed recognized my companion, and greeted him—more often, I am bound to say, with " Guten Abend, Honikol!" than with the salute due to his rank. There was, indeed, very little notion of discipline in this rough, simple militia gathering.

We walked outside the ditch to a grassy clearing toward the Flatts where we could pace back and forth without listeners, and yet could see the sentries posted at the corners of the forest enclosure. Then the honest old Brigadier laid open his heart to me.

" I wish to God we were well out of this all," he said, almost gloomily.

I was taken aback at this. Dejection was last to be looked for in this brave, stout-hearted old frontier fighter. I asked, " What is wrong?" feeling that surely there must be some cause for despondency I knew not of.

" *I* am wrong," he said, simply.

" I do not understand you, Brigadier."

"I wish to God we were well out of this all," he said almost gloomily.

" Say rather that *they*, who ought to know me better, do not understand me."

" They ? Whom do you mean ? "

" All these men about us—Isaac Paris, Ebenezer Cox the colonel of my own regiment, Fritz Visscher, and many more. I can see it—they suspect me. Nothing could be worse than that."

" Suspect *you*, Brigadier ! It is pure fancy ! You are dreaming ! "

" No, I am very much awake, young man. You have not heard them—I have ! It has been as much as flung in my face to-day that my brother Hon-Yost is a colonel with Johnson—up yonder."

The little man pointed westward with his hand to where the last red lights of day were paling over the black line of trees.

" He is with them," he said, bitterly, " and I am blamed for it. Then, too, my brother Hendrick hides himself away in Stone Arabia, and is not of us, and his son *is* with the Tories—up yonder."

" But your brother George is here with us, as true a man as will march to-morrow."

" Then I have a sister married to Dominie Rosencranz, and he is a Tory ; and another married to Hendrick Frey, and *he* is a Tory, too. All this is thrown in my teeth. I do not pass two men with their heads together but I feel they are talking of this."

" Why should they ? You have two other brothers-in-law here in camp—Peter Bellinger and George Bell. You imagine a vain thing, Brigadier. Believe me, I have seen or heard no hint of this."

" You would not. You are an officer of the line

—the only one here. Besides, you are Schuyler's man. They would not talk before you."

" But I am Valley born, Valley bred, as much as any of you. Wherein am I different from the others? Why should they keep me in the dark? They are all my friends, just as—if you would only believe it—they are yours as well."

"Young man," said the General, in a low, impressive voice, and filling and lighting his pipe as he slowly spoke, " if you come back alive, and if you get to be of my age, you will know some things that you don't know now. Danger makes men brave; it likewise makes them selfish and jealous. We are going out together, all of us, to try what, with God's help, we can do. Behind us, down the river, are our wives or our sweethearts ; some of you leave children, others leave mothers and sisters. We are going forward to save them from death or worse than death, and to risk our lives for them and for our homes. Yet, I tell you candidly, there are men here—back here in this fort—who would almost rather see us fail, than see me win my rank in the State line."

"I cannot credit that."

" Then—why else should they profess to doubt me? Why should they bring up my brothers' names to taunt me with their treason? "

Alas ! I could not tell. We walked up and down, I remember, until long after darkness fell full upon us, and the stars were all aglow—I trying my best to dissuade the honest Brigadier from his gloomy conviction.

To be frank, although he doubtless greatly exaggerated the feeling existing against him, it to a degree did exist.

The reasons for it are not difficult of comprehension. There were not a few officers in our force who were better educated than bluff, unlettered old Honikol Herkimer, and who had seen something of the world outside our Valley. It nettled their pride to be under a plain little German, who spoke English badly, and could not even spell his own name twice alike. There were at work under the surface, too, old trade and race jealousies, none the less strong because those upon whom they acted scarcely realized their presence. The Herkimers were the great family on the river from the Little Falls westward, and there were ancient rivalries, unexpressed but still potent, between them and families down the Valley. Thus, when some of the Herkimers and their connections—a majority, for that matter—either openly joined the enemy or held coldly apart from us, it was easy for these jealous promptings to take the form of doubt and suspicions as to the whole-hearted loyalty of the Brigadier himself. Once begun, these cruelly unjust suspicions rankled in men's minds and spread.

All this I should not mention were it not the key to the horrible tragedy which followed. It is this alone which explains how a trained Indian fighter, a veteran frontiersman like Herkimer, was spurred and stung into rushing headlong upon the death-trap, as if he had been any ignorant and wooden-headed Braddock.

We started on the march westward next day, the 4th, friendly Indians bringing us news that the van of the enemy had appeared on the evening of the 2d before Fort Stanwix, and had already begun an investment. We forded the river at Fort Schuyler, just below where Utica now stands, and pushed slowly forward through the forest, over the rude and narrow road, to the Oneida village of Oriska, something to the east of the large creek which bears the name Oriskany.

Here we halted a second time, encamping at our leisure, and despatching, on the evening of the 5th, Adam Helmer and two other scouts to penetrate to the fort and arrange a sortie by the garrison, simultaneous with our attack.

CHAPTER XXXII.

"THE BLOOD BE ON YOUR HEADS."

A BRIGHT, hot sun shone upon us the next morning—the never-to-be-forgotten 6th. There would have been small need for any waking rattle of the drums; the sultry heat made all willing to rise from the hard, dry ground, where sleep had been difficult enough even in the cooler darkness. At six o'clock the camp, such as it was, was all astir.

Breakfast was eaten in little groups squatted about in the clearing, or in the shade of the trees at its edges, members of families or close neighbors clustering together in parties once more, to share victuals prepared by the same housewives—it may be from the same oven or spit. It might well happen that for many of us this was the last meal on earth, for we were within hearing of the heavy guns of the fort, and when three of these should be fired in succession we were to take up our final six-miles' march. But this reflection made no one sad, apparently. Everywhere you could hear merry converse and sounds of laughter. Listening, no one would have dreamed that this body of men stood upon the threshold of so grave an adventure.

I had been up earlier than most of the others, and had gone over to the spot where the horses

were tethered. Of these animals there were some
dozen, all told, and their appearance showed that
they had had a bad night of it with the flies. After
I had seen them led to water and safely brought
back, and had watched that in the distribution of
the scanty store of oats my steed had his proper
share, I came back to breakfast with the Stone
Arabia men, among whom I had many acquaintances. I contributed some sausages and slices of
bread and meat, I remember, to the general stock
of food, which was spread out upon one of Isaac
Paris's blankets. We ate with a light heart, half-
lying on the parched grass around the extemporized
cloth. Some of the young farmers, their meal
already finished, were up on their feet, scuffling and
wrestling in jest and high spirits. They laughed so
heartily from time to time that Mr. Paris would call
out: "Less noise there, you, or we shall not hear
the cannon from the fort!"

No one would have thought that this was the
morning before a battle.

Eight o'clock arrived, and still there had been no
signal. All preparations had long since been made.
The saddle-horses of the officers were ready under
the shade, their girths properly tightened. Blankets
had been rolled up and strapped, haversacks and
bags properly repacked, a last look taken to flints
and priming. The supply-wagon stood behind
where the General's tent had been, all laden for the
start, and with the horses harnessed to the pole.
Still no signal came!

The men began to grow uneasy with the waiting.

It had been against the prevalent feeling of impatience that we halted here the preceding day, instead of hastening forward to strike the blow. Now every minute's inaction increased this spirit of restlessness. The militiamen's faces—already saturnine enough, what with broken rest and three days' stubble of beard—were clouding over with dislike for the delay.

The sauntering to and fro began to assume a general trend toward the headquarters of the Brigadier. I had visited this spot once or twice before during the early morning to offer suggestions or receive commands. I went again now, having it in mind to report to the General the evident impatience of the men. A doubt was growing with me, too, whether we were not too far away to be sure of hearing the guns from the fort—quite six miles distant.

The privacy of the commander was indifferently secured by the posting of sentries, who guarded a square perhaps forty feet each way. In the centre of this enclosure was a clump of high bushes, with one or two young trees, bunched upon the bank of a tiny rivulet now almost dried up. Here, during the night, the General's small army-tent had been pitched, and here now, after the tent had been packed on the wagon, he sat, on the only chair in camp, under the shadow of the bushes, within full view of his soldiers. These were by this time gathered three or four deep around the three front sides of the square, and were gradually pushing the sentries in. Five or six officers stood about the Gen-

23

eral, talking earnestly with him and with one another, and the growing crowd outside the square were visibly anxious to hear what was going on.

I have said before, I think, that I was the only officer of the Continental line in the whole party. This fact, and some trifling differences between my uniform and that of the militia colonels and majors, had attracted notice, not wholly of an admiring sort. I had had the misfortune, moreover, to learn in camp before Quebec to shave every day, as regularly as if at home, with the result that I was probably the only man in the clearing that morning who wore a clean face. This served further to make me a marked man among such of the farmer boys as knew me only by sight. As I pushed my way through the throng to get inside the square, I heard various comments by strangers from Canajoharie or Cherry Valley way.

"There goes Schuyler's Dutchman," said one. "He has brought his *friseur* with him."

"It would have been more to the point if he had brought some soldiers. Albany would see us hang before she would help us," growled another.

"Make way for Mynheer," said a rough joker in the crowd, half-laughing, half-scowling. "What they need inside yonder is some more Dutch prudence. When they have heard him they will vote to go into winter quarters and fight next spring!"

All this was disagreeable enough, but it was wisest to pretend not to hear, and I went forward to the groups around the Brigadier.

The question under debate was, of course, whether

we should wait longer for the signal; or, rather, whether it had not been already fired, and the sound failed to reach us on the sultry, heavy air. There were two opinions upon this, and for a time the difference was discussed in amiability, if with some heat. The General felt positive that if the shots had been fired we must have heard them.

I seem to see him now, the brave old man, as he sat there on the rough stool, imperturbably smoking, and maintaining his own against the dissenting officers. Even after some of them grew vexed, and declared that either the signal had been fired or the express had been captured, and that in either case it would be worse than folly to longer remain here, he held his temper. Perhaps his keen black eyes sparkled the brighter, but he kept his tongue calm, and quietly reiterated his arguments. The beleaguering force outside the fort, he said, must outnumber ours two to one. They had artillery, and they had regular German troops, the best in Europe, not to mention many hundreds of Indians, all well armed and munitioned. It would be next to impossible to surprise an army thus supplied with scouts; it would be practically hopeless to attack them, unless we were backed up by a simultaneous sortie in force from the fort. In that, the Brigadier insisted, lay our only chance of success.

"But I say the sortie *will* be made! They are waiting for us—only we are too far off to hear their signal!" cried one of the impatient colonels.

"If the wind was in the east," said the Brigadier, "that might be the case. But in breathless air like this I have heard the guns from that fort two miles farther back."

"Our messengers may not have got through the lines last night," put in Thomas Spencer, the half-breed. "The swamp back of the fort is difficult travelling, even to one who knows it better than Helmer does, and Butler's Indians are not children, to see only straight ahead of their noses."

"Would it not be wise for Spencer here, and some of our young trappers, or some of Skenandoah's Indians, to go forward and spy out the land for us?" I asked.

"These would do little good now," answered Herkimer; "the chief thing is to know when Gansevoort is ready to come out and help us."

"The chief thing to know, by God," broke forth one of the colonels, with a great oath, "is whether we have a patriot or a Tory at our head!"

Herkimer's tanned and swarthy face changed color at this taunt. He stole a swift glance at me, as if to say, "This is what I warned you was to be looked for," and smoked his pipe for a minute in silence.

His brother-in-law, Colonel Peter Bellinger, took the insult less tamely.

"The man who says Honikol Herkimer is a Tory lies," he said, bluntly, with his hand on his sword-hilt, and honest wrath in his gray eyes.

"Peace, Peter," said the Brigadier. "Let them think what they like. It is not my affair. My business is to guard the lives of these young men here, as if I were their father. I am a childless man, yet here I am as the parent of all of them. I

could not go back again and look their mothers in
the eye if I had led them into trouble which could
be avoided."

" We are not here to avoid trouble, but rather to
seek it," shouted Colonel Cox, angrily.

He spoke loud enough to be heard by the throng
beyond, which now numbered four-fifths of our
whole force, and there rolled back to us from them
a loud answering murmur of approval. At the
sound of this, others came running up to learn what
was going on ; and the line, hitherto with difficulty
kept back by the sentries, was broken in in more
than one place. Matters looked bad for discipline,
or wise action of any sort.

" A man does not show his bravery by running his
head at a stone wall," said the Brigadier, still striving to keep his temper, but rising to his feet as he
spoke.

" *Will* you give the order to go on ? " demanded
Cox, in a fierce tone, pitched even higher.

" Lead us on ! " came loud shouts from many
places in the crowd. There was a general pushing in of the line now, and some men at the back,
misinterpreting this, began waving their hats and
cheering.

" Give us the word, Honikol ! " they yelled.

Still Herkimer stood his ground, though with
rising color.

" What for a soldier are you," he called out,
sharply, " to make mutiny like this ? Know you
not your duty better? "

" Our duty is to fight, not to sit around here in

idleness.   At least *we* are not cowards," broke in
another, who had supported Cox from the outset.

" *You !* " cried Herkimer, all roused at last.   " *You*
will be the first to run when you see the British ! "

There was no longer any pretence of keeping the
square.   The excited farmers pressed closely about
us now, and the clamor was rising momentarily.   All
thought of order or military grade was gone.   Men
who had no rank whatever thrust their loud voices
into the council, so that we could hear nothing
clearly.

There was a brief interchange of further hot words
between the Brigadier, Colonel Bellinger, and John
Frey on the one side, and the mutinous colonels
and men on the other.   I heard the bitter epithets
of " Tory " and " coward " hurled at the old man,
who stood with chin defiant in air, and dark eyes
ablaze, facing his antagonists.   The scene was so
shameful that I could scarce bear to look upon it.

There came a hurly-burly of confusion and tumult
as the shouts of the crowd grew more vehement,
and one of the refractory colonels impetuously drew
his sword and half turned as if to give the command
himself.

Then I heard Herkimer, too incensed to longer
control himself, cry : " If you will have it so, the
blood be on your heads."   He sprang upon the
stool at this, waved his sword, and shouted so that
all the eight hundred could hear :

" VORWÄRTS ! "

The tall pines themselves shook with the cheer
which the yeomen raised.

There was a scramble on the instant for muskets,
bags, and belongings. To rush was the order. We
under-officers caught the infection, and with no dignity at all hurried across the clearing to our horses.
We cantered back in a troop, Barent Coppernol
leading the Brigadier's white mare at a hand-gallop
by our side. Still trembling with excitement, yet
perhaps somewhat reconciled to the adventure by
the exultant spirit of the scene before him, General
Herkimer got into the saddle, and watched closely
the efforts of the colonels, now once more all gratified
enthusiasm, to bring their eager men into form. It
had been arranged that Cox with his Canajoharie
regiment should have the right of the line, and
this body was ready and under way in less time,
it seemed, than I have taken to write of it. The
General saw the other three regiments trooped, told
Visscher to bring the supply-wagon with the rear,
and then, with Isaac Paris, Jelles Fonda, and myself,
galloped to the head of the column, where Spencer
and Skenandoah with the Oneida Indians were.

So marching swiftly, and without scouts, we
started forth at about nine in the morning.

The road over which we hurried was as bad, even
in those hot, dry days of August, as any still to be
found in the Adirondacks. The bottom-lands of
the Mohawk Valley, as is well known, are of the
best farming soil in the world, but for that very
reason they make bad roads. The highway leading
to the fort lay for the most part over low and
springy land, and was cut through the thick beech
and hemlock forest almost in a straight line, regard-

less of swales and marshy places. These had been in some instances bridged indifferently by corduroys of logs, laid the previous spring when Gansevoort dragged up his cannon for the defence of the fort, and by this time too often loose and out of place. We on horseback found these rough spots even more trying than did the footmen ; but for all of us progress was slow enough, after the first excitement of the start had passed away.

There was no outlook at any point. We were hedged in everywhere by walls of foliage, of mossy tree-trunks covered with vines, of tangled undergrowth and brush. When we had gained a hill-top, nothing more was to be seen than the dark-brown band of logs on the gully bottom before us, and the dim line of road losing itself in a mass of green beyond.

Neither Herkimer nor Paris had much to say, as we rode on in the van. Major Fonda made sundry efforts to engage them in talk, as if there had been no recent dispute, no harsh words, no angry recriminations, but without special success. For my part, I said nothing whatever. Surely there was enough to think of, both as to the miserable insubordination of an hour back, and as to what the next hour might bring.

We had passed over about the worst of these patches of corduroy road, in the bottom of a ravine between two hills, where a little brook, dammed in part by the logs, spread itself out over the swampy soil on both sides. We in the van had nearly gained the summit of the farther eminence, and were rest-

ing for the moment to see how Visscher should
manage with his wagon in the rear. Colonel Cox
had also turned in his saddle, some ten yards farther
down the hill, and was calling back angrily to his
men to keep in the centre of the logs and not tip
them up by walking on the ends.

While I looked Barent Coppernol called out to
me: " Do you remember ? This is where we
camped five years ago."

Before I could answer I heard a rifle report, and
saw Colonel Cox fall headlong upon the neck of his
horse.

There was a momentary glimpse of dark forms
running back, a strange yell, a shot or two—and
then the gates of hell opened upon us.

CHAPTER XXXIII.

THE FEARSOME DEATH-STRUGGLE IN THE FOREST.

WERE I Homer and Shakespeare and Milton, merged all in one, I should still not know how fitly to depict the terrible scene which followed.

I had seen poor headstrong, wilful Cox pitch forward upon the mane of his horse, as if all at once his spine had been turned into limp string; I saw now a ring of fire run out in spitting tongues of flame around the gulf, and a circle of thin whitish smoke slowly raise itself through the dark leaves of the girdling bushes. It was an appalling second of mental numbness during which I looked at this strange sight, and seemed not at all to comprehend it.

Then Herkimer cried out, shrilly: " My God! here it is!" and, whirling his mare about, dashed down the hill-side again. I followed him, keeping ahead of Paris, and pushing my horse forward through the aimlessly swarming footmen of our van with a fierce, unintelligent excitement.

The air was filled now with shouts—what they were I did not know. The solid body of our troops on the corduroy bridge were huddling together like sheep in a storm. From the outer edges of this mass men were sinking to the ground. The tipping, rolling logs tossed these bodies on their ends off into the water, or under the feet of the others. Cox's horse had jumped side-long into the marsh, and now, its hindquarters sinking in the mire, plunged wildly, flinging the inert body still fastened in the stirrups from side to side. Some of our men were firing their guns at random into the underbrush.

All this I saw in the swift gallop down the hill to rejoin the Brigadier.

As I jerked up my horse beside him, a blood-curdling chorus of strange barking screams, as from the throats of maniac women, rose at the farther side of the ravine, drowning the shouts of our men, the ping-g-g of the whistling bullets, and even the sharp crack of the muskets. It was the Indian war-whoop! A swarm of savages were leaping from the bush in all directions, and falling upon our men as they stood jammed together on the causeway. It was a horrible spectacle—of naked, yelling devils, daubed with vermilion and ghastly yellow, rushing with uplifted hatchets and flashing knives upon this huddled mass of white men, our friends and neighbors. These, after the first bewildering shock, made what defence they could, shooting right and left, and beating down their assailants with terrific smashing blows from their gun-stocks. But the throng on the sliding logs made them almost powerless, and into their jumbled ranks kept pouring the pitiless rain of bullets from the bush.

By God's providence there were cooler brains and wiser heads than mine, here in the ravine, to face and grapple with this awful crisis.

Old Herkimer seemed before my very eyes to wax

bigger and stronger and calmer in the saddle, as this pandemonium unfolded in front of us. His orders I forget now—or what part I played at first in carrying them out—but they were given swiftly and with cool comprehension of all our needs. I should think that within five minutes from the first shot of the attack, our forces—or what was left of them—had been drawn out of the cruel helplessness of their position in the centre of the swamp. This could never have been done had not Honikol Herkimer kept perfectly his self-control and balance, like an eagle in a tempest.

Visscher's regiment, in the rear, had not got fairly into the gulf, owing to the delay in dragging the wagon along, when the ambushed Indians fired their first volley; and he and his men, finding themselves outside the fiery circle, promptly ran away. They were followed by many of the Indians, which weakened the attacking force on the eastern side of the ravine. Peter Bellinger, therefore, was able to push his way back again from the beginning of the corduroy bridge into the woods on both sides of the road beyond, where cover was to be had. It was a noble sight to see the stalwart Palatine farmers of his regiment—these Petries, Weavers, Helmers, and Dygerts of the German Flatts—fight their path backward through the hail of lead, crushing Mohawk skulls as though they had been egg-shells with the mighty flail-like swing of their clubbed muskets, and returning fire only to kill every time. The bulk of Cox's Canajoharie regiment and of Klock's Stone Arabia yeomen were pulled forward to the rising ground on the west side, and spread themselves out in the timber as well as they could, north and south of the road.

While these wise measures were being ordered, we three horsemen had, strangely enough, been out of the range of fire; but now, as we turned to ride back, a sudden shower of bullets came whizzing past us. My horse was struck in the head, and began staggering forward blindly. I leaped from his back as he toppled, only to come in violent collision with General Herkimer, whose white mare, fatally wounded, had toppled toward me. The Brigadier helped extricate himself from the saddle, and started with the rest of us to run up the hill for cover, but stumbled and stopped after a step or two. The bone of his right leg had been shattered by the ball which killed his steed, and his high boot was already welling with blood.

It was in my arms, never put to better purpose, that the honest old man was carried up the side-hill. Here, under a low-branched beech some two rods from the road, Dr. William Petrie stripped off the boot, and bandaged, as best he could, the wounded leg. The spot was not well sheltered, but here the Brigadier, a little pale, yet still calm and resolute, said he would sit and see the battle out. Several young men, at a hint from the doctor, ran down through the sweeping fire to the edge of the morass, unfastened the big saddle from his dead mare, and safely brought it to us. On this the brave old German took his seat, with the maimed leg stretched out on some boughs hastily gathered, and coolly lighting his pipe, proceeded to look about him.

"Can we not find a safer place for you farther back, Brigadier?" I asked.

"No; here I will sit," he answered, stoutly. "The men can see me here; I will face the enemy till I die."

All this time the rattle of musketry, the screech of flying bullets, the hoarse din and clamor of forest warfare, had never for an instant abated. Looking down upon the open space of the gully's bottom, we could see more than two-score corpses piled upon the logs of the road, or upon little mounds of black soil which showed above the level of the slough, half-hidden by the willows and tall, rank tufts of swamp-grass. Save for the dead, this natural clearing was well-nigh deserted. Captain Jacob Seeber was in sight, upon a hillock below us to the north, with a score of his Canajoharie company in a circle, firing outward at the enemy. Across the ravine Captain Jacob Gardenier, a gigantic farmer, armed with a captured Indian spear, had cut loose with his men from Visscher's retreat, and had fought his way back to help us. Farther to the south, some of the Cherry Valley men had got trees, and were holding the Indians at bay.

The hot August sun poured its fiercest rays down upon the heaps of dead and wounded in this forest cockpit, and turned into golden haze the mist of smoke encircling it. Through this pale veil we saw, from time to time, forms struggling in the dusk of the thicket beyond. Behind each tree-trunk was the stage whereon a life-drama was being played, with a sickening and tragic sameness in them all. The yeoman from his cover would fire; if he missed, forth upon him would dart the savage, raised hatchet gleaming—and there would be a widow the more in some one of our Valley homes.

"Put two men behind each tree," ordered keen-eyed Herkimer. "Then, when one fires, the other's gun will be loaded for the Indian on his running forward." After this command had been followed, the battle went better for us.

There was a hideous fascination in this spectacle stretched before us. An hour ago it had been so softly peaceful, with the little brook picking its clean way in the sunlight through the morass, and the kingfisher flitting among the willows, and the bees' drone laying like a spell of indolence upon the heated air. Now the swale was choked with corpses! The rivulet ran red with blood, and sluggishly spread its current around barriers of dead men. Bullets whistled across the gulf, cutting off boughs of trees as with a knife, and scattering tufts of leaves like feathers from a hawk stricken in its flight. The heavy air grew thick with smoke, dashed by swift streaks of dancing flame. The demon-like screams of the savages, the shouts and moans and curses of our own men, made hearing horrible. Yes—horrible is the right word!

A frightened owl, I remember, was routed by the tumult from its sleepy perch, and flew slowly over the open space of the ravine. So curious a compound is man!—we watched the great brown-winged creature flap its purblind way across from wood to wood, and speculated there, as we stood in the jaws of death, if some random ball would hit it !

I am writing of all this as if I did nothing but look about me while others fought. Of course that could not have been the case. I recall now these fragmentary impressions of the scene around me with a distinctness and with a plenitude of minutiæ which surprise me, the more that I remember little enough of what I myself did. But when a man is in a fight for his life there are no details. He is either to come out of it or he isn't, and that is about all he thinks of.

I have put down nothing about what was now the most serious part of the struggle—the combat with the German mercenaries and Tory volunteers on the high ground beyond the ravine. I conceive it to have been the plan of the enemy to let the Indians lie hidden round about the gulf until our rear-guard had entered it. Then they were to disclose their ambuscade, sweeping the corduroy bridge with fire, while the Germans and Tories, meeting our van up on the crown of the hill beyond, were to attack and drive it back upon our flank in the gulf bottom, when we should have been wholly at the mercy of the encircling fusilade from the hills. Fortunately St. Leger had given the Indians a quart of rum apiece before they started ; this was our salvation. The savages were too excited to wait, and closed too soon the fiery ring which was to destroy us all. This premature action cut off our rear, but it also prevented our van reaching the point where the white foe lay watching for us. Thus we were able to form upon our centre, after the first awful shock was over, and to then force our way backward or forward to some sort of cover before the Germans and Tories came upon us.

The fighting in which I bore a part was at the farthest western point, where the remnants of four or five companies, half buried in the gloom of the impenetrable wood, on a line stretching along the whole crest of the hill, held these troops at bay. We lay or crouched behind leafy coverts, crawling from place to place as our range was reached by the enemy, shooting from the shield of tree-trunks or of tangled clumps of small firs, or, best of all, of fallen and prostrate logs.

Often, when one of us, creeping cautiously forward, gained a spot which promised better shelter, it was to find it already tenanted by a corpse, perhaps of a near and dear friend. It was thus that I came upon the body of Major John Eisenlord, and later upon what was left of poor Barent Coppernol, lying half-hidden among the running hemlock, scalpless and cold. It was from one of these recesses, too, that I saw stout old Isaac Paris shot down, and then dragged away a prisoner by the Tories, to be handed over to the hatchets of their Indian friends a few days hence.

Fancy three hours of this horrible forest warfare, in which every minute bore a whole lifetime's strain and burden of peril!

We knew not then how time passed, and could but dimly guess how things were going beyond the brambled copse in which we fought. Vague intima-

24

tions reached our ears, as the sounds of battle now receded, now drew near, that the issue of the day still hung in suspense. The war-yells of the Indians to the rear were heard less often now. The conflict seemed to be spreading out over a greater area, to judge from the faintness of some of the rifle reports which came to us. But we could not tell which side was giving way, nor was there much time to think of this : all our vigilance and attention were needed from moment to moment to keep ourselves alive.

All at once, with a terrific swoop, there burst upon the forest a great storm, with loud-rolling thunder and a drenching downfall of rain. We had been too grimly engrossed in the affairs of the earth to note the darkening sky. The tempest broke upon us unawares. The wind fairly roared through the branches high above us ; blinding flashes of lightning blazed in the shadows of the wood. Huge boughs were wrenched bodily off by the blast. Streaks of flame ran zig-zag down the sides of the tall, straight hemlocks. The forest fairly rocked under the convulsion of the elements.

We wrapped our neckcloths or kerchiefs about our gunlocks, and crouched under shelter from the pelting sheets of water as well as might be. As for the fight, it ceased utterly.

While we lay thus quiescent in the rain, I heard a low, distant report from the west, which seemed distinct among the growlings of the thunder ; there followed another, and a third. It was the belated signal from the fort !

I made my way back to the hill-side as best I could,

under the dripping brambles, over the drenched and slippery ground vines, upon the chance that the Brigadier had not heard the reports.

The commander still sat on his saddle under the beech-tree where I had left him. Some watch-coats had been stretched over the lowest branches above him, forming a tolerable shelter. His honest brown face seemed to have grown wan and aged during the day. He protested that he had little or no pain from his wound, but the repressed lines about his lips belied their assurance. .He smiled with gentle irony when I told him of what I had heard, and how I had hastened to apprise him of it.

" I must indeed be getting old," he said to his brother George. " The young men think I can no longer hear cannon when they are fired off."

The half-dozen officers who squatted or stood about under the tree, avoiding the streams which fell from the holes in the improvised roof, told me a terrible story of the day's slaughter. Of our eight hundred, nearly half were killed. Visscher's regiment had been chased northward toward the river, whither the fighting from the ravine had also in large part drifted. How the combat was going down there, it was difficult to say. There were dead men behind every tree, it seemed. Commands were so broken up, and troops so scattered by the stern exigencies of forest fighting, that it could not be known who was living and who was dead.

What made all this doubly tragic in my ears was that these officers, who recounted to me our losses, had to name their own kinsmen among the slain.

Beneath the general grief and dismay in the presence of this great catastrophe were the cruel gnawings of personal anguish.

" My son Robert lies out there, just beyond the tamarack," said Colonel Samuel Campbell to me, in a hoarse whisper.

" My brother Stufel killed two Mohawks before he died; he is on the knoll there with most of his men," said Captain Fox.

Major William Seeber, himself wounded beyond help, said gravely: " God only knows whether my boy Jacob lives or not ; but Audolph is gone, and my brother Saffreness and his son James." The old merchant said this with dry eyes, but with the bitterness of a broken heart.

I told them of the shooting and capture of Paris and the death of Eisenlord. My news created no impression, apparently. Our minds were saturated with horror. Of the nine Snells who came with us, seven were said to be dead already.

The storm stopped as abruptly as it had come upon us. Of a sudden it grew lighter, and the rain dwindled to a fine mist. Great luminous masses of white appeared in the sky, pushing aside the leaden clouds. Then all at once the sun was shining.

On that instant shots rang out here and there through the forest. The fight began again.

The two hours which followed seem to me now but the indistinct space of a few minutes. Our men had seized upon the leisure of the lull to eat what food was at hand in their pockets, and felt now refreshed in strength. They had had time, too, to learn something of the awful debt of vengeance they owed the enemy. A sombre rage possessed them, and gave to their hearts a giant's daring. Heroes before, they became Titans now.

The vapors steaming up in the sunlight from the wet earth seemed to bear the scent of blood. The odor affected our senses. We ran forth in parties now, disdaining cover. Some fell; we leaped over their writhing forms, dashed our fierce way through the thicket to where the tell-tale smoke arose, and smote, stabbed, stamped out the life of, the ambushed foe. Under the sway of this frenzy, timorous men swelled into veritable paladins. The least reckless of us rushed upon death with breast bared and with clinched fists.

A body of us were thus scouring the wood on the crest of the hill, pushing through the tangle of dead brush and thick high brake, which soaked us afresh to the waist, resolute to overcome and kill whomsoever we could reach. Below us, in the direction of the river, though half a mile this side of it, we could hear a scattering fusillade maintained, which bespoke bush-fighting. Toward this we made our way, firing at momentary glimpses of figures in the thicket, and driving scattered groups of the foe before us as we ran.

Coming out upon the brow of the hill, and peering through the saplings and underbrush, we could see that big Captain Gardenier and his Caughnawaga men were gathered in three or four parties behind clumps of alders in the bottom, loading and firing upon an enemy invisible to us. While we were looking down and hesitating how best to go to his succor, one of old Sammons's sons came bounding down the side-hill, all excitement, crying:

"Help is here from the fort!"

Sure enough, close behind him were descending some fourscore men, whose musket-barrels and cocked hats we could distinguish swaying above the bushes, as they advanced in regular order.

I think I see huge, burly Gardenier still, standing in his woollen shirt-sleeves, begrimed with powder and mud, one hand holding his spear, the other shading his eyes against the sinking sun as he scanned the new-comers.

"Who's there?" he roared at them.

"From the fort!" we could hear the answer.

Our hearts leaped with joy at this, and we began with one accord to get to the foot of the hill, to meet these preservers. Down the steep side we clambered, through the dense second-growth, in hot haste and all confidence. We had some friendly Oneidas with us, and I had to tell them to keep back, lest Gardenier, deeming them Mohawks, should fire upon them.

Coming to the edge of the swampy clearing we saw a strange sight.

Captain Gardenier was some yards in advance of his men, struggling like a mad Hercules with half a dozen of these new-comers, hurling them right and left, then falling to the ground, pinned through each thigh by a bayonet, and pulling down his nearest assailant upon his breast to serve as a shield.

While we took in this astounding spectacle, young Sammons was dancing with excitement.

" In God's name, Captain," he shrieked, "you are killing our friends!"

" Friends be damned!" yelled back Gardenier, still struggling with all his vast might. " These are Tories. *Fire!* you fools! *Fire!*"

It was the truth. They were indeed Tories— double traitors to their former friends. As Gardenier shouted out his command, these ruffians raised their guns, and there sprang up from the bushes on either side of them as many more savages, with weapons lifting for a volley.

How it was I know not, but they never fired that volley. Our muskets seemed to poise and discharge themselves of their own volition, and a score of the villains, white and red, tumbled before us. Gardenier's men had recovered their senses as well, and, pouring in a deadly fusillade, dashed furiously forward with clubbed muskets upon the unmasked foe. These latter would now have retreated up the hill again, whence they could fire to advantage, but we at this leaped forth upon their flank, and they, with a futile shot or two, turned and fled in every direction, we all in wild pursuit.

Ah, that chase! Over rotten, moss-grown logs, weaving between gnarled tree-trunks, slipping on treacherous twigs, the wet saplings whipping our faces, the boughs knocking against our guns, in savage heat we tore forward, loading and firing as we ran.

The pursuit had a malignant pleasure in it; we

knew the men we were driving before us. Cries of recognition rose through the woods; names of renegades were shouted out which had a sinister familiarity in all our ears.

I came upon young Stephen Watts, the boyish brother of Lady Johnson, lying piteously prone against some roots, his neck torn with a hideous wound of some sort; he did not know me, and I passed him by with a bitter hardening of the heart. What did he here, making war upon my Valley? One of the Papist Scots from Johnstown, Angus McDonell, was shot, knocked down, and left senseless behind us. So far from there being any pang of compassion for him, we cheered his fall, and pushed fiercely on. The scent of blood in the moist air had made us wild beasts all.

I found myself at last near the river, and on the edge of a morass, where the sun was shining upon the purple flowers of the sweet-flag, and tall rushes rose above little miry pools. I had with me a young Dutch farmer—John Van Antwerp—and three Oneida Indians, who had apparently attached themselves to me on account of my epaulettes. We had followed thus far at some distance a party of four or five Tories and Indians; we came to a halt here, puzzled as to the course they had taken.

While my Indians, bent double, were running about scanning the soft ground for a trail, I heard a well-known voice close behind me say:

"They're over to the right, in that clump of cedars. Better get behind a tree."

I turned around. To my amazement Enoch Wade stood within two yards of me, his buckskin shirt wide open at the throat, his coon-skin cap on the back of his head, his long rifle over his arm.

" In Heaven's name, how did you come here? "

" Lay down, I tell ye ! " he replied, throwing himself flat on his face as he spoke.

We were too late. They had fired on us from the cedars, and a bullet struck poor Van Antwerp down at my feet.

" Now for it, before they can load," cried Enoch, darting past me and leading a way on the open border of the swale, with long, unerring leaps from one raised point to another. The Indians raced beside him, crouching almost to a level with the reeds, and I followed.

A single shot came from the thicket as we reached it, and I felt a momentary twinge of pain in my arm.

" Damnation ! I've missed him ! Run for your lives ! " I heard shouted excitedly from the bush.

There came a crack, crack, of two guns. One of my Indians rolled headlong upon the ground ; the others darted forward in pursuit of some flitting forms dimly to be seen in the undergrowth beyond.

" Come here ! " called Enoch to me. He was standing among the low cedars, resting his chin on his hands, spread palm down over the muzzle of his gun, and looking calmly upon something on the ground before him.

I hurried to his side. There, half-stretched on the wet, blood-stained grass, panting with the exertion of raising himself on his elbow, and looking me square in the face with distended eyes, lay Philip Cross.

There, half stretched on the wet, blood-stained grass, lay Philip Cross.

CHAPTER XXXIV.

ALONE AT LAST WITH MY ENEMY.

MY stricken foe looked steadily into my face; once his lips parted to speak, but no sound came from them.

For my part I did not know what to say to him. A score of thoughts pressed upon my tongue for utterance, but none of them seemed suited to this strange occasion. Everything that occurred to me was either weak or over-violent. Two distinct ideas of this momentary irresolution I remember—one was to leave him in silence for my Oneidas to toma-hawk and scalp; the other was to curse him where he lay.

There was nothing in his whitening face to help me to a decision. The look in his eyes was both sad and savage—an expression I could not fathom. For all it said to me, he might be thinking wholly of his wound, or of nothing whatever. The speechless fixity of this gaze embarrassed me. For relief I turned to Enoch, and said sharply:

"You haven't told me yet what you were doing here."

The trapper kept his chin still on its rest, and only for a second turned his shrewd gray eyes from the wounded quarry to me.

"You can see for yourself, can't ye?" he said.

"What do people mostly do when there's shooting going on, and they've got a gun?"

"But how came you here at all? I thought you were to stay at—at the place where I put you."

"That was likely, wasn't it! Me loafing around the house like a tame cat among the niggers while good fighting was going on up here!"

"If you wanted to come, why not have marched with us? I asked you."

"I don't march much myself. It suits me to get around on my own legs in my own way. I told you I wouldn't go into any ranks, or tote my gun on my shoulder when it was handier to carry it on my arm. But I didn't tell you I wouldn't come up and see this thing on my own hook."

"Have you been here all day?"

"If you come to that, it's none of your business, young man. I got here about the right time of day to save *your* bacon, anyway. That's enough for *you*, ain't it?"

The rebuke was just, and I put no further questions.

A great stillness had fallen upon the forest behind us. In the distance, from the scrub-oak thickets on the lowlands by the river, there sounded from time to time the echo of a stray shot, and faint Mohawk cries of "Oonah! Oonah!" The battle was over.

"They were beginning to run away before I came down," said Enoch, in comment upon some of these dying-away yells of defeat which came to us. "They got handled too rough. If their white officers had showed themselves more, and took bigger risks, they'd have stood their ground. But these Tory fine gentlemen are a pack of cowards. They let the Injuns get killed, but they kept darned well hid themselves."

The man on the ground broke silence here.

"You lie!" he said, fiercely.

"Oh! you can talk, can you?" said Enoch. "No, I don't lie, Mr. Cross. I'm talking gospel truth. Herkimer's officers came out like men, and fought like men, and got shot by dozens; but till we struck you, I never laid eyes on one of you fellows all day long, and my eyesight's pretty good, too. Don't you think it is? I nailed you right under the nipple, there, within a hair of the button I sighted on. I leave it to you if that ain't pretty fair shooting."

The cool brutality of this talk revolted me. I had it on my tongue to interpose, when the wounded man spoke again, with a new accent of gloom in his tone.

"What have I ever done to you?" he said, with his hand upon his breast.

"Why, nothing at all, Mr. Cross," answered Enoch, amiably. "There wasn't any feeling about it, at least on my part. I'd have potted you just as carefully if we'd been perfect strangers."

"Will you leave us here together for a little while, Enoch?" I broke in. "Come back in a few minutes; find out what the news is in the gulf—how the fight has gone. I desire some words with this—this gentleman."

The trapper nodded at this, and started off with his cat-like, springing walk, loading his rifle as he went. "I'll turn up in about a quarter of an hour," he said.

I watched his lithe, leather-clad figure disappear among the trees, and then wheeled around to my prostrate foe.

"I do not know what to say to you," I said, hesitatingly, looking down upon him.

He had taken his hand away from his breast, and was fumbling with it on the grass behind him. Suddenly he raised it, with a sharp cry of—

"I know what to say to you!"

There was a pistol in the air confronting me, and I, taken all aback, looked full into the black circle of its barrel as he pulled the trigger. The flint struck out a spark of flame, but it fell upon priming dampened by the wet grass.

The momentary gleam of eagerness in the pallid face before me died piteously away when no report came. If he had had the strength he would have thrown the useless weapon at me. As it was, it dropped from his nerveless fingers. He closed his eyes under the knit brows, upon which cold sweat stood out, and groaned aloud.

"I do not know what to say to you," I went on, the episode of the pistol seeming, strangely enough, to have cleared my thoughts. "For two years—yes, for five years—I have been picturing to myself some such scene as this, where you should lie overthrown before me, and I should crush the life out of your hateful body with my heel, as one does with snakes. But now that it has come about, I am at a strange loss for words."

"That you were not formerly," said the wounded man. "Since I have known you, you have fought always exceedingly well with your mouth. It was only in deeds that you were slow."

He made this retort with a contemptuous coolness of tone which was belied by his white face and drawn brows, and by the troubled, clinging gaze in his eyes. I found myself looking with a curious impersonal interest upon this heavy, large-featured countenance, always heretofore so deeply flushed with color, and now coarsely blotched with varying depths of pallor.

"Doubtless it would be best to leave you here. None of your party will straggle this way. They have all fled. You can lie here and think of your misdeeds until——"

"Until the wolves come, you mean. Yes, go away. I prefer them to you."

The sky to the west was one great lurid, brassy glare, overhung with banks of sinister clouds, a leaden purple above, fiery crimson below. The unnatural light fell strongly upon us both. A big shadow passed for an instant across the sunset, and we, looking instinctively up, saw the circling bulk of some huge bird of prey. I shuddered at the sight.

"Yes, leave me to *them* !" he said, bitterly. "Go back and seize my lands, my house. While the beasts and the birds tear me to bits here in the forest, do you fatten upon my substance at home. You and they are of a kidney."

"You know I would touch nothing of yours."

"No—not even my wife !"

The thrust went home. There was a world of sardonic disdain in his voice as he spoke, but in truth I thought little of his tone. The words themselves seemed to open a gulf before my feet. Was it indeed true, in welcoming this man's death, that I was thinking of the woman it would set free—for me?

It seemed a long, long time before I found tongue again. I walked up and down among the small cedars, fighting out in my own mind the issue of honor which had been with such brutal frankness raised. I could not make it seem wholly untrue —this charge he so contemptuously flung at me. There was no softening of my heart toward him; he was still the repellent, evil ruffian I had for years held him to be. I felt that I hated him the more because he had put me in the wrong. I went back to him, ashamed for the source of the increase of temper I trembled under, yet powerless to dissemble it.

" Why should I not kill you where you lie ? " I shouted at him.

He made an effort at shrugging his shoulders, but vouchsafed no other reply.

" You "—I went on, in a whirl of rage at myself, at him, at the entire universe—" you have made my whole manhood bitter. I fought you the first time I saw you, when we were little boys. Even then you insulted, injured me. I have always hated you. You have always given me reason to hate you. It was you who poisoned Mr. Stewart's mind against me. It was you who stole my sweet sister away

from me. Did this content you? No. You must
drive the good old gentleman into paralysis and
illness unto death—out of his mind—and you must
overwhelm the poor, gentle girl with drunken
brutality and cruelty, and to cap all, with desertion.
And this is not enough—my God! think of it!
this is not enough!—but you must come with the
others to force Indian war upon our Valley, upon
your old neighbors! There are hundreds lying
dead here to-day in these woods—honest men
whose wives, parents, little children, are waiting for
them at home. They will never lay eyes on them
again. Why? Because of you and your scoundrel
friends. You have done too much mischief already.
It is high time to put an end to you."

The wounded man had listened to me wearily, with
his free hand clutched tight over his wound, and the
other tearing spasmodically at the grass beside him.

" I am bleeding to death," he said, with a voice
obviously weakened since his last preceding words.
" So much the better for you. You would like it
so. You are not bold enough to knock me on the
head, or merciful enough to go about your business
and leave me in peace. I ought to be above bandying words with you ; nor would I if it did not take
my mind from my hurt. You are right—you have
always been my enemy. You were jealous of me as
a little boy. You had an apron, and you envied me
my coat. When, like a fool, I came again to this
cursed wilderness, your sour face rose up in front of
me like an ugly dream. It was my first disagreeable thing. Still you were jealous of me, for I was

25

a gentleman ; you were a skin-pedler. I married a maiden who had beauty and wit enough to grace my station, even though she had not been born to it. It was you who turned her mind against me, and incited her to unhappiness in the home I had given her. It was you who made a damned rebel out of her, and drove me into going to Canada. She has ever been more your friend than mine. You are of her sort. An English gentleman could rightly have had no part or lot with either of you. Go back to her now—tell her you left me here waiting for the wolves—and that my dying message was——"

He followed with some painfully bitter and malignant words which I have not the heart to set down here in cold blood against him.

" Let me see your wound," I said, when he had finished and sank back, exhausted.

I knelt beside him and opened his green coat, and the fine, ruffled shirt beneath it. Both were soaked with blood on the whole right side, but the soft cambric had, in a measure, checked the flow. He made no resistance, and I spread over the ugly aperture some of the plaster with which my mother had fitted me out, and bound it fast, with some difficulty, by passing my sash under his body and winding it about his chest.

He kept his eyes closed while I was doing this. I could not tell whether he was conscious or not. Nor could I explain to myself why I was concerning myself with his wound. Was it to save, if possible, his life ? Was it to lengthen out his term of torture here in the great final solitude, helplessly facing the

end, with snarling wolves and screaming kites for his
death-watch ? I scarcely knew which.

I try now to retrace the courses by which my
thoughts, in the confused searchings of those few
moments, reached finally a good conclusion ; but the
effort is beyond my powers. I ·know only that all
at once it became quite clear to my mind that I
must not leave my enemy to die. How much of
this was due to purely physical compassion for suffering, how much to the higher pleadings of humanity, how much to the feeling that his taunts of base-
ness must be proved untrue, I cannot say.

I was still kneeling beside him, I know, when
Enoch suddenly stood in front of me. His practised
footsteps had made no sound. He glanced gravely
at me and at the white, inanimate face of Cross.
Emotions did not play lightly upon Enoch's leather-
like visage ; there was nothing in his look to tell
whether he was surprised or not.

" Well, what news ? How has the day gone ? " I
asked him.

" Your people hold the gulf. The British have
gone back. It seems they were attacked in their
rear from the fort. The woods are full of dead
men."

" What is Herkimer going to do ? "

" They were making a litter to carry him off
the field. They are going home again—down the
Valley."

" So, then, we have lost the fight."

" Well, seeing that every three sound men have
got to tote back one wounded man, and that about

half the people you brought here are dead to begin with, it don't look much like a victory, does it ? "

" But the British have retreated, you say, and there was a sortie from the fort ? "

" Yes, it's about six of one and half-dozen of t'other. I should say that both sides had got their bellyful of fighting. I guess they'll both want to rest for a spell."

I made no answer, being lost in a maze of thoughts upon the hideous carnage of the day, and upon what was likely to come of it. Enoch went on :

" They seemed to be pretty nigh through with their litter-making. They must be about ready to start. You'd better be spry if you want to go along with 'em."

" Did you speak to any one of me ? Did you tell them where I was ? "

" I ain't quite a fool, young man," said the trapper, with a gaunt sort of smile. " If they'd caught sight of me, I wouldn't have got much chance to explain about myself, let alone you. It kind of occurred to me that strangers found loafing around in the woods wouldn't get much of an opening for polite conversation just now—especially if those strangers were fellows who had come down from Sillinger's camp with letters only a fortnight ago."

All this time Cross had been stretched at my knees, with his eyes closed. He opened them here, at Enoch's last words, and broke into our conversation with a weak, strangely altered voice :

" I know you now—damn you ! I couldn't think

before. You are the fellow I gave my letters to, there on Buck's Island. I paid you your own price —in hard gold—and now you shoot me in return. You are on the right side now. You make a good rebel."

" Now look here, Mr. Cross," put in Enoch, with just a trace of temper in his tone. " You paid me to carry those letters because I was going that way, and I carried 'em straight. You didn't pay me for anything else, and you couldn't, neither. There ain't been gold enough minted yet to hire me to fight for your King George against Congress. Put that in your pipe and smoke it ! "

" Come, Enoch," I here interrupted, " enough of that. The man is suffering. You must not vex him further by words."

" Suffering or not," returned the trapper, " he might keep a civil tongue in his head.—Why, I even did something you didn't pay me for," he went on, scowling down at the prostrate soldier. " I delivered your message here to this man " (indicating me with a gesture of his thumb)—" all that, you know, about cutting out his heart when you met him, and feeding it to a Missisague dog."

Enoch's grim features relaxed into a sardonic smile as he added : " There may be more or less heart-eating round about here presently, but it don't look much as if it would be his, and the dogs that'll do it don't belong to anybody—not even to a Missisague buck."

The wounded man's frame shook under a spasm of shuddering, and he glowered at us both wildly, with a look half-wrath, half-pitiful pleading, which helped me the better to make up my mind.

Enoch had turned to me once more :

"Come," he said, "we better hustle along. It will be all right with me so long as I am with you, and there is no time to lose. They must be starting from the gulf by this time. If we step along brisk, we'll soon catch them. As for this chap here, I guess we'd better leave him. He won't last long anyway, and your folks don't want any wounded prisoners. They've got too many litters to carry already."

"No," I made answer, with my resolve clear now before me. "We will make our own litter, and we will carry him to his home ourselves—by the river—away from the others."

"The hell you say!" said Enoch.

CHAPTER XXXV.

THE STRANGE USES TO WHICH REVENGE MAY BE PUT.

IN after-times, when it could do no harm to tell this story, people were wont to regard as its most remarkable feature the fact that we made the trip from the Oriskany battle-field to Cairncross in five days. There was never exhibited any special interest in the curious workings of mind, and conscience too if you like, which led me to bring my enemy home. Some few, indeed, like General Arnold, to whom I recounted the affair a fortnight later when he marched up the Valley, frankly said that I was a fool for my pains, and doubtless many others dissembled the same opinion. But they all, with one accord, expressed surprise, admiration, even incredulity, at the despatch with which we accomplished the difficult journey.

This achievement was, of course, entirely due to Enoch. At the outset he protested stoutly against the waste of time and trouble involved in my plan. It was only after much argument that I won him over to consenting, which he did with evident reluctance. But it is right to say that, once embarked on the adventure, he carried it through faithfully and with zeal.

The wounded man lay silent, with closed eyes, while our discussion went on. He seemed in a half-lethargic state, probably noting all that we said, yet under too heavy a spell of pain and weakness to care to speak. It was not until we two had woven a rough sort of litter out of hickory saplings, covered thick with moss and hemlock twigs, and Enoch had knelt by his side to look to his wounds again, that Cross spoke:

"Leave me alone!" he groaned, angrily. "It makes me worse to have you touch me. Are you not satisfied? I am dying; that ought to be enough for you."

"Don't be a fool, Mr. Cross," said Enoch, imperturbably, moving his hand along the course of the bandage. "We're trying to save your life. I don't know just why, but we are. Don't make it extra hard for us. All the help we want from you is for you to hold your jaw."

"You are going to give me up to your Oneidas!" cried the suffering man, raising his head by a violent effort at the words, and staring affrightedly straight ahead of him.

There, indeed, were the two friendly Indians who had come with me to the swamp, and had run forward in pursuit of Cross's companions. They had returned with absolute noiselessness, and stood now some ten feet away from us, gazing with stolid composure at our group.

A hideous bunch of fresh scalp-locks dangled from the belt of each, and, on the bare legs beneath, stains of something darker than vermilion mingled with the pale ochre that had been rubbed upon the skin. The savages breathed heavily from their chase, and their black eyes were fairly aflame with excitement, but they held the muscles of their faces in an awesome rigidity. They were young men whom pious Samuel Kirkland had laboriously covered, through years of effort, with a Christian veneering. If the good dominie could have been there and seen the glances they bent upon the wounded enemy at our feet, I fear me he would have groaned in spirit.

" Keep them off!" shrieked Cross, his head all in a tremble with the sustained exertion of holding itself up. " I will not be scalped! So help me God, I will not!"

The Indians knew enough of English to understand this frantic cry. They looked at me as much as to say that this gentleman's resolution did not materially alter the existing situation, the probabilities of which were all on the other side.

" Lay your head down, Mr. Cross," said Enoch, almost gently. " Just keep cool, or you'll bust your bandages off. They won't hurt you till we give 'em the word."

Still he made fitful efforts to rise, and a faint purplish color came into his throat and cheeks as he strove excitedly. If Enoch had not held his arm he would have torn off the plaster from his breast.

" It shall not be done! I will die now! You shall not save me to be tortured—scalped—by these devils!"

I intervened here. " You need fear nothing from

these Indians," I said, bending over him. "Lie back again and calm yourself. We are different from the brutes in your camp. We pay no price for scalps."

"Perhaps those are not scalps they have hanging there. It is like your canting tongue to deny it."

It was easy to keep my temper with this helpless foe. "These savages have their own way of making war," I answered, calmly. "They are defending their own homes against invasion, as well as we are. But we do not bribe them to take scalps."

"Why not be honest—you!" he said, disdainfully. "You are going to give me up. Don't sicken me with preaching into the bargain."

"Why be silly—you!" I retorted. "Does the trouble we propose taking for you look like giving you up? What would be easier than to leave you here—for the wolves, or these Indians here? Instead of that we are going to carry you all the way to your home. We are going to *hide* you at Cairncross, until I can get a parole for you from General Schuyler. *Now* will you keep still?"

He did relapse into silence at this—a silence that was born alike of mystification and utter weakness.

Enoch explained to the Oneidas, mainly in their own strange tongue, my project of conveying this British prisoner, intact so far as hair went, down the Valley. I could follow him enough to know that he described me as a warrior of great position and valor; it was less flattering to have him explain that Cross was also a leading chief, and that I would get a magnificent ransom by delivering him up to Congress.

Doubtless it was wise not to approach the Indian mind with less practical arguments. I saw this, and begged Enoch to add that much of this reward should be theirs if they would accompany us on our journey.

"They would be more trouble than they are worth," he said. "They wouldn't help carry him more than ten minutes a day. If they'll tell me where one of their canoes is hid, betwixt here and Fort Schuyler, that will be enough."

The result was that Enoch got such information of this sort as he desired, together with the secret of a path near by which would lead us to the river trail. I cut two buttons from my coat in return, and gave them to the savages; each being a warranty for eight dollars upon production at my home, half way between the old and the new houses of the great and lamented Warraghiyagey, as they had called Sir William Johnson. This done, and the trifling skin-wound on my arm re-dressed, we lifted Cross upon the rude litter and started for the trail.

I seem to see again the spectacle upon which I turned to look for a last time before we entered the thicket. The sky beyond the fatal forest wore still its greenish, brassy color, and the clouds upon the upper limits of this unnatural glare were of a vivid, sinister crimson, like clots of fresh blood. In the calm gray blue of the twilight vault above, birds of prey circled, with a horrible calling to one another. No breath of air stirred the foliage or the bending rushes in the swale. We could hear no sound from our friends at the head of the ravine, a full half-mile away. Save for the hideous noises of the birds, a perfect silence rested upon this blood-soaked oasis of the wilderness. The little brook babbled softly past us ; the strong western light flashed upon the rain-drops among the leaves. On the cedar-clad knoll the two young Indians stood motionless in the sunset radiance, watching us gravely.

We passed into the enfolding depths of the woods, leaving the battle-field to the furred and feathered scavengers and scalping-knives of the forest primeval.

Our slow and furtive course down the winding river was one long misery. I recall no other equally wretched five days in my life.

The canoe which Enoch unearthed on our first evening was a small and fragile affair, in which only one beside the wounded man could be accommodated. The other must take his way as best he could through the sprawling tangle of water-alders, wild artichoke, and vines, facing myriads of flies and an intolerable heat in all the wet places, with their sweltering luxuriance of rank vegetation. One day of this nearly reduced me to the condition of our weak and helpless prisoner. I staggered blindly along toward its close, covered to the knees with black river-mud, my face and wounded arm stinging with the scratches of poisonous ivy and brambles, my brain aching savagely, my strength and spirit all gone. I could have wept like a child from sheer exhaustion when at last I came to the nook on the little stream where

Enoch had planned to halt, and flung myself on the ground utterly worn out.

We were somewhat below Fort Schuyler, as near to the first settlements on the German Flatts as we might with safety venture by daylight. Thereafter we must hide during the days, and steal down the river at night. Enoch had a small store of smoked beef; for the rest we ate berries, wild grapes, and one or two varieties of edible roots which he knew of. We dared not build a fire.

Philip Cross passed most of his time, while we lay hiding under cover, in a drowsy, restless stupor, broken by feverish intervals of nervous activity of mind which were often very like delirium. The heat, the fly-pest, and the malarial atmosphere of the dank recesses in which we lay, all combined to make his days very bad. At night in the canoe, floating noiselessly down the stream, Enoch said he seemed to suffer less and to be calmer in his mind. But at no time, for the first three days at least, did he evince any consciousness that we were doing for him more than might under the circumstances be expected. His glance seemed sometimes to bespeak puzzled thoughts. But he accepted all our ministrations and labors with either the listless indifference of a man ill unto death, or the composure of an aristocrat who took personal service and attention for granted.

After we had passed the Little Falls—which we did on our third night out—the chief danger from shallows and rifts was over, and Enoch was able to exchange places with me. It was no great trouble to him, skilful woodsman that he was, to make his way along the bank even in the dark, while in the now smooth and fairly broad course I could manage the canoe well enough.

The moon shone fair upon us, as our little bark glided down the river. We were in the deep current which pushes forcefully forward under the new pressure of the East Canada waters, and save for occasional guidance there was small need of my paddle. The scene was very beautiful to the eye— the white light upon the flood, the soft calm shadows of the willowed banks, the darker, statelier silhouettes of the forest trees, reared black against the pale sky.

There is something in the restful radiance of moonlight which mellows hearts. The poets learned this, ages since ; I realized it now, as my glance fell upon the pallid face in the bow before me. We were looking at one another, and my hatred of him, nursed through years, seemed suddenly to have taken to itself wings. I had scarcely spoken to him during the voyage, other than to ask him of his wound. Now a thousand gentle impulses stirred within me, all at once, and moved my tongue.

" Are you out of pain to-night ? " I asked him. " The journey is a hard one at best for a wounded man. I would we could have commanded a larger and more commodious boat."

" Oh, ay ! So far as bodily suffering goes, I am free from it," he made answer, languidly. Then, after a little pause, he went on, in a low, musing voice : " How deathly still everything is ! I thought that in the wilderness one heard always the night-

yelping of the wolves. We did at Cairncross, I know. Yet since we started I have not heard one. It is as if we were going through a dead country."

Enoch had explained the reason for this silence to me, and I thoughtlessly blurted it out.

" Every wolf for forty miles round about is up at the battle-field," I said. "It is fairly marvellous how such intelligence spreads among these brutes. They must have a language of their own. How little we really understand of the animal creation about us, with all our pride of wisdom! Even the shark, sailors aver, knows which ship to pursue."

He shuddered and closed his eyes as I spoke. I thought at first that he had been seized with a spasm of physical anguish, by the drawn expression of his face; then it dawned upon me that his suffering was mental.

" Yes, I dare say they are all there," he said, lifting his voice somewhat. " I can hear them—see them! Do you know," he went on, excitedly, " all day long, all night long, I seem to have corpses all about me. They are there just the same when I close my eyes—when I sleep. Some of them are my friends; others I do not know, but they all know me. They look at me out of dull eyes; they seem to say they are waiting for me—and then there are the wolves ! "

He began shivering at this again, and his voice sank into a piteous quaver.

" These are but fancies," I said, gently, as one would speak to a child awakened in terror by a nightmare. " You will be rid of them once you get where you can have rest and care."

It seemed passing strange that I should be talking thus to a man of as powerful frame as myself, and even older in years. Yet he was so wan and weak, and the few days of suffering had so altered, I may say refined, his face and mien, that it was natural enough too, when one thinks of it.

He became calmer after this, and looked at me for a long time as I paddled through a stretch of still water, in silence.

" You must have been well born, after all," he said, finally.

I did not wholly understand his meaning, but answered :

" Why, yes, the Van Hoorns are a very good family—noble in some branches, in fact—and my father had his sheepskin from Utrecht. But what of it ? "

" What I would say is, you have acted in all this like a gentleman."

I could not help smiling to myself, now that I saw what was in his mind. " For that matter," I answered, lightly, " it does not seem to me that either the Van Hoorns or the dead Mauverensens have much to do with it." I remembered my mother's parting remark to me, and added : " The only Van Hoorn I know of in the Valley will not be at all pleased to learn I have brought you back."

" Nobody will be pleased," he said, gloomily.

After that it was fit that silence should again intervene, for I could not gainsay him. He closed his eyes as if asleep, and I paddled on in the alter-nate moonlight and shadow.

The recollection of my mother's words brought with it a great train of thoughts, mostly bitter. I was bearing home with me a man who was not only not wanted, but whose presence and continued life meant the annihilation of all the inchoate hopes and dreams my heart these last two years had fed upon. It was easy to be civil, even kind, to him in his pres-ent helpless, stricken state; anybody with a man's nature could do that. But it was not so easy to look resignedly upon the future, from which all light and happiness were excluded by the very fact that he was alive.

More than once during this revery, be it stated in frankness, the reflection came to me that by merely tipping the canoe over I could even now set every-thing right. Of course I put the evil thought away from me, but still it came obstinately back more than once. Under the momentary spell of this devilish suggestion, I even looked at the form re-cumbent before me, and noted how impossible it was that it should ever reach the bank, once in the water. Then I tore my mind forcibly from the idea, as one looking over a dizzy height leaps back lest the strange, latent impulse of suicide shall master him, and fixed my thoughts instead upon the man himself.

His talk about my being well born helped me now to understand his character better than I had before been able to do. I began to realize the existence in England—in Europe generally, I dare say—of a kind

26

of man strange to our American ideas, a being within whom long tradition and sedulous training had created two distinct men—one affable, honorable, generous, likeable, among his equals; the other cold, selfish, haughty, and harsh to his inferiors. It struck me now that there had always been two Philips, and that I had been shown only the rude and hateful one because my station had not seemed to entitle me to consort with the other.

Once started upon this explanation, I began to comprehend the whole story. To tell the truth, I had never understood why this young man should have behaved so badly as he did; there had been to me always a certain wantonness of brutality in his conduct wholly inexplicable. The thing was plainer now. In his own country he would doubtless have made a tolerable husband, a fair landlord, a worthy gentleman in the eyes of the only class of people whose consideration he cared for. But over here, in the new land, all the conditions had been against him. He had drawn down upon himself and all those about him overwhelming calamity, simply because he had felt himself under the cursed obligation to act like a " gentleman," as he called it. His contemptuous dislike of me, his tyrannical treatment of his wife when she did not fall in with his ambitions, his sulky resort to dissipation, his fierce espousal of the Tory side against the common herd —I could trace now the successive steps by which obstinacy had led him down the fell incline.

I do not know that I had much satisfaction from this analysis, even when I had worked it all out. It

was worth while, no doubt, to arrive at a knowledge
of Philip's true nature, and to see that under other
circumstances he might have been as good a man as
another. But all the same my heart grew heavy
under the recurring thought that the saving of his
life meant the destruction of all worth having in
mine.

Every noiseless stroke of my paddle in the water,
bearing him toward home as it did, seemed to push
me farther back into a chill, unknown world of gloom
and desolation. Yet, God help me, I could do no
other !

CHAPTER XXXVI.

A FINAL SCENE IN THE GULF WHICH MY EYES ARE MERCIFULLY SPARED.

JUST before daybreak of the fifth day we stole past the sleeping hamlet of Caughnawaga, and as the sun was rising over the Schoharie hills I drew up the canoe into the outlet of Dadanoscara Creek, a small brook which came down through the woods from the high land whereon Cairncross stood. Our journey by water was ended.

Enoch was waiting for us, and helped me lift Cross from the canoe. His body hung inert in our arms; not even my clumsy slipping on the bank of the rivulet startled him from the deep sleep in which he had lain for hours in the boat.

"I have been frightened. Can he be dying?" I asked.

Enoch knelt beside him, and put his hand over the patient's heart. He shook his head dubiously after a moment, and said : "It's tearing along like a racehorse. He's in a fever—the worst kind. This ain't sleep—it's stupor."

He felt the wounded man's pulse and temples. "If you're bent on saving his life," he added, "you'd better scoot off and get some help. Before we can make another litter for him, let alone taking him up

this creek-bed to his house, it may be too late.   If
we had a litter ready, it might be different.   As it is,
I don't see but you will have to risk it, and bring
somebody here."

For once in my life my brain worked in flashes.
I actually thought of something which had not
occurred to Enoch!

" Why not carry him in this canoe? " I asked.
" It is lighter than any litter we could make."

The trapper slapped his lank, leather-clad thigh in
high approval.   " By hokey! " he said, " you've hit
it ! "

We sat on the mossy bank, on either side of the
insensible Philip, and ate the last remaining fragments of our store of food.   Another day of this and
we should have been forced to shoot something, and
light a fire to cook it over, no matter what the
danger.   Enoch had, indeed, favored this course two
days before, but I clung to my notion of keeping
Cross's presence in the Valley an absolute secret.
His life would have been in deadly peril hereabouts,
even before the battle.   How bitterly the hatred of
him and his traitor-fellows must have been aug-
mented by the slaughter of that cruel ambuscade, I
could readily imagine.   With what words could I
have protected him against the righteous rage of a
Snell, for example, or a Seeber, or any one of a hundred others who had left kinsmen behind in that
fatal gulch?   No!   There must be no risk run by
meeting any one.

With the scanty meal finished our rest was at an
end.   We ought to lose no time.   Each minute's

delay in getting the wounded man under a roof, in bed, within reach of aid and nursing, might be fatal.

It was no light task to get the canoe upon our shoulders, after we had put in it our guns, covered these with ferns and twigs, and upon these laid Philip's bulky form, and a very few moments' progress showed that the work before us was to be no child's play. The conformation of the canoe made it a rather awkward thing to carry, to begin with. To bear it right side up, laden as it was, over eight miles of almost continuous ascent, through a perfectly unbroken wilderness, was as laborious an undertaking as it is easy to conceive.

We toiled along so slowly, and the wretched little brook, whose bed we strove to follow, described such a wandering course, and was so often rendered fairly impassable by rocks, driftwood, and over-hanging thicket, that when the sun hung due south above us we had covered barely half our journey, and confronted still the hardest portion of it. We were so exhausted when this noon hour came, too, that I could make no objection when Enoch declared his purpose of getting some trout from the brook, and cooking them. Besides, we were far enough away from the river highway and from all habitations now to render the thing practically safe. Accordingly I lighted a small fire of the driest wood to be found, while the trapper stole up and down the brook, moving with infinite stealth and dexterity, tracking down fish and catching them with his hands under the stones.

Soon he had enough for a meal—and, my word!

it was a feast for emperors or angels. We stuffed the pink dainties with mint, and baked them in balls of clay. It seemed as if I had not eaten before in years.

We tried to rouse Cross sufficiently to enable him to eat, and in a small way succeeded ; but the effect upon him was scarcely beneficial, it appeared to us. His fever increased, and when we started out once more under our burden, the motion inseparable from our progress affected his head, and he began to talk incoherently to himself.

Nothing can be imagined more weird and startling than was the sound of this voice above us, when we first heard it. Both Enoch and I instinctively stopped. For the moment we could not tell whence the sound came, and I know not what wild notions about it flashed through my mind. Even when we realized that it was the fever-loosed tongue of our companion which spoke, the effect was scarcely less uncanny. Though I could not see him, the noise of his ceaseless talking came from a point close to my head ; he spoke for the most part in a bold, high voice—unnaturally raised above the pitch of his recent faint waking utterances. Whenever a fallen log or jutting bowlder gave us a chance to rest our load without the prospect of too much work in hoisting it again, we would set the canoe down, and that moment his lips would close. There seemed to be some occult connection between the motion of our walking and the activity of his disordered brain.

For a long time—of course in a very disconnected way—he babbled about his mother, and of people, presumably English, of whom I knew nothing, save that one name, Digby, was that of his elder brother. Then there began to be interwoven with this talk stray mention of Daisy's name, and soon the whole discourse was of her.

The freaks of delirium have little significance, I believe, as clews to the saner courses of the mind, but he spoke only gently in his imaginary speeches to his wife. I had to listen, plodding wearily along with aching shoulders under the burden of the boat, to fond, affectionate words addressed to her in an incessant string. The thread of his ideas seemed to be that he had arrived home, worn-out and ill, and that he was resting his head upon her bosom. Over and over again, with tiresome iteration, he kept entreating plaintively: "You *are* glad to see me? You do *truly* forgive me, and love me?"

Nothing could have been sadder than to hear him. I reasoned that this ceaseless dwelling upon the sweets of a tender welcome doubtless reflected the train of his thoughts during the journey down from the battle-field. He had forborne to once mention Daisy's name during the whole voyage, but he must have thought deeply, incessantly of her—in all likelihood with a great softening of heart and yearning for her compassionate nursing. It was not in me to be unmoved by this. I declare that as I went painfully forward, with this strangely pathetic song of passion repeating itself in my ears, I got fairly away from the habit of mind in which my own love for Daisy existed, and felt myself only an agent in the working out of some sombre and exalted romance.

In Foxe's account of the English martyrs there are stories of men at the stake who, when a certain stage of the torture was reached, really forgot their anguish in the emotional ecstasy of the ideas born of that terrible moment. In a poor and imperfect fashion I approached that same strange state—not far removed, in sober fact, from the delirium of the man in the canoe.

The shadows were lengthening in the woods, and the reddening blaze of the sun flared almost level in our eyes through the tree-trunks, when at last we had crossed the water-shed of the two creeks, and stood looking down into the gulf of which I have so often spoken heretofore.

We rested the canoe upon a great rock in the mystic circle of ancient Indian fire worship, and I leaned, tired and panting, against its side. My arm was giving me much pain, and what with insufficient food and feverish sleep, great immediate fatigue, and the vast nervous strain of these past six days, I was well-nigh swooning.

" I fear I can go no farther, Enoch," I groaned. " I can barely keep my feet as it is."

The trapper himself was as close to utter exhaustion as one may be and have aught of spirit left, yet he tried to speak cheerily.

" Come, come ! " he said, " we mustn't give out now, right here at the finish. Why, it's only down over that bridge, and up again—and there we are ! "

I smiled in a sickly way at him, and strove to nerve myself manfully for a final exertion. " Very well,"

I made answer. " Just a moment's more rest, and we'll at it again."

While we stood half reclining against the bowlder, looking with trepidation at the stiff ascent before us on the farther side of the gulf, the scene of the old quarrel of our youth suddenly came to my mind.

" Do you see that spruce near the top, by the path —the one hanging over the edge? Five years ago I was going to fight this Philip Cross there, on that path. My little nigger Tulp ran between us, and he threw him head over heels to the bottom. The lad has never been himself since."

" Pretty tolerable fall," remarked Enoch, glancing down the precipitous, brush-clad wall of rock. " But a nigger lands on his head as a cat does on her feet, and it only scratches him where it would kill anybody else."

We resumed our burden now, and made our way with it down the winding path to the bottom. Here I was fain to surrender once for all.

" It is no use, Enoch," I said, resolutely. " I can't even try to climb up there with this load. You must wait here ; I will go ahead to Cairncross, prepare them for his coming, and send down some slaves to fetch him the rest of the way."

The great square mansion reared before me a closed and inhospitable front. The shutters of all the windows were fastened. Since the last rain no wheels had passed over the carriage-way. For all the signs of life visible, Cairncross might have been uninhabited a twelve-month.

It was only when I pushed my way around to the rear of the house, within view of the stables and slave quarters, that I learned the place had not been abandoned. Half a dozen niggers, dressed in their holiday, church-going raiment, were squatting in a close circle on the grass, intent upon the progress of some game. Their interest in this was so deep that I had drawn near to them, and called a second time, before they became aware of my presence.

They looked for a minute at me in a perplexed way—my mud-baked clothes, unshaven face, and general unkempt condition evidently rendering me a stranger in their eyes. Then one of them screamed: "Golly! Mass' Douw's ghost!" and the nimble cowards were on their feet and scampering like scared rabbits to the orchard, or into the basement of the great house.

So I was supposed to be dead! Curiously enough, it had not occurred to me before that this would be the natural explanation of my failure to return with the others. The idea now gave me a queer quaking sensation about the heart, and I stood stupidly staring at the back balcony of the house, with my mind in a whirl of confused thoughts. It seemed almost as if I *had* come back from the grave.

While I still stood, faint and bewildered, trying to regain control of my ideas, the door opened, and a white-faced lady, robed all in black, came swiftly out upon the porch. It was Daisy, and she was gazing at me with distended eyes and parted lips, and clinging to the carved balustrade for support.

As in a dream I heard her cry of recognition, and

knew that she was gliding toward me. Then I was on my knees at her feet, burying my face in the folds of her dress, and moaning incoherent nothings from sheer exhaustion and rapture.

When at last I could stand up, and felt myself coming back to something like self-possession, a score of eager questions and as many outbursts of deep thanksgiving were in my ears—all from her sweet voice. And I had tongue for none of them, but only looked into her dear face, and patted her hands between mine, and trembled like a leaf with excitement. So much was there to say, the sum of it beggared language.

When finally we did talk, I was seated in a great chair one of the slaves had brought upon the sward, and wine had been fetched me, and my dear girl bent gently over me from behind, softly resting my head against her waist, her hands upon my arms.

"You shall not look me in the face again," she said—with ah! such compassionate, tender playfulness—"until I have been told. How did you escape? Were you a prisoner? Were you hurt?"—and oh! a host of other things.

Suddenly the sky seemed to be covered with blackness, and the joy in my heart died out as by the stroke of death. I had remembered something. My parched and twitching lips did their best to refuse to form the words:

"I have brought Philip home. He is sorely wounded. Send the slaves to bring him from the gulf."

After a long silence, I heard Daisy's voice, clear

and without a tremor, call out to the blacks that their master had been brought as far as the gulf beyond, and needed assistance. They started off helter-skelter at this, with many exclamations of great surprise, a bent and misshapen figure dragging itself with a grotesque limping gait at their tail.

I rose from my chair, now in some measure restored to calmness and cold resolution. In mercy I had been given a brief time of blind happiness—of bliss without the alloy of a single thought. Now I must be a man, and walk erect, unflinching, to the sacrifice.

"Let us go and meet them. It is best," I said.

The poor girl raised her eyes to mine, and their startled, troubled gaze went to my heart. There must have been prodigious effort in the self-command of her tone to the slaves, for her voice broke down utterly now, as she faltered:

"You have—brought—him home! For what purpose? How will this all end? It terrifies me!"

We had by tacit consent begun to walk down the path toward the road. It was almost twilight. I remember still how the swallows wheeled swiftly in the air about the eaves, and how their twittering and darting seemed to confuse and tangle my thoughts.

The situation was too sad for silence. I felt the necessity of talking, of uttering something which might, at least, make pretence of occupying these wretched minutes, until I should say:

"This is your husband—and farewell!"

"It was clear enough to me," I said. "My duty

was plain. I would have been a murderer had I left
him there to die. It was very strange about my
feelings. Up to a certain moment they were all
bitter and merciless toward him. So many better
men than he were dead about me, it seemed little
enough that his life should go to help avenge them.
Yet when the moment came—why, I could not suffer
it. Not that my heart relented—no ; I was still full of
rage against him. But none the less it was my duty
to save his life."

"And to bring him home to *me.*" She spoke
musingly, completing my sentence.

"Why, Daisy, would you have had it otherwise?
Could I have left him there, to die alone, helpless
in the swamp ? "

" I have not said you were not right, Douw," she
answered, with saddened slowness. " But I am trying to think. It is so hard to realize—coming like
this. I was told you were both dead. His name
was reported in their camp, yours among our people.
And now you are both here—and it is all so strange,
so startling—and what is right seems so mingled and
bound up with what is cruel and painful! Oh, I
cannot think ! What will come of it? How will it
all end ? "

"We must not ask how it will end !" I made
answer, with lofty decision. "That is not our affair.
We can but do our duty—what seems clearly right—
and bear results as they come. There is no other
way. You ought to see this."

"Yes, I ought to see it," she said, slowly and in a
low, distressed voice.

As she spoke there rose in my mind a sudden consciousness that perhaps my wisdom was at fault. How was it that I—a coarse-fibred male animal, returned from slaughter, even now with the blood of fellow-creatures on my hands—should be discoursing of duty and of good and bad to this pure and gentle and sweet-souled woman? What was my title to do this?—to rebuke her for not seeing the right? Had I been in truth generous? Rather had I not, in the purely selfish desire to win my own self-approbation, brought pain and perplexity down upon the head of this poor woman? I had thought much of my own goodness—my own strength of purpose and self-sacrifice and fidelity to duty. Had I given so much as a mental glance at the effect of my acts upon the one whom, of all others, I should have first guarded from trouble and grief?

My tongue was tied. Perhaps I had been all wrong. Perhaps I should not have brought back to her the man whose folly and obstinacy had so well-nigh wrecked her life. I could no longer be sure. I kept silence, feeling indirectly now that her woman's instinct would be truer and better than my logic. She was thinking; she would find the real right and wrong.

Ah, no! To this day we are not settled in our minds, we two old people, as to the exact balance between duty and common-sense in that strange question of our far-away youth.

There broke upon our ears, of a sudden, as we neared the wooded crest of the gulf, a weird and piercing scream—an unnatural and repellent yell, like a hyena's horrid hooting! It rose with terrible distinctness from the thicket close before us. As its echoes returned, we heard confused sounds of other voices, excited and vibrant.

Daisy clutched my arm, and began hurrying me forward, impelled by some formless fear of she knew not what.

"It is Tulp," she murmured, as we went breathlessly on. "Oh, I should have kept him back! Why did I not think of it?"

"What about Tulp?" I asked, with difficulty keeping beside her in the narrow path. "I had no thought of him. I did not see him. He was not among the others, was he?"

"He has gone mad!"

"What—Tulp, poor boy? Oh, not as bad as that, surely! He has been strange and slow of wit for years, but—— "

"Nay, the tidings of your death—you know I told you we heard that you were dead—drove him into perfect madness. I doubt he knew you when you came. Only yesterday we spoke of confining him, but poor old father pleaded not. When you see Tulp, you shall decide. Oh! what has happened? Who is this man?"

In the path before us, some yards away, appeared the tall, gaunt form of Enoch, advancing slowly. In the dusk of the wooded shades behind him huddled the group of slaves. They bore nothing in their hands. Where was the canoe? They seemed affrighted or oppressed by something out of the common, and Enoch, too, wore a strange air. What could it mean?

When Enoch saw us he lifted his hand in a warning gesture.

"Have her go back!" he called out, with brusque sharpness.

"Will you walk back a little?" I asked her. "There is something here we do not understand. I will join you in a moment.

"For God's sake, what is it, Enoch?" I demanded, as I confronted him. "Tell me quick."

"Well, we've had our five days' tussle for nothing, and you're minus a nigger. That's about what it comes to."

"Speak out, can't you! Is he dead? What was the yell we heard?"

"It was all done like a flash of lightning. We were coming up the side nighest us here—we had got just where that spruce, you know, hangs over— when all at once that hump-backed nigger of yours raised a scream like a painter, and flung himself head first against the canoe. Over it went, and he with it—rip, smash, plumb to the bottom!"

The negroes broke forth in a babel of mournful cries at this, and clustered about us. I grew sick and faint under this shock of fresh horrors, and was fain to lean on Enoch's arm, as I turned to walk back to where I had left Daisy. She was not visible as we approached, and I closed my eyes in abject terror of some further tragedy.

Thank God, she had only swooned, and lay mercifully senseless in the tall grass, her waxen face upturned in the twilight. 27

CHAPTER XXXVII.

THE PEACEFUL ENDING OF IT ALL.

In the general paralysis of suffering and despair which rested now upon the Valley, the terrible double tragedy of the gulf passed almost unnoted. Women everywhere were mourning for the husbands, sons, lovers who would never return. Fathers strove in vain to look dry-eyed at familiar places which should know the brave lads—true boys of theirs—no more. The play and prattle of children were hushed in a hundred homes where some honest farmer's life, struck fiercely at by a savage or Tory, still hung in the dread balance. Each day from some house issued forth the procession of death, until all our little churchyards along the winding river had more new graves than old—not to speak of that grim, unconsecrated God's-acre in the forest pass, more cruel still to think upon. And with all this to bear, there was no assurance that the morrow might not bring the torch and tomahawk of invasion to our very doors.

So our own strange tragedy had, as I have said, scant attention. People listened to the recital, and made answer : " Both dead at the foot of the cliff, eh ? Have you heard how William Seeber is to-day ? " or, " Is it true that Herkimer's leg must be cut off ? "

In those first few days there was little enough heart to measure or boast of the grandeur of the fight our simple Valley farmers had waged, there in the ambushed ravine of Oriskany. Still less was there at hand information by the light of which the results of that battle could be estimated. Nothing was known, at the time of which I write, save that there had been hideous slaughter, and that the invaders had forborne to immediately follow our shattered forces down the Valley. It was not until much later—until definite news came not only of St. Leger's flight back to Canada, but of the capture of the whole British army at Saratoga—that the men of the Mohawk began to comprehend what they had really done.

To my way of thinking, they have ever since been unduly modest about this truly historic achievement. As I wrote long ago, we of New York have chosen to make money, and to allow our neighbors to make histories. Thus it happens that the great decisive struggle of the whole long war for Independence—the conflict which, in fact, made America free—is suffered to pass into the records as a mere frontier skirmish. Yet, if one will but think, it is as clear as daylight that Oriskany was the turning-point of the war. The Palatines, who had been originally colonized on the upper Mohawk by the English to serve as a shield against savagery for their own Atlantic settlements, reared a barrier of their own flesh and bones, there at Oriskany, over which St. Leger and Johnson strove in vain to pass. That failure settled everything. The essential feature of

Burgoyne's plan had been that this force, which we so roughly stopped and turned back in the forest defile, should victoriously sweep down our Valley, raising the Tory gentry as they progressed, and join him at Albany. If that had been done, he would have held the whole Hudson, separating the rest of the colonies from New England, and having it in his power to punish and subdue, first the Yankees, then the others at his leisure.

Oriskany prevented this! Coming as it did, at the darkest hour of Washington's trials and the Colonies' despondency, it altered the face of things as gloriously as does the southern sun rising swiftly upon the heels of night. Burgoyne's expected allies never reached him; he was compelled, in consequence, to surrender—and from that day there was no doubt who would in the long-run triumph.

Therefore, I say, all honor and glory to the rude, unlettered, great souled yeomen of the Mohawk Valley, who braved death in the wildwood gulch at Oriskany that Congress and the free Colonies might live.

But in these first few days, be it repeated, nobody talked or thought much of glory. There were too many dead left behind—too many maimed and wounded brought home—to leave much room for patriotic meditations around the saddened hearthstones. And personal grief was everywhere too deep and general to make it possible that men should care much about the strange occurrence by which Philip and Tulp lost their lives together in the gulf.

I went on the following day to my mother, and
she and my sister Margaret returned with me to
Cairncross, to relieve from smaller cares, as much
as might be, our poor dear girl. All was done to
shield both her and the stricken old gentleman, our
common second father, from contact with material
reminders of the shock that had fallen upon us, and
as soon as possible afterward they were both taken
to Albany, out of reach of the scene's sad suggestions.

From the gulf's bottom, where Death had dealt
his double stroke, the soldier's remains were borne
one way, to his mansion; the slave's the other, to
his old home at the Cedars. Between their graves
the turbulent stream still dashes, the deep ravine
still yawns. For years I could not visit the spot
without hearing, in and above the ceaseless shouting
of the waters, poor mad Tulp's awful death-scream.

During the month immediately following the
event, my time was closely engaged in public work.
It was my melancholy duty to go up to the Falls
to represent General Schuyler and Congress at the
funeral of brave old Brigadier Nicholas Herkimer,
who succumbed to the effects of an unskilful ampu-
tation ten days after the battle. A few days later I
went with Arnold and his relieving force up the
Valley, saw the siege raised and the flood of invasion rolled back, and had the delight of grasping
Peter Gansevoort, the stout commander of the long-
beleaguered garrison, once more by the hand. On
my return I had barely time to lease the Cedars to
a good tenant, and put in train the finally successful

efforts to save Cairncross from confiscation, when I
was summoned to Albany to attend upon my chief.
It was none too soon, for my old wounds had
broken out again, under the exposure and travail of
the trying battle week, and I was more fit for a
hospital than for the saddle.

I found the kindliest of nursing and care in my
old quarters in the Schuyler mansion. It was there,
one morning in January of the new year 1778, that
a quiet wedding breakfast was celebrated for Daisy
and me ; and neither words nor wishes could have
been more tender had we been truly the children of
the great man, Philip Schuyler, and his good dame.
The exact date of this ceremony does not matter ;
let it be kept sacred within the knowledge of us two
old people, who look back still to it as to the sunrise of a new long day, peaceful, serene, and almost
cloudless, and not less happy even now because the
ashen shadows of twilight begin gently to gather
over it.

Though the war had still the greater half of its
course to run, my part thereafter in it was far removed from camp and field. No opportunity came
to me to see fighting again, or to rise beyond my
major's estate. Yet I was of as much service, perhaps, as though I had been out in the thick of the
conflict ; certainly Daisy was happier to have it so.

Twice during the year 1780 did we suffer grievous material loss at the hands of the raiding parties
which malignant Sir John Johnson piloted into the
Valley of his birth. In one of these the Cairncross
mansion was rifled and burned, and the tenants

despoiled and driven into the woods. This meant
a considerable monetary damage to us ; yet our
memories of the place were all so sad that its demo-
lition seemed almost a relief, particularly as Enoch,
to whom we had presented a freehold of the wilder
part of the grant, that nearest the Sacondaga,
miraculously escaped molestation.

But it was a genuine affliction when, later in the
year, Sir John personally superintended the burning
down of the dear old Cedars, the home of our youth.
If I were able to forgive him all other harm he has
wrought, alike to me and to his neighbors, this would
still remain obstinately to steel my heart against
him, for he knew that we had been good to his wife,
and that we loved the place better than any other
on earth. We were very melancholy over this for a
long time, and, to the end of his placid days of second childhood passed with us, we never allowed Mr.
Stewart to learn of it. But even here there was the
recompense that the ruffians, though they crossed
the river and frightened the women into running for
safety to the woods, did not pursue them, and thus
my mother and sisters, along with Mrs. Romeyn and
others, escaped. Alas ! that the Tory brutes could
not also have forborne to slay on his own doorstep
my godfather, honest old Douw Fonda !

There was still another raid upon the Valley the
ensuing year, but it touched us only in that it
brought news of the violent death of Walter Butler,
slain on the bank of the East Canada Creek by the
Oneida chief Skenandoah. Both Daisy and I had
known him from childhood, and had in the old times

been fond of him. Yet there had been so much innocent blood upon those delicate hands of his, before they clutched the gravel on the lonely forest stream's edge in their death-grasp, that we could scarcely wish him alive again.

Our first boy was born about this time—a dark-skinned, brawny man-child whom it seemed the most natural thing in the world to christen Douw. He bears the name still, and on the whole, though he has forgotten all the Dutch I taught him, bears it creditably.

In the mid-autumn of the next year—it was in fact the very day on which the glorious news of Yorktown reached Albany—a second little boy was born. He was a fair-haired, slender creature, differing from the other as sunshine differs from thunder-clouds. He had nothing like the other's breadth of shoulders or strength of lung and limb, and we petted him accordingly, as is the wont of parents.

When the question of his name came up, I sat, I remember, by his mother's bedside, holding her hand in mine, and we both looked down upon the tiny, fair babe nestled upon her arm.

" Ought we not to call him for the dear old father —give him the two names, ' Thomas ' and ' Stewart ' ? " I asked.

Daisy stroked the child's hair gently, and looked with tender melancholy into my eyes.

" I have been thinking," she murmured, " thinking often of late—it is all so far behind us now, and time has passed so sweetly and softened so much our memories of past trouble and of the—the dead—I

have been thinking, dear, that it would be a comfort
to have the lad called Philip."

I sat for a long time thus by her side, and we
talked more freely than we had ever done before of
him who lay buried by the ruined walls of Cairncross. Time had indeed softened much. We spoke
of him now with gentle sorrow—as of a friend whose
life had left somewhat to be desired, yet whose
death had given room for naught but pity. He had
been handsome and fearless and wilful—and unfortunate ; our minds were closed against any harsher
word. And it came about that when it was time for
me to leave the room, and I bent over to kiss lightly
the sleeping infant, I was glad in my heart that he
was to be called Philip. Thus he was called, and
though the General was his godfather at the old
Dutch church, we did not conceal from him that the
Philip for whom the name was given was another.
It was easily within Schuyler's kindly nature to comprehend the feelings which prompted us, and I often
fancied he was even the fonder of the child because
of the link formed by his name with his parents'
time of grief and tragic romance.

In truth, we all made much of this light-haired,
beautiful, imperious little boy, who from the beginning quite cast into the shade his elder and slower
brother, the dusky-skinned and patient Douw. Old
Mr. Stewart, in particular, became dotingly attached
to the younger lad, and scarce could bear to have
him out of sight the whole day long. It was a
pretty spectacle indeed—one which makes my old
heart yearn in memory, even now—to see the sim-

ple, soft-mannered, childish patriarch gravely obeying the whims and freaks of the boy, and finding the
chief delight of his waning life in being thus commanded. Sometimes, to be sure, my heart smote
me with the fear that poor quiet Master Douw felt
keenly underneath his calm exterior this preference,
and often, too, I grew nervous lest our fondness was
spoiling the younger child. But it was not in us to
resist him.

The little Philip died suddenly, in his sixth year,
and within the month Mr. Stewart followed him.
Great and overpowering as was our grief, it seemed
almost perfunctory beside the heart-breaking anguish
of the old man. He literally staggered and died
under the blow.

There is no story in the rest of my life. The
years have flowed on as peacefully, as free from tempest or excitement, as the sluggish waters of a Delft
canal. No calamity has since come upon us; no
great trial or large advancement has stirred the current of our pleasant existence. Having always a
sufficient hold upon the present, with means to live
in comfort, and tastes not leading into venturesome
ways for satisfaction, it has come to be to us, in our
old age, a deep delight to look backward together.
We seem now to have walked from the outset hand
in hand. The joys of our childhood and youth spent
under one roof—the dear smoky, raftered roof, where
hung old Dame Kronk's onions and corn and per-
fumed herbs—are very near to us. There comes between this scene of sunlight and the not less peace-

ful radiance of our later life, it is true, the shadow for a time of a dark curtain. Yet, so good and generous a thing is memory, even this interruption appears now to have been but of a momentary kind, and has for us no harrowing side. As I wrote out the story, page by page, it seemed to both of us that all these trials, these tears, these bitter feuds and fights, must have happened to others, not to us—so swallowed up in happiness are the griefs of those young years, and so free are our hearts from scars.